Cade
Let us know
what you think
Will

Toby watching m.c.a

STOLEN

LIBERTY

BEHIND THE CURTAIN

Book One

THOMAS A. WATSON

WILLIAM ALLEN

M.C. ALLEN

William Allen

M.C. Allen

Thom P Watson

A special Thank you to the following people for all your help:

Nicholas A. Watson

Leslie Bryant

Yalonda Butler

Steven Smith

Sabrina Jean

William Beedie

Deb Serres

Cora Burke

Clarke Ferber

Joseph Ruffalo

Robert Launt

Britta Victoria

Credits

EDITED BY SABRINA JEAN

www.fasttrackediting.com

A-Poc Press

Malleus Publishing

Dedication

Well here it is, over a year's worth of work from myself, Will Allen and M.C. Allen at long last. I wanted to do this story with them for a long time. We actually talked about it three years ago but each of us had so many projects going at the time we had to schedule this into the works. I love this story and the characters and can't wait to see where this will lead. When I do a story, I do the beginning and the end. Well, this time I only did the outline for the beginning and a very rough outline for the end. Will and M.C. have been adding to the end and it is still evolving. I have to say, I love working with the brothers. When I approached them the only stipulation in taking this project was Tina has the final say and both looked at me and went 'Well duh dumbass'. In my part of this book I'm dedicating it to all of my fans who have made it possible for me to become a full-time author.
Thomas A Watson.

Full credit for this story idea must go to Thomas A. Watson and I am proud to be invited to play in his playground here. This was my first effort writing something as part of a group and I thoroughly enjoyed not just the writing but also the opportunity to hang out with some really interesting people and bounce ideas around as we fleshed out the story. For me, writing this book also gave me a chance to learn more about a unique group of individuals who have sacrificed so much in the name of liberties the rest of us take for granted. I want to dedicate my part of this book to the United States Army Rangers, past and present. Thank you.
William Allen.

When Thomas Watson asked me about working on this project, I'll admit I was not only shocked, but terrified at the prospect. I couldn't wrap my head around something this amazing could ever just drop into my lap. I wanted to honor all of the members of our armed services who put their lives on the line every day. I served with Charlie Company, 82nd Engineer Battalion out of Bamberg, Germany, and we lost three brave souls in Iraq during Operation Desert Storm. Three others in that ill-fated squad suffered horrendous wounds, but they survived and walk among us today. The last member of the squad didn't suffer so much as a scratch, but in a way, his demons tormented him. He was my roommate at the time, and his nightmare screams still haunt me. Sean D., wherever you are, I hope you are well and in a good place.
For my Brothers.
M.C. Allen

Cast of Characters

Randy Gibson (aka Shadow) – Machinist.

Lena and Oliver (Mom and Pop)-Randy's parents.

Cody Marshal (aka Baby Face) Does odd jobs for the trio. Lives with them and has a room at each of their homes.

Charlie Tucker (aka Book)

Robbie (aka Blaster)

Aaron Peterson (aka Cobra. Hates snakes.) Wife Elizabeth (Liz). Kids: Andre 9 and Eli 6.

Bert Travis (aka Pirate)

Frank (aka Wheat) dead and Kristi Wheaton (six years older than the trio) Kids: Clark and Emily

Tabitha (Kristi's younger sister) Husband: Dillion Greenway. Kid: Chase.

Victor- stalker that the boys went and talked to then beat the shit out of for bothering Kristi.

Winston Zimmer – Korean War vet. Widower, old man who lives next to Randy. One that owned the retreat.

Captain Winnfield- CO in the Stan and now Colonel.

Chapter One

Nangarhar Providence, Afghanistan

Trying to pull air into his burning lungs with the high noon sun overhead, Randy spun around, dropping the body he was carrying and bringing up his M4. Seeing movement on the rocky trail, he held the ACOG sight steady and saw the figure wasn't wearing fatigues but was carrying an AK47. Squeezing the trigger, he watched the hadji drop, rolling into a ravine.

"Shadow, we aren't stopping to play!" Charlie shouted at him, running past and carrying a body over his shoulder.

Moving his aim, Sergeant Randy Gibson, aka 'Shadow' to his team, saw another hadji and squeezed the trigger.

"Dude, you heard Book, and I can't carry another one. Move your ass," Robbie said, running past while carrying a body over his shoulder.

Slinging his M4, Randy picked up the body of PFC Griffin, moving it onto his right shoulder. Getting to his feet, he struggled under the weight to follow Robbie in a jog.

He was in the 75th Rangers and had moved out five days ago with fourteen men to take out four HVTs, high value targets, in the eastern part of Afghanistan in the providence of Nangarhar. When they'd taken out the targets last night, it had pissed off a lot of their friends. Since 0310, they had been trying to break contact without luck.

Of the fourteen, only eight were still moving. The others were dead and being carried out. Some, like Pirate, or back in the world known as PFC Bert Travis, couldn't even hold a weapon, but they still bore the weight of their fallen and kept up the pace. They believed in the creed that no Ranger gets left behind. They were now running on a rocky, barren ridgeline under the crest, following a narrow trail.

Holding the body on his shoulder tight, Randy jogged past Robbie. "Eat me, country boy," Robbie huffed with a grin, watching Shadow close the distance fast to Charlie. "That boy can run like a gazelle."

Behind them, an AK47 barked and Randy saw dirt kick up around him. "Thank you, God, for having idiots shooting at us on full auto," Randy mumbled, passing Charlie.

"Don't piss God off or He might tell the hadjis to switch to single shot and they could actually hit us," Charlie snapped. "We've had enough FUBAR on this field trip."

Passing Platoon Sergeant Wheaton, Randy glanced over. "You need to move because none of us can carry your big ass, Wheat," Randy said, passing him. Randy was 6'2" and weighed a lean 224 lbs. Wheaton was four inches taller and forty pounds heavier.

"I'm going to beat your ass when we get back," Wheaton panted, adjusting the body on his shoulder.

Reaching the front of the group, Randy put Griffin down and pulled his M4 up. He snapped off two shots and watched another pursuer's body drop. "They are really pissed off, Book. You and Blaster need to move it," Randy pressed his PTT (Push-To-Talk) box, calling out over the radio.

"Talk to Blaster. He's the one who left the claymore mines for them," Charlie called back.

"Fuck both of you, I was spreading goodwill," Robbie huffed over the radio. "Not my fault they didn't like the fireworks. Besides, Book is the one that started this shit with his sniper rifle."

"I hit my targets, bitch. Each one saw the pink mist," Charlie snapped back.

"Boys!" Wheaton shouted over the radio.

"Boys! We are hard charging airborne rangers; not PX Rangers!" Robbie popped off.

"And I'm an Airborne Ranger Sergeant First Class!" Wheaton snapped. "Close your crumb catchers and move. I'm tired of playing with these towel heads."

As the group filed past him, Randy kept his aim behind them, shooting tangos as they ran into the ravine. "Blaster, do you have any more claymores?" Wheaton called over the radio.

"When have I ever *not* had explosives?" Robbie shouted back.

Letting the comment slide, Wheaton barked, "Ahead, the trail narrows. Book, peel off and cover him. Shadow, hold there as long as you can to slow them down. Then put asshole to elbows because we aren't coming back to get you."

2

"First you want me to run, then stop. You need to make up your damn mind, old man," Randy popped off into the radio, grinning. Wheaton was the 'old man' being thirty, as the next oldest were Book, Blaster, and Randy at twenty-four. None of the others, living or dead, were a day over twenty-two years of age.

With a big grin, Charlie ran past Randy. "You know calling him an old man pisses him off."

"Yeah and life sucks ass, Book," Randy laughed, squeezing the trigger and watching the hadji pitch over to crash on the trail.

"Want my SAW?" Robbie asked, running toward him.

"Hell no, Blaster, I like to send out my love one shot at a time," Randy answered, squeezing the trigger and dropping another body into the ravine.

Running past Randy, "If a bullet has your name on it, that's one thing. I address my love 'to whom it may concern' when I blow their asses up," Robbie snarked as he chuckled.

Dropping down on his right knee, Randy saw four bodies, a hundred yards back, run into the ravine. They all stopped, seeing the bodies Randy had already taken out. "Thank you," he grinned, squeezing the trigger rapidly and watching impacts on all the bodies.

Dropping the empty magazine, Randy tossed it in his dump bag and pulled a fresh one off his vest, slamming it in. Like Charlie, Robbie, and Wheaton, he was wearing a forbidden, self-purchased body armor vest with his gear attached to the webbing that ran around the it. The military demanded its troops to wear the IOTV, Improved Outer Tactical Vest, but that didn't matter to the team. They had seen with their own eyes, the vests they were wearing stopped bullets and weighed ten pounds less, and pounds equaled pain.

Aiming down the ravine, he caught his breath as twenty hadjis ran into the ravine. "Shit," he mumbled and started squeezing the trigger, moving the crosshairs to different hadjis.

It seemed the more he shot, the more poured into the ravine. "I'm out of here," Randy finally huffed, since the hadjis were adding faster than he could subtract. Bending down, he grabbed Griffin's body and threw it over his shoulder. The only thing on Griffin's body was his uniform and boots. Like the other dead members of the team, they had stripped them down to save weight.

Taking off in a dead run, Randy pressed his radio toggle. "Guys, they have a shitload of friends coming."

"Count," Wheaton panted over the radio.

"I took out fifteen, but more came into the ravine and I stopped counting at twenty," Randy replied, forcing his legs to run. "They are fifty yards behind me. Just thought you would want to know because I'm passing you."

Seeing the narrow gap in the trail, Charlie skidded to a stop and laid the earthly remains of PFC Eric Blakely on the ground and pulled his M110 up to his shoulder. Stopping beside Charlie, Robbie set Spec4 Horowitz's body down and yanked a bag from his vest. "I need two minutes," Robbie said, yanking a claymore out.

Seeing Randy two hundred yards back and running like the hounds of hell were after him, Charlie looked over at Robbie. "You have one, and I'm going to be hard-pressed to buy it for you," Book told him, then put his eye on the scope. Hitting his scope with his clear combat goggles, Book moved his head back some. In the rocky hell of the Stan, goggles were needed to protect the eyes from the rock chips the bullets threw up.

"I hate shoddy work," Robbie spat, already setting the claymore up.

Taking a deep breath, Book held the crosshairs steady behind Randy. When the first hadji appeared, he squeezed the trigger. The hadjiman jerked back when the bullet hit him in the face. Barely moving the crosshairs, Charlie squeezed the trigger again, dropping another.

"Fuck me," he gasped at what could only be called a gaggle of men as they ran into his scope view.

Holding on a target, Book stroked the trigger, knocking one down and then moved his crosshairs across the group, dropping a body with each shot until his bolt locked back. Changing magazines, he saw the rest dive for cover while he shoved in a new magazine.

"I'm here," Randy called out, running up the small knoll they were set up on. "Now I'm gone," he said, running past them and jumping over the tripwire Robbie had over the trail.

Bullets started kicking up the dirt around him as Charlie took a slow breath and squeezed the trigger, hitting another in the face. Charlie felt rock fragments hit his cheek. A man beside the last hadji

4

shot, peered over a boulder beside the trail and Charlie hit him in the face for good measure.

"You don't have to hit them in the brain can, they aren't zombies!" Robbie shouted.

"If they can take a 7.62 to the head, then they have earned the right to kick our ass," Charlie mumbled, squeezing the trigger rapidly and dropping four more. "You done?" Charlie barked, seeing the rest of the attackers drop down again and the gunfire stop.

"Bitch, I'm waiting on you!" Robbie shouted, and Charlie turned to see Robbie adjusting the body he was carrying on his shoulder.

Jumping up, Charlie grabbed the body he was carrying, pulling it onto his left shoulder and stood. Seeing Charlie was ready, Robbie jumped the tripwire. "Don't hit it or we are dead," Blaster said with a giggle. "It's a special message of love."

"You have serious problems," Charlie grunted, jumping the tripwire. Gunfire slowly picked up behind them while they ran down the small knoll and around a bend in the trail. "Just what did you leave back there?"

"Everything I had left. A claymore, two pounds of C4, and a hundred feet of det cord with a phosphorous grenade," Robbie huffed out as Charlie ran past him.

Hearing that, Charlie leaned forward pushing his legs hard. "You still good covering our six?" Charlie asked, pulling away from Robbie. He didn't want to be close when that little surprise cooked off.

"Hell yeah, that's why I carry a gun that can fill the air with lead," Robbie snapped back, keeping a ten yard gap between him and Charlie.

Rounding the bend, they saw the others ahead still running, or more appropriately, jogging as fast as they could. The human body could only move so fast carrying so much weight. Everyone had dropped their main packs, so they could carry the fallen team. The only things on their backs now were the small packs with the hydration bladders. Everyone's bladder had long ago been sucked dry, but the packs had room to hold a small amount of extra gear, which they'd stuffed with ammo before dropping their main packs.

A thunderous explosion sounded behind them, then screams filled the air. Rocks started rolling down the hillside in a steady crescendo. "God damn it Blaster! I said one claymore!" Wheaton screamed over the radio.

"That shit was getting heavy and I was going to have to drop it soon, so get off my ass!" Robbie shouted back.

"Shadow, are you in the lead?" Wheaton called out.

"Yeah, that's where you told me to get back to," Randy answered.

"Find us a spot to stop for two minutes, so I can get on the radio," Wheaton ordered.

"You can't use the radio and run? How did you get out of Benning?!" Robbie shouted over the radio. Charlie laughed but had to agree with Blaster on that.

"Little boy, I can't hold the directional antenna, my rifle, a body and run, so excuse me!" Wheaton shouted, and Charlie didn't need the radio to hear that.

Charlie slowed and turned to Blaster. "Blaster, lay off Wheat," he said in a low voice. "He's had enough shit for one day."

"I know, that's why I'm giving him shit," Robbie said, huffing. "I don't want him thinking this shit is on him. If he's bitching, he's thinking like a Ranger should."

Not sure of the reasoning but thinking it sounded good, Charlie nodded and picked up his pace until he was ten yards in front of Robbie.

"Got a spot," Randy called over the radio.

"Hold there and set up security. If you can, when Babyface gets there, move up and check ahead of us," Wheaton said on the radio.

"Shadow is a corn-fed country boy and can run like a deer," Robbie huffed behind Charlie.

Randy stopped and put Griffin down, scanning ahead. Hearing footsteps and heavy breathing, he turned to see Private Cody Marshal, aka Babyface, trotting up and dropping to his knees before collapsing onto his face. Moving over, Randy grabbed his shoulder. "You have to stay alert and be tired later," he said in a low voice. "You are a Ranger and a breed above others, so you must embrace the suck."

Cody gulped in air and grinned at the slogan, giving a nod. Randy looked down at the wound on Babyface's hip and saw the dressing was stemming the blood flow. He wasn't the only one not carrying a body of a comrade, nor the only one that was running wounded. So far, only Randy, Robbie, and Charlie weren't wounded, but the day was still young and there was plenty of suck yet to embrace.

When Cody lifted his rifle, Randy nodded, glancing at his watch as PFC Aaron Peterson, aka Cobra, dropped down beside Cody. The young black soldier was holding a dressing over his left shoulder where he'd gotten hit by shrapnel. Checking Peterson's wound, Randy looked in his face.

"How you holding up, Cobra?" Randy asked. When Aaron nodded, mouthing 'I'm good', Randy stood up, lifting his wrist. Seeing it was 1140, he moved down the trail.

When Charlie and Robbie joined the group, they set down the bodies and saw Wheaton holding up a small dish antenna. "A chopper better be on the way," Robbie panted.

"The last three they sent for us got shot up," Charlie said, moving over to Cody. "You holding strong, Babyface?"

"Yes, Sergeant," Cody panted with a grimace, taking off his helmet.

"You hang tough, troop, and the name's Book in the field or Charlie in the world," Charlie told him, and Cody grinned. Charlie looked at his dressing and shook his head, lifting his eyes back up to the eighteen-year-old face. This was Cody's first outing, and *shit*, did he pick a doozy.

Wheaton had begged Captain Winnfield to hold Cody back, but Babyface had high scores from Benning and the captain wanted him to go. Even when Charlie and the other sergeants spoke up, the captain didn't listen. "Test scores mean shit downrange," Charlie mumbled.

"What, Book?" Cody panted.

Patting Cody's boot, "Nothing, Babyface. Keep an eye out, troop," he said and moved back to Robbie who was looking behind them with binoculars. "You see anything?"

"Hell no, and that is just fine by me," Robbie popped off. "I haven't seen a sexy woman in thirteen months and you know why? There aren't any here. I want to see some hot American women in bikinis."

"You need to be thinking with the head on your shoulders, troop," Charlie grinned, but knew it was a lost cause on Blaster.

Moving his binoculars across the ravine, "Book, I'm telling you. We bring some hot American woman over here, these boys will quit fighting and screwing goats. They will see what true beauty is and start having fun."

"Keep an eye out, Blaster," Charlie chuckled. "I'm going to see what Wheat has come up with."

"Shit, like I have somewhere to be and a date tonight? Women walk around with curtains over them here," Robbie mumbled. "Make a man believe he's chasing Casper the friendly ghost."

Kneeling down beside Wheaton, Charlie looked down at the map in Wheaton's lap as he talked on the radio. "Copy your last, but we need evac now, not move another twenty miles to get extracted," Wheaton snapped in the radio.

Charlie closed his eyes as Wheaton listened. "Sir!" Wheaton snapped. "I have six KIA and five WIA that includes me! We ran fifteen miles to the area you said would be our extraction point. Then we had to take off again, going through a valley and over another mountain."

"I'm shooting the captain when I get back. He definitely qualifies for extinction," Charlie mumbled, looking around. Setting his rifle down, he checked the dressing on Wheaton's upper shoulder where a bullet had passed through, taking a chunk of meat out. Hitting Wheaton between the shoulder and neck, luckily it hadn't ripped open a big bleeder.

Seeing Wheat was okay, Charlie moved around to the other wounded to check them. "Sir, are you telling me there isn't a chopper that can fly here? If you need gas money, we can pitch in for some," Wheaton said in a quivering voice filled with rage.

Closing his eyes as he listened, Wheaton gripped the headset so hard they could hear the plastic cracking. "Can you at least send some fast movers? One fucking plane to get these fuckers off our asses!" Wheaton growled.

Listening to the radio, Wheaton's face turned purple. "Well, sir, when I get back, you can court martial me but be warned, I'm going to stomp your ass. You stuck our asses out here without a plan and we all told you, cocksucker!" Wheaton shouted, throwing the headset down and turning the radio off.

"I take it the captain hasn't called up the chain and informed them he has a team stuck in a clusterfuck?" Charlie said, moving over to Wheaton.

"Fuck no," Wheaton snapped. "He wants us to travel another twenty miles, so the choppers can come in without people shooting at them."

Looking over his shoulder, "Blaster, we good?" Charlie asked.

"Have I said anything?" Robbie replied with his binoculars up, scanning the trail behind them.

"What's the plan, Wheat?" Charlie asked as Randy came running back up the trail. "Oh, shit," Charlie mumbled, seeing Randy's face.

"Good news and bad," Randy said, squatting down.

"Bad," Wheaton barked, shoving the radio in his backpack.

"We have a group of sixty tangos moving down the slope ahead of us, nine clicks ahead," Randy told him, pointing at the map Wheaton was looking at.

"What could you possibly have for good news?" Wheaton cried out, throwing his hands up.

"Five clicks ahead down in the ravine is a small village. I saw several vehicles we can steal and just fucking drive back to base," Randy grinned.

"Where?" Charlie asked, looking at the map and Randy pointed. "Damn, talk about a race," he said, looking at the terrain they would have to cover.

"I suggest we come in first," Randy said. "We hit the village as a group because we don't know if those in the village are tangos."

Glancing back, "The last two villages we passed, everyone shot at us, so why should this one be different?" Robbie popped off, then turned back to glass behind them.

"Listen up!" Wheaton called out. "We are moving five clicks to a village and stealing a fucking ride. There are bad guys ahead trying to cut us off, so this is a race. Let's show them Rangers always win."

"Hooah," Charlie said with a grin.

"Pack up and haul ass. Shadow, you're on point and no playing with the locals. If you see one, light them up fast," Wheaton ordered, getting to his knees.

"I only play when they piss me off," Randy said, grunting as he picked up Griffin. Holding out a hand, he helped Cody up. "Stay frosty, Babyface, because it's not over till we get back to the world."

"Yes, Sergeant," Cody said, grimacing while holding his hip.

"Did you hear Book? You are on this team, Babyface. I'm Shadow or Randy in the world," Randy grinned at him.

"Shadow, kiss him if you're going to, then get your ass moving so you can show us this village," Wheaton barked.

Adjusting his throat microphone, Randy smiled at Cody and turned around, trotting off. "We going to hotwire a ride in this village?" Robbie asked, getting up.

"Piss on that, someone has keys and we'll just take them, and send them a check for the ride," Charlie chuckled.

They formed up and trotted after Randy and saw him running off the trail to the bottom of the ravine. Where the ravine met the valley ahead, they saw the small village. "Damn, that's a steep slope!" Robbie gasped, then followed the others down.

Everyone skidded and slid more than they ran down the steep slope, reaching small trees halfway down. Moving faster in the trees, they reached the small stream at the bottom of the ravine. Randy moved through the trees at a walk and keyed his radio. "Slow your pace, we aren't alone," he warned in a low voice, releasing his toggle switch. Scanning ahead, Randy just felt something out of place.

"Shadow, we don't have long before that big group beats us to the village," Wheaton said over the radio.

Stopping, Randy crouched down, seeing the village through breaks in the trees. "Wheat, I think the guys behind us dropped down into the valley and got ahead of us. I'm going to slip into the village at a walk. Keep your pace down in case we have to move back up the mountain," Randy said softly, releasing his radio.

"Copy, but you spot trouble, you call before acting," Wheaton called back.

Shifting Griffin's weight on his shoulder, Randy pressed the radio toggle. "Oh, they are there, I just don't know how many."

"Shadow, you need me to move up?" Charlie called over the radio.

"Yeah, I'm dropping a bottle cap on the trail, Book. Thirty meters to the right is a boulder you can set up on. Have Blaster move in to cover our six. I think they are trying to catch us between a hammer and anvil," Randy said in a low voice, digging in his pocket and dropping a bottle cap. It was a trick Wheaton had taught them. When they wanted to mark something, they dropped a bottle cap. They were light and didn't arouse suspicion if someone else saw it.

"Copy, moving," Charlie called out, easing up through the team. "Blaster, did you hear Shadow?"

"Yeah, and I think he's right. I hear movement and it's not goats," Robbie replied.

Easing forward and moving from tree to tree for sixty meters, Randy paused hearing something brush up against metal off to his left. Lowering his body until he was resting on his left knee behind a bush, Randy slid Griffin's body down to the ground. Dropping to his belly, Randy eased his head around the bush, looking where he thought the noise had come from.

He froze at seeing a head pop up from behind a fallen tree twenty meters away on the other side of the stream. With his heart rate speeding up, Randy pressed his radio toggle twice, letting the others know he'd seen the enemy but was too close to talk.

"I'm set," Charlie whispered over the earbud in Randy's ear.

The man's head popped up again and looked to his left, then his right and Randy saw several men step out from behind trees, looking at the man behind the log. "Shadow, I have a hadji forty meters to my front behind a tree armed with an AK. He's looking to his left like he's talking to someone." Charlie called over the radio.

Easing his rifle up, Randy pressed his toggle twice and aimed at the one furthest away. Resting his crosshairs, he slowly squeezed the trigger and watched the man's head jerk back as his gunshot broke the quiet. No sooner than his gunshot had sounded, another hadji broke as Randy dropped his aim to the man behind the log.

The man stood up, aiming toward Charlie and Randy squeezed the trigger, watching the man grab his chest. Squeezing the trigger two more times quickly, Randy smiled to see the man jerk and fall back. Swinging his rifle over, he saw the one closest to him missing most of his head.

"Three down and we need to haul ass," Randy called over the radio as automatic gunfire erupted behind him up the ravine.

"Contact! Big time!" Robbie yelled over the radio with thunderous gunfire in the background. "Are we making a last stand and dying, or we gettin' out of Dodge?"

"Blaster, fall back down to the village. We can stand there if we can't get out!" Wheaton shouted.

Moving onto his knees, Randy picked up Griffin, rolling the body onto his shoulder. Getting up with a grunt, he eased to the village as more gunfire sounded up the ravine. "Blaster, you need me to come back?" he called over the radio.

"You do, and you'll be alone. I'm running to you," Robbie huffed out over the radio.

Glancing back, Randy saw Charlie stand and pick up the body he was carrying and start toward the village. Turning toward the village, Randy took off at a fast walk, trying to scan everywhere as the tempo of the gunfire behind them increased in intensity.

Reaching the village and moving between two huts, he saw goats and chickens running around with a teapot smoking over a fire, but no people. "Not good," he mumbled, stopping beside a hut. Pressing his radio, "Bad guys are close, village is empty," Randy said.

"Fucking get in a hut, then!" Wheaton shouted.

"Moving to your left," Charlie said, coming up behind him and moving to the side of the other hut.

"They are close," Randy said in a low voice, then his eyes moved to an ancient white Toyota Pathfinder.

Dropping to one knee, Charlie looked around and then raised his rifle up as the gunfire behind them got closer. "Can you hotwire? I'm not in the mood to look for keys," Charlie asked.

"Yeah," Randy huffed.

"Leave Griffin and I'll cover you. Get the ride started, so we can get the hell out of this damn place," Charlie said.

Sliding the body down, Randy took a deep breath and bolted from the side of the hut. Gunfire erupted as he jumped over the fire with the teapot, heading for the Pathfinder.

With bullets kicking up dirt around Randy as he ran, Charlie saw two men on the hillside to his right overlooking the village. Swinging his rifle up and squeezing the trigger twice, Charlie watched both drop. Hearing more gunfire on the left, he swung his rifle and saw a man with an RPK machine gun resting on a boulder chasing Randy with his aim. When his crosshairs centered on the man, Book squeezed the trigger and watched the man's head snap back.

The gunfire in front of him stopped, but the gunfire behind him became louder. When he saw Shadow reach the Pathfinder, he spun around, seeing the rest of the team moving towards them. Lifting his gaze up the ravine, Charlie's heart froze to see hadjis, lots of them, moving between the trees and coming towards them.

Lifting his rifle, Charlie started shooting and heard bullets impacting on the hut. "Got our ride started! Let's get the fuck out of here!" Randy yelled over the radio.

Bringing up the rear, Robbie weaved around trees, hearing bullets impacting around him and slapping the trees. Seeing a boulder up ahead, he skidded to a halt and spun around behind the boulder and rested his SAW on it before squeezing the trigger. He wasn't aiming, he was just trying to get the tangos to slow down and hide for a second.

"Shit!" Robbie yelled, seeing a hadji pop out from behind a tree twenty meters away and swung the barrel of his SAW over as he held the trigger down. Watching bullets stitch the body, Blaster moved the barrel and just sprayed up the ravine.

Seeing men stop and dive behind trees, Robbie smiled, lifting up his SAW and taking off running. "You better be glad I'm out of explosives, goat lovers!"

Skidding to a stop beside Charlie, Wheaton saw Randy running over. "Where are you going?" Wheaton shouted.

"Getting Griffin," Randy answered, skidding to a halt and picking the body up.

Nodding as Randy took off carrying the body, Wheaton motioned for the others to follow. "Book, can you hold until we load up?" Wheaton asked, bringing his rifle up and spraying bullets behind them to try and slow them down again.

"Don't know for how long," Charlie admitted, dropping an empty magazine. "I'm down to forty rounds."

"Buy us what you can," Wheaton said, turning for the Pathfinder and saw Randy tossing Griffin in the back. Patting Charlie on the shoulder, he took off to the Pathfinder and saw the others stacking the dead in the back and on the roof tying them down quickly. Then he noticed Randy running back to Charlie. "Where are you going now?"

"We need accurate covering fire, and Book can't do that moving back fast and carrying a body!" Randy shouted, running past him.

Jumping over the fire again he looked up the ravine, and time slowed for Randy while he was in midair. A man stepped out from behind a tree holding an RPG. Starting his descent, Randy saw the projectile fire off with an explosion, streaking through the air at him.

When he landed, the rocket impacted to his front, propelling him back and pain shot from his left leg. Landing hard with his ears ringing, Randy shook his head and smelled burning clothes, and felt his back getting hot. Realizing he'd landed in the fire, he rolled away blinking his eyes.

Looking down, Randy saw bone sticking out of his left ankle and his foot twisted ninety degrees to the right. Seeing it with his eyes, the pain became very intense when he sucked in a breath, seeing blood pulsing from his ankle.

Feeling someone hit him in the chest with a sledgehammer, Randy grunted as the air was knocked out of his lungs. Crawling fast, he moved over behind the low stone wall beside the fire. Yanking his small hydration pack off, Randy dug out a dressing and put it on his ankle, then looked down at his vest to see where a round had hit him dead center. "It *is* bulletproof," he huffed, tying the dressing on while the gunfire continued.

Looking at his ankle, he shook his head and then looked around, seeing a wooden chair beside him. Pulling his M9, Randy shot the back of the chair, splintering the wood. Snapping the two pieces off the back, he pulled out a roll of duct tape from his small pack. Glancing at his ankle, he saw the dressing was soaked.

"This is FUBAR," he said, grabbing another dressing and a tourniquet. Blinking tears out of his eyes and gritting his teeth, Randy grabbed his foot and moved it until it was pointing straight, then duct taped the dressing over his ankle. Next, he taped his ankle and foot to hold it straight. He took a breath and wrapped the tourniquet below his calf muscle and taped it down. Grabbing the sticks from the chair, he duct taped the sticks to make a splint, so he could use his foot.

14

Looking around, Randy saw his M4 was still attached with the one point sling. "Well, I still have you," he said, checking his rifle.

When the explosion had hit, Charlie had been knocked flat and Robbie had skidded to a halt, turning around and spraying the ravine again. Shaking his head, Charlie looked back and didn't see Randy. "Where's Shadow?" he yelled over the ringing in his ears.

"I was covering our six, I don't know!" Robbie shouted back when his SAW ran dry. Letting it hang, he grabbed Charlie and pulled him around the corner of the hut.

"I'm good, where is Shadow? He was running up behind me!" Charlie shouted, checking his weapon.

Looking back, Blaster saw Randy working on his leg. "He's behind that stone fence beside the fire," Robbie said, dropping to one knee and letting the body on his shoulder hit the ground. Yanking out another box of ammo, he popped his feed tray open as Book raised his rifle, shooting in a steady rhythm.

"Go check on him, I'm on my last mag," Charlie said, ejecting the magazine.

Slamming the feed cover closed, Robbie spun around and bolted over as bullets whizzed past him. Jumping up, he dove over the wall and saw Randy jerk, lifting his rifle but stopping. Hitting the ground hard, Robbie rolled over and crawled back. He looked at Randy's duct taped leg, shaking his head. "I don't think that's one of the thousand and one uses for duct tape."

"It is now," Randy said, grunting through the pain before getting up on one knee and lifting his rifle up. "We are getting Book and leaving!"

"You won't hear me bitching about staying," Robbie said as Randy opened fire. "Book, moving to you!"

Charlie heard Blaster yell and heard a 'whoosh', then his world turned to bright light, thunder, and heat. His entire being screamed in pain.

"BOOK!" Robbie and Randy screamed, jumping over the wall and seeing a burning body rolling around. The hut Charlie had been kneeling by had a huge hole blown in the wall and the inside was on fire.

Seeing men pouring down the ravine, Blaster raised his SAW, squeezing the trigger and watching the running figures get mowed down. "I have cover!" he yelled as Randy ran over on his destroyed ankle.

Jumping in the air, Randy dove on Charlie while smelling diesel fuel and kerosene, trying to smother the flames with his body. Seeing Book's face on fire and knowing that had to be put out first, Randy covered Book's face with his hands, feeling the fire eat through his gloves. Gritting his teeth, Randy reached up and pulled his shemagh off, using it to help smother the flames.

Grabbing Book's melted combat goggles, Randy pulled the melted burning mess off his face, tossing them aside as he held the shemagh over Book's face. Knocking Charlie's burning helmet off, he smothered the smoldering hair on the left side of Book's head.

Feeling the flames still burning under him on the left side of Charlie's body, Randy moved over, trying to smother the flames with his own body. Suddenly, he felt a hand grab his and looked up to see Charlie trying to pull Randy's hands off his face. Moving his hands, Randy sighed to hear Charlie take a deep breath when his hands uncovered Book's face. "I wasn't trying to smother you," he said.

Looking down, he saw Charlie's right sleeve all the way to his glove was still on fire. Randy felt his hands burning and realized his gloves were on fire. "Blaster, put out the rest of the fire!" Randy shouted, rolling off and beating his hands on the ground, burying them in dirt to smother the fire.

Robbie turned around to see Book's left side still burning and dove, covering Charlie's body with his. Unfastening Charlie's burning vest, Blaster glanced over as Randy got the fire out on his hands. Robbie rolled Charlie out of the burning vest, beating at the fire burning Charlie's uniform. When the fire was out, he looked in Book's face and saw the outline of the melted glasses Randy had pulled off. The skin was burnt over the left side of his face but his left eye, except for being swollen shut, looked okay. Hearing gunfire very close, Robbie looked up as he smothered the fire on Charlie's legs with his body. Randy was aiming up the ravine as the hadjis charged.

"Book, can you hear me?" Robbie yelled, seeing the fire was out and grabbed his SAW while rolling off of Book.

"You're yelling in my face! Yes, I hear you!" Charlie shouted in a hoarse voice.

"Can you move? We need to evac," Robbie said, raising his SAW and firing off a burst.

"I can't move fast, but I'm not staying here," Charlie said, getting up and realizing he couldn't see out of his left eye. Hearing a wet slap, he turned to see Blaster spin around, diving to the dirt.

"Shadow, Blaster is down!" he yelled and tried to reach out with his arm but pain shot through his body. Letting out a yell, Charlie pulled his body over and saw Robbie crawling around the corner of the hut the RPG had hit, holding his left arm.

"I'm still here, butt monkeys!" Robbie yelled as blood squirted in his face. He looked down and saw his left gloved hand dangling, only held on by a strip of flesh. A bullet had impacted just above his wrist where the glove stopped, nearly severing his hand completely. "Don't think they sell that at Walmart," he huffed, yanking a dressing out.

Randy rolled around the corner gasping and looked at Robbie putting a dressing on. "Shit," he mumbled before leaning around the corner and shooting.

"Where's your damn duct tape?" Robbie yelled, turning to Randy and saw the roll of duct tape on his hydration pack. Grabbing the roll, he wrapped it around the dressing. "I take back what I said, it works pretty good," he gasped, seeing the bleeding stop.

A figure ran over before dropping down and all three jerked, spinning with their weapons. "I leave you three alone for two minutes!" Wheaton shouted, looking at the wounded trio. "Can everyone move?"

Randy spun around to look at Wheaton. "Want to see me run on my hands? How's the rest of the team?" he snapped, then leaned back around the corner firing.

"Had a kid jump out with an AK," Wheaton said, shooting a man trying to move around them. "Babyface is the only one mobile. Aaron and Travis look bad. Book, can you move?"

Seeing the burnt side of Charlie's body, Wheaton cringed and looked at Book as he pulled up his rifle. "I can move, but don't know for how long," Charlie replied with a wheeze, pulling the trigger. "On my last mag."

A loud grunt sounded out and everyone turned to see Randy fall back while grabbing his hip. "I'm getting tired of this shit!" Randy yelled.

"Then quit acting like a bullet magnet. That's not being ninja-like, Shadow!" Robbie shouted, squeezing the trigger and firing a long burst when two charged them.

"I'll cover and you three move to the ride," Wheaton told them, standing up.

"Book, can you help cover? Blaster and I'll take the bodies," Randy panted, crawling over and getting to his knees.

"My right eye can see," Charlie said, trying to grin but the burnt skin on his face didn't move and sent pain radiating through him.

"Move!" Wheaton yelled, squeezing his trigger and Randy grabbed the body Book was carrying while Blaster grabbed his. "Leave them!"

"I didn't carry Horowitz's ass across the Stan just to leave him now," Robbie grunted, dragging the body away with his right hand as he cradled the stump of his left.

Raising his rifle, Charlie used the remains of his left hand to hold up his rifle, shooting a fighter that popped around the corner.

The group moved back to the Pathfinder and loaded up the bodies in the back, then saw Cody stand up out of the sunroof shooting. They turned to see a figure that was charging them from the front, drop. "Good shooting, Babyface," Blaster said, closing the back hatch.

"Wheat, we are leaving!" Randy shouted, moving to the passenger door.

Wheaton took off in a run, then turned to fire behind him when he felt pain below his armpits and burning in his chest. Grabbing his chest, he felt his legs get weak, and hammers started hitting him in the back.

"Cover!" Robbie yelled, lifting his SAW up and used the stump of his left hand to brace the barrel.

The three turned as eight fighters rounded the corner of the house shooting, and saw Wheaton go down. Charlie jerked his rifle up, squeezing the trigger as Robbie and Randy hosed down the area and saw two go down. Moving his sight, Charlie didn't see any more standing and lowered his rifle, seeing the other fighters down.

18

"Wheat!" Robbie yelled, running over and saw pink frothy blood on Wheaton's lips. "Dammit," Blaster huffed, grabbing Wheaton's vest and dragging him. Feeling something bump him, he glanced over as Randy grabbed Wheaton to help him pull the body.

Seeing movement, Charlie spun to his right and squeezed the trigger, watching a man grab his chest before crumpling over and falling face first. Two more came around the corner they'd left, and Charlie squeezed the trigger, watching both fall over and his bolt lock back. "Out of ammo!" he yelled, pulling his pistol.

"Book, get in the damn ride and you drive!" Randy yelled.

"I can only see out of one fucking eye!"

"I only got one foot, Blaster has one hand and it's a standard. You're out of bullets and we aren't!" Randy screamed as they reached the Pathfinder. Robbie looked in the backseat.

"Where is a Suburban when you need one," he grumbled at the packed backseat, closing the back passenger door. Shoving Wheaton's feet in first, Randy climbed in the passenger seat pulling Wheaton's body in. Robbie moved up, pushing Wheaton and helping Randy get him inside while Cody grabbed Wheaton's legs, pulling them between the front seats. Slamming the door, Robbie climbed up on the roof and dropped his legs down in the sunroof.

"Go!" Robbie screamed, seeing a large group come out between the huts and squeezed the trigger.

With his charred left hand, Charlie braced it on the steering wheel, shoving the shifter into first and popping the clutch as Blaster opened up. The concussion radiated down, making everyone's ears scream in pain. About to roll down the window to relieve the concussion from the gun blast of Blaster's SAW, Randy crouched down in the seat, hearing the windows exploding when bullets shattered them.

"I'm sick of your shit!" Randy shouted, maneuvering his rifle out the passenger window. Cody saw Wheaton's torso was blocking Randy from leaning out the window and pulled Wheaton's body back, resting Wheaton's back on the center console.

Leaning out, Randy started shooting as Robbie changed belts in his SAW. Keeping his head turned with his right eye facing more toward the driver's door so he could watch the left side with his right eye since his left was swollen shut, Charlie shoved the shifter in third. "Sharp curve!" he shouted but didn't hit the brakes.

Cutting the wheel, the rear barely skidded out with the weight of fourteen men as the Pathfinder's frame rubbed against the tires, it was riding so low. When they rounded the curve, the village disappeared from sight and Randy pulled back inside and Blaster dropped down from the sunroof but couldn't sit down.

"Feel like I'm in a clown car," Robbie said grimacing, cradling the stump of his left arm. He felt something bumping his back, and turned to see an unconscious PFC Bert Travis, known universally as 'Pirate' for his maritime lineage and exploits while on leave, shot through both arms and still bleeding through the hastily-applied bandages. Behind Travis, he could barely make out Corporal Cabrera, clutching at a fresh wound on the outside of his left thigh. Then he heard a grunt and turned his head slowly.

Trying to grin, Wheaton coughed up frothy blood. "Trust Shadow to find a rice burner," he said as blood ran out of his mouth.

Leaning over and panting through pursed lips from the pain in his ankle, Randy tried to grin. "Hey, they had a tractor, but I didn't take it for us, did I?" he joked, searching for wounds on Wheaton.

Robbie leaned over to help and watched Randy drop his head, looking under Wheaton's left armpit. "Entry left side under the arm," Randy announced, and Robbie moved his right hand under Wheaton's vest feeling the right side.

With a grimace, he felt a large exit wound on the right chest wall. "Blew through," Robbie said, yanking his hand out and grabbing a dressing from Wheaton's vest. Shoving his hand back under to stuff the dressing over the wound and trying to stem the flow of blood, Blaster looked down at Wheaton's hip. "Right hip," he said, seeing a hole in Wheaton's hip.

"Troops," Wheaton coughed, holding up his right hand. Charlie took his hand off the shifter to grab it and Blaster yanked his hand out, grabbing theirs. Grabbing Wheaton's hand with them, Randy looked at Wheaton.

"We're here, brother," Randy said as Wheaton struggled to breathe.

"Can you guys watch out for Kristi and the kids? Please? I know they're mine, but..." he said, struggling to breathe and gasping for air.

"Wheat, you don't have to ask," Charlie said, glancing down at Wheaton.

"Yes, I do. Please ... for me..." he gasped, then coughed up frothy blood. "I promised I would be there. They will never know me."

"I will watch her," Charlie promised, squeezing his hand.

Squeezing Wheaton's hand, "I will," Robbie vowed.

Randy nodded, also squeezing, "We are family, brother. I'll be there for them."

A peace filled Wheaton's face and a soft smile split his lips. "Thank you, guys," he murmured, closing his eyes with a gurgling sigh.

Chapter Two

Hardin County, Ohio

Lunging up in his bed and gasping for air, Randy looked around, panting. Blinking his eyes, he looked around for Wheaton and then realized he was in his bedroom in his own house. Feeling wetness, Randy looked down at the sweat-soaked sheets. Tossing the covers off, he spun around while throwing his legs off the bed and his foot touched the floor.

Scooting to the edge, he grabbed his prosthetic foot, sliding the nub of his left lower leg into the boot housing. His foot had been amputated two inches above his left ankle. Standing up, he felt the nub slip into the boot that extended up almost to his knee. The boot compressed against his lower leg, distributing the weight of his body off the bottom of his stump. This boot was only designed to be put on when walking around the house and wasn't strapped on; like a house shoe.

Randy walked out of his bedroom and down the hall into the bathroom. Turning on the light, he walked up to the sink and stared into the mirror. "You would think after more than a decade, the dream would lose potency," Randy informed his reflection.

Turning on the water and cupping his hands before splashing water on his face, Randy rubbed his hands over his silver-streaked shoulder-length brown hair. "Need to shave," he said, looking at the stubble around his goatee.

Glancing at his watch while he turned on the shower, "Well, had to get up soon anyway," he mumbled.

On Randy's return home, he'd stayed on the family farm in Hardin County, Ohio, during his rehab. Learning to walk again with a prosthetic was harder than he'd imagined, but learn he did. Now, he had several prosthetics and could run just as fast as he did before that fateful mission. While he rehabbed, Randy got an Associate degree in Machining and Manufacturing.

His mom and dad helped him build a small house and shop on the farm, and when he wasn't helping his dad work the farm, Randy ran his own business out of the shop. He really liked being a machinist; working with metal appeased him.

Stepping into the shower, he looked down at the pure carbon fiber appendage with a sigh. Then his eyes moved up his body to the scar on his right hip where he'd been hit, then his right shoulder. It wasn't until they'd pulled into an Army outpost and a medic had stripped him, that Randy saw where a bullet had passed through his deltoid.

"Had bigger wounds that generated more pain to think of," he said, grabbing a rag.

Everyone else, like him, discovered they had more wounds than they'd thought. The biggest wound was on the inside. Seeing your team killed and injured was the most difficult to deal with. Like the others, he'd made peace, but the memories still hurt.

Out of everyone, Charlie's, or Book to the team, rehab was the longest.

Grabbing a towel when he got out and dried off, Randy sat down on a chair he kept in the bathroom. Taking his 'boot' off, Randy grabbed the rag and washed his stump. Drying the stump off, Randy shoved a towel down into the boot, soaking most of the water out.

Putting the boot back on, he stood up and moved to the sink. Lathering his face, Randy grabbed the razor. "We kept our word, Wheat," he said, nodding at his reflection and then started shaving his face.

Even during rehab, the three had kept tabs on Wheaton's wife and kids. Once a week, each talked to her on the phone and visited at least once a month.

They'd been there for every birthday Clark and Emily had since they'd gotten back. Emily, now eleven but would turn twelve this weekend, only had pictures of Wheaton. Little Emily was born six months after Wheaton died. Wheaton had been allowed to stay back from deployment for Kristi's first pregnancy. They had been in a car wreck on the way back from the doctor's office doing a one month checkup on Clark. Wheaton and Kristi were banged up but luckily,

Clark wasn't hurt. Then Kristi came up pregnant in the months they were recovering. The first sergeant tried to keep Wheaton stateside after the doctors released him for duty from the injuries he'd received in the wreck, but higher ups sent him to the Stan. Randy, Charlie, and Robbie had already been in country for almost a year but stayed for another deployment after seeing Wheaton show up.

The trio had been together since Ranger School, and Wheaton had been a sergeant in the 75th Rangers when they were first assigned to his platoon. For five years they stayed together, only being separated for advanced schools. Rinsing his razor off, Randy smiled, thinking about when he'd attended Pathfinder school.

Keeping a watch over Kristi, she'd never asked them for anything, nor did the kids. At times, Randy thought they should give her some space but until she told them, they would hold on to the vow. But truth be told, now they saw her as part of their family. Hell, even his mom called Kristi more than he did.

The kids thought of the trio as uncles and called them that. Cody, or Babyface, found them when he was released from the hospital and discharged from the Army. The day Cody showed up at Randy's family's farm, he'd stayed part of the group.

In the twelve years since hell, the vow they'd pledged was slowly replaced by a family commitment they felt for Kristi and the kids. Though she was a few years older than them, they saw her as a little sister.

Six years ago, Randy had called Kristi to check on her and Kristi had answered the phone crying. To say the least, Randy felt panic grip him when she answered. Come to find out, the sewage had backed up and no plumber could make it for ten days. The one plumber that did, quoted her a price that was the equivalent of a new mid-sized sedan to fix the problem.

"We'll see you in a few hours," Randy told her and hung up. Yelling for Cody to pack up and load the toolbox, Randy called Charlie, who was in law school and told him what was going on and he was heading to Chicago with Cody to help. After hanging up, Charlie went to his professors and told them it was a family emergency and jumped in his car, never waiting for approval.

Randy called Robbie as he and Cody threw suitcases in his Blazer. Robbie just heard, 'Kristi's in trouble'. Hanging up on Randy before finding out anything else, Robbie jumped on his Harley, speeding to Chicago.

What did they know about plumbing? Not a damn thing.

Stopping at a Lowes before reaching Chicago, Randy bought some tools he thought he would need for plumbing. Seeing they had books on the subject, he bought one of each. The books weren't for him, they were for Book. That was where Charlie got the handle 'Book'. He didn't read; he soaked up a book.

Randy loved to read and could've done it, given enough time. But Charlie could sit down, read a damn book in a few hours, and then teach it.

Even though Robbie lived the furthest from Chicago at the time, when Randy drove up to Kristi's house in Oak Lawn, Robbie was in the front yard with a shovel, digging. Robbie never told them until a few years later, he had evaded two cops who had tried to pull him over.

When Charlie showed up, Randy held out the bag of plumbing books, only to see Charlie had already stopped and bought some. For five days, the four dug up the yard and fixed the plumbing, then the floor of the house that had been ruined.

They bought what was needed for the repairs. Since Charlie was still in school then he couldn't buy much, but he bought what he could. Kristi was beyond tearful for their help. But when she tried to pay them for their time and the mountain of supplies they'd bought, the four carried her outside and rolled her around in the muddy yard. Seeing the four 'uncles' and their mom playing in the mud, Clark and Emily ran out and joined them.

Randy laughed, remembering the neighbors watching them with wide mouths when they'd rolled around in the muddy yard with Kristi and the kids.

Everyone that had made that trip out of hell, all stayed in touch. The others didn't check up on Wheaton's family like the trio did, but they hadn't made the vow. Cody had adopted the vow since the trio followed it, and he stayed with one of them depending on who needed him. All the rest of the team saw Kristi and the kids when they made the trip up to the retreat several times a year or during birthdays.

The retreat was over two hundred fifty acres in Meigs County, Ohio. An old farmer, Winston Zimmer, who lived next to Randy's dad had the land and kept a small herd of cows. One day, Mr. Zimmer had asked Randy while he was in rehab if he would look after the place. It was a hundred and sixty miles away, but Randy agreed. When he got there the first time, Randy was in heaven. The 'herd of cows', turned out to be ten cows and one bull.

Over half the land was covered in timber and a small river ran through the western side. The other half was field and had an old barn. Walking the property, Randy felt at peace for the first time since coming home.

Returning to his truck, Randy saw he didn't have cell service and drove to the town of Lookout before he got service again. When he saw bars on his phone, he pulled over and called Robbie and Charlie. It took them both some time to understand because Randy was talking a thousand miles an hour. Charlie was living in San Antonio for rehab and Blaster was in Atlanta. Hearing the excitement in Randy's voice and him saying he'd found 'peace', both loaded up after hanging up and drove to Ohio.

The next day, Randy showed them the property and like Randy, they'd felt peace walking the field and woods. Walking the property, they found where the river formed an oxbow that covered twenty acres and made camp. For three days the trio camped, feeling more like their old selves.

When he got home, Randy talked to Mr. Zimmer, who like his dad, was a vet. The old man saw the excitement in Randy's eyes and Randy begged him to let them build a small cabin. Just seeing Randy, the boy he'd watched grow up get excited again, the old man said he didn't care as long as Randy checked the land often.

A year after that peaceful day, and what Randy still didn't know, his father went to Mr. Zimmer and bought the land, putting it in a trust in the old man's name. Seeing how much it helped his son and his team; Randy's dad, Oliver, couldn't run the risk of them not being able to have a place to recuperate.

The land was just called 'the retreat'. When Cody showed up at his house, Randy took him to the retreat that day and Cody felt whole again. They invited the others, and like the trio and Cody, they fell in love with the retreat. Like visiting Kristi, the trio and Cody now visited the retreat once a month most of the time. They hunted, fished, rode four-wheelers, or Randy's horses when he brought them down, sat in the clubhouse watching college football, or just walked the woods.

Out of everyone from the team, Cody was the only one who'd never popped back socially. He always lived with one of the trio, helping them with work. It depended on the time of year to which one he lived with. During the fall, he always lived with Randy to help with the harvest and moved between Charlie and Robbie. A few times, Cody had even stayed with Kristi because her schedule changed, and the kids needed someone at the house. Cody was never a burden. Wherever he was, Cody worked, and like the trio, he was a bachelor. Only a few years younger than the trio, his gentle face and small stature made him still look like he was a teenager.

Not to say they didn't date, except for Robbie. If it was female, Robbie would chase it. To date, Robbie's longest relationship with the same woman that Randy knew about was sixteen days. Randy had dated several women but had never connected with one. Most got pissed at his relationship with the others and Kristi. When he saw that, it was over. The team, like Kristi and her kids, were family and were part of him. If a woman couldn't accept that, then he didn't need her.

Walking out to the living room that held his gym, Randy looked out the window and saw his parents' house was still dark. "Dad doesn't get up till five," he said, turning to the clock on the wall and saw it was 0330.

Working out for an hour, Randy went to his room and grabbed his clothes. On his dresser, he saw pictures of the group at the retreat. The next picture was Aaron and his family standing in front of his cabin at the retreat. Aaron had been wounded in the chest and abdomen loading up in the Pathfinder. It took four months before he was able to return to active duty, but Aaron didn't re-enlist. A year after that trip, he'd exited the military and went to college, getting a degree in accounting. While he was in school, he got married and everyone liked Elizabeth, or Liz. They had two kids now; both boys, Andre who was nine and six-year-old Eli. Glancing over the other pictures and seeing only the trio and Cody not married, he sighed. "Maybe one day," he said.

Walking into the kitchen and turning on the coffee pot, the phone rang. He turned to the phone smiling. "That is Book because Blaster will be shacking up with some woman at this time."

Not even looking at the caller ID, he grabbed the phone. "Hey, Charlie," Randy answered.

"You alright?" Charlie asked in a groggy voice. It was weird or maybe not, but whenever one of them had a nightmare or was feeling down, the other two knew and would call. Most of the time, it was within hours, case in point, right now.

With a grin, "Yeah, I'm good, Charlie. Just reliving that last day in hell. Was it last week you made the trip?" Randy asked, trying to remember when he'd called Charlie.

"Week before," Charlie answered with a yawn. "You want to head to the retreat this weekend?"

"Brother, Emily's birthday party is Saturday, we can't miss that."

Charlie laughed, "We can leave after the party if you need a trip."

"I can't remember the last time we didn't spend more than one day at Kristi's," Randy mumbled, thinking of all the times over the years they had been to Kristi's.

Silence filled the phone for several minutes. "Um, I don't think we ever have," Charlie finally answered. "But I don't have court for a few days, so we can drop by the retreat."

Laughing, "Charlie, I promise, it's all good," Randy said. "You sure you just don't want to go back and try to catch that fish you missed last weekend?"

"I told you, that wasn't a fish, it was a whale," Charlie said in a stern voice, suddenly very awake.

Grabbing a coffee mug, Randy poured a cup. "Babyface up yet?"

"No, I had him type up some requests for production and a set of interrogatories last night."

"Oh, come on, he's a Ranger. Can't you find him something cool to do?" Randy chuckled, taking a sip.

"F.O., Randy. He asked, and I showed him how last year. Don't worry, he's going to work on my truck tomorrow. That stud enough for him?" Charlie laughed.

"Yeah, I guess," Randy said, putting the cup down. "Tell Cody, Dad was asking if he would be coming over soon to help start plowing the fields."

"When Babyface wakes up, I'll tell him," Charlie said, knowing Cody would take off after hearing Randy's dad needed him.

Several seconds passed and Randy became serious. "Has Cody talked about going to see his family? His dad is in the hospital."

Letting out a long sigh, "No," Charlie answered. "I asked him yesterday and he just blew me off. Then last night he told me he was *with* family."

"His dad shouldn't have said what he did when Cody was in the hospital," Randy said, more to himself than Charlie.

"Yeah, having your father tell you that your sacrifice didn't mean shit, even for your team, really puts a damper on the family dynamics," Charlie admitted. "Like the kid said, he's with family."

"Yeah," Randy groaned. "Well, I have to go over to the Richard's farm today and work on his tractor. If I miss Blaster's call, tell him I said thanks for checking."

"You're a machinist, what are you working on tractors for?"

"He broke the axle and I'm going to fix it, so he doesn't have to spend ten grand for a new one," Randy laughed.

"Yeah, that seems a bit steep for an axle," Charlie chuckled. "Call if you need me."

"Will do, Book."

"Hey, tell Mom and Pop 'hi'," Charlie said. Out of everyone's families, Randy's was the only ones who understood. Randy's dad Oliver had served in the Army and been downrange. He understood and helped more than anyone. Randy's mom, Lena, was just loveable and holy crap, could she cook!

"Can do, Book. If you need me, call," Randy said, hanging up.

Chapter Three

Cleveland, OH

Charlie sat by the pool and sipped his orange juice, eyes focused on the iPhone as he read the e-mail message. Ignoring the few curious looks coming his way from the early morning crowd at his gym, the young man took a few seconds to swallow his juice and digest the words on his screen. He gave a little sigh before setting the device aside, locking the screen, and padded barefoot over to the edge of the pool.

With his pale white skin, evidence of his Irish and English roots, the mottled brown and dark gray scars showed in graphic detail. Like a map of some undiscovered continent, or a particularly gruesome series of tattoos, the scars covered him front and back on the left side in a scrollwork of pain and horror. He knew people looked away. Charlie couldn't really blame them. He wanted to look away himself, but he was trapped on the inside looking out.

Only here, at the pool, did Charlie allow others to see. Probably went back to his rehab time at the Burn Center at Brookes Army Hospital in San Antonio. With his burns came surgeries, multiple surgeries, and then rehab between the surgeries. As the burns healed and the skin grafts took, or not, the patients needed to be engaged in some sort of physical therapy. Those tissues and muscles needed to be pulled and stretched regularly, or the patient might never regain any range of motion. For Charlie, his favorite therapy was time in the pool. Now, twelve years after his last battle, he still found his peace at the pool, or on the range.

He used the first few laps as warm-ups, getting the blood flowing and doing that all-important stretching as he let his mind go. Charlie focused on his breathing and motion, allowing the concerns of the day to slip away. After that, in a relaxed, almost Zen state, he hit the next ten laps hard. Exploding through the water like a knife, he stroked through the length of the lane and then pushed off smoothly on the flips. Pushing his body past its limits, he then throttled back, languidly paddling through another lap as his body began to cool down and recover from the exertion.

He longed to kick it back up, do more sets, and work his body to complete exhaustion. He wanted that razor's edge he used to feel, but it was a Friday and he still needed to go to work. Charlie wasn't a soldier anymore, and he had bills to pay.

Floating over to the tiled steps, Charlie gripped the edge of the pool with his left hand and pulled as he rose from the slightly chilly, chlorinated water. The choice of hand was no accident. The same explosion and fire that'd transformed his body into a patchwork of twisted scar tissue and slightly more regular stretches of harvested skin grafts, also cost him most of the last two digits on his left hand. Most, because he retained the last joint; the proximal phalanx as one of his physical therapists had called it, of his ring finger while the pinky finger had been amputated down to the knuckle.

With just the index and middle fingers left whole, along with a stub of the ring finger, to balance out his heavily-scarred thumb, Charlie knew his left hand more resembled a lobster's claw than anything else. Them's the breaks, he told himself, and lessons learned, hard lessons involving copious amounts of sweat and tears where no one else could see them fall, taught Charlie not to baby that hand. So, by leaning into his left hand, he shifted his weight into the palm as he leveraged himself out of the pool and onto the skid-proof concrete and tile of the apron. From there, he rose on slightly shaking legs and tottered over to his gym bag, robe, and towels arrayed around his chair.

"That was some workout," a stranger's voice stated, coming from behind him. So much for my situational awareness, the swimmer chided himself as he forced himself not to react. Female, he thought, and with a familiar accent. Not exactly Southern, he decided. Texas, maybe, he thought. Youngish, but not juvenile. Educated.

"I was in a hurry today," Charlie replied, reaching for the towel and wrapping it around his neck. Finally turning with his robe in hand, he caught sight of the speaker. She was tall, maybe five feet nine inches, and wearing one of those sleek, black one-piece suits favored by serious swimmers. That seemed likely, given her well-

31

defined shoulders and tight, muscular build. Her hair was up in a cap, but from her pale brows, high cheekbones and almost Elfin Nordic features, he was willing to lay any amount of money she was blonde. That contrasted nicely with the dark blue eyes, he concluded.

He took everything in at a glance, rather than ogling the hot chick who dared speak to him. And yet...

"You done checking me out?" she asked, but there was no challenge in her voice.

"Actually, just trying to place you," Charlie replied, his voice steady as he spoke. "Not many show up this early to the gym on a weekday, and the ones that do generally try to avoid the Phantom whenever possible."

"The Phantom?"

"Of the Opera," he answered, and to punctuate his statement, Charlie theatrically shook out the terrycloth robe in a flutter of fabric and donned it like he was stepping into a cape.

That seemed to catch the woman off guard, and she wrinkled her brow for a moment. Charlie thought it was cute and then had to fight the smile. She was attractive, though not normally what he would have considered his type. More honestly, what he would have considered in his league. Even before he'd gone bobbing for French fries in the deep fryer, he thought wryly.

That's what one wag had called it, back at the burn center in Texas. There was some grisly truth to the joke, in Charlie's case, as the best they could tell was he'd been caught by an exploding fuel oil bomb. Somebody's cooking oil tank, his surviving squadmates insisted. Staff Sergeant Mallory might not have coined the phrase, but he was willing to steal it for his own use. Where Charlie suffered mainly from surface burns to about thirty-five percent of his body, Mallory had been blown up in an IED attack and then burned, so he'd been subjected to a 'shake and bake'.

Mallory, in addition to the third degree burns on his chest and face that claimed his right eye and part of his nose, also suffered with the traumatic amputation of his right leg above the knee and his right arm at the elbow. Man was a physical wreck on the outside, but still had the morbid sense of humor common in frontline troops. He'd also served as a pillar of strength for the mostly young men who sought care at the hospital.

Thinking of Staff Sergeant Mallory made the smile slip out anyway and yet, this hot blonde was still standing there. Looking a little confused but not frightened by his appearance. He wanted to just turn and walk away, but he didn't dare. Attractive women seldom stuck around in his presence, and even if she wasn't interested, he needed to treat her politely. What the locals referred to as the Cities might take up a sizeable chunk of real estate but in some ways, the four cities reminded Charlie of a small town. At least, in the way the gossip mill worked, anyway.

Despite his concerns, the young lady in question just shrugged off his attempted joke and addressed his earlier comment.

"I actually just started this week. Like you, I prefer to get my workout in early." Then she paused and stuck out her hand like it was the most normal thing in the world to do.

"My name is Joan, by the way. Joan Norgren," she said, and despite her slight accent, she shook hands like a Midwestern farm girl. Firm grip and looked him straight in the eye as she pumped his arm.

"Charlie Tucker," he managed to say. "It is a pleasure to make your acquaintance. I'm sure I'll be seeing you around. This is a good gym, and most folks are very friendly."

Joan flushed for some unknown reason at Charlie's words before replying and Charlie again felt a twinge of unease. After the last round of plastic surgery, the exposed bone in his jaw was no longer visible and finally the built-up shelf of tissue that was his left cheek nearly matched the natural one on his right side, but nothing could really cover or fix the raw-looking, discolored patchwork of skin stretching from his left temple to the bottom side of that surgically repaired chin. His doctors finally admitted what he could clearly see, which was his rough and tattered scars might never smooth out, and the tight quirk to his lips gave him an almost sinister twist when he wasn't careful. Even after hours practicing in front of the mirror, he knew he still screwed up at times, even after all these years.

"I, uh, better get going," Charlie announced, almost tripping over the aluminum chair in his haste to leave the area. He was getting himself spun up, he realized, but did not seem able to stop his flight. "See you around."

So intent on leaving, he almost missed her parting words.

"I look forward to seeing you again, Charlie Tucker."

Gathering up his gear, Charlie retreated back to the changing room and away from this beautiful, interesting woman. He felt conflicted, and the thought of her looking forward to seeing him again made the hair on the nape of his neck stand up.

"Rangers lead the way," he whispered to himself as he headed for the showers.

Chapter Four

Chicago, Illinois

"I hate this damn city," Randy snarled, fighting the urge to hold his middle finger out the window as a car driving forty crossed over to the center lane, pulling in front of him from an entrance ramp. Glancing in his rearview mirror, he pursed his lips barely shaking his head in trembling anger, seeing he wasn't getting over any time soon. Taking a deep breath and trying to calm down, Randy narrowed his eyes and just gave up as another slowpoke pulled onto the highway.

"I would buy Kristi a new house from my own pocket if she left this damn town," he said, still glancing in his mirror, and the first slow car he was still behind actually slowed down more while the rest of the traffic zipped past.

Watching his side mirror at the line of cars passing, Randy spotted a gap coming in the line of cars. Randy yanked the steering wheel to send his lifted Blazer into the outside lane and the small gap widened as the truck he cut off hit the brake when it saw the massive 4x4 was coming over regardless. Stomping the gas, he looked out the passenger window, but couldn't see the pokey driven car because his truck was too high. Glancing in his rearview mirror, he saw he had scarcely passed the car and jerked his steering wheel right, pulling only feet in front of the slow car.

Hearing a honk, Randy smiled, pressing the gas and fighting the urge to stomp the brake. "If you can't stop, smile as you go under," Randy sang out with a smile.

Pulling onto the exit lane an hour later and feeling very proud of himself for only flipping off three drivers, Randy guided his truck off at the Oak Lawn exit. Traffic for a Saturday at eight in the morning wasn't bad, but it was more than he liked dealing with. Guiding his truck through the affluent neighborhood, Randy moved to the turning lane.

It never ceased to amaze him at all the nice houses in this neighborhood where Kristi lived. The house, she got from her grandparents just before Wheat died. She'd gotten her nursing degree while Wheaton was in the Army. With a kid still in diapers and six months pregnant, Kristi had moved from Washington State back to her hometown.

The move had nothing to do with nostalgia. When Wheaton died, the military told Kristi she had thirty days to vacate the base. At the time, Randy was in Walter Reed with most of the team. Charlie had been sent to Texas to the military burn center. Randy's parents came to the hospital and he'd begged them to help Kristi.

They'd left Randy and had driven to Chicago and met Kristi, helping her move in. That was when Randy's mom became endeared to Kristi. Since Kristi's parents had moved to Florida and her younger sister was in college at the time, nobody in her family helped. They did come for the funeral but didn't even return when Emily was born. Kristi's sister, Tabitha, did move back to Chicago after school, but only came to Kristi when she needed something.

Randy's parents, Lena and Oliver, more or less adopted Kristi then and there. His mom stayed with Kristi for the last month of her pregnancy, then didn't come back home until Emily was two months old. Many times, Randy told his parents thank you for that, but they just told him it was the right thing to do. The fact Kristi's family never showed up made Randy and the team realize why Wheaton had begged for the vow, and come hell or high water, it would be kept. The only living relative Wheaton had was a brother in jail.

Rather excited, Randy had left his house at 0500 as had his parents, but his mom and dad took the RV. His mom didn't like riding in his Blazer since you literally had to climb up into it. What Randy really thought was they didn't like how fast he drove because his parents always took their own vehicle. They made the trip to Kristi's almost as many times as he and the trio did. None of the team could remember a month that at least one of them hadn't come to Chicago to stay a few days. Oliver still hadn't forgiven Randy or the others for not telling him about the plumbing incident. Thinking back, Randy really wished he had because his dad would've been a big help, saving them a lot of money and time.

Slowing down, Randy guided his truck next to the curb in front of Kristi's house. It was a nice-sized, two-story brick home. Kristi made good money as a nurse but couldn't have afforded to live there if her grandparents hadn't willed her the paid-for house. Even with the house paid for, Kristi was pressed just covering the taxes and insurance. Over the years, he and the trio did many upgrades. Most Kristi loved because she was going to do them anyway when money allowed. A few improvements she didn't want but would give in because they would just show up with the supplies.

The two main ones she hadn't cared for were they had replaced all the entrance doors with steel doors and frames. Next, they had installed storm doors on all the entrance doors. Then they had replaced the ground floor windows with storm windows, then put bars on the windows. When they had finished, Robbie had noted if Chicago got hit with a hurricane, Kristi and the kids would be safe.

The neighborhood association didn't like the upgrades because nobody had cleared it with them, but the boys didn't care. To shut the HOA up, Charlie had filed suit against the management company and then served them a stack of discovery, including requests for admissions and a whole volume of requests for production. As far as Randy was concerned it was mumbo jumbo, but Charlie insisted they would back off once he scheduled the depositions for the President of the Homeowners Association, and he had been correct. Randy, Cody, and Robbie just wanted to burn down the HOA building and beat the board members with baseball bats. None of them liked Chicago and more than once, all of them had begged Kristi to move, telling her it was too dangerous here. They didn't like a city that made it illegal to defend yourself, and cost an arm and a leg to live in.

Kristi was a very pretty woman at five-foot-five with short black hair. The death of Wheat had aged her, along with being a nurse and single mom, but she wore it well. Six years older than Randy, Robbie, and Charlie, she actually looked younger.

Opening the door of his Blazer, Randy dropped out, taking most of the weight on his left side. The prosthetic took the impact better than his foot did. The prosthetic he was wearing today was the main one he wore. Like all his prosthetics, a shoe could be worn on it and he bent over adjusting his pants that had pulled up, exposing the flexible joint.

Grabbing one of Emily's presents, he shut the door and walked around his truck and grinned, seeing Robbie's Harley in the driveway. Before he could think about when Blaster got here, "Uncle Randy!" he heard and turned to see Clark and Emily charging out of the house at him.

Kneeling and putting the wrapped box he was carrying on the ground, Randy held his arms wide. They crashed into him, almost taking Randy to the ground as they wrapped their arms around his neck, squeezing tight. "Man, I was just here two weeks ago, and I swear you two have grown," he said, hugging them tight.

They leaned back, looking at him with grins, "We haven't grown in two weeks," Clark laughed. Randy looked at Clark's face and smiled with remorse. He was the spitting image of Wheat. He had just turned thirteen but was big like his dad. Clark was already as tall as his mom and stout. Looking at little Emily, she was demure like her mom but had Wheat's bright green eyes. It wasn't hard to see his friend in these two.

"Where's Granny and Grandpa?" Emily asked, looking down the road with a worried expression.

"Emily, you know they never ride with me," Randy laughed, hearing the door open and looked up to see Kristi step out on the porch.

"You need to get a ladder, so Granny can get in your monster truck," Clark smiled, letting Randy go as he stood up. Randy glanced behind him at his truck. The bottom of the truck was over four feet off the ground and the huge tires made it look taller.

"I don't think Granny likes how fast I drive," Randy laughed, turning back to the kids.

"You drive the best," Emily said in a cheer. "When people drive stupid, you wave your middle finger at them and honk your horn, yelling you're going to run over them."

Walking over, Kristi laughed, "Yes, like a little girl did yesterday."

With a pained look, Randy leaned down. "I told you not to do that when your mom was around," he said in a low voice to Emily.

"She did it, too," Emily whined.

Clark looked back at his mom. "And Mom rolled down her window yelling a lot more than she would run them over," he chuckled.

"Kids," Kristi said, raising her eyebrows and both stopped smiling. "I'm grown."

"That's right," Randy agreed, pulling the kids beside him. "Only do that when you are with me," he said with a serious face and nod.

Kristi laughed, stepping over and hugging Randy. "Don't know what I'm going to do with any of you," she laughed. Letting Randy go, the laugh turned into a smile.

Behind them, the door opened up. "I don't remember a welcome like that," Robbie commented, coming out on the front porch.

"Robbie, you got here before seven and the kids ran out in pajamas," Kristi snapped, glancing back at him. "I was brushing my teeth. I swear, none of you sleep."

Watching Robbie come trotting down the porch steps, Randy laughed. "I want to know how Robbie can party all night and still get up before sunrise."

"Sleep is overrated," Robbie said, walking up and Randy moved over as they engulfed each other in a bear hug.

"Momma is going to yell at you, Blaster, for driving your motorcycle," Randy chuckled, letting Robbie go.

Lifting his left arm up and pointing at his bike, "Mom can yell at me all she wants to, but not at my bike," Robbie said, pointing at his bike with his prosthetic hook.

Looking over at the massive chrome-covered Harley, Randy shook his head. "Momma would've broken it by now but can't believe how much money you have invested in it."

"Pop likes it," Robbie huffed.

"Yeah, because Momma made Dad sell his when I was born," Randy grinned.

Shaking his head, "Sometimes, Ms. Lena needs a spanking," Robbie said.

"You can try to spank her," Randy laughed.

"Nope," Robbie said with a straight face. "I've had enough beatdowns in my life."

"Is that my present?" Emily asked, clapping her hands.

Looking at the big box, Randy nodded. "One of them," he said, and Kristi looked up at him, narrowing her eyes.

"I told each of you, one present," she almost growled and waved her hand at Robbie. "UPS delivered his yesterday."

"I couldn't carry them on the bike," Robbie cried out. "Putting a trailer on a hog is like putting training wheels on; it's sacrilege."

Looking at Robbie with a flat expression, "Yeah," Randy snapped. "You have proven that point."

Kristi busted out laughing, slapping her leg. Last year, she and the kids met up at the Grand Canyon with Randy, Cody, Charlie, and Robbie to go backpacking and kayaking for a week. At the parking area, a young man had pulled in riding a Harley that had training wheels and Robbie had spun off on the young man. Charlie and Randy had to tackle Robbie before he attacked the young man. As they'd held Robbie down, the young man had jumped on his training-wheeled Harley and sped away.

"I can't believe you threatened to beat him to death with his own bike," she howled, stumbling around laughing.

"Kristi," Robbie said, holding his chin high. "There are some things that just can't be overlooked."

Clasping Robbie's shoulder, "Brother, you're lucky we didn't get thrown in jail," Randy grinned.

"Book's a lawyer," Robbie huffed.

"Yeah, that's why he wanted us to hurry up and get on the river before the park rangers showed up," Randy replied.

"I'm not apologizing," Robbie snapped with a straight face. "The kids didn't need to see a Harley with training wheels. I'm sure it scarred them mentally."

Taking a step back, "I didn't ask you to," Randy said. "I just wish you would've kept your mouth shut and we could've thrown the bike in the canyon."

"Oh," Robbie said, raising his eyebrows and nodding. "You need help getting your stuff?"

"With the presents, but I'm going to go to a hotel-," Randy started, and the laughter left Kristi's face and the kids gasped.

"What are you talking about?!" she snapped, very close to a yell. "We have room for everyone!"

"Well, with the entire group here again with Momma and Dad, it's kind of crowded," Randy tried to explain, taking a step back from Kristi.

"Mom and Pop are bringing the RV, aren't they?" Kristi asked, crossing her arms and Randy nodded. "There's more than enough room and even if they weren't... Troop!" she snapped, making everyone jump. "Your ass will be staying here."

Robbie stepped up. "You remember, I never said I was going to a hotel. This is all on Shadow."

"Blaster!" Kristi snapped, making him jump back. "You learned your lesson last time."

"Kri-," Randy started, and Kristi held up her hand stopping him.

When Randy closed his mouth, she crossed her arms again. "This is your home here and if you have a problem, we can settle up."

A grin split Randy's face. Even after all the years, he could still see and hear Wheat acting the same way Kristi was now. "You win," Randy gave in, and the kids started cheering.

Cutting his eyes to Robbie, Randy saw Robbie hold up his hand and hook. "Brother, don't look at me," he cried out. "When I asked last Christmas, Kristi grabbed a broom to hit me."

"I would've caught you if the kids hadn't latched onto my legs," Kristi admitted, then slowly started to grin.

Leaning over, Robbie hugged the kids, "Thank you again for that," he whispered in a low voice. Leaning up, "Let's get your stuff," he said, looking at Randy.

Everyone came over as Randy climbed up in the passenger door, passing out two more presents and grabbed his bag. When he jumped out, moving to the back of the Blazer and opening the back, he purposely kept his eyes diverted from Kristi. He could feel the hard stare burning the side of his face.

"Blaster, need your help carrying this one," Randy said, handing his small suitcase to Clark. The burning on the side of his face from Kristi's stare intensified.

As Randy helped Robbie carry the box, Robbie looked at him while shaking his head. "Just to warn you, she's going to pull you in the kitchen and give you a lecture. She's in that mood because I already got mine," he said in a low voice.

"What is that?" Kristi asked, nodding at the box they were carrying.

"A present," Randy scoffed. "Kristi, I can't tell you with Emily right here."

"I should of thought of that," Robbie mumbled, walking up the porch steps.

Running to the door, Emily held it open. "Can I open one now?" she asked Randy with pouty eyes.

Just as Randy was about to say yes, Kristi barked. "Emily!"

"Um, how about we wait till the party. Granny and Grandpa will want to watch you open your presents," Randy offered wisely.

The pouty face dropped off and a smile sprang up on Emily's face. "Okay," she said and they carried the box in. Kristi put the present she was carrying down and Randy saw a stack of presents in the dining room.

"Those from you?" Randy asked Robbie as they set the box down.

"Hell yes!" Kristi snapped, making both jump. "I told each of you, one present. I have told all of you that since they were babies, one present, but do any of you ever listen?"

"Um," Randy said looking away. "I only got you one present for Christmas this year," he said proudly.

"I told you not to get me any!" Kristi snapped.

"Oh, yeah," Randy mumbled. "Why don't you tell that to Momma and Dad?" he asked.

Giving a startle, the hostile expression on her face dropped as Kristi shook her head. "Uh-uh. Mom and Pop would spank my butt."

"Yep," Robbie grinned as he gave a nod.

Hearing a car pull up, the kids took off out the door. "You two can wait on us!" Kristi yelled out, chasing them and Robbie and Randy followed.

Moving to the door, Kristi thought of the four and couldn't help but smile. She didn't know how she would've made it without them, or Mom and Pop for that matter. It wasn't the help they provided that she loved so dearly, it was the sense of family they brought to her and the kids.

Granted, if the kids weren't so well-mannered, there was no doubt in Kristi's mind they would be spoiled brats. Cody, Charlie, Robbie, and Randy spoiled the hell out of them, along with Mom and Pop. Every Christmas and birthday, the two had mountains of gifts and almost every time the trio came to visit, they brought the kids something.

She loved the rest of the group but those four with Mom and Pop, she looked at them as her family. Her parents visited once a year and she took the kids to see them in Florida once a year, but the four were here all the time. Just visiting, following the kids in activities, working on the house or her car. Hell, Kristi saw them more in a month than she saw her younger sister Tabitha in a year, and Tabitha *lived* in Chicago.

Stepping outside, she saw Clark and Emily charging Cody as he climbed out of his 1966 red Camaro. When his feet hit the ground, the kids latched on, hugging him. "Uncle Cody!" they cried out, squeezing him.

"Hey guys," he smiled, hugging them. Kristi walked down the steps, shaking her head while looking at Cody. He was thirty now and still had the young face of a kid. It didn't help that he wasn't much taller than her with a slight build that accentuated his child-like face. She had known him for more than a decade and still couldn't believe he was thirty. Unlike the others, she didn't know Cody until he came over with Randy that first time. Cody had been assigned to the unit while it was in Afghanistan.

Walking off the porch and heading over, she watched Cody release the kids and move to his trunk, pulling out a present and his suitcase. "Cody, I'm so proud of you!" Kristi cried out and broke into a run. She hugged him tight. "You listened and only got one present."

"Well, uh, Kristi, I couldn't fit the rest in because I'm heading back with Randy, his dad needs me," Cody stuttered. "Um, Charlie has the others."

She released him as a big quad cab truck pulled up. Kristi turned and her mouth fell open, seeing the bed was covered with a tarp. "Told you she would get pissed because we bought them a swimming pool," Robbie mumbled, walking down the steps.

"I still say, we don't let Kristi know we bought Emily a four-wheeler until they come up to the retreat," Randy suggested again.

"We got Clark one when he was twelve," Robbie objected.

Walking across the yard, Randy nodded. "I know, I'm just saying. I already have a lecture coming if the routine doesn't work. I don't want it to last all day. She acts like we are spoiling them rotten."

"They need this stuff," Robbie protested throwing his hook up in the air.

Randy smiled. "I know and when we get them, Kristi's lectures aren't as bad as Momma's."

"I want to crawl under a rock when Mom lectures," Robbie huffed.

"Tell me about it," Randy chuckled as they reached Cody. They both hugged him as the kids and Kristi met Charlie, hugging him.

Cody looked at them grinning, "Guess I get a lecture," he said.

"Well, you can join me for mine if the routine doesn't work," Randy laughed.

"No way, I took mine alone," Robbie snapped with a grin.

Putting his arm over Cody's shoulders, Randy led him over to Charlie as he talked to Kristi and the kids. "So, what's this I hear about you typing up legal mumbo jumbo?" Randy asked. "You thinking of becoming a lawyer?"

"No," Cody said with a serious face. "I couldn't even pronounce the words I was typing. Charlie's secretary was sick and he asked if I could do it."

Randy and Robbie walked with Cody between them. They knew, like Lena and Oliver, Cody loved the feeling of being needed. They paid him, forcibly most of the time, as they made up jobs for him to do to help out. Each did their best to make Cody feel indispensable.

"How much longer you got on your degree?" Robbie asked.

"One more semester," Cody grinned. The guys had finally talked Cody into getting a computer programing degree online. It took some effort, but they all told him it would help them out tremendously. He loved computers and had one at each of their houses. That's why the guys bugged him to take computer courses. Cody didn't like being away from them and online courses were a Godsend. They wanted to make sure, if something happened to them, Cody would be able to survive.

They reached Charlie's truck as he knelt beside Emily. "One of the presents is for you and Clark," Charlie told them and both kids' eyes grew big as they slowly turned their gaze to the truck.

"Charlie, I'm going to punch you," Kristi said with a flat voice.

"Glad we voted him to bring the pool," Robbie whispered to Randy.

Nodding, Randy glanced at Robbie. "After I brought that eighty-inch TV last year, I knew I wasn't bringing it," Randy said in a low voice.

Passing Kristi, Randy walked over, wrapping his arms around Charlie. "Brother," he said, squeezing tight. "I haven't got my lecture, so you can join Cody and me in the kitchen. That way, Kristi can get all three out at one time."

Releasing Randy, Charlie hugged Robbie. "You would think Robbie would quit getting here first, so he wouldn't take his lecture alone," Charlie said. "Kids, will you carry the presents in the backseat inside for me?" The kids took off, grabbing presents and running inside.

"Nah," Robbie chuckled, letting Charlie go. "Kristi's lectures, when she first wakes up, aren't that bad."

Charlie looked from Randy and then to Cody. "I'm getting here earlier then," Charlie concluded.

Seeing Kristi taking a deep breath and narrowing her eyes, Randy moved up beside her. "Kristi, I hate to ask but, I skipped breakfast. Can I get something to eat? I'll take a bowl of cereal. I'm really starving."

Shock hit her and the anger left Kristi's face. "Randy, I'll fix you some breakfast. You're not eating cereal," she gasped. Kristi turned and patted the side of Charlie's scarred face, then headed to the house.

"Kristi, can I get something to eat?" Cody asked with a pleading look.

"Charlie, are you starving him?" Kristi asked, spinning around.

"No, he eats more than I do," Charlie grinned. "But we forgot to go grocery shopping and just left last night. We stopped and got a bag of chips when we filled up with gas."

"Hey, since you're cooking, can I beg for a plate?" Robbie said, winking at Charlie.

"Well, yes," Kristi answered, turning to the house and moved at a fast walk.

When she went inside, Charlie held out his hand palm up and the other three slapped it one at a time. "You think she'll ever figure that out?" Charlie asked as the others turned to him.

"Book, we've done that for eight years and she hasn't figured it out," Robbie grinned. "Doesn't mean she won't, but we can hope."

Hearing a diesel engine growling, they turned to see a Class-A RV pulling down the road. "Robbie, you may want to move your bike, so Mom doesn't tell Pop to run over it," Charlie offered with a grin.

"Oh crap!" Robbie cried out, taking off in a run. Kicking the kickstand up, he pushed his bike up to the house.

"Cody, remember, you have to tell Kristi you are going to get a motel room when we come for Clark's birthday," Randy said.

Letting out a sigh with a groan, "Oh man, I hate it when she gives me that look then she crosses her arms and starts tapping her foot," he whined.

"Buck up, troop, and embrace the suck," Randy said, grinning.

A grin split Cody's face. "When she figures it out, we are going to have hell to pay."

"Nah, I'll tell Momma," Randy laughed as the RV pulled up into the driveway. "You would think since they own a big ass RV, they would use it more than just coming here."

"Hey, they took that trip to Oregon last year," Charlie said.

"Yes, with Kristi and the kids," Randy chuckled.

"That was the only way we could get her out of the house, so we could put in an electric garage door," Charlie reminded him.

Nodding as the RV came to a stop, "You don't know how happy I was that it was Momma and Dad who dropped her off," Randy chuckled.

"I didn't answer my phone for two days when she called," Charlie grinned.

"Neither did I," Randy said.

"Yeah, you made me answer it," Cody huffed.

"Babyface, nobody can stay mad at you for more than a few minutes," Charlie laughed.

Waving at the RV, "Mom can," Cody admitted with a straight face and Charlie stopped laughing.

"You got me there, but Kristi works stupid hours and needed that garage door. I don't like her living here in a city that says criminals can go armed but not the citizens," Charlie said.

"If Kristi's not going to move, she just has to accept us turning her house into a bunker," Randy fumed as the side door of the RV opened. "I want concrete walls."

Lena, a spry, elderly lady, stepped out of the RV, walking toward them. "Cody!" she cried out, shaking her head. "You haven't been eating."

"Mom, I swear I have," he groaned, holding up his hands. "Charlie almost force-fed me a second plate every night. He said if you spanked him, I was getting taken outside."

Lena stopped and hugged Cody tight. Closing his eyes in bliss at the motherly hug, Cody hugged her back tight. "He won't do no such thing," Lena promised, then kissed Cody's cheek. "I'll take care of getting you fed when you're at the farm," she promised, letting him go. Lena, like everyone, knew Cody would be coming to the farm. Someone asked for his help and Cody would be there.

"Yes ma'am," Cody smiled as Lena hugged Charlie.

"Charlie, you need to spend some time with us as well, you're losing weight," she told him firmly, hugging Charlie's muscular frame.

"Mom, I have to go on a diet when I leave your house," Charlie laughed as he let her go. Lena turned around as Robbie walked over.

"You're lucky you moved it because I told Oliver to run the damn thing over," she snapped, waving at Robbie's motorcycle. "I wish you would stop riding that thing, you could get hurt."

"Mom," Robbie whined, coming to a stop. "I like riding it."

"Oh, shush," Lena said, stepping over and hugging him tight. Letting him go, Lena turned to the others. "Is Kristi already in the house cooking?"

"Yes, ma'am," Charlie said grinning.

Turning back to Robbie, Lena gave him a studying stare. "She wasn't too rash in her little rant, was she?" Lena asked.

"No, Mom, she had just woken up," Robbie chuckled.

"That's good," Lena said. "She needs to understand those are our kids as well and if we want to get them something, we can," she said, lifting her chin high.

"I ain't telling Kristi that," Randy mumbled.

"If you do, don't come crying to me when she spanks your bottom," Lena snapped, then moved toward the house. "I need to go help her cook."

Halfway to the house the door busted open. "Granny!" Clark and Emily cried out. They ran and wrapped their arms around Lena.

"Oh, how are you doing?" Lena said, squeezing them tight.

Hearing the door of the RV open, they turned to see Oliver, a robust, older man, step out. "Hey Pop," Cody said, walking over. "Got my stuff in the car."

Stepping out of the door, "That's good, Cody," Oliver said, closing the door. "Randy has so many jobs lined up, he won't be able to lend a hand getting the fields ready. You don't know how much I appreciate this."

Wrapping his arms around Oliver, Cody gave him a hug and then stepped back. "It's no problem," he said, smiling.

"Pop, would you have really run over my bike?" Robbie asked with a pained face.

"No," Oliver scoffed. "I told Lena to stop being mean to that bike on the way over and almost pulled over at the state line, so we could get out and tussle."

Letting out a long, relieved sigh, "Had me worried," Robbie admitted, hugging Oliver.

"We need to unload that swimming pool, so I can go to the store and get some lumber for the deck," Oliver said, walking over and hugging Charlie.

Releasing the hug, Charlie looked at him hard. "You're the one telling Kristi about the deck, Pop," he snapped.

"Nope," Oliver replied curtly, spinning away as the kids charged him and the others gasped.

"Grandpa!" they cried out.

"I'm making Lena tell her," Oliver said, wrapping the kids in a bear hug.

As Oliver walked in the house with the kids, the four looked at each other. "I like that Mom is telling her," Robbie said.

"Nobody disagrees with Mom," Cody grinned.

Randy nodded, heading for the house. "Not even Dad," he said with a grin.

"That's because Pop is a smart man," Charlie laughed.

48

Chapter Five

Chicago, IL

Stepping out back that afternoon, Kristi shook her head at the very big above ground pool the men had put up. The men went out with shovels after the birthday party, leveling an area and setting up the pool while Oliver left in Charlie's truck.

Along with the boys, of course, Kristi had allowed Emily to invite several of her nicer girl friends from school, and two of their fathers had shown up for the party. They'd suddenly found themselves put to work performing a little manual labor. That was okay, since the boys had plenty of iced drinks plus listening to Robbie's constant patter of crazy stories was payment enough for a little shovel work. The scary thing was, Charlie and Randy knew most of their friend's stories were true.

"So, you guys served together in the Army?" Chet Mahorn asked, trying not to stare at Robbie's prosthetic and Charlie's scars.

"Oh, yeah," Aaron replied, taking a break and leaning heavily on his shovel. He wasn't breathing hard yet, but unlike the others, he'd not kept in quite the same shape as the other four. "We are brothers from way back."

"Except Aaron got a little too much sun," Robbie popped off. "I swear, when we got to Afghanistan, that man was whiter than Charlie. We tried to get him to stop laying out with that baby oil, but did he listen? Nooooooo."

Aaron and Charlie exchanged a look and then busted out laughing, while Randy just shook his head in mock disgust. Mustering up his dignity, he spoke next.

"Brothers? Aaron, Charlie, and Cody are my brothers. That one," Randy aimed a thumb in Robbie's direction, "he's like that cousin who shows up at the family reunion and nobody's sure how he's related, except that his parents had to be brother and sister."

"Oh, you wound me," Robbie recoiled in horror. "And after I sacrificed my hand to save your life. And ruined my modeling career."

"What?" asked an incredulous Mike Selfridge. He was a prosperous, very tall and robust black man in his early forties, and he was still trying to figure these men out. They looked hard, even the slightly paunchy Aaron, but they played and picked on each other just like Mike remembered doing with his own brothers, even after they were all full-grown and out of the house.

"Oh yeah," Robbie continued. "See, Randy accidentally shoved a grenade down his pants and I had to reach in and...well. You can see what happened," he concluded, holding up his clearly artificial, five-fingered prosthetic. "And it ruined my career as a hand model."

Charlie started laughing and had to bend over to catch his breath. Then, holding up his own maimed hand, concealed by the black gloves he usually wore, he made a stop motion.

"Come on, guys, you all know to play nice," Charlie chided, then turning to the other two men, he continued. "Please excuse my friend Robbie. We checked him out of the hospital to visit today, but he's still not completely housebroken."

That got the laughter going again, and the men turned back to digging with the occasional chuckle.

When Oliver got back, Kristi took a deep breath to start, only to have Lena step in front of her. "Kristi, I'm the one who said the pool had to have a deck. I don't want these babies having to climb a shaky ladder to get in the pool." Seeing a challenging glare in Lena's eyes, Kristi only nodded and smiled.

Now, the men were building a nice deck around the pool and Kristi wasn't going to say a thing.

The party, like all the others, involved tons of gifts. It took a now twelve-year-old girl almost two hours to open all the gifts. Aaron and Bert Travis usually only got her two gifts since they had their families, and that was the main reason Kristi didn't want the boys, Randy, Cody, Robbie, and Charlie, buying so many for the kids. She didn't want anyone to feel pressured. That, and she prayed the kids never came to expect it.

The thought of saying something to Mom and Pop never entered her mind. Kristi respected them more than her own parents.

50

When Emily was seven, they had stayed a week with Mom and Pop. Lena had freaked when they'd unloaded their suitcases at Randy's small house.

Lena only had to look at Pop and Randy for them to move the suitcases from Randy's house to her house.

One day after Randy had taken the kids horseback riding, Emily came running in and begging for a horse. Before they'd left, Pop had driven up with a horse trailer and a young horse. Clark got one the next month. Now, the kids spent a few weeks every summer on the farm. When Kristi took the kids to the retreat, Randy would load up their horses.

Like the kids, Kristi loved the retreat. It was very relaxing to just be around the group, and the land just seemed to take your worries away. At first, she'd felt like she was intruding. Then she began to realize, if she went there, so would the boys; her boys. The boys were Cody, Randy, Robbie, and Charlie. She could tell this land was what took their pain away and where they found joy again. They were at the retreat every chance they got.

So, to keep them from coming to Chicago, Kristi would ask if they could go to the retreat. Not to say they didn't come to Chicago a lot. The kids were in sports and other activities, so the boys had to come. Again, this helped Kristi out. If she was working, someone would be there to take the kids and she rarely asked.

A part of her wanted the boys to stop because she felt they were spending too much time with her and the kids, and not looking to start a family of their own. Then she had a selfish part that enjoyed the help and being a part of this new family.

Yes, she knew of the vow Randy, Robbie, and Charlie had made and told them they had honored it, but they didn't think so. She also knew Randy and Charlie had several girlfriends they had broken up with because of that vow. The women didn't like the fact they would drop what they were doing and jump in a vehicle if they 'thought' Kristi or one of the others needed them.

Cody had had two girlfriends but hadn't stayed with them for long. Kristi believed Cody didn't feel they needed him like the group did. Kristi knew for a fact, one girlfriend left Cody because Lena had told the little tramp if she hurt Cody, she would be fed to the hogs. To be honest, everyone was glad for that intervention because the girl had been a tramp.

Then there was Robbie. Kristi knew Robbie, Randy, and Charlie before her husband Frank had died. They were his boys. When the three arrived at base right after Ranger School, they'd been assigned to her husband, and the group stayed together.

Robbie, as long as she had known him, had always been a ladies man. Frank had always called Robbie a male whore. That, coming from a fellow Ranger, was funny to Kristi until she got to know Robbie. After she did, Kristi agreed with Frank.

Never once had she ever heard Robbie say he had a girlfriend. He had a Miss 'Right Now'.

Hearing the door open, Kristi looked behind her and saw Lena bringing out more food for the table. "Where's your sister?" Lena asked, and Kristi could hear the edge in her voice.

Forcing a smile, "She went to an art showing today. Tabitha said she would bring Emily's present over later in the week," Kristi said, trying to sound cheerful. Tabitha, her younger sister, was the only person in her family she talked to regularly. This was because of Kristi making the effort, not Tabitha.

Putting the food on the table, Lena turned to Kristi and saw the forced smile. Reaching up, Lena caressed her cheek. "That is five birthday parties she has missed," Lena reminded her, and Kristi noticed Lena's eyes narrow slightly.

"Mom, that's just Tabitha. She has made it here every Christmas and Thanksgiving," Kristi offered, turning to look at the men working. Kristi knew nobody in her new family liked her sister, but always went out of their way to make Tabitha and her family feel welcome.

Shaking her head, "An art show doesn't compare to family," Lena huffed, carrying an empty tray inside.

Moving the food from the tray to the picnic table, Kristi smiled at everyone and then headed back inside.

"Why was she looking at us so hard?" Randy asked as everyone stopped working.

Shaking his head and shrugging his shoulders, "Shit, I don't know. But she was smiling, so we won't get a lecture," Robbie reasoned. "I swear, she sounds just like Wheat."

"You don't think she found out it was us that talked to Victor, do you?" Cody asked in a low voice.

"Not unless you told her," Charlie huffed, wiping sweat off his face. He glanced over at the wives and kids and saw one of the younger ones staring at him. None of the others did because they were used to the scars.

Four years ago, Kristi had started dating a nurse she worked with; Victor. At first they'd liked him, then he'd started acting jealous about them. Charlie couldn't blame him, with men coming to see and help Kristi without being asked. Each one had keys to the house and codes to the alarm.

They did try talking to Victor several times. One at a time and then as a group, Kristi was a sister to them.

It was Clark and Emily who'd brought the situation to a head. One day when he came over, Victor told Kristi he didn't want the guys over anymore unless he was there. Oh boy, did the kids throw a fit. The guys had gone to their games, competitions, carried them to Boy and Girl Scout meetings and to karate classes, and Emily to gymnastics.

They had helped them become better in any activity they did. Not to mention all the trips to the retreat, vacations, camping and hiking trips.

Then Victor comes along and says no, the group who the kids called 'uncle' with 'granny and grandpa' can't come over anymore unless *he* said so? What really didn't help was the kids blew up at Victor when he'd said it. Victor started yelling at the kids and Kristi told him to leave. He did leave when the cops came after Victor shoved her around. After that, Victor started following Kristi.

When the kids told the boys, because Kristi wouldn't, the boys started staying closer to Chicago. Robbie was the one spending the weekend at the house when Victor started calling. Of the four, Robbie was the one with the shortest fuse and the quickest to act when his fuse was lit, so that didn't go well for Victor.

The only thing that saved Victor from a beatdown and disappearing right then was Kristi hiding Robbie's motorcycle keys, and Robbie refused to hotwire his beloved Harley.

Several weeks after that, Victor showed up at Emily's school when she got out. He told her he was sorry and wanted to come back and live with them. That evening, Kristi called Charlie and talked to him about Victor showing up at Emily's school. Out of the four, Charlie was the slowest to get angry and was very level-headed. This was the reason Kristi discussed her fears with Charlie. He talked to Kristi for several hours in a calm, soothing voice and told her it wasn't anything to worry about.

It was true Charlie was the slowest to anger, but when he got there he would stay angry for weeks. And the object of his anger was forever on his shit list.

When Charlie hung up, he grabbed the keys to his car, calling the others on his cell phone. They met up in Chicago. Using his computers, Cody found out everything there was to know about Victor. The next night when Victor got home, four men were inside his house and beat the ever-loving shit out of him.

Then Victor was gagged, stripped, held down, and painted bright yellow. When he wouldn't be still so they could paint him, one mean man took a hammer, hitting Victor's toes until he stopped moving. It only took two toes for Victor to get the message.

Painted and gagged, Victor was pulled out to his front yard and chained butt naked between two trees. That's how the neighbors found him the next morning. There had even been news coverage.

The boys had all hauled ass back to Randy's house, getting there before sunrise and sat down around the kitchen table playing poker. When she woke up, Lena saw their cars and she ran over, wanting to know when they'd gotten there because they hadn't come over to say hi. Everyone told her they got there yesterday evening and thought she was asleep.

Getting to work that afternoon, Kristi found out about Victor and called Charlie. Not getting him, she called the others until she called Lena. When she asked where the boys were, Lena told her the boys had played poker all night and were sleeping now. Relieved the boys were cleared, Kristi thought it was because Victor was an asshole and someone else had come calling.

"She finds out, we are in deep," Cody mumbled, sitting down.

Oliver walked over and smiled. "I should tell her because you didn't invite me."

The four all paled. "Pop, if you would've come, Mom would've known," Charlie offered carefully.

A big grin split Oliver's face. "I know, and you boys did good," he chuckled, then grabbed a board. "Think Victor knows who did it?"

"Yep, *someone* took their mask off when they pissed in his face," Charlie snapped, and everyone turned to Robbie.

"What good is a warning if they don't know who delivered it?" Robbie shrugged.

"He never told the cops?" Oliver asked shocked.

"Nope. I went to school with one of the ADAs and he got a hold of the report. I did a little snooping, and confirmed Victor never said anything," Charlie chuckled.

Helping his dad line up the board on the deck, Randy grinned. "He moved from Chicago two days after he was released from the hospital."

"I hope he never shows up here," Oliver said, grabbing his hammer.

"He won't, he lives in New York now. He's under the impression if he comes back to Chicago, someone will cut off his dick and make him eat it," Randy said as his dad nailed the board down.

"Wonder why?" Cody laughed, pulling a knife out and flicking the blade open.

Hearing a squeal, they turned to see all the kids playing chase. "If he would've hurt Emily, Clark, or Kristi, he never would've lived till morning," Robbie said with a stern face.

"Got that right," Randy nodded.

Pounding the nail in, Oliver looked up at his son and then turned to look at the others. A part of him wished one of the boys would go out with Kristi, but he knew they viewed her like a sister. Even though Robbie, Charlie, and Randy were thirty-six and Kristi was forty, they viewed her like a little sister. Turning back to Cody, Oliver could see even Cody, at thirty, looked at Kristi like a younger sister.

The funny thing was, Kristi looked at them like younger brothers and had even told Lena so.

Standing up, Oliver watched as they pulled over more boards, finishing the deck off. Turning back to the pool, he saw the water level was rising faster than he'd thought it would. Charlie and Randy had gone to the neighbors' houses and had given them a hundred dollars, then ran water hoses from their backyards and over the privacy fence around Kristi's backyard. With three water hoses going full blast, it wouldn't take much longer.

55

Randy turned to the others. "Just to tell you, I'm not swimming until that water gets warmer."

"You are a Ranger, punk," Robbie snapped.

"Yep, and that means I know that water is cold and there is no mission, so I don't have to get in."

Shyly looking up, "Randy, the kids will want us to swim with them," Cody said in a soft voice.

"I will tomorrow. We bought a heater," Randy told everyone with a straight face.

"Guys, let Randy wear his dress," Charlie chuckled.

Robbie and Cody broke out laughing. Hearing the laughter, Aaron and the others came over to find out what was so funny.

Hearing what was going on, Aaron looked at Randy. "You swam across a river during the spring thaw. There were chunks of ice the size of cars," he chuckled.

"Had a mission," Randy nodded with pride. Even out of the Army for this long, the group still had that same bearing in life.

"Yeah, he climbed out and yelled over the radio he couldn't find his manhood and had to wipe after he peed!" Robbie yelled out, laughing.

The group busted out laughing as the wives came over to listen. The only element really missing from normal military banter was the swearing. When the kids were near, everyone watched their mouths. A few words would sneak out but for the most part, to military standards, the conversations were clean.

It wasn't always that way. That started when Emily was five and she asked what a 'bitch boy' was. The language stopped. Kristi never said anything, she laughed more than the others. She was a nurse and cussed as bad as the boys did. The boys just didn't like the fact the little girl had said that word. Charlie gave Emily twenty dollars and bought her half a dozen toys to never say the word again.

Walking out the back door, Kristi saw everyone gathered around the almost finished deck. Seeing them laughing, she smiled and grabbed a tray, loading it with bottles of beer. Carrying it over, Kristi held it out as everyone took one.

"You remember what Shadow said when Captain Winnfield told him to swim back across?" Charlie chuckled, taking the top off the bottle. Kristi smiled, watching him put the cap in his pocket. That was what Frank had taught them to use to mark a trail.

Robbie collapsed in laughter and shocked everyone that he never even spilled his beer. "What did he say?" Elizabeth, Aaron's wife asked, laughing.

Standing up straight, Randy lifted his chin. "I told the captain I would be more than happy to swim back, once he went in the river and found my balls that had frozen and broke off."

"I thought Wheat was going to wet his pants," Aaron laughed.

"He did, Cobra!" Robbie howled from the ground.

"Why did Shadow need to get back across?" Cody asked, laughing.

Wiping his eyes and taking a drink. "We were playing war games and the captain wanted to call in an artillery strike because Shadow had found the enemy's camp," Charlie explained in several octaves.

"Hey, I told the captain to call in real artillery, at least I could've gotten warm," Randy huffed. "I have *never* been that cold."

"Yeah," Robbie laughed, setting his beer down as he stomped the ground. "The captain threatens Shadow with an article fifteen for disobeying a direct order. Shadow gets on the radio and tells the captain if he wants his damn stripes so bad, he would put them on a log and float the damn things back across the river because he wasn't swimming it again till the end of summer. Because he had to squat to take a piss!"

Spitting out a mouth full of beer, Aaron howled out. "The captain started yelling at Wheat to get him to talk to Shadow, but Wheat was rolling around in the snow laughing because Shadow started singing *My Ding a Ling* over the radio."

When the laughter died down, Clark looked up at Randy who was wiping his eyes. "Did you get in trouble?" Clark asked.

"Yep," Randy laughed. "Had guard duty for the next month."

"Yeah," Kristi chuckled. "It's really a shame a horse broke into Captain Winnfield's apartment while he was gone for the weekend."

The men busted out laughing as the wives turned and looked at her. "Frank didn't like anyone messing with his troops. So somehow, a horse broke into the captain's apartment," she explained, chuckling.

"It was ankle deep in shit when the captain got back!" Robbie bellowed.

Randy stood up as the laughter died down and held up his beer bottle. "To the Wheat!" he cried out.

The others held up their bottles and the kids held up cups of Kool-Aid. "To the Wheat!" they all yelled out to the toast.

Chapter Six

Cleveland, OH

After a quick shower at the gym, Charlie took thirty minutes to painstakingly shave the creases and folds of his face before "suiting up" in his best work outfit. Wearing a suit was second nature to Charlie after three years of law school, two years at the DA's office, and another four years in private practice, but there were degrees of formality when it came to the business suit you wore. For a simple hearing, you wore the average, off-the-rack Sears number.

For a mediation with retired Judge Myers on a million-dollar case, Charlie broke out the navy Brooks Brothers number, a crisp white shirt from the same source, and a red tie with subtle stripes that caught the eye. He remembered the tie had been a gift from Emily and Clark, and that thought made him smile as he remembered Emily's birthday party. Then he fished out a new pair of leather dress shoes from the tree in his closet, and he checked the shine. Perfect.

After jockeying his truck into a pay lot nearly three blocks from the Judge's office, Charlie pulled his heavy rolling briefcase from the rear seats and shouldered his padded computer bag for the hike. Nothing to it, he thought with a sly half-grin as he watched his portly counterparts huffing and puffing down the sidewalk. Even after all the years since his discharge, Charlie kept himself in good shape, and the swimming was only half of the workout.

The receptionist, an older woman named Molly, who according to the rumor mill followed the judge from his long stint at the courthouse into private practice, gave him a pleasant smile when he arrived. She was in her early fifties and maintained a pixie-cut hairstyle that somehow reminded Charlie of Joan's short cut blonde locks.

Get your mind off the girl and onto the case, he chided himself as he followed Molly into the small office set aside for his use. The room boasted a six seat conference table, a modern speaker phone claiming a place of honor in the center, and a whiteboard mounted on one wall he could use as a projection screen.

"Anyone else here yet?" Charlie asked, his voice deferential and polite to the older lady. Always be nice to the staff, his current employer and mentor, Billy Carpenter, constantly preached.

"Just you, hun," she replied. "Well, and the Judge, of course. He always gets here early. Turns the lights on and starts the coffee."

"Thank you. This will be perfect."

"You want some of that coffee?"

"Yes, ma'am. Just point me in the right direction, please."

Molly smiled, showing a dimple. "No trouble, Mr. Tucker. How do you take it?"

"Just black and call me Charlie."

"You got it, Charlie. I'll leave you alone now, so you can get set up."

Charlie, as was his practice, showed up at least twenty minutes early for anything, including this mediation. That gave him enough time to lay out the marked deposition excerpts he wanted to use with opposing counsel, as well as multiple copies of the lost earnings reports, medical documents, and still gave him time to cue up his PowerPoint.

For their part, the 'three wise men', actually two men and a lady representing the power plant, arrived ten minutes late for the scheduled nine a.m. start time. Typical. Through the heavy wooden door of his temporary office, Charlie heard the familiar deep but somehow whiny voice of Nelson Bentson in the reception area, complaining about the lack of parking and the overall inconvenience.

Charlie knew Nelson all too well. The lead partner at Foley, Fley & Bentson, Nelson Bentson was a fine figure of a man in his mid-fifties, with a headful of dark hair going artfully gray at the temples. As head of the litigation department at FF&B, Nelson seldom darkened the courthouse steps anymore, but he was a rainmaker for the large defense firm. Since Luminous Power, one of the largest power plant operators in the northeast after their merger with Great Northern, Inc., was hip deep in this case, Nelson took a personal interest in the ongoing litigation.

Maybe too personal. Charlie remembered the way Nelson went after Mrs. Melton in her deposition and involuntarily flexed his fingers as he remembered the deposition exchange from nearly four months prior. When asking about whether the widow was dating since the death of her husband of nearly twenty years, he'd listened to the poor woman explain how she didn't know how she would go on without her Floyd. That question had skirted the edge of politeness, Charlie had thought at the time, but he'd let it pass. Nelson, however, had been just getting started. Next, he had produced a copy of a change of address form for one Stanley Obregon moving to the same residence and went on by insinuating the firm's investigators had uncovered Mrs. Melton moving her new lover in just weeks after burying her husband.

Charlie knew the truth and had exploded. Interrupting the proceedings, he'd escorted the weeping woman from the room, leaving her with his paralegal Donna, and had returned to the conference room. Nelson, seeming somehow pleased by the turn of events, tried to engage Charlie in conversation, but the younger man had no time for pleasantries at this stage. Instead, he'd immediately gotten on the speaker phone in the room and had called the judge.

Judge Womack had shared Charlie's lack of amusement when he heard how Mr. Bentson, in receipt of the interrogatory responses from three months before listing Mrs. Melton's brother Stanley as a current resident of the house, had questioned the widow. Charlie knew Stanley, and knew the only reason he'd moved in was to assist his grieving sister who was now solely responsible for raising her two sons. Charlie, given his relationship with Sarge's family, could certainly relate.

Bentson, for his part, had acted surprised and defensive, lashing back at Charlie for setting him up this way. Charlie, relying on reserves of calm he seldom needed in recent years, proceeded to flay the older, apparently underprepared Bentson in front of the judge.

In the end, Judge Womack had threatened sanctions but stayed his hand when Bentson managed a show of contrition and blamed his conduct on miscommunication, after throwing his secretary under the bus by claiming he'd never received the amended interrogatory responses. Such tactics, on top of his previous misconduct, left Charlie convinced this Nelson Bentson was scum of the lowest order. His actions since had simply confirmed this judgment.

Charlie came to the mediation forewarned that Judge Myers liked to hold first, an informal get-together of the parties as an icebreaker before beginning the presentations and the attendant round-robin of negotiations. So, he was not surprised that five minutes after hearing Nelson's voice, Molly came in to invite him to join the judge in his office with the people from Luminous Power. Charlie, despite his antipathy for Bentson, agreed. He was here for Mrs. Melton and her children, he reminded himself.

In Judge Myers' plush office, Charlie found himself introduced to Bryan Akkard, general counsel for Luminous, and Paige Bishop with the insurance company, Reliant. Akkard's name appeared all over documents held in the company's Privileged Log, as apparently no one at Luminous took a bathroom break without consulting with their lawyer, before and after. So went the story, as the power company worked hard, in Charlie's opinion, to hide reports and meeting minutes where the safety deficiencies of the company's Delhouser Power Plant were discussed. As for Akkard, he was a golf-fit man in his early sixties, a regular country club and boardroom type who, according to Charlie's research, hadn't set foot in a courtroom in thirty years.

The wildcard was Ms. Bishop. A tall, severe-faced woman dressed in a plain pantsuit and minimal makeup. The fortyish woman wore no jewelry and though her shoulder-length, ash-blonde hair looked to be well maintained, she wore it in a simple French braid. Charlie had never heard of the woman throughout the year plus the case had been pending, and he wondered how much authority she carried. A thoroughly modern man, Charlie's concerns had nothing to do with her gender and everything to do with the depth of her pocketbook.

After a bit of pleasant chitchat, mainly centered on the Browns and their chances this upcoming season, Charlie caught Ms. Bishop's comment about her preferred team, the Jets. After the two sides were once again separated, Charlie took the time to do a little search for Ms. Bishop in the New York, New Jersey area. By the time the numbers started going back and forth, he also knew a bit more about the lady who could successfully resolve this matter.

Charlie came with authority from his client to settle the case for two million dollars. For Ohio, that was high. In Illinois, he knew he could get twice that figure, but Ohio had experienced recent changes in the law, meant to cap damages. Coupled with a massive media campaign aimed at tort reform, this resulted in a jury pool that had been compromised by the ever-present television ads designed to "curb lawsuit abuse" to save jobs.

Charlie, more than most, knew the system wasn't perfect. However, he knew this case was trial-worthy, and he'd worked long hours getting all his ducks in a row before the court-ordered mediation. He'd sat for all the depositions, attended all the hearings, and he knew his industrial experts were solid when they pointed the finger at Luminous Power and their penny-pinching maintenance practices. Couple that with a deceased forty-seven-year-old boilermaker, a forty-two-year-old widow who was a stay-at-home mother of two young children, and he felt confident the jury would award a fair amount.

From the beginning of the mediation though, Charlie could tell Nelson Bentson didn't want the case to settle. From the way he postured, Charlie wondered if he wanted to really try this case, or...was it all a show for the Luminous folks? The more he mulled over that idea, as negotiations stalled at one and a half, the more he wondered if there was something else going on here. Was Nelson playing hardball in an attempt to hold on to a very valuable client? Or was he simply trying to run up FF&B's billable hours?

Finally, Charlie asked Judge Myers for one last session and this time, he asked to meet with Ms. Bishop privately. The request was met with an angry response from Bentson, but somewhat out of character, Akkard seemed interested when he offered a compromise. Akkard, as general counsel, and Ms. Bishop would meet with Charlie together. Bentson continued his complaints but Bishop, seemingly frustrated, agreed immediately.

"He really has taken a dislike to you, Mr. Tucker," Bryan Akkard confided when the three sat down in the temporary office set up for Charlie. By now, Charlie had managed to consume two pots of coffee and had eaten his way through the supply of danish that came with the room.

"Well, the feeling is mutual," Charlie replied, "as you no doubt can tell from the transcripts."

"I suspect it had to do with when you called Judge Womack during Mrs. Melton's deposition. I've known Nelson a long time, and he really is sensitive when it comes to losing face in front of a judge."

"We don't have time for this dickbeating, gentlemen," Ms. Bishop announced, and the room fell silent.

Charlie, at least, wasn't surprised by the outburst. For all her fancy education while Ms. Bishop had both a law degree and a Master's in Business Administration, in addition to her undergraduate degree in accounting, she was a straight-forward person. A bean counter, based on what Charlie could dig up. Her interests laid in getting this problem for her insured resolved. Period.

"What's your last offer, ma'am?" Charlie finally asked.

"Do I look like a ma'am to you? Seriously, what century are you from, Tucker?" Bishop responded testily.

"This century, Ms. Bishop, but apparently I spent more time in the south than I realized. Okay, last time. My number is $4.25 million, all cash. And you are now up to offering a million and a half," Charlie recapped and then sighed theatrically. "Honestly, I think we are done here. We are too far apart at this point. Want me to go get Judge Myers and give him the news?"

"There is always room for negotiation," Akkard chimed in, and Charlie almost rolled his eyes. Yeah, now that the insurance company is footing the bill, the in-house is ready to break out the checkbook.

"No," Charlie replied instead, "I don't think so. We'll let the jury decide. Time for Luminous to carry their own dead."

The comment just slipped out. A combination of frustration and exasperation would have been the only reason Charlie might utter such words. Akkard didn't seem to notice, but Bishop stiffened.

"And is that some kind of threat, Mr. Tucker?"

"No, ma'am, I mean, Mizz Bishop. That's just an old saying." Charlie replied, and then decided to press forward one more time, but Bishop started the festivities early with her response.

"Well, I find it offensive," she spat back.

"Really?" Charlie shot back. "I think, killing a man on your job site who was hired to fix a piece of your antiquated equipment, so you can continue charging outrageous rates, is pretty darned offensive. But we are done here. This case will be going to trial in sixty days and we'll let the jury decide."

"You're seriously going to try this case? In this country, with the political situation the way it is? No chance you are getting more than the $1.5 million we are offering today," Akkard said, his voice sounding strained as he delivered the words. This was his first time dealing with Charlie this closely, without Nelson and his clutch of yes-men clustered tightly around.

Charlie turned to the man in his five-thousand-dollar suit and his voice was low when he replied, "Yeah, I think my client would like to see a little justice done. Since the State of Ohio has only seen fit to levy a fine, Mrs. Melton has been dissatisfied with that process anyway. I'll see you in court."

Picking up his paperwork and exhibits, Charlie almost missed what came next.

"Three million," Bishop said softly, not looking up. Instead, she was reading something off her iPhone. She was standing still now, her face blank but Charlie could somehow tell she was troubled by what she'd learned.

"Four million," Charlie countered, his voice casual as he continued to fill his briefcase. In his mind, he was already focusing on the motions in limine that would be due in one week. He had a great trial paralegal for the grunt work of prepping the motions, but he still reviewed every word that went out in his name.

"I can't do four million," Bishop said, and Charlie registered the difference in her demeanor. In ten minutes, something had happened to turn this hardcase number cruncher into something approaching human. She caught Charlie's eye and flicked a glance at Bryan Akkard.

She didn't have the authority. Over the years, Charlie had learned to read their faces and decipher the tells from the ones with the money. Everything else was window-dressing, after all.

"Three million, nine hundred ninety-nine thousand," Charlie snapped back, and he thought Bishop almost cracked a smile.

"Smartass," she replied, and after a pause, she continued. "I think I can sell $3.75 million, if you will accept payment in one hundred and twenty days," Bishop said, and then she subtly shook her head at the same time. This was wrong, Charlie realized, oh-so-very wrong. Charlie was no novice in the practice of law, but this seemed to be something else.

"I think I can get my side on board with three point seventy-five, but paid-in-full within thirty days," Charlie countered.

"Three point seven five million, full release, standard confidentiality order, and sixty days." Bishop replied, "and I need you to answer one question unrelated to this case."

Quirking his good eyebrow, something he'd practiced while going through physio-rehab, Charlie felt the situation somehow slipping out of his control. On one hand, three million, seven hundred fifty thousand dollars was a lot of justice for the Melton family. Well, minus the firm's thirty-three percent in attorney's fees and expenses, but still well more than his authority from Mrs. Melton for the whole thing.

On the other hand, what the hell came over Bishop? Charlie pondered that question while he stepped out into the hall to call Wanda Melton and give her the news. He knew she would accept the offer. She'd been trying to talk Charlie out of going to trial almost from the start.

Wanda was a sweet lady, and sharp as a tack about some things. But, like many who'd never advanced beyond a high school diploma, she was not at all comfortable about being around lawyers, strangers, or crowds of any type. Her husband Floyd had taken care of her before his death, down to filling out the checks to pay their bills and making most of the major decisions for the family. Now, she was finding out how to make her way in the world on her own; and starting out in the deep end of the pool.

"Take it, Charlie," Wanda said immediately. "Does this mean I won't have to come down to the courthouse again?"

Charlie almost laughed into the phone, but he resisted the urge. "Yes, Wanda, this means you don't have to come back down. All done."

"Then do it, Charlie," the widow said, her voice going heavy for once. "You've dragged them through the mud, and now you're making them pay for killing my Floyd. How can I thank you enough, Charlie?"

Then Charlie did allow himself a smile before answering.

66

"Just tell Billy how happy you are. That will be enough. Trust me."

After that, signing all the paperwork seemed anticlimactic. He had a full and final release for Wanda to sign, which he would drop by her house later to be signed and notarized, and that would be it. Nelson Bentson exited the office once he found out a deal had been struck, and Charlie wondered if his firm would ever see any more work from the power company. Probably, he decided. FF&B carried a lot of sway in local legal circles, and the political ones, too.

For his part, Akkard seemed relieved the whole sorry episode was over, but remained noncommittal when Charlie asked if the company was going to go about replacing or overhauling the steam generators like the one that killed Floyd Melton. Which answered the question. Cheaper to pay almost four million dollars, most of it their insurance company's money, than to fix the problem in the first place.

Bishop still puzzled him, though. She was a solid, no-nonsense bean counter and yet, something had her spooked. Charlie remembered seeing that look before in officers who, scuttlebutt later claimed, received troubling, contradictory intelligence right before sending their boys out into the shit.

Shrugging it off, Charlie finished gathering up his materials and placing them in the correct order in his briefcase. Everything had a place, and Charlie Tucker was meticulous about the order, even in the smallest details.

As he headed out the door, planning to swing by the Melton's humble little one-story rancher on his way to the office, Charlie was surprised to see Bishop waiting for him.

"Ms. Bishop, what can I do for you?"

"I could use a ride to the airport. The boys didn't seem so happy with my company after 'caving in' to you. Plus, I still have that question I need answered."

"As long as it doesn't pertain to this case or anything privileged, then I'm up for giving you a ride." As soon as he said it, Charlie thought about Blaster, since it'd sounded like one of his lame pick-up lines.

Bishop gave a nod and gathered her own briefcase and made no complaint as Charlie led the way back to his pickup in the nearby parking lot. He noted she didn't seemed winded in the least

67

by the walk or his brisk pace. She did hesitate when Charlie went around to open the door for her but kept any complaints to herself.

The drive out to Hopkins passed in relative silence, each absorbed in their own thoughts, right up until Charlie turned at the last exit.

"What did you really mean by carrying your own dead, Mr. Tucker?"

The question caught Charlie off guard, and he tried to blow it off.

"Just an expression, Ms. Bishop. That's all."

"No, I think you meant something more, Mr. Tucker. I saw it in your eyes. So, what does it mean?"

Charlie found himself trapped after agreeing to answer her question, but he couldn't think of a way to avoid telling her the truth. Or at least part of it.

"When I was a Ranger, there were things we said and codes we lived by, ma'am. One of those was if possible, we always brought back the bodies of our boys. Didn't leave anything for the enemy, you know? So, that's all I meant."

"Once you've carried the body of someone as close to you as a brother, then you start to value life a whole lot more. Your guys there at Luminous, they haven't ever learned that lesson. Probably never will."

"Thank you for telling me that," Bishop said. "I had my suspicions, and it wasn't just the scars that gave you away. Something about the way you move or carry yourself still says military. I did a hitch with the Air Force right out of high school to help pay for college."

Charlie nodded, encouraging her to continue. She wasn't finished yet. He could tell the lady had more to say. He pulled the long bed truck up to the Passenger Departing doors and shifted into park, then turned to listen again.

"I'm not afraid of losing at trial, Mr. Tucker. We have a whole appellate firm on retainer, just sitting around and waiting for something to come their way. But while we were in that mediation, I received a message from an old friend still in the Air Force. Just a simple e-mail, but it was also a private code. I don't know any details, but something is up. And I don't want to be stuck in

Cleveland, no offense, when whatever he was trying to warn me about goes down."

"So, what was your MOS, Ms. Bishop?"

"I was in Intelligence, Mr. Tucker. An analyst. Not much different from what I do now. So, get your money in sixty days and stay out of trouble."

"Any idea about what your friend was warning you about?"

"No, and he might not know either. But whatever it is, I think we still have a few months before it really hits the fan."

And with that she was gone, leaving Charlie with more questions than when he'd started the day. He decided to give Randy a call on the way home that night. Maybe it was nothing, and maybe it was the start of something. He decided to start paying more attention to the news, for what good it did. Maybe he should start checking some of those alternate news sites he'd heard Cody mention. Couldn't hurt, he thought.

Chapter Seven

Parma, OH

For Charlie, the weekend came and went far too soon, and the next week looked to be more of the same. He worked for a successful plaintiffs' firm with their main offices in downtown Cleveland and a satellite office in Parma, and Charlie ended up spending most of the week there. He was meeting with two potentially new clients and Thursday, he was defending the deposition of a treating physician in one of his older cases.

The doctor was an interesting older man, a pulmonologist by trade who had been treating Charlie's client for over a year since he'd been overcome by ammonia while working at the liquefied natural gas processing plant just outside Cleveland. Had he been an employee, this would have been a worker's compensation case, but Mr. Santos worked as a laborer on site for a maintenance contractor. This was a very common practice these days, since the refinery could pay contractors much less than they did their employees without having to hassle with things like the Affordable Healthcare Act or other niceties. That was the contractor's problem, after all. Unless someone got hurt, like Mr. Santos.

The oil company operating the refinery proved to be old hands at dealing with these kinds of claims, after decades of handling the nightmare that was asbestos litigation. To Charlie's surprise, their in-house counsel had taken an enlightened approach once they had determined the accident was a legitimate injury and one caused by the failure of the aging machinery in their plant. But, Charlie still had to earn his pay and show that given the extensive scarring in his airways, Mr. Santos was actually never going to be able to work again.

The deposition lasted all day, with Charlie's firm providing sandwiches from a local deli and sodas from their small kitchenette. He ate lunch with Dr. Hammar in his cramped little temporary office, and they chatted about everything but the case at hand. For Charlie, he was extremely pleased by the morning session, as the good doctor never wavered from the findings in his voluminous medical file. Hammar might be old as dirt, Charlie thought, but the old bird still had his claws and his mind remained razor sharp as well.

"So, Charlie, what do you think about this water bill Congress just passed?" Dr. Hammar asked as he slid away the paper plate holding the decimated remnants of his turkey on wheat. Charlie, fastidious as always, quickly policed up the slightly soggy disposable containers and tossed them into his wastebasket. As another holdover from his military days, Charlie tended to wolf his food down like someone was waiting to steal the last bite from him. Given the pranks Robbie liked to pull, that wasn't out of the realm of possibility.

"Water bill? Sorry, Doc, you got me there," Charlie replied as he used a squirt of hand sanitizer to clean his hands before wiping them on his last napkin. "I haven't seen anything about a new water bill. Is it something they are considering in the State House? Those guys in Columbus never seem to stop poking at things."

Doctor Hammar chuckled, and then cleared his throat.

"No, Charlie, not here. In Washington. I heard mention of it on CNN last night, but when I looked this morning, I couldn't find any details about it online. Just that a House bill had been passed and that the Senate had a similar one being considered. Nothing about any debate, or frankly any details, other than it would be directed at ensuring safe public water."

Charlie shrugged. "Sorry, Doctor, this is the first I've heard of this new bill. But after what happened in Flint and then in that little town outside Phoenix, I can't say I'm surprised."

Flint, Michigan had been a cluster from the get-go. An example of politicians playing 'the blame game' and manipulating the press to the point that by the end of the fiasco, no one could be 100% sure of the facts, or who had dropped the ball. Then, it had faded from the public perception as the infotainment industry had moved on to tout some new celebrity love triangle.

The cholera outbreak in the small community of Dana, just on the outskirts of Phoenix, AZ was a different story. A private water provider, one operating a small fleet of water delivery trucks to water tanks in the near desert community, was eventually found by the EPA to have been using water reclaimed from an unapproved source. This finding came too late for seven locals, including three children under the age of five, who had succumbed to the ancient bacterial killer. With another sixty-odd seriously ill victims overwhelming local hospitals, the media once again found something to preach about besides the actual news.

"Well, as a physician, I am hopeful this effort will prevent more senseless deaths, but I am puzzled why the federal government isn't making more of an effort to make political hay out of this," the doctor said, then paused for dramatic effect. "You know, clamoring to get in front of the camera and claim to have invented safe drinking water?"

Charlie had to chuckle at that one. Leave it to the nation's elected officials, Charlie thought to himself, to make the craziest claims to the American public, and then backtrack and obfuscate on the few occasions where they get called for their bull.

The afternoon session rolled on to nearly four o'clock before the last question was posed, and the court reporter was busy packing up her kit while Charlie saw the doctor out before he sat at his desk to respond to the dozens of e-mails accumulated while he'd been in deposition. He sat drinking the latest cup of coffee while composing his e-mail report to Billy and the client file, regarding the just-completed examination.

Charlie knew some lawyers spent most of their time in deposition working on their phones or other mobile devices, but for Charlie, listening to what was actually being said by the witness seemed a better use of his time. He'd lost track of how many times he'd corrected opposing counsel for misstating prior testimony, simply because they'd been typing on their keypads when the information had been previously solicited.

While he was busily responding to yet another email from his paralegal back at the main office, Charlie paused when he heard the muted hum of his cell phone. Not in his pocket and not on the neat work surface, he discovered the phone in the top drawer of the desk on what he thought was the fourth ring. Barely beating voicemail,

Charlie thumbed the answer icon on his phone and didn't even think about the number being an unfamiliar one. In his job, Charlie took a lot of calls from many different people, but he did note the number was a Texas area code.

"This is Charlie Tucker. How can I help you?" he answered, smiling inside at the memory of Randy busting his chops the first time he'd given that greeting. For years, Charlie had the habit of answering with a terse, "This is Book. Go." Even Kristi stopped commenting on his method after a while. But then there was that one time when Judge Greeley had called him personally, a rarity up there with Sasquatch sightings, and upon hearing those words, "This is Book. Go.", and thinking he'd dialed a wrong number, Judge Greeley had immediately hung up.

"Mr. Tucker, this is Joan Norgren," came the reply, and Charlie felt himself sitting up straighter in his seat. He could still detect a faint accent in her voice. Texas, he finally decided. After all the time he'd spent in San Antonio, he should have picked up on the accent sooner.

"Ah, Miss Norgren. A pleasure to hear your voice. Remember, please call me Charlie."

"Okay, Charlie. I didn't catch you at a bad time, did I?"

"No ma'am. Not at all. Just responding to some emails that can wait. What can I do for you?" Charlie replied. He wanted to ask how she'd gotten his cell number but decided to hold that thought for the moment.

"Oh, that's great," she said, and then the long pause that followed made Charlie wonder if the call had been disconnected. That'd been happening more often, and Cody insisted it was because the infrastructure was rapidly losing the race to keep up with the demand. Robbie, for his part, had said it was the NSA hanging up on calls they found too boring for all involved to continue.

"Ms. Norgren, are you still there?"

"Yes, and please, call me Joan. I was just wondering how to ask this next question without sounding like a stalker."

"I think you will find me refreshingly forgiving of such an offense, Joan. But what makes you say that?"

"Because I'm sitting outside your office right now," Joan replied with a bit of a catch in her throat that made Charlie want to smile.

"Well, that is a bit of a problem, since I'm not downtown today," Charlie responded, wondering what her reply would be to that tidbit, but Joan laughed nervously before speaking again.

"I know. Hence the stalker comment, since I'm in the parking lot of your office in Parma."

Charlie had to laugh then. An attractive young woman stalking him sounded like one of Robbie's 'no shit' stories, but now he would be able to hang in there the next time they started one of their bullshit sessions.

"Well, as long as you don't mean me any harm, Joan, you might as well come on in," Charlie said. Despite the odd nature of the call, he didn't feel threatened by the idea. In fact, when he'd first met the woman less than a week ago, he'd gotten the feeling she wanted to ask him something. Maybe today she would work up the courage to verbalize her question.

"Well, as long as I'm not imposing," Joan replied carefully, "then I'll be right in."

With that, she terminated the call and Charlie finished packing up. The office manager here, in practice a glorified receptionist and paralegal working for Brian Neff, Carpenter & Associates' one-man estate planning department, left at three p.m., so it was up to Charlie to shut down the office when his deposition ended. Fortunately, he had a key to the small suite so once he had all the lights off except for the one in the reception area, he was ready to go.

Charlie was seated in one of the overstuffed office chairs when he saw Joan's figure darken the smoked glass panel of the front entry door, so he jumped to his feet before Joan had the door open. He'd told Billy once how the glass insert made the door much more vulnerable to forced entry, but the old man had merely laughed and asked, "Who's going to break in, Charlie?"

Billy had a point. The quiet office park located near Parma Community General Hospital wasn't exactly a high foot traffic area, but even after all these years, Charlie looked to see what could be done to improve security. Hell, bad enough Billy insisted on posting his offices as gun-free zones, though Charlie had little qualm about breaking that rule from time to time, like every time he walked through the door.

"Oh," Joan said as she stepped into the quiet entryway, and her piercing blue eyes scanned the deserted professional space quickly before setting on Charlie. If he could read her reaction, he would say she appeared shocked, but not frightened by the empty state of the satellite office.

"I didn't realize..." she started, and then stopped again.

"Welcome to the Carpenter & Associates Parma office," Charlie announced, spreading his arms in a grand show before stifling a small chuckle and continuing. "This place is just a glorified conference room, Joan. Melba left at three to go pick up her kids, so I'm all that's left to lock the place up."

"Gotcha," Joan responded, clearly recovering from her surprise. "I didn't realize there wasn't anybody else here. Not a problem. Look, do you have time to talk?"

Charlie didn't bother to consult his phone or the heavy watch on his wrist. His day was officially over at this point, and all he had to look forward to was a quiet dinner back at his condo.

"All the time you need, Joan. You want to sit out here or in one of the offices?"

"How about the conference room you mentioned?"

Charlie nodded. That would work, and he was curious to see what this attractive woman wanted with him anyway. Unlike Robbie, who they considered a walking gland, Charlie knew he wasn't God's gift to the ladyfolk. Some of his friends generously attributed his failed relationships in recent years to his devotion to Kristi and the kids, but Charlie knew. It was staring back at him, every time he looked in a mirror.

Once inside the wood paneled conference room and with the lights turned back on, Charlie could see the tension in Joan's face as she claimed a seat in the corner. Charlie, as was his habit, claimed a chair across from the woman where he could keep an eye on both doors. Not that he was armed of course, that would be breaking office policy. He just had access to a piece of machinery that could protect him.

"What's up?" he finally asked as Joan continued to watch him. She was worried about something, clearly, and it wasn't him.

"Well, I don't know how to say this, and I really don't know who else to talk to. I just moved to town a month ago after landing a job as briefing attorney at the Northern District," she explained. "I have to admit something first. I didn't bump into you by accident at the club. I heard you liked to work out in the early morning and I set my alarm clock, so I could see you the other day."

Charlie had a good poker face before the fire, and his expression remained unreadable as Joan made her admission. He merely waited for her to continue.

"Sally Birdsong mentioned you," Joan said, picking up the thread of her explanation. Charlie did offer a nod at this, remembering the woman. She'd worked at Carpenter & Associates for a few years as a legal assistant before receiving her certification as a paralegal and taking a job at the Federal Courthouse. They'd overlapped by a few months, but Charlie could scarcely recall more than a name.

"She said you...she said you were in the Army, and that you were in Afghanistan."

Now that part made Charlie look pointedly at the speaker, as he never remembered mentioning anything of the sort to the plump, forty-something woman while they'd worked together.

"Why would that matter?" Charlie asked evenly, his voice pitched down low as he watched Joan squirm in her seat for the first time.

"I wanted to talk to you the other day about something. Something not work-related. Correction, I wanted to talk to somebody, and Sally suggested I talk to you. She's the one who told me about your gym membership, Charlie. She said you were a good listener, and you might be willing to answer my questions."

"Well, you now have my full attention, Miss Norgren," Charlie replied, and the use of her last name wasn't lost on the woman.

"Charlie, it's still Joan. And I wasn't going to ask you about anything...look, I had an older brother, Sean. He was in the Army, over there, and I just had some questions. I was still trying to work up the nerve to call you, about those questions, but that's not why I called you today."

Joan seemed to run out of steam at that point, and Charlie felt like an ass for putting her on the spot. Clearly, Joan had more than something minor truly troubling her. And, Charlie clearly caught the past tense when referencing her brother.

"Joan, just spit it out, okay? Just tell me why you came over here today first. We can talk about the other later. When you feel up to it. Now, what happened today?"

Charlie's words, slow and careful, seemed to break through whatever barrier the younger attorney had erected.

"All right. All right," she began, "like I told you, I recently started work at the Federal Courthouse as a briefing attorney. Money sucks, but the experience is great for a young lawyer. Anyway, there was a meeting this morning. Unscheduled, or at least, not on the agenda I saw."

Charlie shrugged, clearly not getting it.

"Which judge?"

"All of them. All of the District Judges, and the Magistrate Judges as well," Joan explained, and Charlie started to get a bad feeling as Joan continued.

"I didn't get an invite, but the meeting started at ten o'clock and these men in black suits, you know, like the Secret Service or the FBI agents wear, went to each office and escorted each judge back to that lecture hall-sized conference room they have on the sixteenth floor. Just the judges were allowed inside. They had armed security manning the doors, keeping everybody out."

Not liking anything he was hearing, Charlie leaned forward, his face set in hard lines that made his scarring stand out even more. "Who manned the doors? Was it the guys in the black suits?"

Joan shook her head in the negative before answering. "Federal Protective Services, but not our local guys. Or at least, none of the longtime local staffers I spoke to recognized them."

"Please tell me you didn't draw any attention to yourself when you were asking around," Charlie said, more of a statement than a question.

"No, I didn't. That was Reggie who did all the talking. He's an old bird, and he handles Judge Seaver's court as his coordinator. He was really pissed. Anyway, they were in the meeting for over two hours, and afterwards, I saw some of the judges just after they walked out. Judge Huntley was as pale as a ghost, and old Judge McNamara looked like he was five kinds of pissed-off. After that, the coordinators canceled all business in the courthouse and sent us home."

"You got any idea what they talked about in there?"

Kneading her hands as they rested on the table, Joan shook her head again. "Not a clue. I know Judge McNamara a little bit, since I'm working on a project for him, but he wouldn't even look me in the eye when I asked if there was anything I could do to help. I swear, Charlie, he looked scared, and I thought nothing in the whole wide world could do that."

Charlie thought about what Joan had described and he felt the beginnings of a headache starting behind his eyes. Like Joan, Charlie knew that Federal District Judges were literally a law unto themselves. The new American ruling elite, with individually more power than any single legislator.

With lifetime appointments and powers only limited by their own brethren in the appellate courts, and ultimately the Supreme Court, these few men and women wielded the might of the federal government in their courtrooms. Some federal judges maintained a strict interpretation of the Constitution while in recent years, many had taken it upon themselves to expand upon a living document. Essentially, they put on their 'Founding Fathers' thinking caps and ruled on what they thought the law should be. Sometimes this was to address an issue unimaginable when the Constitution had been written and other times, this judicial legislation came to pass when the judges found the need to reverse some past injustice.

"Off the top of my head, I can't think of anything either, unless it had to do with some imminent natural disaster. They cannot make an earthquake go away, for instance. No matter what the Supreme Court might fancy," Charlie opined, more to distract Joan than anything else while he thought.

Charlie spent little time in Federal Court. Not a lot of justice for the little guys getting meted out in those marble halls, and Charlie liked to think of himself as a champion for the underdogs. At least, in his city. So he didn't have a lot of connections there, but he did have someone he could call. Later, he thought.

"So, what do you think is going on here, Charlie? I'm not embarrassed to admit, I'm scared by what I saw today. Those men, they just marched in like they owned the building, and everyone in it," Joan said, and shivered before continuing. "There was something in the way they moved, and in the way they looked at us. Made me feel like they actually wanted someone to protest or make a scene. The way they ordered the judges around like small children was clearly a statement, but for what?"

Charlie didn't comment right away, but when he did, he spoke with a decisive tone.

"I might know some people I can call, but it will need to be later this evening. In the meantime, if it will make you feel better, you can come back with me to my place. No strings. I may have some more questions for you anyway. Things neither of us have thought about yet."

Joan looked hard at Charlie.

"No strings? I mean, you seem like a nice guy and Sally said I could talk to you, but I hardly know you."

With a slight nod, Charlie offered, "Absolutely. If you'd rather, I can just see you home to your place and check in with you later. Your choice."

That was the right move, Charlie realized when he saw Joan's eyes. Giving her that option sealed the deal for her. She was scared, more so than she wanted to let on, and Charlie just seemed too good to be true. Just by being a decent guy, which Charlie realized said a lot about the current state of mankind.

"I'll go with you. If that's okay?"

"I wouldn't have offered if I didn't mean it, Joan."

"Yeah. I can see that about you," Joan replied, and before he knew it, the woman was in his arms, clutching at him like he was the last life preserver on the Titanic.

Chapter Eight

Parma, OH

Charlie's condo was a three-bedroom unit, with a two-car garage on the ground floor and the living space on the second floor. He liked living in a fairly secure, gated community not too far from the Parma office. He might work in the revitalized Cleveland downtown, but he still preferred a place in the suburbs with trees and grass. As long as he didn't have to trim the limbs or run the lawnmower. Not that he wasn't handy, finally, after all those years of helping out with Kristi and the kids, but if he had the weekend off, he was either at the retreat or in Chicago.

After he parked his extended cab pickup in the cramped garage, he got out and showed Joan where to park her Jetta on the street. Joan got a peek into a meticulously organized garage, including a tiny pop-up camper adjacent to the truck and rows of pegboards running around the room, holding a wide variety of tools and big boy toys neatly arranged. She was almost disappointed when Charlie closed the garage with a remote and instead, led her up the steps to the front door.

Once inside the foyer, Charlie moved quickly to disengage the alarm and then guided Joan into the spotless kitchen and eat-in nook. Heading for the chromed wine chiller, he opened the glassed door to pull out two bottles of water.

"Would you care for something to drink?" he asked, offering one of the bottles. "I've also got ginger ale, orange juice, and maybe a bottle or two of Shiner Bock. Anything harder, and I'll have to hit the bar."

Joan, distracted, took the offered water bottle and continued to inspect the well-equipped kitchen. She was admiring the stainless-steel refrigerator when she saw the colorful, child-like crayon drawings affixed to both doors with magnets shaped like ladybugs and bullfrogs.

"Oh, I didn't know you had kids. Are they gone somewhere with your wife?" Joan asked, her voice going a touch uncertain. The last thing she wanted to do was cause a problem here, after all. She was looking for answers, and yes, maybe a little reassurance, but not to get in the middle of someone's marriage. She knew if the neighbors saw him come in with her, then the wife would know within minutes of her return. Rather than opening the water bottle, she set it aside and started to head for the door, thinking this had been a terrible idea after all.

Charlie just laughed, obviously enjoying her discomfort just a tiny bit.

"Joan, relax. No wife, and no children, at least, none that I know of. Those pictures are from Emily and Clark, who are sort of my niece and nephew."

Feeling foolish for her snap judgment, Joan turned away from Charlie, so he couldn't see the color rising in her cheeks. With her pale complexion, a blush was almost impossible to hide.

This isn't me, Joan told herself. I'm not some flighty little girl, and this is not a date gone bad. I came to this man for help, and maybe, she had to admit to herself, just maybe a little comfort.

Joan wasn't accustomed to being menaced by thugs with guns. Menaced, she mused, was just the way it had felt, too. Threatened without a word being uttered, by men who looked at her from behind those black sunglasses that made the wearers look like insects.

"Ah, sorry. I just don't know anything about you is all, Charlie. I mean, Sally said you were hard-working and smart, but she didn't know anything about your personal life. Married, engaged, gay, straight or what. She said you worked long hours when she was at the firm, but she said she seldom saw you on weekends. You just disappeared."

"Yeah," Charlie responded, gesturing at the artwork on the refrigerator and then to several framed photographs scattered on the walls in the kitchen and on through into the living room. Stepping over, she took a close look at one such photo and saw a pretty, petite woman wearing a baseball cap and kneeling next to two small children. A boy of maybe six years old and a little girl maybe a year or two younger. Not having children and being the youngest child in her family, Joan had no experience at guessing the ages of children.

"Cute kids," she said. "Is their mom your sister?"

"Not exactly. She is a friend, a very close one."

"But you two aren't dating..." Joan continued, for some reason curious about this mystery woman. Not that she had designs on Charlie, she told herself, but out of sheer curiosity.

"No," Charlie answered without hesitation, then stopped, opening the bottle of water and taking a long sip before continuing. Though the friends never made any secret of the initial reasons for their concern for Kristi, he still felt a moment's pause before giving even a brief summary.

"Her husband was our senior NCO, our platoon sergeant. We lost him on my last mission, the same one where I got burned. When he died, Kristi was pregnant with Emily, and Clark was just barely walking."

Charlie's words, though lacking inflection, masked a pain that Joan could sense. And relate to, in a strange way. They'd both lost someone they held very dear.

"That's horrible," she replied, involuntarily touching her fingers to her lips, as if she could call back the offending question. This wasn't the first time her curiosity had resulted in hurt feelings. "I'm sorry I brought it up."

"Don't be. I'm not." Charlie said simply, and when he continued, his tone sounded like it was coming from a long distance away. "That was a terrible day, but those of us that survived, we did so only because First Sergeant Wheaton was there. So, if I try to keep his memory alive for his children, for his son that doesn't remember him or his daughter who he never had a chance to hold, then that's the least I can do."

"Can...can you tell me about what happened that day?" she asked timidly.

"No," he replied after a beat. "I can't. Not today. And why would you want to hear something like that?"

"To try to understand," Joan replied, picking up the bottled water again and absently spinning the plastic cap between her fingers. "To try to make sense of what it was like over there, and why he did it once he was home."

Even with so many other things on his mind, what Joan said had tumblers clicking in Charlie's head.

"Your brother, Sean, he had something happen after he got home," Charlie's words weren't a question. He knew.

"The Highway Patrol labeled it an accident," Joan said, her voice cold as she rattled off the dry details. "He hit the bridge abutment going over one hundred and twenty miles per hour. No alcohol in his system, which was a first, and no sign of skid marks or anything that might indicate a loss of control."

"And that's what you originally wanted to talk about," Charlie supplied, and Joan nodded before continuing.

"But now, I want to first find out what the heck is going on. The more I think of it, the more it bothers me. Those judges, when they got out, the ones I saw weren't just upset. The more I think about it, the more I realize I was seeing something on their faces that should never have been there. Fear. Who has enough power to terrorize a group of entitled, head-in-the-clouds jurists, and why? Why try to scare one district full of judges into jumping a certain way?"

Charlie snapped his fingers at that question, as Joan's words triggered another thought and a recent memory.

"I don't know anybody here I could call who might know more than you do. But you just gave me an idea."

Charlie pulled out his cell phone and fiddled with the device, even as Joan was waving her hand in his face, trying to get an answer. What idea, she wanted to know, but Charlie never paused as he hit the send key and pressed the phone to his ear. The line sounded clear and he heard the distinctive pulse that used to be called a 'ringing' as the call went through.

"Charlie!" the voice on the other end of the phone gushed, "How are you doing, old man?"

Rolling his eyes at the other man, Charlie responded as politely as he could manage, given the nervous energy he suddenly felt running through his body.

"I'm doing great, Bryce," Charlie responded, trying but failing to get the same level of enthusiasm in his voice. "And how are things with Rodger?"

"Wonderful as always," Bryce responded. "But you didn't call me out of the blue to ask me about my love life, did you?"

83

Despite the way he sometimes let months go between calls, Charlie actually liked Bryce McKentrick, and always felt guilty for not staying in better contact with his friend. In many ways, he thought of Bryce like one might a puppy that sometimes piddled on the carpet but was just too amusing to be punished. Especially when Bryce had been drinking in law school, and there had been a carpet pissing incident that had gone unreported but well remembered. That boy just couldn't handle his booze. Bryce had become more than just a law school classmate of his, and they'd somehow become friends in spite of the culture clash. Or maybe because of it.

Charlie came from poor, blue collar roots, the son of an oft-unemployed welder who was more fond of the liquor bottle than his kids. Bryce, on the other hand, came from a wealthy and sophisticated family of professionals who encouraged their only son to explore his passions while backpacking through Europe before enrolling in law school.

They'd met their first year of law school at Marshall, and quickly found their common areas of interest in Constitutional Law and history gave them something to talk about while they waded through the byzantine world of Contracts and the Uniform Commercial Code. Eventually, Charlie's interests drew him into criminal law while Bryce finally decided to focus on the corporate route.

After a few frustrating years as a prosecutor, Charlie managed the jump into personal injury work without too much head scratching, but he still relied on Bryce's help from time to time when he needed to dig deep into the corporate shell games that some of his opponents utilized. Bryce, for his part, knew he could rely on Charlie's tutelage if he got himself too deep into a liability or coverage issue for one of his corporate clients.

They represented different ends of the spectrum: socially, politically, and even sexually, as Bryce was a proud, openly homosexual male, and Charlie remained, as Bryce put it, hopelessly hetero.

One night had sealed their nascent friendship, when Charlie, for once overindulging in alcohol, had delivered an impassioned defense of the homosexual lifestyle that had all of his small study group helplessly rolling on the floor.

"I love gay men," Charlie had proudly announced, much to the surprise of the half dozen law students gathered at their favorite low rent bar. That proclamation had received boos from several of the other patrons, until Charlie proceeded to deliver the basis for his statement.

"Look, even before I had my little 'accident'," he continued, gesturing vaguely to his face while undeterred by the naysayers, "I wasn't exactly a superstar with the ladies. But look at Bryce," he waved at his friend. "That guy has perfect teeth, perfect hair, and he talks real, real smooth. If he was straight, I'd have zero chance if we set our sights on the same little lady.

"But fortunately, he likes the salami, and more power to him," Charlie forged ahead, his voice growing stronger as he spoke. "Because that puts him out of the running when it comes to female companionship. So, the more gay men, the better my odds. Simple mathematics, you see?"

Charlie, allowing his crooked grin to show in recollection of that night, brought his attention back to the here and now.

"Actually, I am calling to check up on Rodger. You know, making sure he is good enough for my buddy Bryce."

"Puh-leeze," Bryce responded, "like you care. I don't hear from you for months and then all of a sudden, I get a call from my favorite knuckle-dragging right-winger. How are things 'in the Bubble'?"

"Har-Har," Charlie deadpanned, accustomed to his friend's knee jerk conservative bashing. "Seriously, I *was* calling to ask about Rodger. He's still working for Judge Wallenstein?"

"Yes, he is," Bryce confirmed, his voice getting a little more serious as their conversation continued. "You have a case in Illinois now? You know, he can't do anything, right?"

"Bryce, Bryce, I would never ask something like that," Charlie said, sensing his friend's discomfort.

After graduation, Bryce took a job with one of the biggest corporate transactional firms in the country and relocated to Chicago. After the move, he eventually started seeing Rodger who, the last Charlie heard, was working as court coordinator for one of the District Judges in the Northern District of Illinois situated there in Chicago. Even though Bryce made crazy money at his firm, Rodger wanted to keep making his own way and not become the prototypical housewife. Charlie could respect that attitude. This call was a longshot, but Charlie still felt like he should ask.

"Nope, Bryce, I was just wondering if Rodger came home early today. You know, if the principal let the kids out early from school?"

Bryce laughed then. "What? Are you in town? Is this some pathetic way of asking if we want to go out for dinner this evening? Hey, you can bring that lady friend of yours again. She's adorable, don't you know? Or you can leave it to me to round you up some suitable female companionship."

Charlie had to admit, for a gay man, Bryce had a good eye for the ladies. And matchmaking tendencies that would make Charlie's own Irish grandmother sigh with envy. Since Bryce was an old married man, he now thought all his friends should be joining him in wedded bliss.

"No, honest. I was just curious. A friend of mine mentioned her court received a surprise visit today from some unexpected guests, and I was just wondering if this was an isolated incident."

The line was silent for several seconds before Bryce replied. Now the man was serious, and all attempts at levity were absent from his voice.

"No, that was yesterday. Rodger didn't say much about it, but he was plainly bothered by something he saw or heard. He called me on the way home, saying the staff had been dismissed for the rest of the day. But he's right here if you want to ask him."

After making quick pleasantries, Charlie managed to confirm basically the same information as Joan had shared from this morning's meeting. At least on the surface, the same entourage had showed up the day before in Chicago to deliver some kind of briefing. Or something.

When Rodger handed the phone back to Bryce, Charlie heard a quick conversation take place, but he couldn't make out the words. Then, Charlie's friend came back on the line.

"Is this something we should be worried about, Charlie? Is there something you're not telling me? Some super-secret military plan in place?"

Charlie had to fake a laugh this time, but his words remained serious as he replied.

"Bryce, you know I'm out. All the way out. This is just weird because it sounds just like something that happened here today. At our federal courthouse. Maybe you can find out something, but I've got nowhere else to look."

"Yes, maybe I will. You know, maybe I can have my friends take a look too."

Charlie managed not to sigh at that. In addition to his long hours and hard work for his corporate masters, Bryce somehow found time to be active as a volunteer with the local chapter of the ACLU. As a skilled legal researcher and writer, Bryce contributed several hours per week just writing amicus briefs and the ever-constant Freedom of Information requests.

Thinking about his conversation from earlier with Doctor Hammar, Charlie made one last comment before he ended the call.

"Longshot suggestion, Bryce, but look for what you can find out about the water bill that Congress just passed. Unlikely, but that's the only other odd thing I can think of right now."

"What water bill? Why is this the first time I am hearing of this?"

"Maybe nothing, Bryce. Only other oddball event I can think of that comes close to coinciding with the dates."

"I'll do that. And I'll be in touch."

After that, Joan and Charlie talked more about what had happened, but before they lost the light, Joan needed to get back to her apartment. Charlie walked her out and made sure she buckled her seat belt.

"Well, that wasn't much of a first date," Charlie groused to himself as Joan pulled away. "But now I know why she originally wanted to talk to me. To find out why her brother killed himself."

Charlie knew there were as many reasons as there were stars in the nighttime sky. And whatever was coming, his brothers needed to know about it.

Chapter Nine

Retreat

Pulling off the back-country road, Kristi turned onto a small dirt drive. She stopped and looked over at Clark. "Will you open the gate for momma?" she asked with a smile.

Grabbing the door handle, Clark just pushed the door open while undoing his seatbelt, jumping out and took off running. "It's my turn, Mom," Emily whined from the back seat.

"Sorry, baby," Kristi said, looking in the rearview mirror. "When we leave, you can do the gate."

A smile popped up on Emily's face. "Okay," she beamed.

Dropping her eyes, Kristi saw Clark holding the gate open. She eased her SUV through the gate and stopped. She watched Clark close the gate in the mirror and made sure he pushed the bar all the way, closing the gate. A few years ago, he hadn't closed it good and everyone had to get on four-wheelers and chase the cows back into the field.

When Clark was back in, Kristi drove through the pasture while looking at the cows around the old barn that was used to house the hay. She had no idea how big a farm used to be here but from the size of the barn, it must have been colossal. "Mom, can we go fishing?" Emily asked.

"Baby, let's see what the others are doing," Kristi smiled, pulling through the pasture. The dirt drive passed the barn, then passed into a stand of oak and cedar trees. Letting out a sigh, Kristi relaxed in the tranquility the retreat always brought to her. If it did this for her, she knew the boys needed it.

In the years she had come here, it had only taken once to fall in love with it and she was thankful the boys had brought her down. It had helped her heal as well, and let the kids grow up with a family.

The property was two hundred and fifty acres with a river running through the west end. Over half was covered in tall trees with the fifty acres near the road as pasture. Her first year to come down, the boys had put a fence up to keep the cows, all eleven of them, from entering the woods. The kids were still toddlers and even then, they'd loved this land.

The boys had taught them how to fish and hunt here. And of course, shoot. That was one thing that was done every time anyone came to the retreat; shoot. They had built a nice five-hundred-yard range and had put in a skeet range two years ago at the north end of the pasture.

Frank, her husband, had taught her how to shoot and Kristi had her own weapons that he'd bought her. Her kids had their own arsenal; thanks to Mom, Pop, and the boys. Unlike most people from Chicago, Kristi loved firearms and was happy that the kids were taught right, even if she had to jump through hoops with the state for the right to own or even touch ammunition at an Illinois sporting goods store. She just got upset that the boys kept buying the kids more. The pink AR Randy bought for Emily for her birthday two weeks ago was in its case in the back.

Emily already had two .22s that Mom and Pop had bought her, a 20ga shotgun Robbie had bought her last year for her birthday, and a rifle Book had bought her to hunt with last Christmas. Kristi knew weapons and knew the ones they'd given Emily weren't cheap.

Then there was Clark, and they had bought him more guns than Kristi even owned. The gun safe Frank had was packed now. So packed, Kristi bought another gun safe and put it at the cabin the boys had put up for her here at the retreat.

Four years ago at Christmas, Randy had bought her another AR. She didn't understand why, she had two that Frank had owned and the one Frank had built for her. But when Kristi started to complain, Randy went and tattled to Mom and Pop. The complaining from Kristi stopped instantly.

That was when Charlie and Robbie had both given her new pistols. Robbie, being the lover of oddball guns, went against his normal grain and got her a Colt 1911 that he had tuned and upgraded for her. When Kristi looked at Robbie with a glare, Robbie just shrugged and told her. "Hey, I wanted a project gun to learn on, and I didn't need another in my safe." Charlie, being Charlie, gave her a compact Glock in .45 ACP, something useful and light enough for her to carry.

"We promise, we didn't plan this," Charlie had chuckled and held up his damaged hand. "Scout's honor."

Like it was yesterday, Kristi remembered looking at both of them, then over at Mom and Pop. She'd bit her tongue and hugged them both. Like they did for the kids; Mom, Pop, and the boys bought Kristi more than she wanted them to. How they could, she didn't know. If her house wasn't paid for, Kristi would be living somewhere else and she still had trouble making ends meet.

A nurse made good money but for a single mom with two kids, it wasn't that great. Driving through the trees, Kristi let out a sigh as her mind returned to the here and now. She knew without the boys; her kids would've lived a totally different life and wouldn't have had near the experiences. They were the ones who paid for the kids to do extra activities, a lot of extra activities.

When Book found out the kids couldn't swim six years ago, both were enrolled in lessons within a week. Oh no, not at the local Y like Kristi wanted and even looked into. Charlie had found a former U.S. Olympian to teach the kids to swim. Even while he'd been in law school, Charlie had made sure each kid made every lesson. If he couldn't take them, one of the others did.

All the improvements made on the house were done by the boys, along with Pop. A smile broke out on Kristi's face, remembering when her BMW had started acting up. Cody was there that day, tearing it apart. At dark, she'd told Cody to come in and he could continue tomorrow, but Cody had refused.

When she'd woken up the next morning, she'd found all the boys in her garage working on her car. Stepping out into the garage, Kristi almost passed out to see the entire front end taken apart with Charlie reading a manual. Robbie and Randy were taking apart the engine and Cody was looking at his laptop that was hooked up to her car.

That was one time, Kristi didn't protest. She just hoped they could put it back together. Cody threw her his keys, so she could get to work. Holding the keys, Kristi had watched the four working and remembered how none of them slept more than a few hours a day.

Pulling into the driveway that afternoon, Kristi saw the Suburban she was currently driving, sitting in the driveway. When Kristi got out of Cody's Camaro, Charlie had walked over and handed her the keys. "You will drive this until we fix your car," Charlie had told her with his scarred face in a scowl. "Why Wheat wanted a beamer beats the hell out of me, but you have to have one American ride here." Wisely, Kristi had kept her mouth shut and the boys had her BMW back together the next day.

When Kristi had tried to give the keys to the Suburban back, Robbie had looked at her with a grin. "Mom and Pop bought that for you. YOU can tell them YOU don't want it," Robbie had told her.

"What are you smiling about, Momma?" Clark asked, looking over and breaking the memory.

Turning to look at Clark, Kristi's smile turned into a grin. "Oh, just that I love this weird family we have," she answered, slowing for a turn. The kids knew what she meant.

"We have the best family ever!" Emily cheered, throwing up her arms.

Turning her head back to the front, Kristi nodded and mumbled, "We're just missing one."

Slowing down, Kristi drove around a small knoll and into the camp area. It was twenty acres set in an oxbow. A large double wide that served as a clubhouse sat in the center of eight manufactured buildings, the type seen on construction sites. They all ranged in size with each person having their own, and Kristi's being the largest.

On that, Kristi had thrown a fit and it'd been a good one. So good, the boys almost hauled the large building out just so Kristi would shut the hell up, but luckily, Mom and Pop had showed up. That was the one and only time, Kristi had argued with Mom and Pop. It took an hour, but Kristi had finally let it go because it turned out, Mom had forgotten more about bitching than Kristi would ever know, even if Kristi lived two lifetimes.

Each building had a small bathroom, living room with a kitchenette, and bedroom. The boys each had an extra room in theirs and used it to store equipment and reloading supplies. Behind each of the buildings everyone called cabins, sat at least one forty-foot shipping container. This was where everyone stored

ATVs, ammo, and put their gun safes because the containers were harder to get into than the buildings.

The retreat had never been bothered, but it just felt safer to leave the expensive stuff more secure. Randy did come down every few days just to check and they had wireless game cameras everywhere that Cody had put up. It wasn't until last year that Kristi had found out, when Cody was staying with her to take the kids to their ball practice, that he could get on his laptop and check the cameras.

Pulling around the clubhouse, Kristi sucked in a breath as Emily let out another cheer. Randy, Robbie, Cody, and Charlie were standing around a new four-wheeler that had a big red bow on it. "Is that mine?!" Emily screamed.

"I'm going to kill them," Kristi mumbled. Seeing movement out of the corner of her eye, she turned to see Mom and Pop walking over to the boys. "Later, after Mom and Pop go to bed," Kristi amended.

The SUV was barely stopped before Emily jumped out in a dead run. Randy kneeled, holding his arms open. "Uncle Randy!" Emily cheered, running at him. She hit him hard, wrapping her arms around his neck.

"Hope you like it, tadpole," Randy said, squeezing her tight. "They didn't have one in pink, so you had to get Mossy Oak like everyone else's."

Emily kissed his cheek and let him go and charged Cody who caught her in a hug. "I love it!" she said and kissed Cody's cheek. Cody put her down and Emily ran at Charlie. "Uncle Charlie, thank you!"

Charlie picked her up, hugging her as Clark got out and ran over to hug Randy. "Mom's mad," Clark whispered.

"That's why Granny and Grandpa are here," Randy whispered back, letting Clark go. As Clark ran to Cody and Emily charged Robbie, Randy turned to see Kristi get out. Standing up straight and poking his chest out, "I can outrun you, so bring it on," he challenged.

Crossing her arms over her chest, Kristi started tapping her foot as Robbie put Emily down. "Which one of you bought it?" Kristi asked with an icy stare. Randy pointed at Cody and Cody pointed at Charlie and Charlie pointed at Robbie who pointed at Randy.

Knowing that each had chipped in like they'd done for the swimming pool, Kristi bit her bottom lip to stop the words she wanted to come out.

Emily stepped back as the four pointed at each other and turned to look at her mom, then at the four-wheeler. "Moooooom, come on. You have one and Clark has one," Emily moaned.

"Yeah, that we didn't buy," Kristi snapped, staring at the four still pointing at each other.

"Kristi, you hush now," Lena said, but all present interpreted it as a command. Walking over, Lena put her arm over Kristi's shoulders. "The boys think she needs her own. They bought Clark one last year and Emily has driven every person's four-wheeler out here. She's safe, so you let the boys pamper those kids."

"Pamper?" Kristi cried out, dropping her arms and turning to Lena. "How about spoil?"

"Hush," Lena said, smiling. "It won't be long until Emily starts having boyfriends and stuff-"

"Boyfriend?!" Robbie, Randy, Charlie, and Cody shouted and charged over at Kristi. Turning to the shouts, Kristi saw each one had a very hostile expression on their face as they stormed over. Not liking the way they were coming over, Kristi moved behind Lena who promptly got the hell out of the way.

"You let her have a boyfriend?!" Randy barked with his face turning purple.

"Who the hell is this little butt-wipe?!" Robbie snarled, pulled a knife, and tested the edge with his thumb. "I know how to cure this," he mumbled.

Cody got in Kristi's face. "Where is he planning on going to college?!"

Shoving Cody out of the way, Charlie got in Kristi's face. "Who are his parents?!"

Looking from Charlie's face to the others, Kristi tried to swallow but her throat was too dry. "She doesn't have one yet," Kristi said rather timidly.

The four glared at her, then turned to Emily. "You have a boyfriend?" Charlie asked.

"Ewww," Emily cried out, shaking her hands. "Boys have cooties."

"That's right and don't you forget it," Cody said, walking over to her. "Granny and Grandpa got you a helmet."

"Granny, Papaw, thank you!" Emily cried out and ran over to them.

Kristi took a step back and Charlie whipped his head around, looking at her. "We are going to talk about this later," he almost growled. "Boyfriend, indeed," he huffed and lifted his chin high, strolling off.

The others moved over as Emily climbed on her four-wheeler. "I'm sorry, baby, but your future dates are going to have hell, going through four who see you as their daughter," Kristi said, shaking her head.

"Oliver sees her as his grandchild, so don't leave him out," Lena chuckled.

"I thought they were about to spank me," Kristi exhaled with relief.

Seeing Kristi as her daughter, Lena smiled and patted her back. "If it would've been true, I'm sure they would have."

Giving a big sigh, "Mom, I don't like the boys always buying them stuff. Hell, they are always doing something for us," Kristi moaned as Emily started the engine. "What about Aaron's kids? They might get jealous."

"I doubt it, but they are only six and nine. And the boys buy stuff for them too," Lena said as Emily took off.

"Not like they do for Clark and Emily. Hell, or me, for that matter. Do you know Clark's and Emily's college is almost paid for?"

With a sigh, Lena grabbed Kristi's shoulder and spun Kristi to face her. "They see Clark and Emily as theirs, so you have to deal with that. Yes, I know about the college fund, Oliver and I put in what we could. They see you as a little sister," Lena explained, with a stern face. "Oliver and I see all of you as ours, so you let the boys and us have our fun. It makes us happy."

Wrapping her arms around Lena's neck, "I love you, Mom," Kristi wept as tears ran down her cheeks.

"We love you too, dear," Lena said, patting her back as she hugged her tight. "Now, don't be mad at Oliver because he bought the kids new saddles."

Feeling her legs go numb, Kristi leaned back and looked at Lena in shock. "He just bought them some last year," Kristi mumbled.

"Those were used. Oliver said they needed new ones, and the tack needed to be replaced anyway. Now the saddles and riding gear all match!" Lena claimed, patting Kristi's cheek. "I'm going to start some supper."

As Lena walked away, Kristi looked up. "They aren't you, Frank, but they are the closest thing, baby. Thank you."

Chapter Ten

Retreat

"So anyway," Charlie began, sitting on his four-wheeler and watching the kids cutting back and forth on the trail. "I haven't heard anything more about what happened at the federal courthouse, but it was weird."

"Define 'weird' when it comes to the Feds, man. Maybe it has something to do with the President's immigration reforms. Or some other garbage he's spouting. This guy makes Obama look like Reagan," Cody said, leaning back on his four-wheeler.

Robbie gave Charlie a shrug. He was not really following what his legal eagle friend was talking about today, but he wasn't exactly a fan of the new guy in the White House. Randy, though, looked perplexed before he spoke up.

"I don't know, guys. Doesn't sound like anything I've ever heard of. Maybe some kind of security briefing, about some terrorist threat to the judiciary? Cody, you see anything with your buddies online?" Randy asked.

Cody looked off in the distance, and for someone who didn't know him, the younger man might have appeared to have missed the question. All three knew that expression when it came to Babyface. He was checking his memory banks, as Robbie called it.

"No, nothing legit," Cody finally said. "A few of the fringe folks are honking their horns about some United Nations school we have going at some of our bases, but heck, we've been running some of those classes for years. All it takes is one Belgian paratrooper to wear his blue helmet for a photo op, and metaphorical tongues start wagging. A few years back, a trainload of armored vehicles were loaded on a rail line, and the internet blew up with all sorts of conspiracy theories."

They all nodded at that idea. Cody still made fun of the rumor spreading through West Virginia several years ago over social media about how the Federal government was mobilizing to take over their local gas stations. This had come in the wake of a gasoline pipeline breaking, depriving the area of fuel shipments for a few days. It had all begun with some black 'military vehicles' being photographed in the parking lot of a Hampton Inn in Beckley, West Virginia.

The posts had gone viral on Facebook and had gotten hundreds of thousands of views before someone, Cody couldn't remember who, announced the teams were actually there to attend a three-day course at a nearby military reservation. Happened every year, but this time, they had pictures and a story made up to fit the local concerns, and the rumor mill had done the rest.

"I don't know," Charlie continued. "My friend who was there was pretty upset by what she saw. Said she felt 'menaced' by the Men in Black."

"Oh," Robbie piped up. "Now it all makes sense, gentlemen. This is about Book chasing some tail. Is she hot? I'll bet she's hot. And dirty, too. Is she a beast in the sheets, my man?"

Charlie had to fight to keep from rolling his eyes. Robbie was sometimes a bit too much, but he was never boring. So, Charlie decided to tweak him right back.

"Man, is she Hot! I mean. Tall, blonde, with gorgeous blue eyes. Fit, as the Brits might say. Smart, too, so Robbie wouldn't last five minutes with her. She actually speaks in complete sentences and has her own place. You know, she doesn't still live with her parents." Charlie threw in the last part, grinning at the others.

"Dude," Robbie replied indignantly, "that was *one* time. One freaking time! And she was twenty-seven and living with her folks after her divorce. Just trying to get back on her feet."

"Or back on the pole," Cody interjected with a snicker. "You know, down at the Pink Pussycat Cabaret where she worked."

Robbie snorted, but in mirth, not objecting because it was simply the truth, before retorting, "That was some shock, I admit. What self-respecting stripper still lives at home?"

"And I rest my case, Your Honor," Charlie deadpanned, before getting serious again. "Look, if it was one courthouse, I could see the Federal Protection personnel coming out to give a warning, but two different courthouses? Doesn't sound right."

"Outside my bailiwick," Randy said, "but I agree, it is something peculiar. And anyway, you guys are missing the important part: Charlie has a girlfriend."

Charlie groaned as the good-natured ribbing went into full swing. He went along, his crooked lips twisted up in a smile as he listened to his friends, his brothers, give him shit. That was to be expected, and he wouldn't have it any other way.

"Too bad Bert couldn't make it this year," Randy said, finally changing the topic.

"Hard to get away, I'd imagine," Robbie added. "He's kind of having to run the whole business since his dad had his heart attack. Plus, you know, the whole 'wife and kids' thing. Must suck something awful having to run every decision past the C.O. before you can put your pants on in the morning. So much for the unstoppable Pirate. It's just sad."

"Come on, guys," Charlie interjected, "Lydia's cool. She had Kristi and the kids stay with her when she went down to surprise her parents last year. That was pretty nice, considering they've never met. Well, except on Facebook."

That got a groan from the others, mentioning the social networking site that everyone on the planet over the age of thirty, present company excluded, held a membership.

"Maybe they can make the trip in the fall, after the charter business slows down a little," Cody mused. "Be good to see those kids again. They were just tadpoles that last time."

Thinking about it, Charlie agreed with Cody. It would be good to see their old comrade, and Charlie knew Bert, salt water running through his veins and all, still found their retreat to be a place to find his peace.

"Would be nice to see them," Randy chimed in, and his voice sounded heavy as he continued. "Would be nice to see all our old friends one more time."

Knowing he was speaking of Wheat, and the rest of the men they'd lost on that last mission, as well as others that'd come before, Charlie and Robbie managed a somber "Amen" while Cody, lost in his own thoughts, continued to stare off into the distant green hills.

***

Walking into the clubhouse, Kristi looked around and saw Lena heading to the kitchen. Every wall in the double wide had been ripped out and the only closed rooms were the two bathrooms. At this end, next to the kitchen where the master bedroom once sat, a huge screen dominated one wall with a projector mounted on the ceiling. Recliners were arranged in rows with a sectional on the back wall like a movie theater. She knew basketball and hockey would be on that screen this weekend.

In the center of the clubhouse when you walked out from the kitchen was a game area. A pool table sat in the middle of the floor with a card table off to the side. On the other wall sat two flat screen TVs that had game consoles hooked up.

Then at the far end, a rather nice gym was set up. All the boys worked out and had gotten Kristi back into exercising. The only people not in shape were Aaron and Tyrone. They weren't fat, just not in shape. Tyrone, for his part, had worked construction for years, but he lacked the physique for running.

It didn't take a rocket scientist to see what the clubhouse really was. A really big and nicely set up man cave.

"Need any help, Mom?" Kristi asked, moving over to the stove.

"No, you go get your stuff set up," Lena said as the sound of engines sounded outside.

"Okay, but I'll come back and help," Kristi said, and Lena only nodded.

Walking back out onto the massive deck, Kristi looked at the gas grill and one of the biggest hot tubs she had ever seen. Giving a sigh she moved to the steps and stopped, seeing her Suburban had been moved and was sitting next to her cabin. "Just once, I wish they would stop," she groaned, reaching the ground.

Off the back deck were two buildings. She walked past the small building on the right that Robbie and Cody had built to house batteries. In the stream that ran around the oxbow, Robbie and Cody had built a small dam and put in several turbines. Kristi didn't know how much power they put out, but they didn't have to run generators.

There was power on the property at the barn next to the road, but the boys didn't want to run it to the camp at the back. So that's why they'd put in the turbines. There was no cable, they had put in satellite for TV and Cody put up a relay to use a hotspot for internet. The relay also helped with cell service because without it, there was none.

Granted, you could only use a cell phone in the camp, but you could use one. Although most put their cell phones away as soon as they arrived.

On the other side of the deck was another building. It was smaller but led to a large and deep root cellar. There was food down there, but it mainly held liquor, beer, and wine to be used in the clubhouse.

Between the two buildings was a large fire pit with chairs surrounding it. On many nights a fire would be built, and everyone would just sit around the fire talking.

Walking around the fire pit to her cabin, Kristi walked in and saw all their luggage already unloaded and sitting on the living room floor. Giving a sigh, she grabbed her suitcase and moved through the living room that had a small kitchen on the other side of the room. A small bathroom sat off in the far corner.

There wasn't a TV in the living room, only a coffee table, couch, and a recliner with a bow rack on the wall. On the opposite wall from the door were three doors to their bedrooms. Walking in the far left door, Kristi put her suitcase on a small stand at the foot of the bed.

The only other thing in the room was a bar mounted on the wall to hang clothes on and an empty gun rack. Like everyone else, they used gun racks in the cabins because when they left, they put the guns back into their gun safes in the storage containers. "Wonder if Emily will let me leave her AR here?" Kristi mumbled, going back to the living room. Knowing Emily would throw a fit to take her pink AR home, Kristi just gave up on that idea.

Grabbing the kids' stuff, she carried it to their small rooms. Like her own, the rooms were just the same. Small with one bed, since that's all that could really fit inside. It didn't matter because when anyone was at the retreat, you were outside or in the clubhouse.

Taking her cell phone out, Kristi set it on the coffee table and headed back outside. She looked over and only saw the boys' vehicles there. Wondering where they were, Kristi headed back to the clubhouse. Looking out in the woods across the stream, she saw the boys and her kids riding four-wheelers through the trees.

Changing course, she walked between Cody and Randy's cabins and stopped at the deep ravine the stream had cut around the oxbow. The stream was only six feet across, but the ravine was twenty feet deep and three times that wide. Looking at the clear stream at the bottom, Kristi stared at the water as it flowed over a two foot waterfall. The soft roar was very comforting.

"I swear, this place is a small piece of heaven," Oliver said, walking up beside her.

Giving a sigh of content, "Yes, it is," Kristi said, then turned to Oliver. "Pop, I've always wanted to ask, why don't you and Mom have a cabin?"

Oliver moved closer and put his arm over her shoulder, pulling her close. "The boys wanted to get us one, but we told them no," he said, then waved over at the RV. "Don't really need it when you have that."

"True," Kristi said, resting her head on his side.

Squeezing her tight, Oliver looked across the ravine at everyone riding around. "Don't be too hard on the boys. They love you and those kids," Oliver said with a grin.

Giving a snort, "I know, Pop, and if I do start on them, they run and tattle to Mom," Kristi chuckled.

"You going to ride with them?" Oliver asked. "They pulled your four-wheeler out."

"No, I told Mom I would help her with supper," Kristi said with disappointment.

Dropping his arm, Oliver popped her on the butt lightly. "Now you get, don't make me take my belt off," Oliver laughed.

Turning around, Kristi broke into a run around her cabin and saw the double doors of her container open. Sitting outside the doors was the four-wheeler the boys had bought her. Grabbing her helmet and pulling it on, Kristi jumped on the seat before hitting the start button and took off.

The boys would ride through the ravine to the other side and each time they did, Kristi's heart would stop. The walls of the ravine were almost vertical, and she had forbidden the kids to even try it by telling them she would break the four-wheelers if they ever attempted it.

Speeding out of the camp, Kristi turned right to follow one of the many trails that had been made across the land. She slowed when coming to a bridge the boys had made out of trees across the ravine where it narrowed down to only twenty feet across.

Stopping on the bridge, Kristi looked down in the small thirty-foot gorge the stream had worn away and at the small building that housed the turbines. Hitting the throttle, she sped over the bridge and saw the gun range off to the left. She had been to many ranges and only a few could even come close. There was a covered awning with cables running down the three-hundred-yard-long range.

Even if it was raining, you could hook your target up on the cable and push a button to a motor. The target would zoom down the range until you wanted it to stop. Beside the long range was a popper range with different steel targets set up.

Speeding past the range, Kristi thought of the skeet range at the front of the property that also served as the long rifle range. Once you made sure the cows were out of the way, you could shoot seven hundred yards across the field at the front of the property near the road.

Seeing movement, Kristi slowed and saw Emily zoom across the trail Kristi was moving on. Giving her mom a small wave, Emily zoomed past with Clark behind her and the boys following along in single file. Turning her handlebars, Kristi hit the throttle and joined at the back of the line as they sped around the property.

Chapter Eleven

Cleveland, OH

After a fairly interesting week following a visit to the retreat, Charlie found Friday at ten a.m. back at the downtown office to be glacially slow-going. After the long hours he'd been putting in working on the Melton case, he could probably just take off the day and no one would say anything. There was a big, fat fee coming in and it had been generated in-house, so Billy wouldn't need to chop it up with any other firms.

But work marched on, and Charlie saw he had a mountain of interrogatories in his inbox to review and sign for several cases. Judging from the stack, he might be finished by lunch if he knuckled under and focused on the matter at hand. That way, he might be able to cut out at one and still get a little range time in this week. He didn't have any client meetings scheduled for the rest of the day after all.

Like a machine, Charlie plowed through the first half of the stack and was reevaluating his departure time when his phone buzzed with an incoming call. Looking at the computer screen, he saw the caller was Billy Carpenter himself, and snatched up the receiver on the second ring.

"This is Charlie Tucker. How can I help you today?" Charlie practically sang with fake enthusiasm in his greeting.

"Tucker, don't pretend like you didn't know it was me calling," the old man groused good-naturedly. "Get down here when you get a chance."

"Yes, sir," Charlie replied crisply. 'When you get a chance' was Billy-speak for as soon as possible. 'Right now' meant just that, and don't worry about running someone over in the hallway. Logging off his computer and securing his files, Charlie shut the door to his office and took off with a purposeful stride down the plushily carpeted main thoroughfare that ran through the middle of the offices. He passed the front desk, also known as Grand Central Station when they had more than one deposition or settlement conference going on at once, and headed for the power corridor where Billy Carpenter and his chief associates claimed their offices.

Billy had three long-time associates that he allowed to call themselves partners, but only Billy Carpenter ran this show. Charlie figured the three junior partners had no more than 10% equity in the firm, and he would not have been surprised to know their actual ownership stake was zero. Such things were above his pay grade, though he admitted to himself he was a little curious.

Billy Carpenter's office was a sprawling, glassed-in monument to ego and success. The office was a diamond-shaped space, half wood panel and then half floor-to-ceiling glass, with the outward facing point like the prow of a ship jutting out into space or at least, the thirtieth floor of the building. The glass windows offered a nearly 180 degree view of downtown Cleveland and out into the lake. Autographed pictures lined the pale wood paneling from floor to ceiling and in them, Charlie could see everything from candid snapshots to elaborate, professionally-shot photographs.

Most of the pictures were of Billy shaking the hand of some sports celebrity or political figure. When he'd first been hired, Charlie spent a bit of time surreptitiously examining the pictures and knew they featured everything from the obligatory 'presidential handshake' from most of the last thirty plus years, from Jimmy Carter to Ronald Reagan to the current inhabitant of the White House. No shocker there, since Billy knew while the Democrats carried water for his causes, he needed to spread the wealth to both sides of the aisle.

Billy's craggy, progressively more sun-spotted features seemed much more animated in the pictures where he was posing with football greats Jim Brown, Paul Warfield, and even Bernie Kosar. These seemed to have been at various charity events sponsored by the stars, and Billy had a reputation in the local legal community as being a soft touch. Especially when it came to charities aimed at helping children. That was the rumor. But after working for the man for over four years, Charlie still couldn't say he understood the man or what really motivated him to come to work every day. The man was at least seventy years old.

This time when Charlie entered the office, accompanied as always by Billy's watchdog secretary Felicia, he was surprised to see the old man stand up and come around the desk, his hand outstretched. Charlie took the soft, baby smooth hand in his and returned the hard-pumped shake as Billy went so far as patting him on the other shoulder.

"There he is," Billy said, speaking to Felicia but with the door open, he knew everyone on this side of the building could overhear Billy's words at this volume. "The man of the hour."

"Thank you, Mr. Carpenter," Charlie responded. He figured this had to do with the Melton case, and he was correct. The wire transfer of funds must have come through today.

"You not only delivered a great outcome to our client and the firm, you also managed to give that asshole Bentson a right reaming in the process. Never could stand that man," Billy continued and gestured for his associate to follow him over to the massive glass and steel monstrosity the old lawyer used as a desk.

"Here you go, son," Billy Carpenter announced, his voice still boisterous but somehow more subdued in volume as he thrust an envelope in Charlie's direction. Charlie wisely accepted the cream-colored envelope and slipped it into his suit pants pocket without looking at it. "That's just a little taste for you, but rest assured, I'll be thinking of you come bonus time if you keep up this quality of work. Yes, indeed."

Sensing his audience with the Emperor was at a close, Charlie thanked his boss for thinking of him and made a graceful exit. He managed to avoid opening the envelope and looking at the check inside until he was back in his office.

"Huh," Charlie said to himself, looking at the check for fifty thousand dollars. "That will pay for a lot of Match Grade ammunition, the new scope, and leave some over for the kids' college funds."

Being on the plaintiffs' side of the bar, Charlie was accustomed to seeing a large chunk of his compensation come from the year-end bonus and last year, he'd banked over twice that in December when the checks had come out. Oh his salary was more than sufficient for his needs, but the extra had made paying off his student loans a much easier burden.

"Yep, this is definitely a day to play hooky," Charlie decided and dove back into the stacks of paperwork occupying his inbox. If he skipped lunch, he could still be out by one o'clock.

Chapter Twelve

Cleveland, OH

The range was a bit windy this afternoon, but Charlie compensated for the steady breeze as a matter of course and he made minute adjustments to his posture on the mat. Memories of hot, muggy days spent in a similar setting at Fort Benning while he learned the trade and later, hotter but much drier days and nights while he plied that trade, crowded into his head. After years of experience, Charlie managed to banish those intrusive recollections to the back of his mind and he focused on the now.

Reading the wind, timing the gusts, and regulating his breathing occupied Charlie for a short span of eternity, and his eye never strayed from the site image in his Leupold scope as he acquired the target.

The two-stage trigger, as smooth as glass, worked as the Gods of War intended, and Charlie found his happy place there on the six-hundred-meter range.

The rifle wasn't the same one he'd carried in Afghanistan. Oh it was close, and the manufacturer guaranteed the same level of accuracy as the one he'd hauled all over Hell and beyond but today, something felt different. Nothing wrong with the rifle, he thought, after the range went cold and he made the long walk back from retrieving his target. The group was tight, almost as small as what he'd shot when still in the Army, and he used his Sharpie to mark the date and time at the bottom of the perforated paper.

Maybe it was something in the air, he mused. Some undercurrent his subconscious was picking up that his rational mind was still processing. Almost three weeks had passed since his conversation with Bryce McKentrick, and he'd heard nothing from his old friend. In fact, his last two calls to Bryce had gone straight to voicemail, and his emails had also gone unanswered. He'd gone up to see Kristi and the kids the weekend before and his excitement at spending time with his surrogate family might have distracted him, until now.

As he closed up his long rifle in its hard-sided case, Charlie looked over to the other shooting stations and noticed the dearth of activity at the normally popular outdoor shooting range. Usually, there was a wait to get a lane but today, he'd just walked up, paid his money, and managed to jump right in without a pause. Maybe half of the lanes were active, he thought. Strange.

Suddenly, Charlie felt an itch he needed to scratch. Something, again, was touching that primitive part of his brain, the old reptile that crouched in the back. He'd learned a long time ago to pay attention to that sense, and he felt his feet involuntarily pick up their pace as he neared his truck.

By the time he reached his condo, Charlie had a plan in mind. When he had deposited his bonus check, he'd pulled out $5,000 in cash as his mad money. He never knew when he was going to see something he just had to buy for Kristi or the kids. Emily's birthday might have just come and gone, but there was always next year, Clark's birthday would be here before he knew it, and of course, Christmas.

This time, Charlie was paying attention to that little voice in the back of his head, the one that had told him when hadjis were setting up an ambush in the next valley, or that the wooden crate lying next to the dirt trail contained an IED. While not foolproof, the instincts had a track record he needed to respect.

Booting up his home desktop, Charlie looked up a number for one of his favorite stores. It was a Friday afternoon, but he hoped he could catch someone before they went home for the day, so he quickly dialed the number on his landline.

"AIM Surplus, this is Ronnie. How can I help you?"

"Hi Ronnie, this is Charlie Tucker from up in Cleveland. Did I call in time to get an order placed today?"

"Cleveland? Is this for pickup or delivery?"

"Pickup, if I can come get it tomorrow."

"Hold on," Ronnie replied, "let me pull this up."

Charlie knew the salesman was looking up his name to make sure they already had his information on file. He knew they did but waited patiently to be confirmed.

"Yes sir," Ronnie said when he came back on the line thirty seconds later. "What can we get for you today?"

"First, do you have any more of that .308 Serbian match grade in 175 grain?"

"Yes sir, we sure do. How many boxes can I get for you?"

"That comes in 500 round cases, correct?"

"That's correct. And we can let you have that at $362.50 plus tax."

Charlie paused for a second. In addition to the five grand he'd pulled from the bonus check, he thought he had about eight grand cash in his .338 Lapua fund. He'd been meaning to get one for a couple of years, but after dropping nearly $25,000 for the Knights Armaments M110, Charlie was feeling a bit gun-shy. His face twisted into a grim smile at the thought.

"Alright. I'll take ten cases of that. Now, let me see..."

In just under five minutes, he managed to spend a total of almost ten thousand dollars on more .308. This time, some of the soft point hunting ammunition, as well as five thousand rounds of 5.56x45 split between the 55 grain and the 62 grain. Oh, and some hollow point .45ACP, and 9mm for his pistols.

He could have gotten ammunition closer to home, but not in this quantity and in the quality he was looking for. The Serbian stuff was really good. New manufacture, instead of some old surplus that might have been sitting around in a warehouse for years. Plus, he still had over three hundred rounds of high quality, Sierra King Match Grade for the M110, but something told him he needed to lay in a supply. Maybe he would even pick up a case of the premium stuff on his way out of town.

Assuring Ronnie that he would be there at three p.m. the following day to pick up his order from the loading dock out back, Charlie then breathed a sigh of relief and felt some of the pressure in the back of his head abate.

Next, he hauled his rifle case into the second bedroom and set the hard-sided case on one of the benches he'd installed. The next hour would be spent cleaning and detailing the rifle, and then he would think about grabbing something to eat. Maybe call Joan, he thought.

They'd gone out twice since that weird meeting at his office. Once, just for a bite to eat at a barbeque place he knew in Avon, and then the following week, she'd picked a Vietnamese restaurant situated just outside downtown where Charlie watched in awe as the blonde-haired Texas transplant calmly ate a tray of those killer yellow peppers that always made him cry.

Each time, Charlie was aware of the looks he received from the other restaurant patrons. He could always feel the eyes on him when out in public, but this time, he hadn't cared. He was sitting at a table with the prettiest girl in the place, and his watchers could look all they wanted.

Joan, unsurprisingly, was as intelligent as she was attractive and in addition, she was also blessed with a good dose of common sense as well. At first, they'd picked around the issues and the elephant in the room, for once, wasn't Charlie's disfiguring scars.

No, the touchy subject for both was Joan's brother. Sean was like a ghost at the table when they'd started eating their pork ribs at Dusty's Barbeque, but before the night was over at the Vietnamese restaurant, Joan was telling funny stories about her older sibling and describing how proud she felt when she saw him in his uniform when he was home on leave.

"He was captain of the football team, but he also lettered in debate and had several schools offering at least partial scholarships. But he knew the money wasn't there for school and joined the Army as a way to pay for it."

Charlie nodded at that.

"I was the same way. I mean, not the captain of the football team or Homecoming King," he said. "But without the G.I Bill and the enlistment bonus, I knew I would never be able to afford to get my undergraduate degree. Still," he continued, with not a little pride, "I managed to take dual coursework in my high school, taking classes at the local junior college so when I graduated, I had the freshman classes knocked out as well."

"That is impressive," Joan agreed, "but why did you stay in after you had your four years done?"

"First, the bonus they offered for re-enlistment was nice, plus I managed to knock out another year of classes while in the Army. And second, I honestly don't know if I would have gone for twenty, but..."

Joan gave him a moment as he looked down at his empty plate of spring rolls, but after he remained silent for over a minute, she prompted him.

"But what, Charlie?"

"Well," he said, finally finding his words. "See, I didn't have much in the way of a home life growing up. Mom tried, but it was hard, with my father being a drunk and all. But in the Army, it was like I had a fresh start with a new family. And after I graduated from Ranger School, that was just the best thing in the world, being with Blaster, Shadow, Cobra and Wheat, it was like we were brothers."

"Wow," Joan exclaimed. "I don't think I've ever heard you say that much at one time. For a lawyer, you can be rather sparing with your words. So graduating from Ranger School was a bigger deal than graduating from law school?"

Charlie laughed at the question. Not in a mean way, but in real humor.

"Joan, you have no idea. I thought the instructors were trying to kill me. Forget about the grind of finals. I was so tired, sometimes I was beginning to hallucinate. And so hungry, I would have fought a coyote over a week-old armadillo roadkill."

"Yeah, that will do it. Did you go to any other schools in the Army?"

"Oh, the Army has schools for everything. But the one that sticks out for me was completing sniper school. That was also at Fort Benning, but it was a very different environment. There was plenty of physical, but also a lot of mental, too. Classroom subjects, but not like we had in college."

"So, all of your friends had nicknames? Sounds like something out of, I don't know, G.I. Joe? I mean, come on, Cobra? Is that wrong for me to say? And what was yours?"

Charlie laughed again before answering.

"I don't know about everybody, but yeah, most had a nickname or handle they picked up. Cobra? Well, that was easy. Aaron was, and still is, scared to death of snakes. Nearly got dropped from Ranger school because of it, but he managed to fake it well enough to fool the instructors. Blaster, well, he was always wanting to blow stuff up, even before they sent him to school for it, and Shadow was like a freakin' ninja. As for me, well, the boys got to calling me Book."

"Book? That's not a very scary nickname."

"Most of them aren't, really," Charlie said with a shrug. "I was always reading something, so it kind of stuck. Plus, the guys knew I was always taking classes online, whenever we were in one place long enough for me to sign up. But no, not all of the nicknames were something intimidating. I mean, come on, we all called Cody 'Babyface', so that should tell you something."

"You mentioned Wheat. Was that a nickname?" Joan asked innocently. "I think I heard you mention that one before."

Charlie nodded slowly before speaking.

"That wasn't really a nickname. He was always just Wheat. Our platoon sergeant, Frank Wheaton. The best man I ever had the honor of serving with. You heard me talking about his wife, Kristi, and their children."

"Oh," was all Joan could say. "I can tell you were very close."

"Yeah. If we were brothers, then Wheat was our big brother. He took care of us that way."

And the evening went on like that, except Charlie managed to turn the tables on Joan and got the young woman to talk about herself. As Charlie suspected, Joan had been a competitive swimmer in high school and college, and she'd attended undergrad and law school at the University of Texas at Austin. Her parents were Ohio transplants, moving to Texas when her father's work with automated production systems brought him to the attention of one of the high-tech firms near Austin.

"So, you were law review and competed in moot court?" Charlie remembered commenting. "When did you have time to sleep?"

"Oh, come on, Mr. 'I Stayed Awake Until I Hallucinated'," Joan shot back playfully. "I managed by not becoming a statistic. You know, the drunken college party girl. I just kept my head down and lived in the library, where it was safe."

"Oh, I'm sure you could have found a way to have a little fun in school," Charlie had said with a challenging tone, and then they were off again. It'd been a good time, and Charlie knew he was starting to develop feelings there.

"Yeah, maybe I should give her a call," Charlie said to himself. If they were going to go out, Charlie knew he would need a shower first. His clothes would smell like Hoppes No. 9 oil before he was finished.

Chapter Thirteen

Cleveland, OH

Going out with Joan turned out to be a good idea, as it allowed him a chance to find out more about the woman and her background. Now that they had breached the barrier that was Sean, he felt her grow more comfortable with their conversations. They talked about movies, art, and their favorite books. The owner of the little Italian restaurant, a corner establishment that boasted of being in business since 1956, finally had to come out and let them know they would be closing in ten minutes. He seemed apologetic with breaking into their private moment, and Charlie thanked him profusely as he left a fifty-dollar tip to go with the bill.

Joan protested, of course, and he gently explained that she could pick up the bill next time. She seemed mollified by this provision, and when he walked her out to her car, she rewarded him with a kiss on the cheek. He wondered if it was by accident that she picked his left cheek, the one rippled with scars, and decided he didn't care. He'd caught her examining his scars a few times, but she didn't seem repulsed by what she saw, or morbidly turned on by the sight.

Gathering his courage after she stepped back, he asked the question that had been nagging at him for a while now.

"It doesn't bother you?" he asked softly, gesturing vaguely to encompass the visible damage. He knew it was a painful sight for some, despite all the best efforts of the doctors in San Antonio.

"Yeah, it does bother me in a way," she replied. "I hate what happened to you, Charlie. But these scars, they aren't you. They are just something you survived."

"Dang, ma'am, you sure are a sweet-talker," he replied, and turned away to hide the mist in his eyes. Giving her hands a last squeeze, he promised to call her soon.

Back at home, Charlie paused before bed and checked one of his e-mail accounts, and quickly discovered he'd received an e-mail from Cody. It was a brief note, drawing Charlie's attention to the attachment, which turned out to be a link to a news website with which Charlie was unfamiliar. From anybody else, Charlie would have feared a virus, but he knew Babyface would stomp all over anything dangerous before sending it to him.

The link led Charlie to an article about HR 2121, a bill proposed to protect and secure America's drinking water, referring to it in the article as the Safe Drinking Water Act. Whoever wrote the article, the byline was blank, clearly wasn't a professional reporter. Too many errors in the text, and not enough meat to the analysis, but he was still riveted by what he found.

Charlie was a long way from parsing bills in his classes, but once he waded through the high-sounding rhetoric at the beginning, he was immediately struck by the long-range implications.

"Public water" was already subject to testing, and taxing, and varying degrees of scrutiny. Charlie paid his water bill every month, and he knew part of the money went to pay for the municipal water system. That was to be expected.

This bill went so much further, it made Charlie's head hurt at the idea. Charlie recalled one of his law school classes had dealt with the issue of water rights, and he knew that different states had vastly different laws with regard to water and the rights of private citizens. Some states treated the water under someone's property as their private property and inviolate. Others took a broader approach and used a balancing test for determining private versus public ownership of water.

Here, essentially, the federal government was pre-empting the states and claiming all fresh water sources as property of the Federal Government. Period. If you wanted to pump water from a private well, you had to have a meter installed, and the users would be liable for a tax based on the gallons used. This tax money was supposed to be reserved for repairing the nation's aquifers and waterways.

Likewise, people who owned any waterfront property would be assessed a tax based on the square footage of the property as a

115

"land use" tax, and the definition of waterfront seemed darned elastic to Charlie's reading.

Charlie saved the entire bill to a file, noticing in passing, the sponsoring congressmen were a pair of far-left leaning ideologues who routinely introduced such ridiculous legislation that never saw the light of day. This bill, however, had already been passed by a narrow margin and sent on to the Senate. Without any media scrutiny and no discussion that Charlie, or Cody, could find.

"No way the Senate will sit still for this," Charlie whispered. The Senate, the old-boys club of vested interests and the gatekeepers of public policy, would never go along with this. This damned thing would bankrupt every corporate farm and factory in the country, Charlie realized.

If this was what got Bishop so worked up, Charlie said to himself, then her source was either paranoid as a cat in a house full of rocking chairs, or there's something else going on. No way those rich bastards would vote for a law rendering their own beachfront property either prohibitively expensive, or worthless.

Scanning through the document, Charlie quickly realized all he had here was an abstract of the bill, since the actual verbiage ran over two thousand pages. Maybe her friend wasn't so paranoid after all. Who knows what's really hidden from public scrutiny in there?

Opening another window, Charlie ran a LexisNexis search and found, to his surprise, that the bill wasn't available for public view.

"Curiouser and curiouser," Charlie muttered. He prepared a short email back to Cody, ccing Randy, and gave his summary. It was a worrying bill, but not something the Senate would ever entertain. Most disturbing, though, was how closely some of the language mirrored some of the position papers and agenda memoranda he'd seen coming out of the United Nations' more active social justice committees.

After his shower that night, Charlie laid awake for several hours, thinking about that damned water bill. No way could it pass, he reminded himself, but why did two of the President's fair-haired boys introduce such an obviously unconstitutional bill, and how did they manage to ram it through the House? Was it a trial balloon, to see how the public would react to the idea of having their water rights stolen by the government, or something else?

Not by coincidence, once he did manage to fall asleep, Charlie found himself back in the dusty hell of Afghanistan, once again hauling the cold, dead body of PFC Eric Blakely. This was a recurring nightmare for Charlie, and something that he'd never discussed with his counselors at the hospital. He would talk about the nightmares he had about his own wounds, but for some reason he couldn't bring himself to talk about this one. It seemed disrespectful of the dead.

Blakely had suffered a neck wound early on, a chunk of shrapnel from a mortar round chewing out most of his neck, and the only way Charlie could keep the head attached to the body was tying his shemagh in a tight loop. As their flight had stretched on for hours, he kept having to stop and tighten the neck scarf. Charlie remembered having to do this several times, but in the nightmare, his friend would talk to him while he worked.

"Stop, Charlie, it hurts," Eric would whine, his voice somehow audible despite the absence of vocal cords. Every time Charlie awoke from the nightmare, he would remember that point, but while he was in the grip of the horror, that fact never penetrated.

"Stop it, Eric," Charlie begged as rounds snapped past his head and the distant rumble of incoming told him more mortar rounds were incoming. "You're dead, brother."

"We're all dead, Charlie," Eric insisted, his voice now slurred and straining. "We're all dead."

When Charlie finally awoke the next morning, he was off the bed and on the floor, and he had no memory of falling out. But he knew he would have to wash the sweat-stained sheets before the mattress was ruined.

True to form, as Charlie was drinking coffee before leaving, Randy called, and he and Cody talked to Charlie for half an hour. Before walking out the door, Charlie answered his cellphone, "I'm good, Blaster."

Chapter Fourteen

Kenosha, Wisconsin

Robbie Lennox stared at the high-definition flat screen television over the bar and grimaced as the team managed to go another three and out. So far, they'd had to rely on their world class kicker to put any points up on the board. Their rivals in green didn't seem to have the same lack of offense and kept finding new ways to score. Robbie sipped his lukewarm drink and ignored the annoying conversations coming from the table of drunks near the unused dartboard. So far, the group had left the pair alone at the bar, but Robbie picked up that one of the women had glanced their way several times from the reflection of the mirror behind the bar.

"Why do you always want to come here and watch those losers throw another game? Man, we can do so much better than this shithole." Jerome rolled his eyes as he glanced at the worn-out bartender, wiping away at invisible spots at the end of the bar in the Polka Dot Tap.

The two had started coming to the corner bar two years ago when Robbie did a listing four houses down. The buyer had wanted to meet and discuss items on the inspection report that Jerome had worked up for the sale. The seller complained that Jerome had nitpicked some of the minor issues, and the buyer wanted a face-to-face meet. The buyer ended up hiring Jerome's crew to fix most of the issues after the sale went through. Somewhere in the mountains of rules and regulations in Wisconsin's codes on real estate, there must have been a clause that made Jerome's repair work for the buyer a conflict of interest ethics violation, but the buyer had read over the inspection report and realized that Jerome had literally crawled all over that house finding items that would need to be addressed in the near future. Jerome and Robbie made the small bar their Sunday ritual during the football season. During the off-season, the owner let Robbie watch the retro channel. For some reason, his team still found a way to lose, even in the past.

"This place is where your inspection business really took off, and they will let me watch the 'Boys try to find their asses with two hands'. Call it tradition. As a bonus, nobody messes with us, and Mr. Wojciechowski keeps my glass topped off. He's not very personable, but he never complains when we ask to watch the game." Robbie finished off his pint and Mr. Wojciechowski ambled down and pulled another pint from the tap. The blockish man, with gnarled fists that came from a background in either masonry or beating other men into puddles of blood and urine, nodded and stepped away from the duo perched near the middle of the small brass-trimmed bar.

"Why don't you change the channel, you two?" a woman slurred and sauntered over to Robbie's side.

"What were you wanting to watch?" Jerome eyed the dishwater blonde with a chubby face and a dark green sweater two sizes too small to show off her ample chest.

"I don't care if it's two dogs taking a crap, anything has to be better than watching these morons. Why don't you put on something we can all enjoy?" She leaned in and brushed herself against Robbie. He hadn't taken his eyes off the game yet. "Do you have plans later? I'm off tomorrow and I want to celebrate some. You interested?" the woman purred.

Jerome coughed and choked on his drink looking at the woman. "Not to be a blocker or anything, but we do have a job tomorrow morning."

"Well then, we'll just have to start this party up a little sooner, so Mr. Quiet and Handsome can make it home before bedtime. You his mommy or daddy? You don't look related, some kind of adoption service?" She laughed at her own joke and nudged Robbie and rocked him slightly on his stool. "Come on, I don't bite…much."

Robbie sighed and watched the rookie running back break a tackle and make the first down. They didn't have enough time, even running their hurry up offense to score three touchdowns in the remaining few minutes, but he had become a sucker for the underdogs over the years. They called a timeout to stop the clock and delay the inevitable. Robbie looked away from the game and took a closer look at the intoxicated woman throwing herself at him for the first time.

"You seem like a wild one. What's your name, honey?" Robbie settled his brown eyes on her and waited.

"I'm Carrie. What's your name?" she slurred as she smiled at his attention.

"I'm Robbie, and my friend here is Jerome. What brings you out to this fine establishment today?" Robbie glanced at her leather pants and her sweater threatening to ride up her abdomen. He didn't recognize Carrie or her friends, but he and Jerome only came to the Polka Dot on Sundays.

"We are going to the rally in a bit at the courthouse. We're gonna tear some shit up!" Carrie whooped and her entourage at the back table saluted with their drinks and murmured, "Heck, yes!"

"What the hell are you protesting? This is the first I'm hearing of it," Jerome asked from his barstool.

"The government. They just keep taking and taking, and we're not lying down for it anymore. Do you guys want to join us for some fun? We could use some big guys like you to intimidate the pigs." Carrie ran her hand up Robbie's bicep and leered at him. "Can I ride with you on your bike?"

"How do you know I ride?" Robbie shook his head at the woman.

"I saw you last week when you pulled in. We were just leaving." The dumpy woman shimmied up onto the stool and eyed Robbie like he was a slab of meat.

"We aren't what you would call the 'protesting' types. Jerome and I come here to watch the game and relax before we jump into it each week," Robbie tried to politely rebuff her, but the woman persisted.

"So, you are free after the game? It's almost over. Can you?" She leaned in and whispered to Robbie, "Maybe afterward we can go to my place for some fun times." Carrie's breath scorched Robbie's nose with the reek of cigarettes.

"I can't let you ride with me, Carrie."

"Why not? Don't you like me?" she whined.

"It's got nothing to do with that. I can't let anyone ride with me because I'm still not sure of myself with this new arm." Robbie placed his left "hand" on the bar. After several surgeries and different models, the doctors at the Veterans Administration settled on his three-fingered "claw", socketed below his left elbow and strapped in place. He had several different attachments, including a lifelike hand that lacked the functionality of his "claw".

"Aw, that's freaky. Can you like, change it out to other things? Or, you know, take it off completely?" Carrie practically purred at the thought.

"Okay, well, this conversation took an unexpected turn. Most women take this moment to beg off and find something better to do when I flash my hand." Robbie finished his drink and glanced at Jerome sitting with his mouth open. "You ready to blow, buddy? We have a full week in front of us."

"Yeah, I'm going to need to take a mental shower after that. I thought of some things that I can't delete from my mind." Jerome reached for his wallet and counted out enough to cover his tab. Mr. Wojciechowski quietly moved over and took the payment and made change. Jerome, as always, left a hefty tip. Next week, Robbie would do the same for Jerome.

"You aren't leaving yet, are you? The game is still on," Carrie whined.

"What's your deal, lady? We were minding our own business over here. What do you really want? I can smell a con a mile away, and this stinks to high heaven." Robbie and Jerome settled and waited.

"Like I said, we could use some muscle, and you two are pretty big guys and we want to send a message that we are not going to be pushed around." Carrie didn't sound as sloppy drunk as she had a minute before. Robbie glanced to Jerome, who had also noticed the shift in the woman's speech.

"How many people do you have right now? What's your objective?" Robbie replied with a quick look at Carrie's tablemates.

"We spread out to different places around town. Mostly bars. Most of our core supporters are from the country, but we don't have the numbers to attract attention. The farmers are the ones with the real grievances." Carrie waved over a tiny man with hipster glasses and skinny jeans. Robbie groaned to himself in anticipation with the coming onslaught of political rhetoric.

"I take it he is the intellectual power in your team of misfit toys? What are you, the recruiter?" Jerome asked Carrie.

"I'm not too proud to use my feminine ways to pull in some extra numbers. It almost worked. What, did I come on too strong?" She lightly brushed at Robbie's sleeve.

"I told you, it didn't smell right. Ladies don't throw themselves at me like they used to, and yes, you did come on waaay too strong for my broken-down self. Plus, the game was on."

"But they were losing. Who the hell even watches them anymore?" Carrie waved at the television screen showing a beer commercial.

"I lost a friend who admired their grit and determination. No matter how bad things get, they keep plugging away. Jerome humors me and shares in my insanity of watching them every Sunday, even if it's a rerun and I already know the outcome. The Polka Dot Tap is just our latest place to watch, but it is close to home and comfortable."

"Are they going to help us?" Carrie's friend interrupted. Robbie had forgotten he had come over to stand beside her barstool. Robbie would have ignored the man in public since he didn't make much of an impression, except for his small stature and choice of clothes.

"I don't just volunteer for things anymore. What the heck is going on, just give it to me straight." Robbie watched the pair's expressions, and Carrie looked to her friend to step in and explain.

"The EPA has essentially taken control of the water resources nationwide with a decision that they have jurisdiction over both surface water and groundwater. The majority of the American populace have no idea what has been happening in the rural areas, and the news outlets have never bothered to report on the implications." The man took a second to let his announcement sink in before continuing. "All private water wells are now required to have a meter on their well and pay taxes on their consumption. Failure to install the correct monitoring device will result in fines and orders to cease all operations on the property. People in cities and municipalities were not affected because they already pay water bills."

"That's ridiculous! When the hell did that happen?" Robbie slapped the surface of the bar with his hand loud enough to draw Mr. Wojciechowski's attention.

"Problem, Robbie?" The owner had stayed out of the conversation. Robbie had noticed that the old gentleman never got into arguments on politics or religion with his patrons, but he would have heated conversations about the Brewers management.

"Have you heard about the EPA taking over all water in the U.S.?" Jerome asked.

Mr. Wojciechowski wiped the bar and grunted, "I've heard rumblings that have gotten louder lately. Seems the Feds have started shutting people down out in the country, but nobody knows how many have been affected yet."

"I had several calls to work on wells out in the suburbs in the last few days. I got them in contact with some plumbers out their way, but I thought the meters were some new local code and not a federal law," Jerome scratched his chin in thought.

"That's because it got passed without any fanfare. This was done at the behest of unelected officials and it affects a huge swath of the country. Nobody knows about this, and most importantly, nobody bothered to report about it in the major news sources. Internet boards have been screaming over this for weeks, how did you not hear about it?" Carrie's friend dropped that nugget on the group.

"Who the hell are you?" Robbie laughed and thought about Charlie. He sounded like his old buddy and fellow Ranger.

"Dexter Fowler. I'm a blogger who has been reporting about this ruling since I got fired from my job over it."

"What did you do that got you fired for trying to tell the truth?"

"I worked for the county Agricultural Extension office. When I graduated from the University of Wisconsin, I went to work for them to help other farmers. What I found out got me fired."

"Dexter, what have you found out, and do I need to ask Mr. Wojciechowski for some tinfoil to wrap around my head after you tell me? I hear the feds can read our minds, too," Robbie smirked and waited for the typical conspiracy theory from a wide-eyed true believer.

"The whole water controversy is both a money-making scheme and a land grab. Pay for your water or have your land seized. If the government takes the land, it is then sold for pennies on the dollar to one of their receivership corporations who then takes over the operations. Small farms are being consumed at an unprecedented rate and turned over to corporate friends. Can you imagine what that does to a family that has to have a decent crop just to pay the bills each season?" Dexter's cheeks started to turn red as he worked himself up.

Jerome cleared his throat and asked, "What proof do you have?"

"I was able to download a few files that track the farms being confiscated by the change in ownership from an individual or family to a corporation. They are all being listed as TriCorp Holdings after the takeover. That's how I knew something funny was going on. I used to meet with these people and help them with things like pest eradication and soil surveys. These family farms range from thousands of acres or as small as a few hundred, but they are being gobbled up if they can't pay for the water they use. If they refuse the meter, they get shut down. The most horrible aspect of this regulation was when I found out the supply of meters ran out long before the deadline for compliance. The deadline for compliance was today."

Robbie rubbed at his beard and thought for a second. "So, the drought last summer…"

"Absolutely devastated the local farming community. I wrote about what was going on, and my director got a visit from a 'suit' who told him to fire me or lose his own job. He took a risk and told me why I was being let go. I haven't been able to find another job, except pouring coffee at a diner on 57th where the owner pays me off the books."

"So, what is your objective for your rally today? I don't see any signs or megaphones. Who brought the gas masks for when the riot cops show up?" Jerome asked.

"I called the local news outlets to let them know about our protest, so even if only one camera crew shows up and broadcasts anything, I'll consider it a win. We are going to assemble at the county courthouse and march down to the harbor. We don't have a permit, so we will stick to the sidewalks and try to make ourselves seen and heard."

"If you want to get attention, why not do this during the week? The courthouse is closed on Sunday," Robbie asked.

"We, well, most of the supporters, have jobs. Can you believe that a lot of protests you see on the big news stories have paid protesters bussed in from out of state? We can't afford to do

124

something that underhanded. This is the only day we could agree to come together for this. The sports bars are open, so we spread out to recruit more before we meet up. And yes, we have another team working on making signs. Can we count on your support?" Dexter waited for Jerome and Robbie to make their decision. He didn't pressure or go off the rails talking about crazy conspiracies. Well, the corporations taking over the farms was nothing new and had been happening for decades.

"Tell you what, I'll sit here and watch the news later and see if anything pops up. How do you contact the rest of your team of rising anarchists?" Robbie offered.

Dexter gave him his number and Robbie programmed it into his phone. Cassie went back and collected the rest of his group from the back table.

Cassie lingered for a minute, waiting for Robbie and Jerome to possibly change their minds as the small band of protesters filed out.

"Go on, Cassie. I'm not the joining type anyway. For the record, I don't like the taste of cigarettes, so that was a deal breaker from the word go." Cassie shrugged and headed for the door.

"The offer still stands, but you can keep the prosthetic on. I'm not that freaky, that was an act."

"Noted. Until then." Robbie saluted her with his empty glass and watched the group file out, leaving the Polka Dot Tap empty except for Mr. Wojciechowski and his two regulars.

"They are going to get themselves killed," Mr. Wojciechowski grumbled.

"You think?" Jerome asked.

"If Dexter was being honest with you, then he has already attracted too much attention. A tyrant once said that 'the nail that stands out gets the hammer', and he is crossing a dangerous line by putting himself out in the public eye." The aged bartender leaned against the shelves at the back of the bar area and his eyes glazed over for a second.

"Shit, I agree with you, but we can't do much to help, can we? We both have our own businesses to protect. Hell, Jerome, your ex would love to see you get locked up over some stupid protest. She's just looking for a reason to pull your visitation rights." Robbie flexed his left arm and articulated his prosthetic enough to make the triple metal "hooks" open and close.

"Yeah, and I still can't get why the judge gave her primary custody over my parents. I mean, yes. I know with my history, I'm not winning any awards for Daddy of the Year, but she is a hot mess even off the pipe." Jerome glanced down as he thought about his own failings that led to him not having his children at home with him full time.

"That's why you are staying here while I scout this out." Robbie pulled out his phone and checked the address of the condominium he had listed across the park from the courthouse.

"You are going to their protest rally? That's risky," Jerome warned.

"Not really, I have practice at this. Can you hang tight? I'll be back in a few, and I'm not going to be using my phone."

"Do you need some foil?" Jerome glanced to Mr. Wojciechowski.

"I'm just being cautious. You ever get that tingling at the back of your neck like someone is watching you?"

"What, you having paranoid delusions of grandeur? That's a sign of a deeper psychosis, you know?"

"It's not paranoia if they really are watching you. Mr. Wojciechowski, do you mind if I call you using your landline? I don't think anyone will be monitoring those just yet, but if Dexter is right, they may be surveilling cellular signals." Robbie pulled out his phone and handed it to Jerome.

"Mr. Wojciechowski, will you wrap this up in multiple layers of foil and then plaster some around his dome? I think he's lost it." Jerome took Robbie's phone and laid it on the bar.

"He may be onto something." Mr. Wojciechowski turned and walked to the cordless phone behind the counter and laid it before Jerome. "Be cautious, Robbie."

"This isn't my first rodeo, guys. Man, I hope I'm wrong about this." Robbie zipped his leather jacket and pushed his way out of the Polka Dot Tap, walking to his bike parked in the adjoining parking lot next to Jerome's blue pickup with a white camper shell over the cargo bed. He cranked the bike over and let it idle as he pulled on the full faced black helmet and snapped the visor down. Robbie took his seat and shifted the bike to the right and raised the kickstand with his left booted heel. Working his prosthetic to activate the clutch took practice, and he hadn't been lying to Cassie. Robbie didn't want to risk a passenger throwing off his balance while he learned to work through the gears.

Robbie took the one way street down a block and cut over to double back to the center of Kenosha. The harbor area had been revitalized in the last twenty years and retro streetcars ran along the trendy shops. The blocks around the county courthouse were currently an "up and coming" neighborhood where Robbie had several properties listed for sale. The one he had in mind had a clear shot of the city park and the courthouse from the living room windows. The sixth floor condo also would give Robbie unobstructed views of the streets around the municipal buildings.

The garage for the building, accessed from a side street, allowed Robbie to motor directly up to the parking ramp and use his garage opener from the owner to access the building. The owner, currently living in an extended stay hotel in Seattle, had left his condo with all of the furnishings until it sold. As Robbie parked his bike and used the access card to open the elevator, he smiled to himself. Mr. Janick, his client, had also left his telescope in the living room. Robbie punched the right button and waited for the car to reach the sixth floor.

Mr. Janick might have been a peeping tom, or he might enjoy amateur astronomy. Robbie didn't care as long as he got his commission at the time of the sale. He also remembered he was doing an open house here next week, so Robbie had an excuse for being here anyway. He paid a sweet older lady, Margaret Reid, to run a crew of eager beavers to do his open houses when he had other things to do. Getting tied down at a single property for three hours when he could be doing paperwork was a waste of his valuable time. Besides, having a few drinks with Jerome and watching the game took priority.

The elevator door opened to a beige hallway with slate-colored carpeting. The condominium association was in charge of the common areas, so he couldn't do anything to help the bland décor. Mr. Janick did a great job himself with his own space, though.

Robbie pushed his access code into the key storage box hanging from the door handle and retrieved the deadbolt key. Robbie unlocked the door and pocketed the key, so he didn't make the rookie mistake of leaving the key on the counter when the door shut behind him. That had happened to him once, and he'd learned from that embarrassing mistake, with the cost of a locksmith on the weekend hammering the point home. Keep the key with you until you leave.

The blinds in the living room and the drapes were closed, so Robbie pulled the drapes aside and peeked through the horizontal blinds. The sun, coming from the west, shined on the green park and the trees still without leaves. In a month, Robbie would not be able to see the gathering crowd on the steps of the courthouse.

Robbie pulled a chair from the cozy eating area and perched himself at the window with only a single slat pulled up. It limited his field of view, but Robbie didn't want to give away his position.

The snipers on the rooftop next to the courthouse didn't seem to notice him watching. Robbie jerked away from the window in a reflex move before he processed the scene. Someone had people on a roof in black tactical gear watching the protestors. Robbie pulled the chair out of the way and pulled the tripod mounted telescope into position. The scope needed a bigger opening in the blinds to be effective, so Robbie pulled the string and raised the blinds just high enough for him to see out.

The black-clad individuals on the rooftop didn't have sniping weapons, but they did have cameras with long lenses. One of the teams had a directional microphone scanning the crowd with a separate technician monitoring it with headphones and what appeared to be a recording device of some type. Robbie scanned the gathering crowd holding signs and he watched Dexter mount the courthouse steps with a cheap megaphone. Dexter stood front and center and gave his speech, but Robbie could not hear a word of it through the insulated double pane windows. The signs carried by the protestors had unusual demands. "Free the water" and "Freedom" and "Save our Farms!" were the most common themes to the signs. "EPA let us be" caught Robbie's attention. Robbie continued to scan the crowd and the rooftops for other observers.

"Now, why the hell would these obviously violent thugs need to be monitored instead of arrested?" Robbie muttered to himself. He scanned the cars moving along the square until he saw the one he'd hoped he would not see. The blacked out Suburban crept along the street and paused at each car before moving along.

"They are scanning the plates of every car around the square, and I'll bet they are also going through the parking lots." He knew that if the government had a team on the ground, the cell towers in the area also had surveillance. Robbie went to the kitchen and got the phone to call the Polka Dot Tap.

"Can they monitor cordless calls too?" Robbie stopped and stared at the handset. The signal could be intercepted, but probably only if the team had someone closer to the condo. Robbie took a risk and called anyway.

"Polka Dot Tap, this is Jerome," his friend answered the call.

"Do you have a crazy old Polack named Wojciechowski working there? He's my baby's daddy, and I want child support." Robbie used his goofy high-pitched voice that Jerome had heard many times in the past.

"No, but we do have a crazy Mandingo on the line who can show up and relieve your needs, ma'am," Jerome replied with a laugh.

"Stay there. I'll come back to you. Make some calls for me, would you? Cancel everything we can for the next few days. And yes, I said 'we'. You need to clear your schedule, too."

"What's going down, Robbie?" Jerome sounded panicked.

"No names. I'll tell you in a few. Get the ball rolling before I get back."

Robbie hung up and put everything back in place. He paused and took another look at the protestors standing before the courthouse. He estimated less than a hundred people had gathered there to voice their complaints peacefully. They had definitely gotten someone's attention, but he didn't see a news crew or any expensive cameras shouldered by one of the major networks. That bothered him more than the troops on overwatch. A slow news day would have drawn someone out to fill in some airtime. Kenosha didn't get a lot of protestors.

He relocked the door and replaced the key before heading back to the basement garage and his bike. Robbie took a more circuitous route back to the Polka Dot Tap and avoided the streets anywhere close to the courthouse protest. It took him longer to get back because he took the block twice to check for tails.

A block away from the Tap, Robbie heard sirens converging off in the distance and a chill went up his spine. Something had gone down, and it couldn't have been good. He parked his bike in front of the bar in an empty spot and hurried inside, struggling with the chin strap of his helmet and finally pulled it off as he pushed through the door. His one hand shook as he fought back the adrenaline rushing through his system.

"What happened? I heard sirens on the way back." Robbie dumped his helmet on the bar.

"It just broke on the news. Protestors tried to storm the courthouse and set it on fire. Local law enforcement fired into the crowd when they were themselves fired upon." Jerome stared at the television as the feed from the courthouse came through over the air. The angle of the camera told Robbie the real story.

"The news never showed up. I just left, and nobody was covering it."

"Well, who is filming this?" Jerome gestured at the ambulances and police cars converged on the scene, and several bodies laying in a tangle near the top of the steps.

"Look at the angle of the camera, they filmed this from the rooftop. I saw them there. I didn't see the sniping team or the protesters rushing the doors. All I saw were people waving signs and Dexter giving a speech. Nobody looked agitated or ready to storm the barricades." Robbie rubbed his stubble of hair on his head and thought for a second.

"Did the video show where it started? I mean, who rushed the doors?" Robbie stared at the screen, trying to piece the scene together.

Jerome replied, "They didn't show that part. All we saw were the cops rushing the scene and taking charge. What are you thinking, Robbie?"

"I need to call Charlie. He will know what to do. I don't want to use my phone, though. Mr. Wojciechowski, can I call my buddy in Toledo? I'll pay you for the long-distance charges." Robbie got his phone from the bar and checked the number for Charlie.

"We don't worry about long-distance, Robbie. It comes with the plan. Just call him. This sounds wrong to me, too. Those kids were not looking for a fight, no matter what the news is screaming." Mr. Wojciechowski pulled another drink for Robbie and placed the pint on a coaster for him with a nod.

Robbie started to dial when the riot broke out. Someone in the crowd threw a drink at the local police cuffing protestors. The police responded by wading into the crowd and trying to arrest someone. A shot rang out, and all hell broke loose on the steps of the Kenosha courthouse. The camera didn't pan away and captured everything.

"Oh shit," Jerome muttered.

"Jerome, go home and load up. We have to get out ahead of this."

"What do you mean?" Jerome's voice shook.

"We gotta get our families out of Chicago and to the retreat."

"You sure, Robbie?"

"Man, I don't know. I can't tell if I'm just paranoid, or if we are staring at the beginning of something horrible rolling down the hill. Do I take a risk of looking like an ass and scaring everyone with my Chicken Little cry, or do we sit and wait for the other shoe to drop? I have that old feeling it has hit the fan for all of us."

Robbie unlocked his phone and went to his favorites to get Charlie's number. Grabbing the bar phone and punching in the numbers, he waited for Book to pick up and tried to calm himself as lists of items ran through his head like a jumble from a chemistry textbook. He heard a click on the line after three rings.

"Book, no names, I'm considering bugging out and taking the family to the farm. Tell Mom and Pop to expect some packages in the next few days."

"Hold on, Blaster, I'm seeing some crazy shit over here too, but is this the right move? I was about to call you and give you a heads up."

Chapter Fifteen

Kenosha, WI

In the end, Book convinced Robbie to sit tight and avoid doing anything rash, for now.

"Call me if you see anything else that looks squirrely on your end. I'm going to suggest that you get an evac plan together. If things go south, that entire metro area could go on lockdown," Charlie advised. "Just get momma bear and the cubs out if this goes sideways."

"My partner is here right now in the bar, and he's up to speed on this. I haven't asked him yet, but do you think there is room for him and his kids? He can use my cabin or the clubhouse if we need the room." Robbie glanced at Jerome and shrugged.

"I don't even know if I can get to my kids, but I would be willing to help out and contribute. I know we are just making plans, but are we actually thinking the crap is about to go down?" Jerome raised his glass and took a sip. Robbie noticed Jerome had a case of the shakes. Robbie understood and felt his own heart drumming along from the adrenaline dump from earlier.

"You and your kids are welcome, Mr. Partner. You know we probably can't take in your ex, though. She's too much of a wild card," Charlie said through the speaker.

"There is no way in hell I'm letting that woman come and mess up your retreat. I agree with you wholeheartedly. Why couldn't you have been my divorce attorney?" Jerome chuckled.

"Now, you get run over by a runaway tanker truck or have an industrial accident, and I'm your man. I don't do the family law. There's only pain there, buddy."

"No kidding. Hey, me and Ladies man will handle this end of it. Between the two of us, we'll keep them safe. I know they are like family to you guys, and I would be honored to help."

"It's settled then. I'll let the rest of the crew know to expect three more. I agree with you. Let's keep the chatter down and avoid acronyms as much as you can. We have players involved that might have some deep pockets and even bigger ears." Charlie and Robbie bantered back and forth for a few more minutes before Robbie hung up.

Jerome looked across the bar and caught Mr. Wojciechowski's eye. "You have an opinion, sir? I'm all ears." Robbie leaned into the bar and waited as the gentleman thought.

"What you need to worry about is how to avoid detection. They are going to monitor phone calls and track license plates where they can. Toll roads are out." He paused and pointed at Robbie. "You are a veteran, and even though you can't use but one arm, they will want to keep up with you for no other reason than to see if you are connected to anti-government activists. With the way things are going, they can easily label you as a domestic terrorist and lock you up. Keep your nose clean and fly close to the ground." The older man wiped his hands with the bar towel and walked to the register, took a key from his pocket and inserted the key into the register. He twisted the key and hit a button. The register started spitting out a long sheet of paper.

"Are you closing up early?" Jerome asked as he took the hint and drained his glass.

"You aren't the only ones who need to get their ducks in a row, gentlemen. I have a cabin I need to see about stocking up for what's coming. I don't plan on being anywhere close to a major city when the idiots in power start trying to divide by zero. When they initiate door kicking and confiscation, they will start something they can't back away from." Jerome and Robbie looked at each other in amazement.

"Mr. Wojciechowski, have you been through this before?" Jerome asked.

"I was a boy, but I remember enough. My father filled in the blanks for me when I was old enough to understand. You've had a good run but look at what is going on here in our small city."

"Thank you, Mr. Wojciechowski. We've enjoyed coming to your establishment." Robbie offered his hand to the man.

"Call me Frank. Mr. Wojciechowski was my father." The bartender squeezed Robbie's good hand and nearly crunched some bones in the process. Robbie grinned back and tried not to wince.

"If I hear anything, is there a way to contact you?" Robbie asked.

"Nope, after tonight, you boys will not see me again. I'm 'heading for the hills' as they say."

Robbie and Jerome walked out, and Frank locked up behind them. He didn't come out, so Robbie assumed he lived over the bar.

"You still want me to clear our schedule?" Jerome asked.

"Not just yet. I've got to switch out my ride and pick up some items. How much can your truck haul? My Ford is just a quarter ton, so I can't take too much of a load."

"The Beast is rated as a three quarter ton truck. I can tow around ten thousand in a trailer." Jerome pointed at the Harley. "Your bike is not going to carry much, will it?"

"Nope, but it can go on a sidewalk and split lanes if I get caught in a traffic jam. I'm off, man. Keep this between us, though."

"I'm not tellin' nobody nothing, Robbie. You going to let your newest 'old lady' in on it?" Jerome prodded Robbie.

"Heck no. It's Sunday. I keep the Sabbath holy, man. No honeys on my free day," Robbie chuckled as he started up the cruiser and let it idle. He did avoid dealing with his rotating stable of girlfriends on Sundays. As a rule, he reserved that one day a week for either himself or Kristi and the kids.

Robbie waved at Jerome before he pulled away from the Polka Dot one last time and headed home. He made a mental map of Kenosha and decided to avoid the parts where the rioting would be getting out of control near the courthouse and the surrounding bars. His home, just south of the downtown area along a quiet residential street, gave Robbie a sense of pride.

He had struggled with school most of his life, but his time after serving and healing up from his wound had given him a clarity of mind. Robbie tried his 'hand' at different trades, but nothing fit him. He worked as a laborer on a job site where the realtor needed some upgrades to flip it quick. The foreman, an old high school buddy, kept Robbie on as a favor, but Robbie saw where the real money could be made. After spending time after work one day talking to

Mr. Peltman, the real estate guy, Robbie knew for sure that he wanted to give it a go.

Using his G.I. Bill money, Robbie attended classes and worked odd jobs while rooming with a sweet little thing who didn't charge him rent. He did have upsets along the way, he had to find another bed to sleep in when his sugar momma got jealous and kicked him out. Robbie slept in his truck a few nights until he found another place to lay his head. Robbie sighed as he remembered Daphne Rutledge. Legs a mile long and jet-black hair down to her sweet bottom. Of all the girls before and after, Daphne had seen straight through his cocky attitude and still let him crash at her place. Her roommate didn't appreciate it, but then again, Philip Morgan did follow Daphne around like a lovesick puppy.

That relationship had lasted long enough for Robbie to save up enough for his own place. After that, the trail of destruction he left in his wake made him smile to himself under the helmet. Daphne and Philip married recently, so at least that was one that really *did* get away.

The real estate license test had been easy for Robbie, but he'd wanted something else to help him succeed. He took his normal core classes required by the university, but he focused on the business side of things. Robbie knew he could talk his way through a business deal, and he knew the basics for buying and selling houses, but he wanted to know how to keep the success rolling.

When he had graduated with his Bachelor's in Business Management, the whole team had showed up to celebrate. Kristi had brought up the kids, and Mom and Pop had made the trip, too. Times had been tough in the beginning with the housing market tanking, but meeting Jerome had really gotten him on the road to being comfortable. The modest home he'd picked up at the lowest point of the housing bubble had been in terrible shape. After the fiasco with the plumbing at Kristi's place, Jerome had taken the time to train Robbie by gutting his own house and completely redoing the pipes and wiring. Robbie discovered that the real hard part was getting the plaster and wall texture perfect.

A year later, Robbie had a brand-new home. The hardwood floors gleamed from the meticulous work he had put into the sanding and multiple coats of stain and varnish. Robbie had camped out in his garage until the fumes had cleared out.

Robbie eased up the drive and pulled to the garage behind the house. He reached into his jacket and pulled out the remote to disable the alarm and raise the single overhead door to the bay where he housed the Harley. He circled the bike around and backed in. He killed the engine and closed the door with the remote. He swung off the bike and worked the helmet off.

Like most garages, he had installed extra shelving and overhead storage. He also had a large powder magazine bolted to the floor near the rear of the bay.

Blaster listened to the engine of his Harley cooling as he cleared his mind. "It's too late to go shopping tonight." He locked up the garage and made his way into his house to plan for the coming collapse. Robbie felt the ground under his feet shift and he knew the time was coming when he would need to gear up for another war. A war in his own country by his own government.

Chapter Sixteen

Ohio

Pulling up to his house, Randy put his truck in park as the tractor pulled up to the barn. Getting out, he saw Cody jump out of the cab of the tractor. "It's only noon, why are you stopping?" Randy called out, grinning.

"Mom called on the CB and told me lunch was ready, and she better not have to come out in the field to get me," Cody huffed.

Randy headed over to Cody and they both walked toward his parents' house. "Trust me, you don't want Mom coming out in the field looking for you," Randy laughed. "I only did it once, and she spanked me the entire way back to the house."

Cody turned to him grinning, "Yeah, Pop told me about that. That's why I'm here."

"Yeah, if I can't outrun Momma, you definitely can't," Randy laughed.

Stepping on the porch, Cody opened the screen door. "You would think, with only one real foot you would slow down," Cody said, holding the door open.

"Hah," Randy huffed. "I'm still just as fast. I'm the bionic man."

Walking into the living room, they found Oliver and Lena staring at the TV. Seeing the look of shock on their faces, Randy froze. "What wrong?"

Slowly shaking his head, "The government has declared the ACLU and the NRA terrorist organizations," Oliver mumbled in shock.

"Do what?!" Randy shouted and ran around the couch to stand beside his parents.

"Sunday there was some shooting in Wisconsin and then twenty minutes later, another in Colorado," Lena said, staring at the

TV. "They said both protests were arranged by the NRA and ACLU. Both houses met Monday and this morning made the announcement."

After talking to Charlie yesterday, Randy knew all that but didn't tell mom. Looking at the TV, Randy saw a reporter talking and in the upper right corner, a small screen showed a riot with police shooting into a crowd. "Why are the cops shooting into the crowds?" Randy asked as Cody moved over beside him.

"Look at the uniforms," Cody said, pointing at the TV. "Those are federal agents, not cops."

"They took an oath to protect and serve!" Randy shouted, watching the officers shooting into a crowd.

"That's from Wisconsin. The riot there only intensified since Sunday. They said the group firebombed the courthouse and shot four officers," Oliver said.

Feeling his heartrate speed up, Randy stumbled back into the couch and dropped down. "Oh, shit," he mumbled, and Cody turned to him with wide eyes.

"Did you see the Polka Dot bar?" Cody asked timidly.

Staring at the TV hard, Randy only nodded. "Isn't that the bar Robbie goes to?" Lena asked.

"Yeah, he was there last Sunday," Randy said, pulling out his cell phone. Tapping the screen for Blaster, he watched the number pop up and ring. After four rings, the automated message came on. Hanging up, he tapped the screen for Charlie.

On the second ring, "Shadow," Charlie answered curtly. "Can't talk now, Blaster is okay. Stay close to home until you hear from me. Stay cocked, locked, and ready to roll hot."

Before Randy could say anything, Charlie hung up. "You get him?" Oliver asked.

"That was Charlie. Robbie's number went to voice mail. Book said Blaster was alright, but to stay close until he called," Randy said, setting his phone on the coffee table. He looked up at his dad. "What is this shit about?"

"Some water bill that was passed," Oliver said.

Getting off the couch, Randy felt constrained and the need to move. "Charlie said that wasn't up for a vote yet."

"Well, it seems they passed it over the weekend behind closed doors," Oliver related, moving over to his chair and sitting down.

"None of the networks are even talking about the bill, all they are covering is the violence."

Lena moved over to her recliner beside Oliver's and sat down. "So, you've heard of this bill?" she asked, but never turned from the TV.

"Yeah, but Charlie said it would never pass and if it did, it would be challenged," Cody said, sitting down. "That's all Book said?" he asked, watching the ticker at the bottom of the TV as it read out other cities where violence was breaking out.

"No, he said stay cocked, locked, and ready to roll hot," Randy answered with sigh. Walking around the couch, Randy headed for the door.

"Where you going, son?" Oliver asked, looking away from the TV.

"Getting ready to roll," Randy said over his shoulder. "Book wouldn't have said it if I didn't need to do it."

Cody jumped up as Randy walked out the door. Breaking into a run, Cody caught up to him as he stepped off the porch. "You don't think Blaster is in trouble, do you?" he asked as they headed to Randy's house. "Surely Charlie or Robbie would've called last weekend if he was."

"Don't know, but if he is, I'm going to help," Randy replied.

"Now you're talking," Cody grinned.

Reaching his door, Randy looked over at Cody's innocent face and smiled, "If this goes down, we are fighting the feds. You ready for that?"

"For my team, I'll fight the ocean," Cody declared, walking past Randy and opening the door. "I may not beat the ocean, but it will damn sure know I was there."

Laughing as a mental image of Cody 'Karate Kid' kicking waves filled his mind, Randy followed Cody inside. Cody headed into his room while Randy went into his small office. Opening his gun safe, Randy started pulling out weapons. "I never thought I would be doing this here at home," he said with a sigh.

After his weapons were laid out, he went to his room and changed into tan tactical pants and a polo shirt. Grabbing his tactical plate carrier vest from the closet and tossing it on the bed, Randy reached up in the top of the closet, pulling down two ballistic plates. After putting them in the vest, he grabbed his XD and clipped it to his waist.

Stepping out, he found Cody in the living room, laying his stuff on the couch. "You think we need our rucksacks?" Cody asked.

"I laid mine out just in case," Randy said as his dad walked in.

"Son, your phone beeped," Oliver said, walking over and holding it out.

Taking his phone, Randy tapped the screen. "It's a message from Book. He says stay in place, but keep sharp," Randy read out.

"Keep sharp for what?" Cody asked.

"Trouble," Randy replied, tapping the screen.

"Momma has food ready," Oliver told them, turning and heading for the door.

Cody went back to his room and grabbed his laptop. "Come on, before she starts looking for us," Cody said, clipping his XD on his hip. All of the team had concealed permits. Even though the permits weren't valid in Illinois, they never went anywhere unarmed. The weapons might not be on them, but they were damn sure close when they visited Kristi.

Walking in the house, they saw Lena eating but still in her chair. "Your plates are on the coffee table," she said, not looking away from the TV. "The President is coming on in five minutes."

"Hell, I barely liked the one they voted out. At least he wasn't a politician," Randy said, sitting down on the couch.

Sitting next to Randy, Cody opened his laptop. "Everyone loves a politician, you can buy one to suit any need," he chuckled, grabbing his plate.

"That's the problem," Oliver commented, sitting in his recliner. "They are worse than a whore. A politician will get in bed with anyone and do anything; a whore only gets in bed for sex."

"You hush," Lena said, popping his arm and Cody stifled a chuckle.

"Got that right, Dad," Randy agreed, reading the ticker at the bottom of the screen. "They are having riots in Columbus?"

"Yeah, reports started coming in after you walked to your house," Lena said, turning back to the TV.

"Momma, I wasn't gone but for fifteen minutes!" Randy cried out.

Staring at the TV, "I know, son, but the riots are spreading fast. Four state governors have called out the National Guard," she related, grabbing a glass of tea.

Lifting his gaze off the ticker at the bottom of the screen, Randy looked at the display beside the reporter showing scenes of riots. "What the hell?" he gasped. These weren't kids rioting, these were adults. Many were wearing uniforms and working clothes. "Where is that at?"

"Billings, Montana," Lena answered, shaking her head. "They are at the federal building."

As Randy watched, a group of officers with shields charged the crowd, then the screen suddenly cut off and showed the emblem of the United States and a steady tone sounded. The ticker at the bottom of the screen read: This is a message from the President of the United States on the Emergency Broadcast Network. Follow all instructions given and comply with all law enforcement demands.

"What the fuck?!" Randy shouted, standing up and staring at the TV.

"Randy, watch your mouth," Lena snapped, and the screen changed to show a small man sitting behind the desk in the Oval Office.

"My fellow Americans, I come before you today with a heavy heart," the President said with a nasal voice, looking down at some papers he was holding. "I have enacted four Executive Orders, one which suspends Posse Comitatus, and I have ordered military units into several major cities to quell the violence that has broken out."

The President stopped and looked up from the paper. "This violence has erupted from a few dissidents complaining about a law the elected legislature has passed. Yes, I signed the Water Act. It safeguards the water for our children and future generations, and I will not tolerate any who would want to jeopardize our children's rights to clean water when they inherit the earth.

"First, the five-cent federal tax on water will go into effect this week on the first of May. All owners of private wells, you will contact your local government for placement of a water meter in the next thirty days. Once your meter is in place, you will be taxed retroactively for the past two years according to your uses from May first. To all homeowners that have water frontage or standing water on your property, you will make an appointment with your

141

local tax office to be assessed your tax per gallon on water touching, standing, or flowing through your property."

The President stopped and looked at the camera hard. "Those not complying within ninety days will face property seizure. We can no longer, not take responsibility in preserving this planet for our children. All businesses with wells will have six months to comply or apply for extensions. Any person, family or dwelling that receives government assistance can apply for exempt status. All you need to do is go to the IRS website and apply. Each person receiving government assistance will be allowed exempt status on five hundred gallons a day. That is what is offered for basic needs and after that, you must pay the tax. All government housing is exempt."

Still staring at the camera, the President put the papers down on the desk. "Now, this morning I signed an Executive Order classifying the ACLU and the NRA, terrorist organizations. The ACLU was trying to justify in court, the reason people had a right to not pay this tax and their right to protest. Many of the protesters you see acting violently have been confirmed to be members or have ties to the ACLU and the NRA. I have been advised that the members of these organizations have been ordered by the leadership to protest with violence. If it is proven otherwise, I will remove them from the terrorist list. Until then, I have enacted an Executive Order limiting the Second Amendment. You may still own firearms, but they must be registered, kept in a safe, stored separate from ammunition and not removed from your residence of registration. All gun owners have thirty days to register your weapons with the Bureau of Alcohol, Tobacco, Firearms and Explosives via their website. Any firearm not registered in these thirty days will be classified as an illegal weapon and the holder will be charged with penalties that carry ten years in prison per weapon.

"Any current or past member of the ACLU and the NRA must register with local law enforcement in the next ten days. After registering, you must turn over all weapons. If you are cleared and found not to be a threat to this great nation, then your guns will be returned.

"As of now, a warrant for the arrest of any standing administrative member of the ACLU or NRA has been issued. I urge you to turn yourself in, to the nearest federal institution. Homeland and the FBI are already looking for you and if you're innocent, you will have your day in court. Unlike you, this government believes in due process of law, but we will not be intimidated by your actions."

Looking away from the camera, the President picked the papers back up and took the top one off, setting it aside. "I have recalled military forces from overseas to help local law enforcement quell this violence. Every member of the UN has passed this legislation, yet only here in America have demonstrations turned violent and disrupted the peace. I know it is only a small fraction of our population, yet it still shames me to call myself an American when this group fights against doing what is right for the children now and future generations. Several members of the United Nations have graciously offered assistance to help suppress these violent few. As President, under Executive Order 13603, The National Defense Resources Preparedness, I am allowing UN forces to assist the United States military in suppressing the violence from this small section of dissidents until this time of crisis has passed.

"All UN forces will be answerable to US military liaisons and will follow the rule of law of the United States," the President said, then looked back at the camera. "It troubles me that this small group has caused this much turmoil, but I can't let them further endanger the citizens and infrastructure of this great nation.

"Let us stand together against these few radicals and any information a citizen can give against these radicals will be rewarded. Contact your local FBI or Homeland office or call the toll-free number at the bottom of the screen," the President said and then smiled.

"Thank you and let's all stand together and support your elected leaders."

The screen blinked to a group of reporters sitting around a table when a clatter sounded in the room. Everyone turned to see Lena had dropped her plate. "Fuck me," Lena mumbled in shock. Wisely, nobody said anything.

Chapter Seventeen

Monroe, OH

The drive towards Monroe was uneventful as Charlie guided his big pickup with the popup trailer to the loading docks around back of the warehouse at AIM Surplus. A clerk checked him in and Charlie began counting out the Benjamins as two men loaded his order; first filling the truck bed up to the top of the camper, then stacking the last few crates into the little camping trailer's available storage space.

"That's a load of ammo there, sir," the clerk commented when he handed Charlie his change and a receipt. He could tell the young man was staring at the scars on his face and neck but pretended like he didn't notice. Charlie had gotten good at ignoring those looks over the years.

"Got a lot of buddies coming over to the range this weekend," Charlie replied coolly, taking the change and stuffing it in his pocket without another word. Today he was wearing his thin black gloves, something he'd been doing more of late when he went out with Joan. Nothing he could really do about the face in public, but he'd be damned if he was going to have someone staring at his left hand and those missing digits if he could help it.

On the drive back, Charlie started by listening to a little Creedence Clearwater Revival on the CD player, followed by a copy of the Eagles Greatest Hits, and he was nearly through the heavy metal mix Cody had prepared for him when he thought about the whim that had prompted this buying spree. Operating the truck on automatic pilot, he saw his exit approaching and realized he'd been wool-gathering for nearly three hours.

He was thinking about Joan when he pulled into his garage and shut down the engine. He'd driven straight there and straight back, stopping at the corner store and filling up his tank. He'd been shocked to see fuel going up again, and that got him to wondering about what else he had missed.

Looking at all the ammunition stacked up in the camper and his truck bed, Charlie wondered if maybe he needed to start seeing a therapist again. Maybe later, he temporized, and transferred everything carefully into the camper. The little twelve-footer seemed to squat on its axle, but Charlie knew if he drove carefully, he could get the load to the retreat without any problems. Randy had customized the little trailer for Charlie years ago, and they'd never managed to overload it. The solid tires helped, Charlie thought with a little grin.

As Saturday came to a close, Charlie spent some time working on the discoveries he would be serving Monday on one of his new cases. Nothing earth-shattering, but he knew he would have to dig a little more than usual to get the facts he needed for this one. The defense firm was one who had a reputation for playing 'hide-the-ball' and he needed to box them in ahead of time. Heck, he already knew he would soon be dusting off an old form and drafting the motion to compel he knew he would be filing in sixty days. Just the nature of the beast.

He called Joan just before bed, checking in, and he was amused to hear how Joan was already looking for a training partner for her swimming. The pair, both competitive in almost everything they did, had already raced a few times at their gym and where Charlie had the edge on endurance, he grudgingly acknowledged that Joan had the God-given talent to dominate anything under 800 meters.

"Well, just go easy on them at first," Charlie warned, "or you will run her off. Or him."

"Definitely a her," Joan replied. "And I think she is going to be pushing me pretty hard as it is."

"You can take her," Charlie encouraged. "And if you end up getting cramped, just give me a call."

"Oh, really?" Joan replied with a suggestive laugh. "Are you making advances, Mr. Tucker?"

"Of course, Miss Norgren," Charlie bantered back, "but in this case, I actually know an excellent massage therapist only three blocks from our gym."

"Well, I guess that will have to do, for now," Joan said with a fake pout that turned into a little purr, and Charlie bit his lip to suppress a groan.

"Goodnight, Joan," Charlie forced himself to say.

"Goodnight, Charlie," Joan replied. "Thank you for calling."

This night at least, if Charlie experienced any dreams, they faded with the arrival of the morning.

For Sunday, Charlie had no plans for working and decided to postpone running down to the retreat for the following weekend. He didn't exactly enjoy the idea of having enough ammo in his garage to cause a major explosion if the block burned, but he'd stored lesser amounts in his garage in the past. At least he wasn't stockpiling bomb-making ingredients.

The next week passed in a blur, as Charlie watched the news with mounting horror. He saw the aftermath of the violent protests and the Federal government posturing, but then, these kinds of scenes were sadly becoming almost commonplace. The main difference being the state government's willingness to use overwhelming violence against questionable provocation.

He'd discussed the situation with Joan several times and he was getting that same sense of foreboding dread as before. His conversations with the boys were much more subdued, avoiding saying anything that might trigger Echelon, or whatever they were calling it these days.

It was a lazy Sunday, and Charlie awoke early from yet another nightmare. After a breakfast of coffee- black, orange juice- chilled, and grapefruit- split, Charlie hit the home gym for a bit of resistance training and pounded out three miles on the treadmill before the sun had risen properly over the trees. He was feeling restless and wondering what else he had to do today when his cell phone rang. Sitting on his narrow deck with another cup of coffee, he hit the Bluetooth function on his phone and listened as the call was accepted.

"Charlie, is that you?"

Bryce's voice had a small echo and at first, Charlie thought it was his phone, but realized it might be on the other end. Whatever was going on, Charlie barely recognized his friend.

"Yeah, Bryce, I'm here," Charlie prompted, then he could hear fumbling on the other end of the phone and the echo faded as Bryce's voice grew stronger.

"Charlie, they're coming for me," Bryce announced, his breathing fast and labored, and Charlie felt a knot of worry form in the pit of his stomach.

"Who is coming for you, Bryce? What are you talking about?"

"The DHS agents," Bryce said softly, almost whispering. Fear edged his every word, and Charlie could sense the panic fast approaching.

At that moment, Charlie nearly ended the call, after watching riots breaking out around the country. Not because he didn't want to hear the rest of what Bryce had to say, but because Charlie knew everything being said on the cell phone was being recorded. Recorded, and likely being used to identify him and his location. Still, Charlie had to know.

"Why, Bryce? Someone eavesdropping on your calls again?" Charlie said forcefully, trying to get his friend to think about the next words out of his mouth before he spoke.

"Judge Wallenstein, he told Rodger what was really happening. And what their meeting was about. It's the water, Charlie. The water bill already passed like the President said. Part of the UN Agreement on Natural Resources," Bryce's voice rose as he spoke, still trying to catch his breath, and he was nearly shouting by the end. "The Administration has been setting this up for months, Charlie. That meeting with the judges, it wasn't just here or in Cleveland. It was everywhere. All of the judges, Charlie. The President and his cronies, they don't just want this implemented, they want to avoid anybody trying to get it held up in the courts. They gave the District Judges their marching orders and told them to toe the line or else. Nobody is going to be allowed to successfully challenge this bill. Charlie, they threatened the judges with everything up to summary execution for failure to comply. And the Senate just passed amendments strengthening the bill this week in closed session."

"Holy Mother of God," Charlie whispered. This was tin-foil hat territory, but he believed the story coming from Bryce. Not just because of who he was, but because suddenly, the pieces started fitting together. There had been rumblings in the media about protests in some of the Western states, something about a change in farm policy, but the media quickly moved on to other stories. In a country where every police stop was a standoff, and every use of force by the local police became tinder for the next riot, Charlie had tuned them out.

"Are you okay? Are you somewhere safe?" Charlie asked, suddenly concerned for his friend, worried that his comments might have gotten Rodger and Bryce in real trouble.

"Judge Wallenstein called Rodger into his office yesterday and told him everything he knew, Charlie. He doesn't know the endgame, but what he does know is terrifying. This water bill, it's only their first step, and it is a way to pay for the rest of the changes they have planned. Wallenstein thinks this was rushed through after their Small Arms Treaty initiative failed." Bryce paused as if winded, and when he started speaking again, Charlie could hear that weird echo once again.

"The Judge, they had something on him, but he was too mad to be blackmailed. And…Charlie, he had some documents he'd managed to acquire, and had Rodger pass them on to me. To go to my friends, you know? Charlie, they are targeting you and your people. They are afraid of resistance, so they are going to strike first and preempt the most likely actors. NRA members, Oathkeepers, certain veteran groups, and even the ACLU. The President wasn't kidding about listing them as terrorists. They have already started rounding them up."

Oh, shit. Thinking of a particularly memorable scene in Pulp Fiction, Charlie wanted to slam his phone against the wall and start screaming, "Prank call, Prank call!" at the top of his lungs. Some things you couldn't unhear, not with Big Brother constantly listening. Of course, Charlie knew Bryce meant the ACLU as 'his friends', but that sounded like too little, too late at this stage.

"What is happening now? Bryce, where are you?"

"I'm almost home, Charlie. We were coming back from lunch over on the Gold Coast," Bryce said, and his voice sounded close to tears. Tears of frustration and rage. "They got Rodger, right there in the middle of the street. No warning, just tackled him to the asphalt, and Charlie, they were beating him. With those batons, hitting him over and over. He told me to run, he told me to get away!"

"Bryce, are you off the streets? Can you see anybody chasing you still?"

"No, I can't see anybody in the hallway," Bryce replied, his panting and huffing somewhat abated. "I just took the back stairs to avoid the security cameras."

"Good man," Charlie said, feeling his own body tense as he listened to his friend's voice. "Look, they are only doing this to protect the children, right? You know how I feel about those kinds of programs."

Praying Bryce would get the meaning, Charlie continued. "This is for the children, Bryce. You need to march down to the closest police station and turn yourself in before they have to come get you. This is for the children, so turn around and don't waste their time. Just get down there and do like I'm telling you, got it?"

In law school, Charlie and Bryce had many funny, stupid, and sometimes heated discussions regarding the shameless use of children in certain political ploys. Gun-free, drug-free schools, requirements for standardized testing and even some vaccine court decisions were all fair game. Both sides of the aisle were guilty, and the refrain, "What about the children?" became a punchline between the two men and their small study group and they would quote: *The state must declare the child to be the most precious treasure of the people. As long as the government is perceived as working for the benefit of the children, the people will happily endure almost any curtailment of liberty and almost any deprivation.* — Adolf Hitler, Mein Kampf.

Controlling his breathing, Charlie hoped Bryce was paying attention as he thought of a plan for Bryce. He needed to get out of that building, abandon his apartment, and disappear.

"Oh God, Charlie, they're here!" Bryce screamed into the telephone, and Charlie could hear shouted voices growing louder in the background. The phone began to get that echo again over the Bluetooth speakers and now, Charlie knew it was the side effect over the microphone of his friend running.

What followed was a jumble of sound as the microphone now picked up cursing and shifting, and the echoes over the phone remained loud and confusing.

"You can't do this! You can't do this! I have rights! I have…"

The boom that followed, and the shrill scream, left nothing to the imagination. The last thing he heard before the phone call died was a murmured, "I told that little bastard not to make us have to chase him. Serves him right."

Charlie ceased taping the call and let his cell phone drop. Acting on instinct, he'd recorded the entire call, and now he was operating on autopilot. Rising carefully from his seat, Charlie opened the glass door and headed back inside as if nothing had happened. His head was spinning with the revelations of the last few seconds, and now Charlie had to decide his next course of action.

Guilt gnawed at the edge of his consciousness, as did a good dose of self-loathing, as he thought about his dead friends. Shit, he'd missed the signs and hadn't taken Paige Bishop's warning to heart. Robbie had seen it coming too, but Charlie had let his normalcy bias overcome his good sense.

Not even entertaining the idea, Charlie knew his cell phone was compromised. No way the Powers-That-Be didn't already have his file pulled up, and now he had a race to get out of sight before the goons came knocking at his door. Charlie needed to move. And move fast.

First, he dialed Robbie. He hoped to light a fire under his friend and get him to evacuate Kristi and the kids. This was only getting started, and Charlie feared the federal government, and this administration in particular, was not above breaking some eggs to make that One World omelet. The President, an avowed Internationalist, had made several statements during his campaign that hinted at his intentions to bringing the United States into the community of nations. After Trump, the lazy and rich had put another giver in office.

Charlie thought the failure of the President's party's renewed gun control bill had set the President straight on the mood of the country. Instead, the little dictator seemed bound and determined to have it his own way, and to hell with the Constitution. Charlie now worried those precious to him might have to pay for the President's hubris.

"Robert, is that you?" Charlie barked harshly, trying to keep his normally chatty friend from getting a word in edgewise, and he continued speaking before Blaster could form a sentence. "I don't have much time, but you need to get the Primaries to the Happy Place posthaste. Chop chop, my friend, and don't stop for anything. Seriously, brother. Anything. See you when I see you."

Tossing the phone on the seat, Charlie turned his attention to getting the garage door open and backing his Ford into position to hook up to his little pop-up trailer. Glad I didn't unload after all, he mused. Hauling all that ammo back out to the trailer would have been a bear of a job.

Killing the engine, Charlie hopped out of the truck and grabbed his phone as he sprinted around to fasten the trailer hitch and get the garage door closed. Fortunately, the garage was deep enough to take both the truck and the trailer in the same slot. That was frankly one of the reasons he'd bought the place when he'd found it for sale. He left the truck where it sat for the moment and charged to the side door, climbing the stairs while managing to simultaneously hit Randy's number from his favorites at the same time.

While the phone rang, Charlie ran into his bedroom and opened the closet door leading to his gun safe. Before he could press his thumb on the biometric pad, he heard Randy's voice on the other end of the phone.

"Brother, don't say anything," Charlie began, again taking over the conversation. Like Charlie and the rest of the men, Randy knew their phone calls were monitored, but his friend likely didn't know how closely they were being scrutinized today. Since last weekend Charlie was sure all vets were on the NSA watch list. After the call from Bryce, he knew everything he said on the cell phone was being recorded for analysis, but he felt the need to give the final warning to his people.

"The pit bull is out of the yard, his owner is on the way, and you need to get a move on to your Happy Place. Go to your Happy Place," Charlie repeated. "And take all our friends. This is a no-shit warning, and you need to be moving. I think we are on the menu."

Charlie was referring to a story Randy had told where he'd been chased by a neighbor's pit bull when he'd returned home from fishing one summer. The owner had been a sheriff's deputy, who according to Oliver, thought his badge meant he could get away with raising fighting dogs out in the country. Despite several complaints to the sheriff, the deputy continued to raise the vicious dogs with only a three-foot-tall chain-link fence to keep the killers inside.

Randy, who'd been maybe eleven at the time, had barely gotten through the front door before the beast had charged in behind him, knocking the flimsy door open. Randy, winded and shaking, got to his Dad's 1911 before the pissed-off dog got a bite in on the boy. When his parents got home from town, they found their son trying to drag the massive dead weight out of the kitchen. So, Charlie figured Randy would get the gist of what he was trying to convey.

"Is little sister on her way?" Randy managed to ask, and Charlie imagined he could hear the wheels turning in his friend's head. Over the years since Wheat's death, Randy had gradually become acknowledged as the leader of their little band of misfit toys, and one of the reasons was his ability to plan for multiple contingencies on the fly, all while keeping a clear head. Randy might act crazy at times, but Charlie knew his friend was a tactical computer when the chips were down.

"I put Cheesehead on it," Charlie replied. "I've gotta go, brother, but watch the idiot box for signs and let Cobra know. They are coming for us, and everyone like us."

That last bit might have been too clear of a reference, but Charlie was counting down the seconds before a squad of black SUVs came barreling into his parking lot. Next, he found the number for Bert Travis and got his voicemail. Travis had moved back to Tampa and had gradually taken over his Dad's charter boat business after he'd gotten out of the hospital, and they all still kept in touch. Mainly Christmas and birthday cards for Bert's kids, but they'd remained tight. In fact, Kristi saw him and his family the last time she'd gone down to see her folks in St. Petersburg.

Like with Randy, Charlie gave Bert a heads-up warning, giving him a shorthand version of the day's revelations. Whether Bert was in any position to utilize the warning, Charlie had no idea, but he felt the need to try. The ties of blood bound them together after all.

With those vital chores out of the way, Charlie threw himself into getting out of the house. He knew someone would be coming, and after he'd heard the fate of his friend Bryce, Charlie wasn't going to give them a chance to take him without a fight. He might die, but he wasn't going to go quietly.

Phone calls done for the moment, Charlie focused the next few minutes on packing up his firearms and loading as many duffel bags as he owned with the extra ammunition in his safe. Unlike Randy or Robbie, Charlie wasn't as eclectic in his firearm collection, plus he kept most of his hunting rifles at the retreat so he only needed three trips up and down the internal stairs to the garage to stow his rifles and shotguns in the trailer.

The SASS would be of little use if the stormtroopers charged his front door, but he did keep out the extended magazine Mossberg and his two personal defense pistols, a Glock 21 and a Glock 30, both chambered in the popular 45 ACP. The pistols, like the shotgun, were nothing fancy, but they functioned properly and he'd used them enough to be comfortable with, should their need arise.

Thirty seconds was all he needed. He was thirty seconds from heading out, when he heard the front doorbell. Checking the closed-circuit camera, he had mounted on the porch, Charlie was dismayed to see it was three uniformed officers waiting at the entryway. Well, three that he could see, along with two City police cars.

Slipping the smaller pistol into his waistband at the small of his back, Charlie placed the Glock 21 on the hallway table out of sight of the door. No matter what, Charlie resolved that he would not be going peacefully. No. He would try to talk his way out of a confrontation, but if the Powers-That-Be wanted to put him in a camp or silence his voice, Charlie would retreat no further. He had little doubt that Bryce and Rodger were already dead and if he was next, he would take a toll before he fell.

Bracing to the side of the door, Charlie took a moment to center himself. He wasn't exactly quelling his nerves so much as preparing his central nervous system for a sudden spike in adrenaline. Adrenaline was fine for a knight fighting with a sword or shield, but that same extra boost could throw off one's aim in a gunfight. He needed ice water in his veins as he prepared to mete out sudden death. Be the Ranger, he reminded himself.

"Yes, sir?" Charlie asked as he swung the door open, and his scarred face tried to mimic surprise while he scrutinized the trio of officers standing on his elevated porch. Wearing navy blue uniforms with a red and yellow flash on one sleeve, the three men seemed to lean forward aggressively as the heavy metal door swung out.

Charlie recognized one of the men immediately from the shooting range, a corporal named Scroggins, and quickly realized Corporal Scoggins was the senior of the three officers, though the man on the end looked to be at least a half a decade older.

"Are you Charles Tucker?" Scoggins asked, though from the flash of recognition when he saw Charlie, the question really didn't need to be answered given the lawyer's distinctive look. Scoggins might as well have been wearing a neon billboard that proclaimed he wished he wasn't here.

"Yes, sir, I am. What can I do for you gentlemen today?"

Charlie remained calm, which seemed to relax the younger two men, but the officer on the end, a patrolman whose nameplate read Domeni, visibly tensed at Charlie's calm words.

"Mr. Tucker, I have a warrant for your arrest," Corporal Scoggins continued and again, Charlie saw the man's lips curl in an unconscious expression of disgust as he spoke.

"On what charges?" Charlie inquired, his voice steady and his body visibly relaxed, which seemed to unnerve the officers.

"You don't need to know, dumbass," Domeni practically snarled as he took a step forward, one hand on his holstered pistol, and the other reaching for the handcuffs. "Just get out here, so we can get this done."

All the slack in Charlie's body went taut, but he focused most of his attention on the corporal.

"Corporal, you know what I do for a living," Charlie said, feigning patience and blinking his eyes lazily. "You also know I was a prosecutor for several years. Before we go one step further, I want to see this so-called warrant. I want to see what the State of Ohio, or the City of Parma, has seen fit to charge me with today."

"Mr. Tucker, this isn't the city, or the state," Scoggins said ruefully. "This is from the United States Attorney for the Northern District of Ohio. It's the feds, Mr. Tucker. She's gotten a federal judge to issue a warrant for your arrest."

"And I am still waiting to see this alleged warrant, Corporal," Charlie continued, his faked good nature wearing thin. "What is the charge?"

Instead of speaking further, Scoggins extended a sheaf of papers towards Charlie, and the lawyer reached out cautiously to accept the documents with his left hand. Charlie, purposefully, had shed his black gloves and left them by the door, exposing his twisted and bent hand as he grasped the pages.

As Charlie took the warrant, Patrolman Domeni started forward at a lunge, handcuffs already out. Charlie, flicking his eyes at the older man, simply stated, "You take one more step onto my private property, Patrolman, in furtherance of these trumped-up and false charges, and I promise, you won't be able to get a job guarding the Claw Machine in the lobby of a Bob Evans."

"Why, you skinny little cripple," Domeni started, but Scoggins didn't let him finish.

"Shut it, Phil," the corporal barked. "You know I don't like..."

"Corporal Scoggins," Charlie said, taking the few seconds he had to scan the documents. "I can't find anything here authorizing this action. There's no charge, and there's nothing under Ohio law authorizing your office to take any action. This isn't anything like a valid warrant. It is defective on its face."

"Mr. Tucker," Scoggins replied with a sigh. "Apparently the President has signed a series of Executive Orders recently, directing the apprehension and detention of certain individuals. That there," Scoggins pointed helpfully to the last page of the document, "are the relevant Executive Orders pertaining to this action. This one is supported by a Presidential Finding, declaring the NRA a terrorist organization."

"On what basis? Contrary to what some people might think, Executive Orders aren't the word of God. They've been successfully challenged in Federal Court. And I still don't know why you are trying to take me into custody. The NRA has millions of members."

"Mr. Tucker, it's about the guns," Scoggins finally said, his sigh deeper this time. "Like I said, the President has signed an Executive Order labeling certain groups to be...well, enemy combatants, I guess that's the term. You are on the list because of your membership in the National Rifle Association, and well, because of other factors."

"He's one of them crazies," Domeni helpfully volunteered. "They have you down as a nut job from your time at the VA, Tucker. Now, can we quit this debating club and get to work? We got a lot more names on that list, and the paddy wagon should be here soon."

Charlie feigned surprise at this news, but in reality, he wasn't. Heck, Charlie realized, the VA records were probably why the Powers-That-Be sent local cops instead of the FBI, or a strike team made up of Marshals. He was considered to be 100% disabled by the review board, after all.

"Gentlemen." Charlie said, "I don't know what is going on, but I do support the local law enforcement. I worked closely with the city and county when I was a prosecutor, so listen closely to what I am about to tell you. This is an illegal warrant, and it has been improperly issued. It is also, frankly, insane. This violates Article 1 Section 4 of the Ohio Constitution which all three of you have been charged with protecting, and so many other state and federal laws, I don't even know where to begin.

"This piece of paper violates both the United States v. Heller on federal grounds under the Second Amendment of the U.S. Constitution, McDonald v. Chicago on the state side, and on Fourth Amendment grounds under unreasonable search and seizure as defined by Jacobsen. I take it that once I've been illegally detained, you officers plan to tear my house apart to seize the legally purchased hunting rifle Corporal Scoggins has seen me sighting in down at the range?"

That seemed to strike a nerve with both Scoggins and the other younger officer, whose nameplate Charlie had yet to make out. Domeni just seemed to grow more agitated and Charlie turned to confront him yet again.

"Doesn't this seem off, Patrolman? Wrong? It's almost like somebody *wants* violence to erupt in the streets. Not from me," Charlie added hastily, "but there's always *that* guy, right? That whack job who wants to fight it out in the street? So you officers are stuck with a no-win situation and the politicians aren't going to end up in prison when this all goes pear-shaped, are they? No, it will be you and these other officers, who end up in Marion, or Elkton if you are lucky."

The mention of those facilities, the Maximum-Security Penitentiary in Marion, IL or even the Club Fed facility in Elkton, Ohio, seemed to change even Domeni's tune.

"So, what are you proposing?"

"You never saw me. Leave my crippled ass here while I draft a motion to be filed in Federal Court today," Charlie answered

156

plainly. "I'm a fairly well-known local, ties to the community and all that, but after working for years as a prosecutor, I don't want to be locked up with some of the scum I've already sent through the revolving door. Let me work with you to get this straightened out, before we have another Dallas on our hands."

Scoggins seemed to make a decision at that point.

"Men, stand down. Porter," he said, turning to the younger cop slightly behind him, "go tell Marcos we are headed back to the house for now. This is bullshit. And Domeni, stick a sock in it."

"What about you, Corporal?"

"I'm going to have a word with Mr. Tucker," Scoggins replied blandly over his shoulder as the other two cops reluctantly clattered down the stairs and back to their squad cars.

"Any of that bullshit you just spun out true, Charlie?" Scoggins asked, and this time his voice sounded tired. He didn't even blink when Charlie stuck the detention order in his back pocket.

"Oh yeah, Tommy. Most of it. And it really is illegal as shit, what they are doing. Those feds are going to get you and your men shot full of holes, and then they will call in the helicopter gunships to fire up the mess you leave behind," Charlie replied.

Though they'd pretended not to know each other that well, Tommy Scoggins and Charlie had spent more than one afternoon shooting the breeze at the clubhouse attached to the indoor range they both frequented. Charlie knew Tommy had done four years in the Marine Corps, including a tour in Iraq, before starting his career in law enforcement.

"Can you get out of town in thirty minutes?" Tommy asked softly, after glancing down to make sure his body camera was turned off.

"I was headed out the door when you showed up," Charlie answered honestly. "I got a tip."

"What about fighting it out in the courts?" Tommy asked, surprised by the lawyer's response.

"That was the tip, Tommy. They've already fixed the courts. All of them on the federal level, I think. Anyone who doesn't toe the new party line is taken out back, and the stormtroopers give them two behind the ear."

"Jeez, seriously?"

Charlie nodded. That was almost a given, with the information he'd received. If they were willing to kill a court coordinator in broad daylight, he had no doubt the threat to judges was sincere.

"Tommy, you need to start planning your own exit strategy. You got a wife and kids to think about. They seriously targeted me for my membership in the NRA? And because I am a vet? Well, guess what, buddy, they know you fit in the same category. Actually, I was expecting the Men in Black when my doorbell rang."

"What would you have done? I mean, if it was FBI or the Marshals?"

When Charlie gave Tommy his dead-eyed scowl, Tommy had his answer.

"I just cannot believe this is happening in our country, Charlie. Not the country we fought for, and so many of our friends died to protect. What the hell is going on?"

"Tommy, I think we've been sold out, and maybe we'll eventually find out the reason why, and maybe not. All I can tell you is this all started with the new Safe Water Bill, Congress just passed. But the why runs deeper, and I fear the true cause will tear this country apart."

"Over water? Seriously? Hey, we all want clean drinking water. That doesn't make any sense."

Charlie nodded. "Why go after the guns and the gun owners, if all you are trying to do is make the drinking water safe? That's like protesting because the stores are full of food. Well, maybe in California," Charlie said, unable stop himself from taking the jab. "But there is another agenda at work."

"Well, hell, Charlie. I wish…well, you need to get out of here and I need to corral these boys before they get me killed. That Domeni, what a piece of work. Been busted down from sergeant twice already. You'd think I was back in the Corps."

"Semper fi, Marine," Charlie said in parting as he stepped back inside the door.

"Rangers lead the way," Tommy replied, his voice nearly a whisper.

Charlie was sweating despite the cool afternoon air, and he palmed the Glock from the hallway table as he walked by. Despite what he'd told Tommy, he was more like two minutes from lift-off instead of thirty seconds but felt the need to call Bert again and let him know he was probably on the list as well. So Charlie left another message, passing on the new warning, and hung up. He'd done all he could on that end and the clock was almost out of time.

Looking around, Charlie wanted to run through the kitchen for some food and drinks before he hit the road. Not just for the trip, but for the days and weeks to come. Who knew when he would have a chance to stock up again?

And he wanted to bring extra food, because he did have one stop before leaving town. He needed to see Joan one last time, and if she would listen to reason, he planned to have her riding with him. He knew Kristi and Lena would love having more female company at the retreat. Plus, if he was being targeted and Bryce and Rodger were dead, would Joan be subjected to scrutiny after the fact? She worked for the Federal Courts after all, and could be a target too, if they were looking for leaks.

Really, now she was in his life, he didn't want to try continuing to survive without her. Survive? No, he could survive, but he might not be really living.

He dialed the phone one last time and despite everything, he had to smile when he heard Joan's voice on the phone.

Joan, for her part, knew something was wrong as soon as she heard Charlie's voice, but Joan Norgren was more than just a pretty face, so she played along as Charlie asked a question she knew was completely out of character.

"Do I want to go see your family? In Loraine?" she bubbled into the handset of her phone. "Why, of course. Since I've got the day free anyway, that sounds wonderful. Just come by and pick me up."

"I'll be there in half an hour," Charlie promised as he disconnected the call.

Barely thirty minutes had elapsed before she found her friend waiting at the front door of her apartment. He still looked tense, but there was also a sense of barely suppressed aggression that seemed out of place for the normally easy-going attorney.

"That was fast," Joan said, by way of greeting, "but I'm ready for a visit to the wilds of Loraine."

"We're not going there," Charlie said sharply, and stepped through the door without waiting for an invitation. Joan started to say something, then stopped abruptly.

"What happened?"

Charlie looked around and spied her cell phone laying on the counter of the kitchen bar. Moving quickly, he pried loose the hard plastic cover and adeptly popped out the battery and SIM card before answering.

"You remember my friends, Bryce and Rodger?"

Joan nodded numbly, watching Charlie disable her phone and her stomach suddenly cramped up in knots of trepidation as Charlie spoke.

"They're most likely both dead. If not, they're being drained of information at this very moment by some very bad men. So, I need to move and fast. I think...I don't know, but I suspect you might be in danger as well."

"Come with me if you want to live," Joan deadpanned in a terrible Arnold impersonation, and Charlie had to bite back a surprised laugh.

"Man, Joan, that was..."

"Impressive?"

"Terrible," he completed the sentence, but sensed the tension in the room dropped a bit.

"Seriously, Joan, this is very bad. I just had a friendly city cop come by with a bill of attainder with my name on it."

Joan blanched. A bill of attainder was something out of the pre-Revolutionary War era and was right up there with things the U.S. Constitution forbade. A bill of attainder was a legislative act that stripped a person or group of all civil rights and all property without trial.

"Are you kidding?" she asked, her voice like that of a small child.

"Well, they wanted to detain me for no other reason than I was a veteran with a history of medical treatment at the VA hospital and a member of the NRA. Here," Charlie paused, withdrawing the rolled-up document from his rear pocket. "Take a look and tell me what you think."

While Joan paused to examine the few pages of the detention order, Charlie prowled through the small apartment. He was fairly certain no one had bothered to bug the place, but he wanted to get a good look outside from all vantage points. By the time he was back near the front door, Joan was regarding him with frightened, tearful eyes.

"This is all real, isn't it? I mean, they killed your friends, and then came after you. What is going to happen next?"

Charlie shrugged. "When the President's reattempt to implement the Small Arms Bill failed to pass, I thought he was going to pull an Obama and simply try to continue chipping away at things with EOs. But, no, this is a Hail Mary move. Using the Safe Drinking Water Bill as a new tax source, as well as a lightning rod for protest, he might get the disaster he needs."

"What are you talking about? How can he *need* a disaster?"

"Remember the former mayor of Chicago? Rahm Emanual said, 'You never let a serious crisis go to waste'. That quote has followed the man around for years now, but what he said next is even scarier. The very next sentence out of the man's mouth was, 'What I mean by that, it's an opportunity to do things you could not do before'. See, if the President can provoke a violent reaction to this bill, which most people don't even understand, then he can use that violence as an excuse to sign yet another Executive Order. By ordering the police and the Feds to round up the NRA and veterans, he's almost guaranteeing that violent flare up he needs."

Joan followed along and frowned at Charlie's last sentence.

"What do you think he is going to do?"

"Well, apparently, he's already tossed the Constitution out the window," Charlie announced grimly, "so my guess is an EO banning sale or private possession of firearms for the duration of the emergency."

"An emergency that he masterminded," Joan whispered, her comprehension dawning. "And the federal courts have already been neutralized. Which means he can simultaneously order the detention of people who the administration feels might pose a threat. People like you."

"Yep. So, what about that detention order? Think we can get it overturned?"

Joan shook her head, her fingers white with tension as she gripped the pages. "If there was an uncompromised judge on the bench, not a problem. This is blatantly, patently illegal. As things stand now? You'd be dismissed without a hearing."

"Good thing we are bugging out, right now," Charlie declared. "I know a place outside town where we can lay low."

"The camp you talked about? The one I saw in those pictures at your place?"

"Yeah, that's the place," Charlie replied, pleased he'd taken the time to pack up all those photographs and pull the hard drive for his computer before leaving. "And we need to hit the road now. Since I'm a wanted fugitive and all."

"Won't the cops run your plates?"

Charlie laughed before answering.

"That's what took me so long to get over here. Picked up a set of plates at the long-term parking place over on Mitchell. Same model truck and everything."

"You are a sneaky one, Mr. Tucker," Joan said, nearly purring.

"You have no idea," Charlie muttered as Joan threw herself into finishing her packing.

Chapter Eighteen

Tampa, FL

For Bert Travis, life was good. He was standing on the deck of his thirty-four-foot Boston Whaler, *Lydia's Fancy*, and returning to the marina after a great day of fishing with three exhausted but still-enthused advertising execs out of Boston. They'd had a great run with Bert's assistance, and now the cooler fairly bulged with the fish the four of them had managed to wrestle into the boat.

"Fishing for tarpon is a full contact sport, guys," Bert had again warned the trio of first-timers, but they'd come to the charter boat operator as the best kind of clients, which was referrals from other satisfied customers. They would be trolling for the big game fish, but strictly as a catch-and-release for the tarpon, as was the custom. They were great fun to fight, but all those bones made for poor eating.

"We can take it, Bert." Bennie, the oldest of the admin, had assured their captain they were up to the challenge, and darned if he wasn't correct.

During a break in the action, one of the guys happened to notice Bert's shirt sleeves rise up when he was wrestling with a mahi-mahi that would be going back home with the guys after being processed. The ragged scar seemed to wrap around the charter captain's left forearm, almost like a three-dimensional tattoo. Bennie had seemed shocked by the sight, but the youngest of the three men, Dale, had just nodded to himself.

Later, when Bennie went below to grab another beer and Leon, the third member of their charter group, was occupied fighting a particularly feisty tarpon, Dale Gilford had approached Bert as he'd emerged from the cockpit.

"If you don't mind me asking, captain, where'd you serve?"

Given the polite inquiry, Bert replied, "Iraq and Afghanistan, with the 2nd of the 75th, a long time ago. How about you?"

"I did four years in the Navy. Did it to help pay for college, you know? I was a machinist mate second on the Iwo Jima, LDH-7. 75th? That's the Rangers, right?"

"Yes, sir," Bert replied with a grin. Despite his wounds and being jacked around by higher ups, Bert Travis was still proud of his service and his old outfit. Rolling up his sleeve, he showed Dale the slightly faded tattoo of his Ranger tab on his upper arm, and further exposed the scars as Dale could now see the puckered divots of gunshot wounds in the charter boat captain's arm.

"Jeez, captain, it's a miracle you kept the arm," Dale blurted out, then colored when he realized what he'd said.

"Miracle alright," Bert replied, not taking offense. He knew the younger man had merely been surprised, and Bert was well past any shyness about the injuries he'd sustained. He'd survived, after all. He might be older now and carrying a bit of extra weight around the midsection, but by God, somewhere inside, he was still Pirate.

"Got pretty much the same on the other arm. And it *was* a miracle. I was in the hospital for near on six months and can't tell you how many surgeries, but here I am, doing what God intended me to do. Reintroducing swabbies to the sea."

Dale, taken off guard by Bert's pronouncement, burst into a fit of laughter that had Bert chuckling as well. Bennie came up in time to see the end of the exchange, but just shook his head and handed Dale a beer.

Yes, it had been a good day, and despite some rocky points along the way, Bert was pleased with the way life had worked out for him. He had a great family and a job he loved. Not much given to introspection, Bert wondered why he suddenly felt a sense of nostalgia roll over him as he piloted the boat into harbor at the Clearwater Municipal Marina.

I guess talking to Dale brought up some of the old memories, Bert thought, as he guided the Boston Whaler into its accustomed berth and he saw his wife standing there to catch the rope, tossed quite expertly by Dale. He grinned at his wife, but quickly noted her tight features and firmly set jaw, and instinctively knew something must be troubling her.

164

Getting the fishermen off the boat took a few minutes and a hearty round of handshakes and manly fist bumps as Bert's two hands, Damon and Sam, hustled to unload the gear and the aluminum coolers filled with the mahi-mahi and grouper that made up their catch of the day. Those coolers would go straight to the marina-side processor before being delivered, packed in dry ice, to the hotel where the three clients were staying. It was an extra expense, and one that Bert routinely recommended for the ease of transport offered by the service.

When Bert finally completed his chores, including making arrangements to get *Lydia's Fancy* refueled, he found Lydia waiting in their small charter service office, glued to the television set behind the counter. Most often tuned into the Weather Channel, he noted the CNN logo in the corner and saw his wife's expression, if anything, had grown more concerned.

"What's going on?" Bert asked, and Lydia bolted from her seat to grab her husband in a tight embrace before drawing back to gaze up at him. He read the apprehension there in her beautiful green eyes, and Bert knew something terrible must have happened.

"Oh, Bert, it's horrible," she murmured, burying her face into his salt-encrusted shirt.

"Was it another terror attack?" he nearly demanded, feeling the room begin to spin at the thought. Not again. "Are the kids okay?"

"Kids are fine," she replied quickly, knowing her husband's first fear. "They're with your mom and dad right now. But, Bert, there's just so many things going on, I'm having a hard time keeping up. This past week has been crazy with all the violence. And the President was on earlier."

"Now I'm really worried," Bert muttered. "Okay, start at the beginning," he continued, his voice louder now. As he spoke, he picked up his cell phone from the charger on the desk. After losing one expensive phone overboard during a squall, Bert Travis had learned his lesson and left the device behind. He had a perfectly good radio on the *Lydia's Fancy*, as well as an emergency satellite phone locked up in the forward compartment, and that was all he needed.

"Well, there were more protests this morning," Lydia began, wringing her hands in a nervous habit Bert had noted over the years but had never mentioned. "Something about some new water bill that Congress just passed. I really don't understand all the fuss, but apparently it got a lot of farmers and special interest groups stirred up."

As Lydia spoke, Bert looked over her shoulder to see what looked like a full-scale riot taking place on the television screen. He saw black-uniformed police carrying shields and batons and behind them, other officers in tactical gear bearing what appeared like M4 carbines. "Not good," he whispered. Then he looked at the bottom of the screen and saw the location listed as Des Moines, Iowa.

"Why the heck is there rioting in Des Moines?"

"Not just there," Lydia continued. "All morning and into the day, the violence has been spreading. I don't know exactly what has been setting these people off, but the reporters have been talking about white supremacists and other hate groups organizing these protests. The Attorney General was on next, talking about former military members in their ranks."

"This is crazy," Bert said with a scowl. "The Aryan Nation is going out stirring up trouble with farmers? I just don't see that happening. Are we having trouble around here? I didn't see any smoke when we were coming back, but then I wasn't looking for it."

"There was a report about trouble in Tallahassee, and then something down in Miami, but not around here yet. But you haven't heard the latest. Honey, when the President was on, he announced other groups were working with the rioters. He said…he said the NRA was working with them, Bert. He said he had signed orders identifying them as domestic terrorists."

"What the hell?!" Bert exclaimed. "He seriously claimed, on national TV, that the NRA was a terrorist organization? That is just insane, Lydia. I know he hates them, but that's just going too far."

"Bert, he didn't just announce it," Lydia replied, looking down at the desk as she gathered her thoughts. "They are going around arresting the leadership. There's already been fighting over that, too. They had video on earlier. It was horrible, honey. It looked like something you'd see in a movie, not in real life."

While Lydia spoke, Bert stood trying to take in everything his wife was saying while also watching the changing scenes on the television screen. Glancing down, he absently noted he had a pair of missed calls and two new voicemails. Entering his passcode, the year of his wife's birth, he recognized both calls had come from the number belonging to his friend, Charlie Tucker. Not one to believe in coincidence, Bert pressed play and speaker, so Lydia could also hear the messages.

Thirty seconds. He listened to Charlie's voice, and heard the worry in the man's voice as he shared what he knew. About the water bill, and the violence and why he thought everything was happening this way. Crazy conspiracy stuff. He looked at Lydia and saw the doubt and fear in her eyes.

Not waiting to discuss the first message, Bert pressed play for the second, expecting it to be a repeat of the first. Instead, he heard a different one, and he felt his skin crawl.

"Uncle is listening, but Bert, get your family and get out. They are sending out teams to pick us up. May have already hit your house. Just talked my way out with the local fuzz, but they could be back with more. I'm gone. Get your family, pack your gear and head for Happy Days. Be safe. Out."

"What does that all mean? Teams? Why would they want you? Or Charlie?" Lydia cried out. "You aren't soldiers anymore, and you sure aren't terrorists."

Robert Travis, Jr., Bert to his friends, just shook his head slowly as he felt his world turn into a nightmare. As he processed the message, he realized the voice he'd heard in the second call was different from the first. The first was from his old friend Charlie, and he'd sounded scared. The second though, was from Book, his brother-at-arms. And he'd sounded ice-cold, just like he did on a mission.

"Get your bugout bag out of your car, honey. Then let's go get Mom and Dad and the kids."

"What are you planning, Bert?" Lydia was better, now. Bert knew from sailing, that his wife was always a steady hand in the worst storms, and he knew a storm was coming.

"What we should have done last week when these riots started. We're going to load up all the food and supplies we can access here, then we are taking the Whaler and the Hansen up to that old fishing camp in Waccasassa Bay. You know, the one Dad showed us that time?"

"What? Are you crazy? We are just going to walk away and leave everything behind? Bert, we've got people coming in tomorrow for charters," Lydia protested, but Bert knew his wife.

Her protests lacked conviction and besides, with the violence only continuing to spread, who knew if those people would actually show up? Just to be sure, though...

"Alright, then. Lydia, call the numbers you have for the charters tomorrow. Cancel them, due to the worsening security conditions. Offer them a refund or to reschedule. I'll get Mom and Dad and we can start from there, but we are casting off before dark."

"What about Bill?"

Bill was Bert's younger brother, and another captain with the charter service. He lived twenty minutes away, with a girlfriend and an Irish Setter named Boo. Bert liked the dog. The girlfriend, not so much.

"I'll call and extend the invite. See what he says. Either way, Mom and Dad are going with us. Dad's a Life member of the NRA and before he started having his health problems, you know he was heavily involved in organizing the state shooting competitions."

Lydia nodded, then said a little prayer. Lydia believed in the power of prayer, and she had a sudden flash of insight that she needed all the help she could get to keep her family safe.

For Bert, he thought about the earlier flashback he'd experienced when talking to Dale and wondered how much he would need to bring back that old swashbuckling persona if his family was going to live. His Ranger career might have been cut short by his injuries, but he knew he still had the heart that had gotten him through everything the Army, and the hadjis, could throw at him.

Chapter Nineteen

Kenosha, WI

Robbie had spent the last few days balancing his real estate business with his final preparations. His credit card took a hit, and he intended to pay off his purchases…maybe. The billing cycle for the biggest ticket items would begin the next month. He tossed his bag in the back of Jerome's truck on top of the mountain of supplies he hadn't dropped at the retreat.

"With my low interest credit cards, I bet I'll have my goodies paid off in a thousand years." Robbie checked the waterproof plastic case and tucked it under his backpack near the rear of the truck bed. "You have to love next day delivery."

"You sure about us taking separate vehicles? I mean, what if we get separated or something?" Jerome closed the tailgate and locked the back window of the camper top.

"They are not looking for you, man. I'm probably a target as far as Charlie knows, but this truck and the company listed on the registration is in your name. I'll go ahead and look for traffic jams since the bike is more maneuverable."

"Yeah, but you are a sitting duck on your Harley."

"I'm not leaving my baby behind. I bet the local PD is going to trash my house looking for me, if they don't torch the place with flashbangs first." Robbie cranked up the Harley and worked to get the radio in the helmet to connect to the radio strapped to the fuel tank of the bike. "Radio check. Come in, Roadrunner."

"Why do I have to be the Roadrunner, Coyote? It's because I'm black, right?" Jerome jerked his chain over the CB radio.

"Nope. You are kinda birdlike." Robbie pulled the garage door transmitter and closed the overhead door and armed the alarm system. "Let's move, Roadrunner. We have miles to cover."

"Roger, Coyote," Jerome replied into the microphone.

"No, it's Coyote, not Roger," Robbie chuckled into the internal mic in the helmet. He felt the pressure to get to Oak Lawn in the western suburbs and get to the retreat with the kids and Kristi. Jerome's kids could ride with him in his truck, and Kristi would use her own car. At least that was how he had planned the exodus from the metro area.

After he got the call to bug out, Robbie had called Kristi multiple times in the next few hours, but she didn't answer her cell phone. The kids should be home since it was Sunday, and Kristi hadn't mentioned anything on the schedule when he'd checked in the day before.

Since the rioting had gotten worse, Robbie had checked in with the family each evening for a solid week. He anticipated a day when he would have to load up and run like hell. In preparation for that day, Blaster had cleared out his house and sanitized it of all connections to the retreat.

Robbie had left a message for the kids to get their camping gear ready and have the house ready for a surprise vacation when he pulled in. Emily and Clark knew how to pack to go camping, but Robbie didn't want to say too much over the phone. This trip may prove to be a permanent move.

Robbie and Jerome kept their speed within the posted limits and Robbie cringed when they passed a traffic camera. His plates on the Harley could be linked back to him, and if what Charlie told him was true, the locals and feds would want to talk to him in a windowless room without the benefit of legal representation. Surviving in the pokey without an arm would mark him instantly, so Robbie avoided the toll roads that looped around Chicagoland, and he led Jerome directly into the belly of the beast. He wanted to go south on Green Bay Road to avoid the tolls on I-94, then hit the Skokie Highway out of Gurnee. Jerome complained about dealing with the lights and traffic, but Blaster had already made the trip multiple times on dry runs to Ohio.

Outside of Northbrook, the pair merged with I-94 until it bottlenecked into the I-90 split. Robbie led Jerome off the interstate and hit Cicero Avenue.

Robbie keyed the mic. "Stay right on my tail, Roadrunner. The neighborhoods get sketchy in a little bit."

"No shit! I had one of my work trucks jacked near Cicero on the West Side. I promised to never come back here again."

Robbie had his own "vibrant" experiences around the Garfield Park area in the past. He'd had to bluff his way through a group of toughs waiting outside of the Green Line stop at Kedzie when a client had mistakenly decided to ride the train to look at a piece of property two blocks from the EL. Robbie had flashed his "claw" at the crew and smiled at them. The youths, confused by the crazy man with the metal prosthetic, had backed off and let him escort the woman to the property unmolested.

Taking their route through the roughest sections of Chicago seemed silly to Jerome until Robbie had explained his thinking. They'd sat around the kitchen table at Robbie's home and hatched the plan weeks ago. "The police basically leave those communities alone to their own devices during the day. I didn't see anyone actively dealing on Cicero because that's a major street, and I think it's a dividing line for some of the GD's and the Unknowns."

"How can you be sure about that?" Jerome asked.

"I ran that stretch during the day and later at night to check it out. Nobody came out at the lights to offer me anything," Robbie shrugged.

"Offered you what?" Jerome scratched his head.

Robbie smiled. "Anything. On the back streets along that stretch, you can find just about anything for sale, but the dealers stay off Cicero. It's too public and well-lit. The stupid police cameras don't hurt either."

"Are you worried about the 'blue light specials' seeing us on the move?"

"Please, that's Chicago PD's cameras. They had to make them bullet resistant to keep the locals from shooting them out faster than they could put them up. Once we cross into Oak Lawn, those things dry up."

"What if we get stopped?"

"If it's local cops, we give out license and insurance and look lost. If it's the feds, we are screwed. Hell, Chicago isn't the problem. We still have to cross Indiana and most of Ohio before we are home free." Robbie had tried to reassure his friend, but he felt the plan's simplicity made it easier to accomplish.

Get the kids and Kristi out of there before the dance started.

The slower surface streets in Chicago decreased their pace and added an extra hour to the drive. Even for a low traffic Sunday, the eighty miles between Kenosha and Oak Lawn dragged on, and the congestion at Midway Airport and the stupid mall down the street from the bustling airport had Blaster chomping at the bit.

When they pulled in front of Kristi's house, Robbie shook out his right hand and stretched. The next leg of the trip would take another six hours to complete if the traffic behaved, but Robbie had a route that took them around the Tri-State Tollway and used Highway 30, instead of the interstates around Gary. His intuition said to stay off the main roads, so he'd scouted the route in advance.

Robbie took off his helmet and checked on Jerome. "We made it, buddy! Do you see your ex-wife's car around here?" Robbie scanned the residential street.

"I don't see her. I gave her the address and asked her to come by with the kids, so we could visit. She had better not screw up our plans."

Robbie clapped Jerome on the shoulder and headed to the front door. "Watch out for them and keep an eye on the truck. Let me see what Kristi is up to." Before Robbie could knock, Clark ripped the door open.

"Where's Momma?" Clark asked Robbie and looked out to the street.

Robbie almost dropped on the porch in a panic attack. "She's not here? Where is your sister?"

"She's packing everything under the sun. How long are we going? What about school?" Clark looked excited to get out and have some fun after the long winter.

Robbie pushed past Clark and raced into the kitchen. He hit the play button on the answering machine. The speaker played the last message which ended up being a hang up. The caller ID displayed a local number with a Chicago area code, but no new messages. He hit the play button again and listened to ten saved messages and skipped through them with Clark standing at the counter. The third from last message was from the hospital. The woman's voice over the speaker informed Kristi that all on-call staff members had been ordered to show up to handle an emergency.

"Where have you guys been? I called earlier to let you know. You got the message, but where were you?"

Clark shrugged. "Mom sent us next door to the Ramirez's. She said she would be home around noon or so because they didn't like her to get overtime. I came in to get some bread for us to make sandwiches and heard your message. We've been here since then, getting our packs ready. Is Momma coming, too?"

Before Robbie could answer, Emily ran in and gave him a hug. "Uncle Robbie, how long are we going to be gone? I have a project for school due this week." Robbie returned the hug.

"I'll write you a note. This is an educational trip anyway, so we can write a report to cover your tail with the teachers. Everybody likes a go-getter. Are you packed?"

"Not yet. I can't decide what to bring. When is Momma getting back? She's been out all day." Emily sounded worried.

"I'm going to call her and check in. Get your bags finished up and..." Robbie's voice trailed off. "She took her SUV into work, didn't she?"

"She did. Why?" Clark asked.

Robbie sat at the table and rubbed at his forehead. "We were going to take that loaded with your stuff. There's not enough room in the truck for all of us and Jerome's kids."

"Are they coming with us? Reese and James are little kids and I like them, but they don't know much about camping, do they?" Clark asked.

Leaning back in the chair, Robbie scoffed, "It's not their fault. Charlene won't let them hang out with their dad and learn some things. She's supposed to be coming by to let their dad see them, but she is a no-show." He pulled out his phone and opened his address book to find the emergency contact number for Kristi's department at the hospital. "Go on up and help your sister. I've gotta talk to your mother."

Clark nodded. "Sure. Hey, do you know what's for supper? It's getting close to that time."

"I have no idea right now. We should be on the highway eating greasy fast food and singing road tunes by now." Robbie picked up the house phone and dialed the hospital and waited as the phone at the nurses' station rang off the hook for a minute before anyone picked up.

"First Floor, this is Marjorie, can you hold, please?" the voice called out and immediately placed Robbie on hold before he could state his business. The background noise from the floor at the hospital had sounded chaotic from that brief second.

"Oh, hell," Robbie whispered to himself. That sound of overlapping panicked voices and the clatter of instruments being trundled around on carts brought back the old memories. The hospital, not five miles away, sounded like a war zone. Robbie carried the phone to the front door and stepped out to the porch. He waved at Jerome before settling into one of the metal chairs.

From their drive in, neither Robbie nor Jerome had heard the distinctive pop, pop, pop, pop from the neighborhoods off in the distance. The sound of distant fireworks, that Robbie knew were gunshots, sent a shiver down the back of his neck and an involuntary injection of adrenaline to his system.

"Jerome! Do you hear that?" he called to his friend sitting in the truck.

Jerome leaned his head out of the driver's side window and cupped his ear. "What is that?"

"It's started." Robbie stared at the phone in his hand as the hold music played on. His plans to race the Wheaton family out of the city to the safety of the retreat slipped away.

The music stopped, and the phone clicked once before a voice cut into his thoughts. "This is Marjorie, how can I direct your call?"

Robbie made a split-second decision. "Marjorie, this is Detective Sparks from the Oak Lawn Police Department. I need to contact Kristi Wheaton concerning her children. This is an emergency. Can you get her for me?"

"We are overloaded with our own emergency over here. I'll try to shake her loose." The line switched over to music again. In the background noise, Robbie had picked up the piercing wail of someone having the worst day of their life at the hospital.

Jerome left the truck and walked up the porch steps. "What's going on, Robbie?"

"I'm guessing here, but the hospitals are getting slammed." Another string of 'fireworks' let off in the distance and had an accompaniment of slower blasts. "Pistol and shotgun, based on the sound." Robbie reached to adjust his pistol, concealed by his leather jacket and under his left armpit.

"It's getting hot out there," Jerome cocked his head and listened to the sirens in the distance responding to the gunfire.

"Kristi got called in early. My question is, how the heck did they know to call in their on-call staff unless someone predicted this was coming?" Robbie mused.

Clark tromped down the stairs with his backpack loaded up and ready to go. "I'm ready. Emily is almost done." He dropped the pack by the door and stepped out to listen to the distant gun battles playing out in the neighborhoods to the north. "What the heck? It's not the Fourth of July yet."

"Clark, this camping excursion is looking more like a permanent move. I've got the hospital on the line, and I'll let your mom know what's going down. Go inside and fill every bottle you can with water and fill up the tubs. This may turn into something bad."

With his mouth dropping open, Clark looked at Robbie first before turning to look at Jerome. "He's serious, son. We came here to move all of us to the camp in Ohio. Some crazy mess is coming our way, and we need to get out of here before it hits," Jerome said as he sat in the chair beside Robbie and listened to the sounds of the city trying to tear itself apart.

Chapter Twenty

Hardin County, Ohio

Sitting in his small living room when he hung up his phone, Randy looked over at Cody. "We need to move," he said, getting up.

"Was that Book?" Cody asked, looking up from his laptop.

"Yeah, he said we need to pack up and head to the retreat," Randy told him, moving over and looking at the screen.

Nodding as he looked back at the screen, "That is smart. We aren't tied to the land, so nobody will know to look for us there," Cody said. "He get in touch with Robbie?"

"Yeah, and Robbie is going to get Kristi with Jerome," Randy answered, seeing Cody was in a chat room. "Who are you chatting with?"

"No one really, but there is a lot of chat about the feds going after any former military. Especially any with ties to the Oathkeepers or NRA," Cody said and held up a small notepad. "I've been keeping tabs since the presidential address and found out they have detained almost a thousand that fit that category, but the worst is I've heard of over two dozen shootings of vets that fit that profile."

"Believe nothing you hear and only half of what you see," Randy said, walking away.

Watching Randy head to the door, Cody got up and followed. "Randy, if it was only one or two I could follow that idiom, but this is coming from different areas of the nation," Cody explained, following him outside. "Think about it, Randy. These are the people they know can fight and know what the government is doing is illegal. Charlie didn't say why we needed to haul ass, did he?"

"No, but it has to be a good reason," Randy said, heading to his parents' house.

"Like they tried to arrest Charlie?" Cody snapped, and Randy froze and looked at him hard. "Randy, Book is the definition of what they are after. He's not in the ACLU, but he's a lawyer, a veteran, and a member of the NRA. He can prove legally that they are wrong but more importantly, he knows how to fight them outside of the courtroom with physical force. Charlie knows every cell phone call is registered in a NSA data bank. Since he is already in that top tier, his number is already being monitored."

Feeling his heartrate speed up, Randy started feeling lightheaded. "Cody, this is the country we fought for," Randy said in shock.

"Yeah, and it's not those in the office. It's the ideas set down by farmers centuries ago. That is what America is; rights of individuals. Rights that can't be limited or taken away by those sitting high and mighty," Cody said as Randy blinked rapidly and turned away, looking out over the fields.

"They can't," Randy finally said.

"Sure they can, if nobody fights them," Cody scoffed. "The means of self-defense is the most precious of rights, and governments have fought to keep the population unarmed, long before firearms."

"Cody, I know commoners were restricted from carrying weapons in the later middle ages-," Randy stopped as Cody held up his hand.

"Yes, because that was the times when empires were established and kings ruled. But if you look further back, you can find many instances of once-small kingdoms established and starting those laws. Once someone got control of an area, they wanted to make sure they were the only ones to have weapons. They could care less if the peasants were raped and killed, as long as the monarchs weren't challenged in their rule. Those in charge had protection, just like now. That's who they are going after now. The ones who can fight but more importantly, the ones who *know* how to fight, legally and with force."

Slowly turning back to look at Cody, Randy studied his innocent face and then smiled. "Babyface, Charlie has truly corrupted you," Randy grinned, and Cody took a breath to speak but Randy stopped him. "No, you're right. I'm just blinded by the fact we live in America. *'If the representatives of the people betray their constituents, there is no recourse left but in the exertion of that original right of self-defense which is paramount to all positive forms of government'."*

Giving a curt laugh, Cody nodded. "Alexander Hamilton, <u>Federalist #28</u>," Cody answered as Randy turned and headed for the house. "Okay, how about: *Guns are completely inappropriate for the kind of sheep-like people the anointed envision or the orderly, prepackaged world in which they are to live. When you are in mortal danger, you are supposed to dial 911, so that the police can arrive on the scene sometime later, identify your body, and file reports in triplicate."*

Trotting up the stairs, Randy thought as he grabbed the handle of the door. "Oh, Thomas Sowell," he replied.

"Damn, I thought I had you," Cody huffed, following Randy inside. This was one game the guys had always played, going all the way back to when they were in the army, reciting quotes and seeing who could answer.

They stopped and saw the kitchen table stacked with boxes of food and crates of jarred and canned food. They turned to see Oliver and Lena watching the TV. On the screen, a reporter was standing outside of a nice house while black-clad federal agents stormed the structure.

"This is Rhonda Tillman, live at the home of NRA executive Timothy Benson, who for the last four hours, has been in a gun battle with federal agents of the FBI, Homeland, and BATFE when they moved in to arrest him. We have not been told how many agents have been injured but just a few minutes ago, several explosions were heard inside the house and the agents stormed it. We have just now been cleared by authorities to come closer to film the apprehension," a young woman said as gunfire roared in the background.

"We have been told by the FBI's spokesman that they tried to apprehend Mr. Benson peacefully, but he fired on the officers," Rhonda said as the gunfire died down and a man walked up wearing a windbreaker with the Homeland insignia on the chest. "Agent Gibson, has the accused been apprehended?"

The man stopped and looked at Rhonda. "That's the report I am receiving," he said as more men rushed the house.

"Can you tell us if any agents have been injured and if they have, how many?"

Gibson adjusted his stance and stood tall. "I can say, some agents were injured but other than that, not until next of kin have been notified."

Visibly taken back, Rhonda's hand holding the microphone dropped to her waist. "Agents were killed?" she asked in shock.

"Rhonda, microphone," someone said behind the camera and Rhonda raised her microphone and repeated the question.

Slowly, Gibson nodded. "Yes. Mr. Benson refused to be detained until cleared and have his weapons confiscated. He sent his family to his brother's home and waited for agents to arrive."

"Is his family in custody?"

"As of now, no. They weren't on the detain list," Gibson explained as men started coming out of the house.

"Have you had any other trouble from other executives of the NRA or ACLU?" Rhonda asked.

"Unfortunately, yes, along with the members of the NRA. They don't understand that the Second Amendment, like all rights of the Constitution, can be suspended for the greater good in times of crisis or at Homeland's request. We have done it repeatedly and now they think we can't anymore," Gibson said while more officers came out of the house. Then, officers came out escorting a middle-aged man in handcuffs and ankle shackles in the 'perp walk'. With a busted lip and swollen right eye, the man's clothes were ripped and barely hanging on him as he continued to fight against the agents.

When they paraded the man past, Rhonda moved from Gibson and thrust her microphone into Mr. Benson's face. "Mr. Benson, what caused you to finally surrender?" she shouted out and Mr. Benson suddenly stopped fighting the agents and turned to Rhonda.

"I didn't surrender! I ran out of bullets!" he bellowed as the agents dragged him to a black van and tossed him in.

"Yep," Randy grinned and nodded, "That's why I'm a member of the NRA."

"They killed the president of the ACLU," Oliver said, staring at the TV. "They claimed he fought back by shooting at agents, but he was the biggest anti-gun lawyer the ACLU had."

179

"Die fighting or under the boot," Randy sighed, then jerked his thumb over his shoulder. "What's with emptying the pantry?"

"Hook up the flatbed trailer so we can load this, and you can take it to the retreat," Oliver said.

"Okay, but where is yours and Momma's stuff?"

Oliver looked into Randy's eyes and Randy felt his knees get weak. "Son, your mom and I are staying here. We can't be living in the backwoods. Hell, we are both on medications and if this doesn't end soon, we would be a burden on the group," Oliver said.

"Pops, come on now!" Cody cried out, moving over beside Randy, who was catatonic. "You and Mom need to come with us. You were in the military and both are members of the NRA."

"Cody, Lena and I are almost seventy. We aren't in danger, but you two and the others are," Oliver told him firmly.

Lena turned away from the TV and wiped tears off her cheeks. "This will blow over in a month or two, but Oliver and I have to go get medicine," she said and patted Cody's cheek. She turned to Randy and smiled at him. "Don't make momma repeat herself, load this up, and you two get. We will be fine if you two aren't here. We'll just tell them you left."

"Mom," Randy protested, and Lena held up her hand.

"Randy, we taught you better manners than that. Now if this lasts longer, we'll try to get more medicine so if we need to, we can join you," Lena smiled at him. "Now, we don't know how long you have, so move."

Reaching out, Randy hugged his mom tight. "I'll check on you," he mumbled.

"No, son. They might watch the house," Oliver said as Randy released his mom. No sooner than Randy released his hug, Cody latched Lena in a tight hug.

"You and Pops stay safe," Cody said in a breaking voice, fighting not to cry.

"Oh, shush," Lena said, hugging him tight. "You don't worry about us. We are just old country folk and they won't mess with us."

Randy hugged his dad and then Cody did. "Son, hook the flatbed to your Blazer and the covered cargo trailer to your work truck. We'll load them, and you and Cody can take them to the retreat. Then you can ride Robbie's dirt bike back. I'll load the horses up to my truck and Cody can drive his car back, and you can take my truck with the horses," Oliver instructed.

"Dad, that's your new truck and it has the diesel tank in the bed," Randy protested.

"My old one works just as well," Oliver said, smiling. "I'll just drive the tractors up here to refuel them."

With a heavy heart, Randy and Cody went outside to hook up the trailers and Lena turned to Oliver. "I'm not being taken from our land," she vowed, holding her chin high.

"After we get them gone we will set up for a fight, but I think they will leave us be with the boys gone. Remember, we are going to tell them the boys went to turn themselves in," Oliver said.

Walking over, Lena wrapped her arms around him. "We can't let them find where the family goes," Lena said softly. "They killed a man who everyone knows didn't have a gun and announced it publicly. I don't think they will feel restrained because we are senior citizens."

"Lena, we would be a burden on them in a few months and if this goes on that long, that would be just the time it will be getting hard on them," Oliver reminded her, then hugged her tight.

"I know, and I agree that we should stay, but they won't make me talk," Lena stated, burrowing her face in Oliver's chest. "If they take me, they can make me talk."

Reaching down, Oliver lifted her chin to look at him. "If it comes to that, we won't run out of bullets. They will have to kill us," he vowed.

Hearing a truck back up, they released their hugs and moved to the table and started moving supplies to the trailer. Each said a silent prayer that this would end soon, and the boys could come home.

In two hours, Randy and Cody met at the trucks after loading up. "I disabled the OnStar," Cody told him. "Turn your phone off and leave it here with Mom and Pop. In case the others call," he said and handed Randy a cheap cell phone. "I gave the number to Mom and Pop, it's a disposable phone. I think you should keep it off and only turn it on every few hours to check for messages, in case they are tracking cell towers."

Too emotionally drained to question Cody, Randy nodded before taking the new phone and climbing in his work truck, and they were soon heading south to the retreat.

Randy's work truck was a small rolling machine shop he used to work on sites where he was needed. It was a one-and-a-half-ton truck with workboxes loaded with tools. There was a small vertical milling machine, CNC lathe, along with a welder and other tools of his trade.

Never in his life did Randy think he had that much stuff in his house that he thought he might need. Emptying his gun safe, Randy had over thirty guns and almost that many at the retreat, but before he let the government take them, he would melt the damn things down.

Driving down the highway, Randy grinned, thinking of Cody loading the computer he had set up in his room at Randy's house. Then he'd chuckled at watching Cody load all the game platforms along with a thirty-inch flat screen TV. Cody only had his XD and AR which he carried with him in his car when he moved from house to house. The rest of Cody's guns were at the retreat.

The retreat was the only real place Cody called 'his'. Granted, he had his own area and room at each of the three's homes, but that small cabin and storage containers at the retreat held most of Cody's possessions.

Each of the group kept a majority of their shooting gear at the retreat, but Randy never realized just how much gear he'd had at his house. When he'd opened a storage box, Randy had found more of his prosthetics that he had quit using but he took them anyway. He had two more like the one he was wearing, and they were the best. The others he could work on and make them almost identical to the ones he liked.

Reaching up, he turned on the radio and the announcer was listing more cities that had riots. Surprisingly, New York wasn't listed, but L.A. had so many fires burning, the fire department had called on the forestry service to start air drops across the city until two tankers were shot up.

Feeling disgusted, Randy punched the CD player and listened to rock. "Book, Blaster, you boys better keep your shit wired tight," he mumbled and settled into the seat.

Chapter Twenty-One

Chicago

Still on hold for Kristi, Robbie set the handset in his lap and hit the speaker button. Light jazz played from the holding call.

"We have to make a decision soon, Robbie. It's going to get worse by the sounds of it." Jerome scanned the empty sidewalk in front of the house.

"Clark, can you go turn on the TV in the living room and crank the sound up, so we can hear it out here? I want to hear if the news outlets are making any announcements," Robbie said as he shifted in the chair and felt the extra magazine dig into his side from the holder clipped to his belt.

Clark didn't reply, but he did go inside and find a local station playing a sitcom. The canned laughter grated on Robbie's frazzled nerves. Jerome's phone lit up and played the cheerful chime.

"This is Jerome. How can I help you?" Jerome answered. He placed the call on speakerphone.

"Mr. Putnam? This is Guardian Security. You are listed as an emergency contact for Mr. Lennox's home. We have detected an alarm at his home, at the first zone in the system. How do you want us to respond?" Robbie sat forward and waved at Jerome. He made a cutting motion with his right hand.

"I'm sorry, this is the wrong number. I do not know a Mr. Lennox, and I am unaware of the circumstances for the alarm. Good evening," Jerome cut the man off and stared at Robbie. "They hit your house."

"They can track that call. Dammit, that was fast. Pull the card out of your phone, Jerome. We have to go dark as shit now. Expect all communications to be tracked from this point forward. Dammit!" Robbie gripped the handset and glared at the speaker, willing it to stop and for Kristi to pick up.

With his large calloused hands, Jerome fumbled with his phone until Clark sat back down and held out his hand. "I got this, Mr. Putnam. Those little SIM cards can be a bugger to get out." The teen pulled the card from the phone and handed it back to Jerome. "Why are you freaked out, Uncle Robbie?"

"They raided my house less than four hours after Charlie called me and warned us to haul ass. Sorry, 'butt'." Robbie shook his head. "Don't tell your momma I slipped up."

"Why isn't she coming to the phone?" Jerome asked.

Robbie shrugged, "It has to be bad over there. Darn it, I'm going to get her!" Robbie stood just as Kristi's voice blasted from the speaker.

"Where are my children?! What's happened to them?!"

Leaning back and almost expecting Kristi to jump out of the small phone, Robbie barked, "Easy, Momma Bear. It's Robbie. We are at your house getting ready to get out of here before the hammer falls. When are you getting home?"

Jerome leaned in and spoke into the speaker, "Hey, Mrs. Wheaton. I'm here to waiting for my kids to show up, so we can all get gone."

"Hello, Jerome. Robbie, the kids are next door with Mrs. Ramirez. Tell her I'm sorry for dumping them on her all day." Kristi's voice faded for a second before she came back. "Robbie, I can't leave. We are swamped with surgeries, and cops are posted all over the place. I think they mean to keep us here. They told us food would be provided and union rules for overtime have been suspended for the duration of the incident."

Robbie took a breath before he responded. "Is there a way for me to come and slip you out? Tell them you have a family crisis or something?"

"They are arresting people left and right for obstructing the police when they try to force their way in. My department head, Janice… Well, her husband tried to come see her and got thrown to the floor and cuffed. It's not safe for you to come up here."

"I can't stay here, Kristi. They are looking for me, and they may have already raided my place. Can I take Clark and Emily out of here?" Robbie asked. Clark and his mother answered at the same time.

"I'm not going anywhere without my Mom," Clark protested.

Hearing Clark, Kristi agreed with Robbie, "They will be safer with you, won't they?"

Jerome split the decision for them. "Robbie, they are looking for you. If they catch you on the road, what happens to them? I'll stay here and look out for them until Kristi can get loose. We'll take her SUV out of the city then."

"I didn't think about that." Robbie relented, "I can't put them at risk." Robbie thought for a few seconds. Glancing away, Robbie thought about how many things could go wrong during a felony stop with Clark and Emily watching their uncle get lit up by anxious feds.

"Robbie, go. I'll be okay," Kristi said quietly through the phone.

Looking at the phone with a scowl, Robbie shook his head, "Wheat would kick my tail for leaving you and the kids here. We made a promise for all of you. I can't turn tail and run when you and the kids are stuck here. It's not safe for you."

Kristi sighed, "I know, but you can't fight this on your own."

"Not alone, I can't," Robbie grumbled.

"Jerome, do you mind watching over the kids until I can get home?" she asked.

Jerome laughed, "Not at all. I'm waiting on my own kids to show up anyway. Robbie can take my truck and I'll wait here for you, if you don't mind?"

"That's fine. The SUV will be cramped, though, with all of us piled in there." Kristi's voice cut out for a second as someone else spoke from near the receiver.

"You need to wrap it up, Kristi. The next case is rolling back in a few, and the room needs to be turned over still. Housekeeping can't keep up, so we are picking up the slack." The voice sounded friendly but brittle.

"Okay, I'm almost done," Kristi responded to the voice. "I gotta go. Jerome, keep my kids safe. I'll be home soon. Robbie, hit the road. Tell the boys we are fine for now."

"Kristi, if I don't hear from you in six hours, I'm bringing the team back in here to extract you and the kids. Call me on Clark's phone when you hear something. He doesn't know it yet, but he is donating it to his Uncle Robbie." Clark smiled and tossed the phone over.

"Why's that?" Kristi asked.

"Don't call any of the boys. I'm betting that most of us are under electronic surveillance. Only call here or Clark's phone from now on. I can't tell anyone else my plan until I see them in person. I hope they have the sense not to call here." Robbie thought for a second. "I'll get down the road and call from a truck stop along the way."

"Well, get going. I'll see you all soon," Kristi promised, then said goodbye to Robbie and told Clark to mind Jerome until she got home.

Robbie hung up and gripped the phone tight. "Jerome, can you get my bike locked up in the garage?" He passed his keys over. "I don't want it out on the street, in case someone comes by running plates. You remember that time we all got ticketed because we didn't have the city permits to park on their beloved streets? If my motorcycle tag gets run, you will have a damn hit squad kicking in your doors and tossing in flashbangs. Hell, take my plates off and hide them if you get a chance."

"If I can figure out your janky clutch, sure." Jerome jingled the keys before pocketing them. "You going to take care of my truck?"

"Man, it's the only way I can see me getting out of here and back without throwing up red flags. I'm not going to speed or wreck it, if that's what you're wondering."

"I'm more worried you're going to drive it into a roadblock and go out guns blazing," Jerome chuckled.

With a long sigh, Robbie shifted in his seat. "No. I have to be all meek and mild, so I can get these kids safe. I made a promise."

"Tell Emily 'bye' then, son. I got this. You guys turned this place into a fortress. Nobody gets in here without a key or my say-so." Jerome clapped Robbie on the prosthetic forearm and smiled.

Robbie stood and went inside to find Emily glued to the television. The news had broken about the "riots" across the major cities. In stunned horror, Robbie watched windows being smashed and stores looted while cars and trash cans burned. A storefront, engulfed in flames, had people still running in to grab hair products in one video clip. Another overhead shot showed crowds of people blocking streets and breaking car windows of stranded motorists.

"This is escalating too quickly," Robbie shook his head, trying to come up with an alternative. Giving up, he leaned over to give

Emily a hug. She focused on him and looked surprised to see him, since she had been sucked into the news broadcast.

"When is Mom getting home?" she asked.

Robbie held her tight and tried not to lie to her, "We just talked to her. The hospital is swamped with cases. Mr. Putnam, Jerome, is going to stay and watch over you and Clark. He is waiting for his kids to show. Keep the doors locked after I leave and don't go outside for anything. Clark filled up the tubs with water in case this turns into something major. Don't bathe in the tubs, just scoop the water out to flush the toilets and to clean up. Only drink from the water bottles Clark filled. Can you remember all of that?"

"Duh, Uncle Robbie. You act like we have never done this before," she smiled at Robbie.

Robbie nodded and hugged her again. "Mind Jerome until your mom gets back. I have to run."

"Are we safe here?" Emily asked.

Robbie hesitated and flexed his prosthetic arm, making the three-fingered claw open and close. "Jerome will keep you safe. These doors are strong enough to stop someone trying to kick their way in, but it shouldn't come to that. I don't need to tell you to stay off your computer and don't email anyone."

Robbie moved back out to the front porch. "Clark, you know the combination to the safe?"

"Yes sir," the teenager replied.

"Crack it open and make sure Jerome has your daddy's shotgun for the house. You okay with that?" Robbie asked the boy becoming a man too soon.

"I think Dad would like that. It kicks too much for me, but I bet Mr. Putnam can handle it," Clark smiled. "Can I get my AR out?"

"Hold off on getting yours or Emily's weapons out, Kristi would roast my hide. Jerome, get anything from the truck you need. I'm out of here. Take care of the kids for me. My family appreciates you for doing this." Robbie shook Clark's hand, but the boy hugged him instead.

"You be careful, Uncle Robbie."

"Shoot. I feel sorry for anyone who gets in my way. If I have to bring the boys back here, there is going to be a reckoning." Robbie headed to the truck with Jerome in tow. The street lamps illuminated the interior of the camper shell enough for Jerome to grab a simple black bag with his basic supplies for a week. The two men had discussed the necessities, and Jerome had followed Robbie's lead when it came time to get his "go bag" together. 'Just the essentials; food, water, ammo, extra socks, and hygiene products for the bag. Everything else just slows you down'.

"I'll check in with you when I stop for gas. I'm thinking three hours until then. The trip there and back puts me at about sunrise when I get here, barring any unforeseen problems. Getting everyone out of here is the goal. Everything else can wait until that happens, Jerome."

"I got you, Robbie. Don't scratch my paint," Jerome warned, shutting the camper shell and tossing Robbie the keys.

Pressing the fob, Robbie unlocked the driver door and cranked the crew cab work truck over and let the engine idle while he took the time to set the power mirrors for himself. In the floorboard of the passenger side, Robbie had his own black backpack with his gear. The older truck lacked a GPS unit, which Robbie didn't mind since he had multiple routes memorized. When he hit the residential street at the end of the block, Robbie took a left and ended up back on Cicero. The sickly yellow sodium vapor lamps lining the major thoroughfare cast deep shadows between the buildings. Robbie paused and looked north and south without seeing any tell-tale glints of flashing red and blue lights.

"No roadblocks, at least not yet," he said to himself. He turned right and headed south and away from the cracking gunfire picking up in the denser neighborhoods inside of the Chicago city limits. Glancing out the side window, Robbie spotted a Southwest flight coming into Midway. "The planes are still landing. Don't know how much longer that is going to happen."

In the suburb of Alsip, Robbie skipped the entrance to the Tri-State Toll Road and headed further south. He didn't want to get Jerome's plates scanned this close to Kristi's house, so he lost time by fighting the mistimed traffic lights. For him, a yellow light was a red. He knew the traffic cameras were all over the place and linked to a central system. At least, that's what he thought. Cicero Avenue paralleled the toll road roughly, so Robbie knew when he reached 183rd Street in Country Club Hills, he could turn left and start heading east. The heavily-wooded Wampum Lake Woods and Brownwell Woods forced Robbie to jog to the south and cut through a secluded residential neighborhood and around a private academy to hit a relatively unknown back road that turned into the Main Street of Glenwood. Robbie found Highway 30 and followed it to I-65.

Feeling he had the time, Robbie pulled over and considered his options. Staying on the surface roads would almost double his driving time, but he could stay under the radar of the Feds. Since they had Kenosha sewn up, Robbie figured they would be beating down every door in Wisconsin looking for him and others like him. Since he'd crossed over into Indiana near Dyer, he jumped onto Interstate 65 and headed toward Indianapolis. He stopped only for fuel at the stations he had scoped out, where they didn't have security cameras worth a flip and he could park the truck away from the cameras inside the store.

He paid cash at each fuel stop, instead of leaving an electronic paper trail of breadcrumbs to the safety of the retreat. Jerome had a line of fuel cans in the bed of the truck, but Robbie opted to save them for the coming troubles he expected.

Outside of Indianapolis, Robbie exited the interstate and pulled his rifle from the case in the back seat. He didn't expect trouble in Indianapolis, but the radio stations had warned about widespread unrest in several major cities.

He didn't want to access the internet on his phone, but he suspected the loop around the city would have issues.

Instead, he called Kristi's home and got Jerome to look for him.

Jerome answered after one ring. "Clark, your mom is still at work. Everything is good here, though."

"Uncle Jerome, can you look up traffic for me around Indianapolis? I want to avoid bad traffic," Robbie asked and cursed the bad news.

Jerome pulled up the information from the laptop. On any given day, the 865 and 465 loops around the north of Indianapolis suffered horrible congestion and accidents.

"It looks like Indie is a complete nightmare. The interstates into downtown and the loops all show red. When I click on the little icons for the alert, the information shows 'ongoing incident', like we don't know what's really up."

"I was afraid of that. Okay, expect me back later than anticipated. I don't want to get stuck in that. Do you see any issues heading east out of the city?"

"Nah, that looks clear, buddy. Just looking around the last few hours, I see traffic going red all over the place in the cities. You made it out of town right before the Mile Long Bridge went down. The news cut in and said a suspicious package had halted all operations on the toll road."

Feeling a hundred years old, Robbie rubbed at his face. "You know that's bullshit, right?"

"Oh, hell, yes. Hey, the kids are antsy for Kristi to get home. I fed them and told them to finish up packing. Anything special we going to need?" Jerome asked.

Robbie thought about the mounds of camping gear the boys had bought the kids over the years. "Jerome, get clothes to fit your boys, in case we have to hoof it. Clark has some decent hiking boots that don't fit any_more in the basement storage. Get packs for you and the boys set up. Clark knows what to bring."

For a few seconds the phone was silent, then Jerome let out a low whistle, "Man, how far you thinking we need to hike?"

"Worst case? We walk all the way to safety."

"Damn. Okay, let me get busy packing." Jerome said goodbye and hung up. Robbie put the truck in drive and searched for the exit that would take him around Indianapolis.

Robbie dropped off south of Lebanon and followed the smaller, but safer state highway east through the fields getting plowed for the spring planting or still fallow from the long winter. He cut south and ran down to Carmel before heading east and south until he found I-70, then picked up speed once again.

Between Dayton and Columbus, Ohio, Robbie threaded his way southeast and into the hills close to the border with West Virginia. Sometime after midnight, he pulled up to the locked gate at the driveway up to the retreat and shifted the truck into park. He waited for a second before flashing his brights twice and then killing the lights.

Shadow tapped his arm and scared the living hell out of him. Robbie jumped off the seat, hitting his head on the roof and let out a small yell before he calmed down.

"Where the hell are they?!" Randy cried out, looking into the backseat. "Why do I see vacant seats, Blaster?" Charlie stepped out from the shadows near the passenger side of the truck.

"Robbie, you had *one* job," Charlie grumbled.

Chapter Twenty-Two

Retreat

"What the hell, Blaster?" Aaron snapped as he unlocked the padlock and stepped out to open the unassuming aluminum gate. The boys didn't want to draw attention to themselves by throwing up a hardened defense that could lead to more curious people showing up.

Robbie, exhausted from the stress of the long drive, popped off at the man. "Hell, Cobra, I didn't see you there. Why don't you smile more, so we can see you in the dark?"

"Hey, I'm not the one who screwed the pooch, hillbilly. Get your narrow ass up to the house so we can fix your screw up." Aaron held the gate and waited. Randy and Charlie hopped into the truck with their weapons and full "battle rattle".

Cranking the truck, Robbie moved it onto the property and waited for Aaron to shut the gate behind them before climbing into the front passenger seat.

Robbie didn't question who would watch the gate. Cody had the entire property wired and set up on a network of cameras with motion sensors. The whole shebang had a dedicated network, disconnected from the internet and with monitors in the clubhouse.

"What was the situation on the roads?" Charlie asked from behind Robbie.

"Rural interstates are still open, but I don't know for how long. Jerome gave me an update four hours ago outside Indianapolis, and the cities are going into lockdown," Robbie informed them.

Leaning between the seats, Randy took in a sharp breath. "You didn't use your phone, did you? They are probably tracking them. Shit! Give it here, we have to shut it down." He reached his hand forward and patted at Robbie's pockets on his jacket.

Lifting his arm off the door rest, Robbie slapped at his hand with the claw. "Ease up, Shadow. I pulled the card and shut it off hours ago. It's not my phone anyway, it's Clark's. Besides, the cell network got funky and I kept losing signal in areas where I normally have 4G."

"Do you think they are pulling the plug on wireless communications?" Charlie asked.

"Let's ask Cody. He is here, right?" Robbie asked as they pulled up to the clubhouse. Robbie backed up to the porch and shut off the truck. "We need to unload the gear back there and load up for an extraction."

The boys piled out and Robbie opened the tailgate and camper shell door with Jerome's keys.

"Jesus, Blaster. What the hell did you bring?" Randy gasped when he shifted Robbie's pack to the side and saw what looked like plumbing supplies.

Undeterred, Robbie pulled the pack further out of the way and set it aside with another large black gym bag and a square Pelican case. "I had some good quality pipe I didn't want to leave behind, as well as some chemicals we may need."

"Classic Blaster. You brought your damn explosives factory down here. Don't you have enough in your storage buildings already?" Aaron chuckled and started pulling pipe from the truck. Aaron's wife, Liz, came out of the clubhouse.

"It's almost two in the damn morning. What the hell are you boys up to now?" She stood in an ankle-length robe and rubbed at her puffy eyes.

"Sorry, Liz. I got caught up in traffic," Robbie smiled at Aaron's better half.

"Why don't you wait until morning to unload? You are going to wake everyone up," Liz complained. Aaron had gone and married a practical woman who shared his love of horses and nature, but she did not like missing out on her beauty sleep. The boys liked to give Aaron a hard time, but they all liked Liz.

Randy pulled another pipe and Charlie helped stack the thick tubing under the porch and out of the elements. "It doesn't matter if it gets a little rain on it," Robbie smirked as he dragged a pipe cutter from the bed.

"Heck, Blaster. I already brought one of those," Randy shook his head.

Cocking an eyebrow up, Robbie laughed, "Two is one, right?" Randy shrugged and took the contraption from Robbie and carried it around the clubhouse to stack it with the rest of the tools.

Cody came out and saw the activity and counted heads. "What happened?"

"We gotta go back. Somebody forgot to do his damn job," Aaron pointed at Robbie. "And for the record, we all agreed that since he lived the closest, it was the logical decision."

"Get off my ass, Cobra. I can't extract them alone. Kristi got called into work *before* the shit got bad and they put her hospital on lockdown," Robbie complained. "They were locking nurses up that didn't report for work."

"Well, that explains Kristi. What about the kids?" Cody asked as he pitched in to unload the truck. Pulling out a five-gallon bucket and reading the label, Cody whistled. "Should you be carrying this much chemical around with you?"

Only answering with a grin, Robbie pulled another pail from the bed of the truck. "Just don't mix it with this. But about the kids, Babyface. You wanted me to risk getting them engaged in a felony stop alone? Jerome is a fighter, but not a trained trigger man."

"No, that was the right call," Cody sighed, turning back to the truck. Cody saw the line of fuel cans in the bed along with other five-gallon buckets of chemicals, and his mouth fell open. "Dear Lord. Are those full?"

"Yes, they are. The gas tank on this beast is not big enough to get here without topping it off. That's my emergency reserve. We are going to need it to get back."

Mumbling to himself, Cody shook his head and carried two of the buckets away. "Put those in my shed, would you?" Robbie called out.

Freezing in his tracks, Cody looked back. "I'm putting them as far away from each other as I can. You are insane, you know?"

Walking around the truck, Randy caught Cody and checked the buckets. "Jesus, Blaster. What the hell?" He shook his head and came back to help with the last of the bags and Rubbermaid totes. "Did Jerome know what he had back here?"

Feeling rather cheerful despite the circumstances, Robbie giggled, "Nope. He did ask why the hell I brought cleaning supplies, fertilizers, mothballs and hair care products in such large quantities. Yeah, he had no clue."

"You have a sickness, Blaster," Randy chuckled and helped his friend carry his gear into the clubhouse. Everyone knew, when Blaster giggled, it was going to be a bad day for someone. Exciting, colorful, and energetic, but a bad day was coming for someone.

"Where are Mom and Pop? I was mostly afraid I'd wake them up." Robbie scanned the big open room and saw a striking woman stand up from a recliner in the theater section and rub at her eyes.

Charlie went to her and leaned close to speak with her.

"Who's that?" Robbie asked Randy in a low voice.

"Charlie picked up a stray. I think she is some kind of legal beagle like Book. He hasn't said much about her except her name is Joan, but I think there is some chemistry there," Randy smiled at the two whispering. "I'm wondering if that's the one he spoke of, but he's not giving the intel on the situation."

Watching Charlie talk to the hottie made Robbie smile. "Good for him. He got himself a gal that he doesn't have to worry about me stealing away from him with my wicked charm." Walking into the living room, Robbie set the gym bag down and unzipped it before he started removing items and laying them out on the floor.

"What? A girl you aren't going to sniff around and try to mount the first time you see her? I'm shocked, Blaster." Walking off, Randy dragged an almost identical bag from beside the door and started assembling his own gear.

"She's got pointy elbows. I like my ladies with extra cushion for comfort," Robbie quipped while he added tape to a magazine to keep it from rattling in the chest rig. Randy had a similar setup. For that matter, they had the same gear, but individualized the pouches for their own preferences.

The door opened and Cody came in with Aaron. Cody had his own bag, but Aaron did not.

"You are staying here to watch out for your family and hold the fort, right?" Robbie asked Aaron.

With a pained expression, Aaron shrugged, "The truck is only so big, and I'm not in shape for an extraction. I think I'm needed here to watch over the place."

"I was going to suggest that, Cobra, but I didn't want to offend you." Randy popped the lens covers on his optic off his AR and checked for dirt or smudges.

Moving over, Aaron sat in a chair and helped Cody get his gear sorted out. "I want to come, but with Liz here and now Joan, we need a trigger puller to keep up security."

Charlie walked over with Joan standing very close to him. "And for that, I'm grateful, Aaron. Joan is a quick study, so put her to work. Will Liz be okay manning the security monitors in here?"

Hearing her name, Liz walked over from where Andre and Eli, her two sons, slept on the floor in their sleeping bags. Even though everyone had cabins, everyone wanted to be close as their world crumbled. "Don't walk on eggshells, Charlie. Yes, I'm fine watching the monitors. As soon as Aaron breaks out the rest of our guns, I'm also going to help with security. I have my own babies to worry about."

"Why aren't the boys in your cabin? Wouldn't they be more comfortable there in their beds?" Robbie asked.

"I wanted them all close to you boys. They are fine 'camping out' in here. They sleep like the dead most times, so don't you worry about waking them." Liz looked at the three men loading magazines and packing their assault packs. "How long do you expect to be gone?"

Letting out a sigh, Randy paused and looked at Robbie. Not about to answer, Robbie shrugged and looked at Charlie. The room went quiet until Cody broke the silence at last. "This could be fourteen hours, or it could end up being weeks." He glanced at Robbie.

"Yeah, he's right. I have several escape routes mapped out and ready to act on, but I can't be sure." Lifting his claw, Robbie pointed to a laptop bag in his duffel. "Cody, check my laptop and pop in the thumb drive I have in the pocket of the carry case. It has all of my routes programmed in."

"Once we get into the city, how are we going to extract?" Cody asked.

"That's a good question. I hope you all have boots that are broken in, because we might have to walk it out. Been a while since we humped combat loads any distance," Robbie looked at Randy. With a grin, Randy looked at his prosthetic foot.

"Shit, son. I can drag myself on my belly that far if I have to. Can you and your stubby legs keep up?" Randy retorted.

Squaring his shoulders back, Robbie stood up in mock anger. "They are not stumpy, Shadow. I'm just big boned!" Liz slapped him lightly on the arm.

"Don't wake the boys!" she hissed.

"I thought you said they were heavy sleepers!" Robbie complained.

Giving a long sigh, Liz rolled her eyes. "Not so heavy that they could sleep through a damn earthquake! Keep your voices down."

"Well, shoot, Liz. I guess we have one more silencer in the group," Robbie said and reached into his bag and pulled out a thick metal tube and locked it into place at the end of his rifle barrel. "Now I'm going to be real quiet for y'all." Randy and Cody followed suit and did a weapon's check.

"Good, now take it all off and pack it up," Charlie told the three.

"What? I don't understand, Book. You want us unarmed when we head back? No way!" Randy's voice went up and Liz gave him a sharp look. Taking a step back, Randy covered his mouth and checked to see that the boys slept on. "That's crazy, man," he whispered.

"We need to go in street clothes. Jeans and work shirts will be our camouflage until we need to go hot. Drawing attention to ourselves decked out as tier one operators will blow this op before we reach Oak Lawn. Blaster, you know the route, but you are tired from the drive. I'm driving. Blaster, take shotgun. Shadow and Babyface will take the backseats and provide suppressive fire as needed. The rifles need to stay out of sight in the bed of the truck and covered up. We wear our pistols, but we keep them concealed. Aaron, we can't contact you because all of our electronic communications will be or already *are* compromised." Looking at each one, Charlie paused and let the suggestions that sounded like orders sink in.

They shrugged and stepped outside to check their night vision on the rifles and their goggles. Robbie pulled out his latest and most expensive purchase. The four-barreled GPNVG-18 night vision system connected to his helmet gave him the look of a demented bug from space.

"How the heck did you get your hands on that?" Randy gasped, standing with his mouth open in the dark.

Looking over at Randy, Robbie giggled, "Can you believe I raised the limit on my credit card and bought it? I paid less for my Harley and damn near could've bought two hogs for what these set me back, but by God, I can see everything! I went with the battery pack that lasted longer. I got extras."

Charlie used his own PVS 14s to look at Blaster standing by the truck. "You look ridiculous in those."

"I know! Don't you wish we had something this cool when we deployed?" Robbie switched the unit off and swung it up to let his eyes adjust to the dark. "I set my bank to autopay my credit card each month, so don't think I'm trying to screw the credit card company. I'm paying it off."

"With what? Do you have that much cash lying around?" Randy asked.

"I took out a line of credit on my house. Anyone want to bet if it's still standing?" Robbie sounded sad at the mention of his now probably destroyed home he had worked so hard to rehab.

"I feel you, Robbie. They probably torched my place too after I left. They sent the locals to do their dirty work in my case, but I'm sure one of the alphabet agencies have shown up by now." Charlie powered his unit down and stuffed it into his bag in the truck.

"Everyone going to the belly of the beast, get ready to move out in five minutes. Grab extra batteries and snivel gear if you feel like you can carry it," Randy announced.

They split up and jogged to their own cabins to get last minute items and take a crucial bathroom break. Once they started the movement to Chicago, they didn't intend to stop for luxuries. They all met back up inside the clubhouse to say their final goodbyes.

"Hey, I have one question, though," Robbie raised his hand like a good little schoolboy.

"What?" Charlie asked.

"Can I bring any explosives I have already made?" Robbie asked like a naughty school boy with his head down.

"I knew I should have just left those buckets outside of his storage locker," Cody mumbled to himself.

With a look that spoke volumes, Charlie shook his head, "You want us branded as terrorists? Because that's how you get branded as a terrorist. One little explosion will have every alphabet organization screaming in on us from every direction. So, to answer your question, no. Leave the things that go boom here." Charlie paused for a second. "Everyone staying here, keep a minimum safe distance from Blaster's cabin and shed." Turning his body, Randy looked at Robbie with an eyebrow raised. Charlie couldn't do that very well, so he crossed his arms and glared at Robbie.

"Okay, fine. Stay about twenty yards from the storage locker unless it catches on fire. If that happens, just run away," Robbie chuckled as Randy groaned and Charlie went to Joan and mumbled something in her ear that had her looking for the nearest exit.

"I'm just kidding, everyone! Relax, will you? Just don't go mixing anything I have in there," Robbie laughed and unhooked his chest rig and placed it back into the zippered bag.

The others watched Charlie hug Joan lightly and headed outside. Nodding to each other, Cody and Randy followed him out. Robbie finished up and went to Aaron sitting in a chair watching the monitors. "Cobra, keep the fort safe until we get back."

He stood and gave Robbie a hug. The big accountant smiled, but Robbie saw a hint of sadness like he wished he could come with them, but he had his own family to protect. Robbie nodded and looked over at the sleeping boys and Liz watching the rest load up the truck. "If we don't make it back, I left instructions in my cabin on how to handle my chemicals. Use it to get us some payback."

"Bullshit, Blaster. If you don't come back, then I expect you took over the country and set yourself up with a giant harem," Aaron chuckled.

Letting Aaron go, Robbie laughed and cocked his head. "I wonder if I could pull that off? I'd need to build up my stamina…" Robbie smiled and headed out the door with his gear to join the rest of the boys at the truck.

"Are we decided to go with multicam for this? Do you have a set in your bag?" Randy asked.

"Yeah, I do. That's probably our best bet for the changing foliage this time of year," Robbie shrugged and then added, "plus it makes me look awesome!"

As the others groaned at Robbie, the boys loaded up and rolled back down the driveway to the gate. Cody got out to open it for them, then closed it back up and locked it before they pulled out into the dark.

Getting comfortable in the seat, Robbie had them take a different route back to the north and west. At one point, he asked Cody to pull up the laptop file he had compiled of routes.

Cody called out from the backseat where he had Robbie's laptop plugged into an adapter, keeping it charged from the truck's electrical system. "Robbie, what's your encryption password for this file?"

"Here, just pass it to me," Robbie reached back.

Cody smiled at Robbie, "No, man. Just tell me. I have it all plugged in and charging. What's the password?"

"Just hand it over, it's easier than trying to get you to do it."

"No, it's okay with me. I have two hands and I type fast. What's the password?"

Not answering, Robbie's face turned redder. Charlie glanced at the big man turning beet red and chuckled, "What's the problem, Blaster? Just tell him the code."

With a small grin, Randy, sensing his discomfort, needled Robbie from behind him, "Is it something embarrassing like, 123456 or password? You know, something you can remember?"

"I need that route information, Blaster. I have a turn coming up, and I need to know if this is the best way. What's the password?" Charlie barked.

Looking out the window, Robbie shook his head, "It was something silly, so I could remember it. I have too many to keep up with through work and all."

"Damn it! I missed the turn! Come on, Blaster! What's the password?" Charlie yelled.

"It's ILoveHelloKitty1," Blaster groaned.

The truck interior went silent as the tires hummed along the two-lane road in the middle of Ohio. Cody tapped in the code and the annotated map popped up for him to see. "That is correct. Now the road we want should be about ten miles up on the left."

The cabin roared in laughter as the three Rangers pounded on Robbie from their seats.

"You are such a weird man sometimes!" Charlie howled in laughter. "Why in the world would you choose that password?"

Holding up the claw, Robbie looked around the cab. "In my defense, Emily went through a cute Hello Kitty phase remember? And I thought that was one password that nobody would guess in a million years for me to use."

They stopped outside of a small town and topped off the tank at a gas station at one point to collect local information, and the cashier said he had heard all sorts of rumors about the riots. He mentioned a convoy of Ohio State Police pulling in to fill up around midnight, but nothing much since.

"Well, you know what they say about midnight?" Randy asked the cashier named Herbert, according to his plastic name badge.

"No, what's that?" Herb asked.

"Nothing good ever happens after midnight," Robbie replied.

"Then what are you folks doing up so late?" Herbert chuckled.

Looking up at Herbert, Randy replied as the two headed for the door, "We are trying to get home to Wisconsin. Our job finished up, and we want to see our families."

"You all be careful in the big cities," Herbert called to them as they left the store.

Coming to a stop, Robbie looked at the deserted parking lot. "Which way did they go?"

"Who?" Randy asked.

Robbie waved his good hand at the road. "The State Police."

"I hope, in the opposite direction. We are driving a vehicle not registered to us with a truck full of military grade hardware. If they pull us over, we are screwed," Randy said, getting back in the truck.

They pulled out of the gas station and stayed alert for anything that might stop them. Robbie pulled out Clark's phone and looked at Charlie. "I'm going to try the house again and see if I can get an update from Jerome."

"Is that wise?" Randy asked, leaning between the seats.

From the backseat, Cody spoke up, "They don't have the manpower to run down tertiary phone numbers from their data dumps. They are probably keying on just primary numbers and their direct contacts. We are far enough away from the retreat, if that's what you are thinking."

Randy listened to Cody and shrugged, "Go ahead. Maybe she's home by now."

Opening the phone up, Robbie popped the SIM card back into the handset and powered up the phone. The signal only had two bars, so Robbie dialed the last number from the recent contacts. The line sounded scratchy, and Robbie put it on speaker for the four to hear.

"This is the Westside Massage Parlor for Dogs, how may I direct your call?" Jerome's smooth voice came through the speaker.

Rolling his eyes, Randy shook his head, "He has been around you waaaay too much."

"This is Huckleberry Hound. Do you have reservations open for four dirty mutts?" Robbie spoke into the microphone.

"Good news! We have room for four more. Our earlier reservation is still a no show at this time, so come on in," Jerome replied.

"See you in five, then!" Robbie made a kissing noise and hung up. He powered the phone down and removed the card again. "Shit!" he hollered. "Kristi's not home yet," he fumed.

"What kind of twisted mess of codes and phrases did I just witness?" Cody asked.

Robbie laughed, "Jerome must figure if the NSA is listening in, then that conversation would have them scratching their heads for a while." He paused, "We go to the house first, then we get her from the hospital if we have to."

"How the hell can they keep her from going home? I mean, yeah, they can force her to stay, but what legal grounds do they have to do that? Book, this is a question for you," Randy asked, glancing at the dark landscape outside.

Racking his brain while he drove, Charlie even tried using the logic the government was using. Finally, he just glanced at the others. "They can't. What they are doing is illegal. Even if martial law is in effect, hospital staff members must be given breaks or their performance will drop to the point where life-threatening mistakes will happen. It's kidnapping or unlawful detainment. Then you have to think about forced labor, which was outlawed in the 1920's."

"Yeah, but if they decide the laws are null and void for the duration of the 'emergency', they can pretty much do anything. Hell, they hung a woman for the Lincoln assassination without her getting a fair trial," Randy thought out loud.

Propping his arm up on the door, Charlie nodded along, "They had a military trial presided over by a military commission. Think about it, guys. They tried civilians in a military court. The defendants were never allowed to testify for themselves. All it took was a simple majority to find them guilty and two-thirds of the jury to approve the death sentence, and they could only appeal to the president. They ended up hanging several of the plotters. I don't disagree with some of their rulings, but they hanged a woman who owned a boarding house where the conspirators had meetings. That's like shooting your pig because he saw the fox eat the chicken."

Closing the laptop, Cody leaned forward in the backseat. "Didn't she deserve it?"

Charlie drummed at the steering wheel for a second. "What about hanging the owner of a motel because the man who shot Kennedy had once stayed there and made phone calls?"

"Yeah, but then you have to go back and argue who actually killed Kennedy," Randy chuckled.

Putting the cell phone away, Robbie laughed, "It was a mob hit. That damn Italian rifle could never make those shots in the time he had."

With a look of dread, Charlie stared out the windshield and thought about it for a second before he continued, "They are going to suspend *habeas corpus,* so if we get pinched, we may never see the light of day before a civilian court."

"Court? Shit, they are going to shoot us along the side of the road if they catch us and leave us for the buzzards," Robbie growled as he tapped at the dash with his claw. "We swore an oath a long time ago, and we have always lived up to that promise. Kristi and those kids are as close to flesh and blood as you can get."

"What's your point, Blaster?" Charlie asked.

"I'm just sayin'," Robbie let his voice trail off.

"I hear you, brother. We'll get them out," Charlie declared as he stared straight ahead.

Chapter Twenty-Three

Westville, Indiana

Less than an hour from Oak Lawn, their luck ran out. A mile south of Westville, Indiana, Charlie passed an Indiana State Trooper car with the lights turned off sitting on the side of the road. Going the speed limit, Charlie slowed the truck and scanned the rearview mirrors. When they entered a curve in the road, the lights behind him popped on and the car pulled out to follow them.

"Company!" Randy called out. "Got a cop car that just dropped in behind us." Randy looked out the back glass and through the rear of the camper shell.

"I saw him. Blaster, prepare for contact to the front. This smells like a setup. Babyface, be ready for action," Charlie called out.

"Wait. Are these local cops or Feds?" Cody asked.

"The car behind is State Police. I don't know what's ahead, but he set up right before this curve. That smells like a trap. How many ambushes have we seen like that? We are in the literal middle of nowhere. I'm not speeding, so something's up." Charlie slowed while going through the curve.

"What's our play, boys?" Robbie asked as he checked his pistol tucked away in his concealment holster. Randy copied the move along his belt. Glancing over, Charlie nodded to Robbie.

"You wanna try the old loopy loo? They aren't going to care that we have licenses to carry. Hell, we are essentially outlaws in their minds," Robbie offered and looked back at Randy. "What do you think, Shadow?"

"Mission comes first, boys. Cody, just follow our lead. This is going to look a little strange, but be ready to send hate downrange if we have to," Randy told him, then glanced away just as two more vehicles blocking the blacktop two-lane road in a V pattern, with their front ends almost meeting at the center line, flashed them with all of their lights, including the post-mounted spotlights on the door frames.

As Charlie came to a stop, a voice boomed through the speakers mounted on the State Police car behind them. "Get out of the car, now, with your hands up! Show me your hands!"

Robbie, nearly blinded by the lights, noticed the shadows of several cars parked behind the police cruisers. A midsized SUV and what looked like a compact car, as well as what could be a pickup truck sat dark without passengers. "I see other civilian cars back there, but no people." The back glass of the camper shell shattered when an officer used his baton to get their attention.

"I said, get the hell out of the car, you bunch of cheeseheads!"

"Remember, Babyface. Follow our lead," Robbie said, taking a deep breath as he reached for his door when the man behind them yelled again.

"You racist fucks had better come out before I light your asses up! Move!"

With a relieved sigh, Robbie paused, "I know our play, Charlie. Randy, get a count. This is going to go down fast. They want a fight, so let's not disappoint." Robbie jumped out of the truck and turned to face the yelling officer behind them.

"How dare you accuse us of being racist! I'm probably the most enlightened person you will ever meet. Just because we come from Wisconsin doesn't make us ignorant fucks sitting around diddling our cousins!" Robbie bellowed.

The rest of the boys stepped out with their hands raised even with their shoulders. Facing the lights but not looking into them, Charlie joined in, "I agree with my friend here. I know for a fact, that he has dipped his wick in every race and religion known to man and a few outside of the species. If he's a racist, then I don't even know what to classify myself as, much less the rest of humanity."

Spinning around and looking over the hood of the truck, Robbie glared over at Charlie. "What the hell do you mean, 'other species'? I keep my pecker reserved only for hot mommas! When we get home, I'm kicking your scrawny ass! I'm about tired of your shit!" Robbie screamed at Charlie.

Taking a step back from the truck, Randy took his opportunity to chime in, "You don't remember that time we worked on the fence at that sanctuary back home. You took a trip on the wild side in the monkey house when you got too plastered on Old Style and whiskey. Oh, man. You should see your face right now, you look like that monkey when you tried to give it your willie." Watching Robbie move in front of the truck, Randy stepped around Charlie and laughed with his hands still raised.

"I'll fucking end you!" Robbie growled, coming around the front of the truck and charged forward taking a swing with his good hand at Randy. The punch missed when Randy ducked and Robbie ended up on his ass, scrabbling back to his feet. "You promised to never tell anyone!"

Rearing his leg back, Robbie tried to kick at Randy's legs, but he dodged away, now on the passenger side of the truck almost out of the bright lights. Charlie and Cody moved to the front of the truck and started laughing before Robbie turned to take out his frustration on Charlie with a wild swing that Charlie dodged.

"What the hell is wrong with you! Stand against the damn truck with your hands up!" a voice called out from their front.

"I've been riding with you for six fucking hours, you moron! I'm kicking your fat ass!" Charlie balled up his fist and drove it into Robbie's face. Not even trying to dodge or block the punch, Robbie fell to the ground and spit out blood.

"Six hours? You think that's bad? I spent twelve hours with your sister last month. She cried and begged for me to keep going!" Robbie smiled. "She knows I like to stick it in the crazy."

"Get your goddamn hands up and back against the truck!" another voice yelled and tried to take control of the situation.

"I don't have to remind you of that whorehouse in Panama where you two tried to tag team that girl who turned out to have a little something extra for ya!" Robbie called out, getting to his feet but wasn't looking at Charlie or Randy. He was counting figures behind the lights.

"Motherfucker! You want some? Then get some!" Randy shouted, with Charlie nudging Cody back along the passenger side of the truck. Turning to Charlie, Robbie charged, making Charlie back up and Randy darted past to the driver's side. The officers stood there and watched while three lunatics with guns pointed at them tried to get into a fistfight. Standing on the driver's side and acting like he was watching Robbie, Randy saw the officers' pistols dip and gave a small nod to Robbie.

Turning to face Charlie like he was readying for another charge, Robbie nodded at Charlie and all three drew their pistols. Bringing his pistol up, Robbie lined up the first shadowy silhouette behind the bright lights in the center of the group and stroked the trigger twice before acquiring the second target. In his mind, Robbie saw the uniformed men as paper targets with interconnected circles noting different scoring. Center mass, or the X ring, gave you a perfect ten in the firing line, but Robbie knew they all wore body armor, so he tried for the next ring worth ten points, the circle above the shoulders, as he continued to move out of the lights.

Charlie, working from the right and Randy from the left, both centered on the shadowy silhouettes and started servicing targets from the outside and worked their way in, with their last shots converging on an officer as he squeezed the trigger of his pistol and hit the windshield of the truck after taking a double-tap to the chest. The officer stumbled back squeezing the trigger again, this time hitting the asphalt as his arms fell. Adjusting his aim when the officer started to fall backwards, Randy brushed the trigger to send one into the officer's head before he hit the pavement.

Robbie's two targets hit the ground like sacks of meat. The .45 slugs punched through their throats and faces and foreheads. The blinding glare from the police lights gave the boys the impression that they had been shooting at ghosts.

Spinning around, Cody fired at the two shadows behind the truck and put them down.

"Clear!" Randy called out from the front of the truck.

A pop from the rear of the truck followed by a "clear!" told Robbie that Cody had to finish one off.

"Robbie, what do you have up there?" Cody called out.

"I see three State Police with standard gear. Sidearm for each is a Sig 227. I'm taking the ammo, we don't need the pistols. We have another bozo in full tactical gear with a face missing. I'll check his pockets and see what's up with him," Robbie shouted back.

"Check the cars. We are cleaning up here," Randy called out while he changed magazines.

Feeling squeamish but not showing it, Cody checked the men he'd shot and then went to the patrol car. He popped the trunk and expected to find a stash of weapons or other goodies. What he found made his yell seem very stressed to the rest of the team. "Check the trunks of those cars and tell me what you think!"

Holstering his pistol, Charlie pulled the keys from one of the cars and shut the lights off, then went back to the trunk. Piled to the top of the space under the deck lid were personal items, wallets, loose money, rings, necklaces, loose credit cards, and guns. In the second trunk, they found a similar stack.

"Okay. Let's do a clean sweep of this scene. Shadow, get personal intelligence and security. I've got radios and documents. Blaster, go with weapons. Babyface, on me. I'm going to show you the ropes, and you are going to help me move the bodies off the road," Charlie called out, then turned to Cody. "Babyface, you have got to shoot and move. You're lucky those fuckers couldn't shoot straight. Are we clear? Shoot and move or do like Shadow, shoot *while* you're moving. We've all done it over the years, so don't let that training go."

Following Charlie as he fought the adrenaline dump, "Yeah, I know better," Cody admitted.

Kneeling in the road, Randy pulled the wallets from the six men and matched their faces to their life stories in the billfolds. The strange one with the tactical uniform was not from Indiana. He had a driver's license issued in Virginia. Randy kept the wallet and moved to check on the remaining crew. They all had Indiana licenses and addresses. With little indifference, Randy overlooked the family photos and shoved that thought to the dark corner of his mind where he kept all the bad shit he had seen and done.

"No fucking grenades!" Robbie spat as he fished the extra magazines from the pistols and unloaded the rounds into a pouch he'd taken off the guy from Virginia. Robbie emptied the .40 caliber rounds from the magazine and considered tossing them aside. Instead, he placed the rounds in a grocery bag and tossed them to the shoulder of the road. "Maybe somebody good will need them. We don't."

Personally happy the group didn't have grenades, Charlie took all the radios and turned them off, except for one which he cranked the volume all the way up to listen to chatter or check-ins on the net.

Jumping in the other cars, Charlie turned the bright lights off and let them work by flashlight to let their natural night vision return over time.

Shaking his head, Randy took a look around the scene and returned with a troubled expression.

"What did you find?" Babyface asked.

"We made the right call. Those cars back there are from earlier victims. The ones caught with guns were handcuffed and marched into the trees over there," Randy grumbled and pointed to a small line of trees along the side of the road. "Single gunshot to the head for each. And this piece of shit did it." He kicked the body of the man in the all black uniform and tactical gear. "I found his fired casings over there by the bodies."

"So, the state troopers were complicit in this?" Charlie asked.

"Does the evidence in the trunks look like they're properly inventoried and ready for collection? Hell, yes, they were complicit. I want to know why they were here." Randy pointed down at the road they were standing on. "In this exact spot, between damn all and nowhere. This road serves no strategic value whatsoever, yet we have a group here with badges, killing for profit. The only people that would use this road would be people trying to get to safety."

"That's a mystery to me," Charlie admitted, walking over with Cody. "We checked the cell phones for messages. I got one to unlock with a fingerprint, but he didn't have any messages for the last two hours, and everything before that was personal messages to someone at home. I won't go into it, but they may not have known what they were here for at first."

"Tell that to the bodies lined up over there. They took the handcuffs off and reused them after they'd shot them in the head. The rings around their wrists indicate that they twitched and writhed in the dirt before they stopped moving," Randy's angry voice went quiet.

"Okay, then. We have our rules of engagement now. Blaster, find anything good?" Charlie asked.

"They have an M4 in the rack of that car." Robbie pointed to the car to their front and left. "The rack didn't survive me, but we have another rifle."

"I'll take the lower and leave the upper behind. That's just more weight to carry," Randy remarked.

"Fine with me. As well as some .45 ACP, I found boxes of ammunition for our ARs, so yay, more ammo to carry," Robbie smiled. "You can never have too much ammo."

"But what if you can't carry it all?" Cody asked.

"Then you shoot until you can carry it. We are about fifty miles from Oak Lawn, and we have to cross some densely-populated areas. We'll have to ditch the truck and go on foot from here," Robbie smiled. "I'm sure they will have more roadblocks set up, unless anyone wants to get a little closer with the truck."

Almost expecting Blackhawks to swoop down, Randy looked around. "Next time, they may just shoot. We'll start the hump, we need to move. Someone will come to relieve them and find this."

"Shit, just load them up in the backseat and drive away. We have four people and four vehicles," Robbie suggested.

"Where do we dump it all? Someone will find it eventually," Charlie asked.

Checking his pistol was secured in his holster, Robbie went to the truck and pulled out his laptop. He squirmed and put in the password to open the file. "Okay, three miles down the road is an area that looks swampy as hell. We can dump them there for now, change into our cammies, and head out. We still have darkness on our side, but we are going to lose that in a few hours."

"How long do you think it will take to get there? This is your town, Robbie," Charlie asked.

"Twelve to fifteen hours, if we can keep up the pace," Robbie shrugged.

Glancing over at Randy and seeing him nod, Charlie gave a long sigh, "Shit, load up with every round we can carry for the rifles. We can resupply at the house, just make sure we have enough to get in. Load up the bodies and let's take a drive down the road to take out the trash."

Working together, they stacked the bodies across the backseats after stripping them of their body armor.

"Why are we bothering? You all have a set of armor already," Cody pointed out.

"We do, but you just have a chest rig with plates, and the kids and Jerome don't, as well as Kristi. These are for them," Charlie reminded the youngest member of the team.

"So we have to carry extra sets of armor too?" Cody asked.

"Think of the good side. We won't be cold," Randy clapped Cody on the back and smiled. "Oh, this is going to be a marvelous suck indeed."

They loaded up and got the cars turned around before speeding three miles to the wooded area that looked more impressive on the map than in real life.

"Man, this sucks! How are we going to hide all these dead bodies in six inches of water?" Robbie complained as he pulled the stick out of the water of the drained swamp.

"We don't need all that extra fuel now, do we?" Randy suggested.

"Hang on, before we fire it up, let me get a few guns from the trunk. I saw a nice shotgun back there that I want to carry too." Robbie fished around in the trunk until he had the Mossberg 930 free. He took the sling from another rifle and attached the shotgun to his vest, so it hung with the rifle.

"Is that going to clank when you run, Blaster?" Randy asked.

Glancing down, Robbie hefted the shotgun and bounced up and down. The rifle stayed attached to his chest by its own sling and didn't impede his motion.

"Fine, just don't go with the shotty unless you have to. We need to move fast and quiet, and that damn thing will rock the neighborhoods," Randy chuckled and smiled when Robbie pulled out boxes of shells for the shotgun and selected the buckshot loads, leaving the smaller birdshot behind.

Tightening his gloves, Charlie looked at the group. "Remember, we are only using the radios for emergencies. Everyone have your hunter's ears in?" Cody, Randy, and Robbie nodded back. Robbie added a "middle finger" with his claw. "Keep hydrated and watch your intervals," Charlie added with a nod and stepped off. Walking past Charlie, Randy took the lead with the map.

Tucking the map into his cargo pocket, Randy sipped from his Camelback tube and sighed as he thought to himself, "Let the suckage begin."

211

Chapter Twenty-Four

Outside of Gary, Indiana

The five to six miles per hour pace along the double train tracks, and the constant attention to the shifting rocks along the line grated on Charlie's nerves. They made good time by avoiding the streets and jogging along the rail line Robbie had mapped out. Twenty yards ahead, Randy stopped occasionally at major intersections, but the suburban areas in Indiana stayed quiet in the near dawn hours, like the world had taken a deep breath and held it for the next trauma. Like an evil dream evolving, as the world brightened, gunfire started barking around them every ten to fifteen minutes.

Staying in his customary point position, Randy led them into the early morning and covered twenty miles in a sweaty, mad dash into the city, but the added light and the potential for trains to run on the start of a busy week, made the team find a place to hole up and survey their options.

In a copse of trees near Burns Harbor, the four took a break and hid out for a few hours. After a breather, Randy took off to reconnoiter the immediate area. Charlie dug into the bag of documents taken from the police cars, and Robbie checked in with Jerome. Next to Robbie, Cody stayed alert and on guard under a scraggly bush, listening to the sounds of sirens and sporadic gunfire in the distance.

Taking a deep breath, Robbie inserted the tiny SIM card and powered up the phone. He didn't have a charger with him, but the simple flip phone had enough juice for what he needed.

Jerome picked up on the second ring. "You had better be close. I'm getting tired of sitting up all night, waiting for you to call."

"I knew you missed me, loverboy. What's the situation at home?" Robbie asked.

"Mamma Bear made it home at dawn. She pulled a Runaway Bride, laced up her shoes, and hoofed it," Jerome yawned.

Letting out a gasp, Robbie almost dropped the phone in excitement. "Is she okay?"

"She's exhausted and sleeping. The kids were chomping at the bit to 'go camping' because the crap is getting closer out here. I mean, like *this* neighborhood."

"Did your kids show?" Robbie asked.

"I never did hear back from Charlene. I don't even know where she is staying now. I'm worried. I called her mom and she hasn't heard from Charlene since yesterday, and has no idea where she could be," Jerome's voice broke over the phone.

"I'm sorry, buddy. I do have good news, though. Expect to see us later tonight." Robbie cleared his throat and glanced around the hasty hide. "We can't move during the day. It's too eventful and we are going to be exposed. We already had to use the smoke poles. Hunker down and hold it together a little longer."

"Will do. Momma Bear broke out her and the kids' toys from the toy box. I still have the boom stick. Hey, where is my ride?"

Cringing, Robbie let the silence stretch for a few seconds before speaking. "I'm sorry, but I owe you a truck." Waiting for Jerome to pop off, Robbie remembered the flames engulfing the patrol cars and Jerome's truck. The team had no better way to erase the evidence, except to dump the fuel cans inside the vehicles and light a match.

When Jerome spoke, it was in a regretful but understanding tone, "Man, I knew I'd never see it again. I'm just glad you are coming."

"Well, get your walking shoes laced up. Looks like we are all humping out and it's going to be interesting."

"Okay, I'll tell the kids when they get up. Kristi is going to be down until this afternoon. She was wiped out, both physically and emotionally. It got bad."

"Hold the fort," Robbie replied, then hung up and took Clark's phone apart and tucked it away in his pack.

"She's home?" Charlie asked from his piles of papers and personal effects they'd hauled from the roadblock.

"Yeah. Jerome says she walked home."

Closing his eyes, Charlie sighed, "The SUV is still at work?"

"Yeah. Admit it, Book. The roads are too dangerous. It's the leather personnel carrier for us." They used to joke that the best way to move in the mountains of Afghanistan was with the LPC's. Keeping low, Robbie adjusted his position to get a better look at their perimeter.

"That's going to be a slow grind," Charlie muttered. "Jerome's kids make it?" Charlie asked, and Robbie shook his head.

Without warning, Randy dropped down next to Charlie and scanned the piles of documents and identification cards. "What do we know?" Randy asked quietly.

After jumping a foot off the ground, Charlie gave him a quick rundown. "Kristi's home and sleeping. She's fine, but she had to abandon her ride at the hospital. The roadblock we hit last night was a roving team guarding a specific boundary on the map. They had orders to stop people from leaving population centers. I don't have any specifics on why they had those orders. The three cars would set up along one road for a few hours before moving south to the next road. My analysis is they don't have the manpower just yet to cover every small dirt road and pig path, but they are expecting reinforcements within a few days."

"Who the hell gave them the orders to execute folks?" Randy asked.

Holding up a handful of papers, Charlie shrugged, "That was not in the official documents I pulled. There are a lot more IDs here than bodies back in the woods. I don't know where the extra people are right now, but they had a set of instructions for processing civilians through to 'safe zones'. Don't ask, because there is nothing more on it."

"You think they went rogue and started collecting ears?" Robbie asked.

"Again, I don't have that evidence in front of me to give you a definitive answer," Charlie answered.

Needing to keep his hands busy, Randy rolled over and adjusted his prosthetic. "We covered a lot of ground last night by following the tracks, and I don't see the trains running today. That's strange because today is a weekday and not a holiday. I also don't see traffic on the roads around here."

"That's nuts, we are close to I-90. We crossed it last night and the rail line parallels it into Gary. If the commuter trains are not

214

running, then there should be a ton of traffic for folks trying to get to work," Robbie said in confusion.

"Do we risk trying to move during the day?" Cody asked from his prone position facing east.

"Too risky. If we get law enforcement on our tails, we might not be able to shake them. Hate to break it to everyone, but they have more guns, bullets, and bodies, not to mention air cover. We don't have anything to take out air assets," Randy explained. "We wait here and hydrate, eat, and rest up. At sunset, we make the push all the way to Kristi's house. I want to move too, guys, but this is the best option."

"Aren't we close to the Dunes? We took the kids there hiking before," Cody said, wanting more cover.

Adjusting his AR, Randy nodded as gunfire sounded in the distance to the north. "Yeah, it's only about four miles north of here. It may as well be on the dark side of the moon. We have an RV park just to the west and an elementary school through the trees of this forest. The school is closed, and the RV park looks full."

"We are so close," Cody responded as a few shots rang out to the east.

They remained in the thick underbrush and listened to gunshots breaking out with greater regularity to their west around noon. A group of people stumbled through the forest around two in the afternoon, laden with backpacks and carrying their belongings, heading east. The former Rangers stayed put and waited for their opportunity. Randy massaged his leg and changed the sock covering his stump before jamming it back into his prosthetic leg. Book smeared ointment on the dried skin of his hand and face to keep his exposed scar tissue moist. As the light faded, the team stood and gathered their gear. They jumped around and used tape to silence any loose gear that made noise.

Reminding himself he was in the USA, Robbie strapped his helmet on and checked his night vision. Charlie checked his sniper system and used the scope to scan the woods before they moved. With the sun setting, Randy gave the hand signals that set Robbie at the rear with his wide-angle night vision goggles and Cody and Charlie in the middle, with himself leading their movement. Satisfied, Randy put his map away and stepped off.

Gripping his rifle, Charlie waited until Randy had a ten meter lead before he and Cody followed. Covering their ass, Robbie walked to the tracks and joined the small team heading west. Cody and Charlie staggered themselves until the entire team covered a compact forty-meter footprint. They could react to threats from any direction, and Blaster practiced scanning their rear while keeping an eye on the trees lining the double tracks. The canyon darkened as the fleeting sun disappeared below the horizon.

With full darkness, Randy picked up the pace until they reached an easy jog and held their rifles at the low ready. The darker it got, the more gunshots sounded off around them. Once they closed with Gary, the tracks entered more urban neighborhoods, and the crossings became street-level with the city lights still working. They picked up furtive movements along the streets and a few shouts of "Five oh!" followed in their wake.

When the shouts started, Robbie called to Randy over the radio, "The natives have seen us. They think we are the cops."

Hearing Robbie's voice over his earbud, "I'm picking up the pace. Keep it together and watch your sides." Randy's voice went up and down as he turned the jog into a run and grabbed the PTT (Push To Talk) toggle again. "Check our rear, Blaster."

"So far, so good. I can still hear them yelling and moving to the tracks. We have to keep going to get out of their area, Shadow," Robbie answered.

They pushed on until they reached an area less developed and wooded. The gunshots from the south, or downtown Gary, increased.

From the back of the formation, Robbie started humming a tune to himself. After a few seconds, Charlie picked it up and chuckled to himself. He keyed his microphone, "Blaster, I never knew you liked musicals. When did you ever see 'The Music Man'?"

"Dude, I'm sorry. I can't get it out of my head," Robbie laughed to himself.

Over the radio, Randy cut in, "Well, I can think of something to take your mind off that damn song. Contact left. Lots of contact. Babyface, watch the right flank. Everybody else, orientate to the left." They broke from the comfort of the double-lined trees and out into the open space where the rail line they'd followed in. Less than a hundred meters from their position, Gary, Indiana's downtown

216

came into view. Furtive movements under the street lights and random gunshots aimed at each other had the four on high alert.

"I'm going to veer to the right and try to take us to the lower ground," Randy told them, then skipped over the tracks and led them down the small embankment, and the city disappeared behind the concrete barrier between the interstate and the rail lines. Everyone noticed, the interstate lacked any traffic. No stalled cars dotted the six lanes of traffic going in either direction. The sound of gunfire increased, and a stray round whined over their heads like a pissed-off bumblebee.

When the others were across, Robbie broke into a trot across the interstate with his head swiveling left and right. "Thissucksthissucksthissucksthissucksthissucksthissucks," Robbie chanted in a whisper to himself. The lack of cover or anywhere to go if they got lit up made the hairs on the back of his neck stand up. They pounded along the uneven siding and hurdled a low concrete wall before entering another line of trees following the rail line. Randy dodged around saplings. A line of trains, loaded with coal, sat on the rails and provided cover between them and threats from the right.

"That fishbowl was not fun," Robbie called out over the radio. The fact that they'd had no cover and the low lights from the city gave away their position as they'd run made him cringe inside. Further ahead, Randy found a denser collection of trees and called for a halt for a few minutes.

Charlie used his scope to scan between the trees to the left. "I don't think anyone saw us, or if they did, they are not crossing that to come at us." He pulled his eye away from the scope. "Can we avoid doing that again?"

"I'll second that notion," Robbie chimed in.

Giving a shrug, Cody scanned the trains and asked, "What was wrong with that? Nobody shot at us, I'll count that as a win."

"That was the worst possible situation, Babyface. One person with a scoped rifle and on one of those downtown buildings could have picked off at least two of us with no sweat. That was a major choke point. Going to the north would have put us in the lake, looping to the south would have brought us through miles of neighborhoods in a rough town. We can't afford to waste time," Charlie responded.

"So why are we just sitting here?" the younger former Ranger smirked as Robbie caught his breath.

Glancing over at Cody, Charlie chuckled, "Smartass. I know for a fact that Blaster has neglected his cardio workouts. He's starting to huff and puff like an old man."

"I'm toting some extra weight, but it ain't around my waist, Book. I'm ready to lighten the load," Blaster retorted. The extra set of vests they had lashed to their assault packs from the dead cops dragged on them, but Robbie knew the kids and Kristi would need them on the way back to the retreat.

"Shadow, how much further?" Cody asked.

"Thirty miles as the crow flies. Six hours, if we keep shuffling on. We can cut time by picking it up a bit. The next few miles will be easier, since it's mostly industrial parks and mixed forests. They were too busy in Gary shooting at each other to notice us slipping through. I didn't hear any sirens, guys. That's not good." Randy stood and adjusted his pack. "Miles to go before we sleep, fellas."

"Well, you know we always did take the road less traveled," Charlie let out a low chuckle.

Checking his weapons, Blaster shook his head, "I hate it when you get all poetic on me. Can we stick with history? I can carry my own water when we discuss the past."

"Ah, Frost was a bit of a dick, but he had some good verse, Blaster. We need to expand your horizons. I think you would like him," Cody smiled and gave Robbie a wink.

"Good God. Book has corrupted you," Robbie sighed.

Not about to get caught up in the chain yanking, Randy stepped off and let them sort themselves out behind him. Handling the easy pace, Robbie called Randy on the radio, "You can pick it up a little, Shadow. I can keep up." Randy didn't reply, but Robbie saw him pull ahead a little by picking up the pace until Cody and Charlie closed the interval. The gunfire faded behind them as they ate away at the miles with lengthened strides. Occasional flurries of fighting broke out along their route, but it was directed against other citizens to the south of their path. As they turned to the left before Buffington Harbor, the battle shifted to their immediate front.

East Chicago sounded like a New Year's and Fourth of July rolled into one hot mess. The rail line dipped under Cline Avenue before the petroleum storage facility, but Randy pulled up short before the overpass.

"Book, check the underpass. I'm seeing movement to the right under the bridge," Randy whispered loud enough for Book to hear with his amplified hearing device.

"I see two tangos on the right and another three on the left. They are armed with rifles or shotguns," Charlie called out from his optic, peering into the darkness. The longer weapons stood out, and they happened to be pointed in their direction. "They heard us coming, but I don't think they can see us in the dark."

"Let me sneak a peek and see if they are friendly," Randy whispered and dropped his pack before taking off to the right and out of sight. Dropping down, Robbie followed Randy's movements until he moved behind some brush next to the concrete bridge abutment.

"Hey, do you five mind not shooting me? I can talk or kill all of you. If that's what you want, I'll help you out," Randy called out in a low voice. Charlie heard the request from his position and laughed to himself from behind his scope.

"Fuck you! You are trespassing! Step out so I can see you," a rough voice responded to Randy.

Adjusting his aim, Randy tried to reason, "We are just passing through. I'm on a time crunch, so I'll just kill you all now and be on my way."

"Bring it, Pig! You have to come through us if you want to get at our families," a different voice yelled.

Ready to drop his finger on the trigger, Randy sighed, "Dumbasses. We are not here to hurt anyone, guys. You have a great ambush spot, but not everyone is out to kill you or your relatives. Can you back off and let us pass so we can get to *our* family, or should I cut over this embankment and just swing around you?"

"We will cut you down on the other side. There is no cover over there," the first voice from under the bridge called out.

"Are you prior service? You have a good spot here," Randy inquired, about ready to tell Charlie to start taking their heads off with his sniping rifle.

"2nd Marines back in the day," the voice responded.

"We were in the other hell hole with the 75th Rangers. My buddies are waiting for my word to cap all five of you. I respect you for protecting your families, but we have to move through your area. If your guys will pull back and form a blocking force, you can be assured that we won't attack your homes. I'm guessing you live in that residential neighborhood just to the north."

"What's your name?" the voice asked.

"My handle is Shadow. The rest of my crew and I go way back. Gary is a free fire zone right now. As you know, help is not coming. They are rounding up veterans, so stay sharp."

"They came for me yesterday. I wasn't home, but they didn't mind tearing my mother's house apart looking for my guns. I dug them up and decided to turn them in when I had emptied them first." One of the men lurking under the bridge chuckled.

"So, do we have a truce, nameless Marine under the bridge?" Shadow asked.

"Shit, just call me Troll. It does fit me, I guess," the former marine responded. "Hey, watch the gangs once you get clear of the oil tanks, they tried to run up in here and we bloodied them good."

"I'll tell my guys to help you whittle them down some more if they get froggy," Randy replied.

"Shit, it ain't an *if*. They light up anyone who comes that way. If you have night vision, then stick to the shadows and nail them before they see you. They will use cars like damn technicals. I'll call my other team to let them know you are moving through."

"Be careful with the radios. I have a feeling that someone is listening, and once they get their troops into place, they will come looking for you," Randy suggested.

Troll laughed, "I know comms security. Someone is always listening. That's why I pulled back from our neighborhood and set up here as a blocking force. Gary is running plenty hot right now."

"Good times, Troll. Stay frosty." Randy admired the guy out here defending his home and family.

"They are pulling back from the bridge. Ease up and make sure they are keeping their word. You know how those jarheads can be about keeping their word," Charlie called over the radio.

Staying low, Randy crept around the concrete columns and caught sight of Troll leading his men away from the bridge.

Impressed, watching the group move, Randy counted a total of ten forms creeping back to the north and forming a line behind cover.

"Damn, he has a couple of fire teams organized over here. Good thing we talked instead of lighting them up. The way ahead is clear as far as I can tell," Randy reported over the radio, then waved the team forward. Handing Randy his rucksack, Charlie waited until he'd pulled it on and they took off at a quick jog.

"The good news is there are more people out here like us, trying to make things safe for loved ones," Randy said loud enough so Cody and Charlie could hear.

The four took off at a jog with their night vision turned off to save the batteries. The glow of the tank farm's security lights would have overloaded the image intensifiers of their units. A mile long row of white steel storage tanks surrounded by chain-link fencing formed an impenetrable barrier to their left. The neighborhoods on the right sat silent, with only a few flickering lights glowing from the windows of the thousands of people waiting for the electricity to come back on.

"Book, who do you think cut the power?" Robbie whispered.

Keeping his breathing at a rhythm, Charlie jogged along and glanced at the houses with his scope. "It could be a power outage caused by a relay station going down or the lines getting cut. There are so many fires burning, I'm sure some have been hit. Hell, who's going out to fix anything with the streets going crazy?"

A red light blinked from the trees adjacent to the tracks. Randy slowed and had them pull into the bushes before he loped ahead to investigate. He called over the radio a quick message, "Clear. Friendlies. Come on forward."

The three rose and advanced to Randy standing near two dark figures. Charlie watched them through his scope, but if Randy said they were friendly, then Charlie took him at his word. The sniper lowered his rifle and watched his step on the uneven ground.

"Troll's guys say we can expect some excitement up the line. The natives are restless," Randy called over the radio, then adjusted his pack and thanked the two men who faded back into the trees.

"Damn, Shadow. Those guys are your people," Robbie noted how the two men had faded into the trees and disappeared.

"They're either trained like I was, or just natural stalkers. Looks like Troll has some folks with him who have experience," Randy nodded as he got them moving again at a slower pace. Once the glare from the tank farm subsided, the team switched back to using their night vision to peer into the darkness of doorways and alleys as the city closed in around them.

The first person to try and take a shot at them, didn't even get the chance to pull the trigger. Charlie saw the man lurking among the trees behind an industrial building. Pulling his rifle up, Charlie called out, "Contact left," and stroked the trigger of his rifle.

"Clear," he called out again when the man slumped down and didn't move. The round through the center of his chest had destroyed his heart and lung.

"Everyone, go weapons free. We can't tell who's friendly, and we don't have time to play twenty questions. Keep it quiet, though. Blaster, no booms yet," Randy called out, just in case Robbie had snuck in some explosives. It wouldn't have been the first time.

"I was denied party favors, thank you," Robbie called back as Randy led them further down the line where the tracks crossed a narrow canal used by barge traffic. One block south of the bridge, flashing red and blue lights marking the bridge for regular traffic were blocked by two ladder trucks from the fire department and backed up by a contingent of police in full riot gear. A glance to the right, and they saw a similar setup on another bridge to the north.

"They are shutting down traffic, but they forgot the rail lines," Cody called out.

Saying a silent thank you to the big Ranger in the sky, Robbie smiled to himself, "Let's hope they keep forgetting."

They jogged under a traffic overpass and ran into one of the "technicals" Troll had warned them about. The gray Nissan Frontier turned right from a rail crossing and straddled one of the rails. The driver and his "crew" were probably trying to avoid the police roadblocks and get over the river.

Instead, they ran into four Rangers with no time to waste.

With the headlights turned off, the driver didn't notice that Randy and Charlie had slid into the bushes to their right. On the left, Robbie and Cody sprinted across the tracks and disappeared into the heavy brush. Two men standing in the bed of the truck fired at Robbie and Cody, but their rounds went high. Charlie put a single round through each of the gunmen in the back while Randy punched the driver's ticket with a double tap through the windshield. The passenger door popped open, and Randy hit the man who tried to bail out.

"Just go. We don't have time to turn out their pockets," Randy called out over the radio. Robbie and Cody ran back to join Randy and Charlie, who cleared the truck by putting a single round through the rear passenger who'd tried to play possum.

The sound of gunfire from the two idiots in the back of the truck had drawn more attention. A dropped Honda stopped at the same intersection where the truck had made its turn. Two more men jumped out, but Charlie lit them up without stopping.

Feeling like the ugly date at a party, Robbie complained about the disparaging distribution of targets, "Could you at least give me a chance, Book? You know, spread the numbers around a little?"

"Take your time, Blaster. I'm sure they are going to sit still long enough for you," Charlie needled Robbie.

They ran into a rail yard and stuck to the deepest shadows until they hit the west side of the facility. Ahead, they saw why the interstate had been empty in Gary. The bridge ahead had been blocked with cargo containers placed sideways across the lanes of traffic.

"Contact, front," Charlie called out. "Snipers on the bridge."

A muzzle flash lit up the night briefly from above as a gunshot rang out. "Who are they hitting?" Randy asked, looking through his ACOG.

"I can't tell, but the line of cars stretches as far as I can see. There must be people trying to make their way on foot between the cars," Charlie replied.

"They are shooting pedestrians? Those are cops! I can see one with a badge spotting," Randy growled in disgust.

"Not for much longer," Charlie replied, settling against a tree and let his sights stabilize on his first target. The two snipers, paired with spotters, and four additional security members brought the total to eight. The snipers both watched the north with their spotters while the security detail orientated to the south to watch their rear.

"I'll engage the snipers first with Shadow hitting the spotters. Blaster, you and Babyface work on taking out the security boys. How does that sound?" Charlie instructed, getting into position behind a large tree and waited for Randy to find his own place to lay up. "I'm ready to engage. Everyone else up?"

223

"I'm good to go," Robbie whispered.

Cody paused for a second, "I have a target ready. Blaster, I'm taking the one on top of the container to the right."

"Cool. I'm going for the one leaning against the rear of the container smoking and joking with my next target. You take the two up top," Robbie answered, then practiced swinging his sights from one target to the next for a few seconds while he waited for Randy to get settled.

"We can't risk leaving anyone up there alive. They will cut us apart on the other side of the bridge before we can get out of sight," Randy spoke up.

"Well, are you up, Shadow? We are all waiting on you," Robbie joked.

Out of options, Randy sighed, "Yes, I'm up. Book, you initiate. Babyface, this has to be coordinated and quick. Drop your target and get to your secondary immediately. Go back and service it again if they start flopping around."

With a distance less than a hundred yards, Charlie had a clear sight picture of the targeted sniper dressed in all black. Through his scope, Charlie settled his crosshairs at the junction between the helmeted head of the target and the base of his neck. The reticle settled on the sweet spot and Charlie squeezed the trigger. "Sending." Charlie's rifle coughed as the sonic crack of the bullet was drowned out by the gunfire in the distance. Watching the impact, followed by the sniper rolling to his side and convulsing on top of the steel container, Charlie moved to the second sniper and performed the same ritual as the first. The second target didn't flop around as much as the first, and Charlie found Randy's second target, the spotter, trying to drop down from the container to the cover of the concrete guardrail before Randy pumped three rounds into his torso. The man leaned back and clutched his chest as Charlie nailed him in the face with a .308 match grade bullet. He fell back and lay unmoving. Cody and Robbie had their targets down by the time Charlie repositioned his rifle.

"Any problems?" Charlie asked the two.

Shaking his head, Robbie stood and gathered his backpack. He changed his magazine out with a full one before dropping the partial magazine into his dump bag attached to his vest. "Nope. They never saw it coming. Let's roll, guys. That's going to get the natives stirred up. If for nothing else, they will be able to cross the bridge now."

The suppressors on their rifles cut down on the muzzle blast from the rifles, but the bullets traveled faster than the speed of sound and left a sonic crack in their wake.

Holding his AR across his body, Randy took off at a moderate pace and let them settle in again before pushing for more speed. Never breaking his stride, Randy checked the map and shook his head. They had just over fifteen miles left to reach Kristi's home. The world's best marathon runners could cover that distance in two hours and some change. But they weren't marathon runners and were carrying heavy gear.

He checked his watch, saw the time and shook his head. They needed to keep up the current pace for the entire time to get there in five more hours. The rail line entered a poor neighborhood and they picked up multiple gun battles flaring up along their left when Randy's voice sounded over the radio, "Close up on me, we are too spread out for this much action."

A group of men ran around the corner ahead of them and ran across the tracks. One of the shadows in the rear pulled a handgun and fired at an advancing group that was chasing after them. The chasing group cut loose with a barrage of bullets that tore into the group trying to get away.

Watching Randy drop to one knee, Robbie picked a side and began picking off the men chasing the smaller group. Thinking about the dynamics of this action, Randy shrugged and did the same. Cody pointed his rifle at the smaller group getting chewed up and shifted to the bigger group. The four former Rangers reduced their ranks into a handful of leakers jumping fences and screaming for help.

"What the hell was that?" Robbie asked as he changed magazines and watched for more.

"I'm calling it urban renewal. I was just going to let them settle it themselves," Randy answered, then turned and started running.

Glancing back, Cody looked at Robbie and shrugged, "I have no idea." He glanced at the smaller group trying to help the injured men shot in the back but decided to let it go.

Robbie checked their back trail but didn't see anyone stupid enough to follow them.

The tracks led them into a wooded area dotted with freshly groomed fields and eighteen holes of mayhem. The golf course had been overrun by bands of roving gangs all moving west. The four watched as groups bumped into each other in the dark. The groups shot it out with rivals, all trying to get at a subdivision on the other side of the course. Not wanting any part of that, Randy had them leave the exposed tracks and follow him through the wooded areas away from the brawling gangs. Without breaking his stride, Randy shot a man who stepped from behind a tree aiming a pistol at them. The body crumbled and each one jumped over it without stopping or wondering why.

When they moved back to the tracks to cross a small stream, a group ran up onto the tracks to block them. "Contact front!" Randy barked out, dropping down and firing. Charlie engaged them from the darkness, and before Robbie could pile on, the targets lay on the bridge leaking their precious blood into an unnamed stream.

"Slow down, Book. You don't have enough ammo to take them all out yourself," Robbie chortled.

Changing magazines, Charlie shook his head and scanned for more problems. "I'm just taking the ones in our way. I've had a target-rich environment since we crossed into this golf course. Did you see the yahoos running around the clubhouse having a blast breaking out the windows and setting fires?"

"Man, don't tempt me. Remember the mission," Robbie griped. "Why the hell are they attacking a damn golf course?"

"They have a bar in the clubhouse, dummy. Plus, the neighborhood next door is easy pickings for them," Randy chimed in from the front of the pack.

Glancing behind them, Robbie laughed, "Every neighborhood here is easy pickings. They expect the cops to stop this, but all I've seen are roadblocks. They want to contain them, not help them."

"Yeah, I agree. This is going to make getting back out even more difficult," Charlie confessed, then scanned his area with his rifle.

Watching his area, Cody had an idea, "Can we boost a car and drive to Kristi's? I don't see any cops prowling around to stop us."

"We can't. A moving car right now is a moving target. All of the good folks are shuttered away at home, waiting for this to blow over. The gangs and predators are roaming the streets looking for the easy pickings," Charlie commented and then swung his rifle up. "Contact, right." He shot a man coming toward them from the right, waving a pistol in their general area. "Clear." He scanned around, but he didn't see any nearby threats. "Pick it up, Shadow. See if we can keep up."

"Yeah, Shadow. I'm ready to stretch my legs," Robbie joked.

"Okay. Try not to cry too much, Blaster," Randy replied.

"Hey! That was just one time, and I really did have a really bad rash."

Unable to let that slide, Charlie jumped in and grinned back at Robbie, "If that's what you call crabs, then fine. You had a bad rash."

"I'll never live that down, will I?" Robbie lamented his misspent youth for a split second before grinning to himself. "It was worth it."

Chapter Twenty-Five

Outside Chicago

They ran through areas dominated by landfills and wastewater treatment plants. With their legs churning, they ran into Calumet on the rail line unmolested and did their best to stay with Randy. Even with a prosthetic leg, the man could still outrun Cody, the youngest member of the team. Robbie held his own and regretted picking up the shotgun and the added weight from the ammunition. He contemplated tossing it aside, but he kicked himself for ever considering putting down a weapon he might need later.

When Randy led them around a stopped locomotive, they entered a massive rail yard, and didn't see a soul moving about. Only slowing the pace, each took sips of water from their drinking tubes and kept going while fires burned in the distance. The sound of street battles from the city around them grew in intensity until Randy called for a break alongside the rail line at Western Avenue.

Dropping down on one knee, Randy looked at the map. "From here, we head north. You can hear the shit is getting heavy all around us. We have been in some shit, but never heard this much scattered gunfire. Load your empty and partial mags and from here, we don't stop until we get to Oak Lawn. Blaster, on the map you have us crossing the Calumet Sag Channel on the rail bridge. How is the neighborhood on the other side?" Randy asked, looking up at Robbie.

"I never did get a great feel for it. You know how a place could go one way or the other, like in Afghanistan? A village would be behind you one day, and planting roadside bombs the next? Blue Island is kinda like that. You want to poke your head over the bridge and take a peek?" Robbie asked while he dug out a box of ammunition and thumbed rounds into a partial magazine until he felt the pressure of a full magazine before moving on to another.

"Yes, I'll do that. When we move this time, let me range out ahead of you by thirty meters or so. The lights are out all over this place, so nobody will be able to pick me up unless they have thermals or night vision," Randy told him, then passed the word to Cody and Charlie. They agreed with the idea and they stood up and let the packs settle back on their shoulders before they started moving once again. Getting to his pace, Randy ran ahead until they had the right separation, then they picked up the pace and held the correct interval. It seemed to take forever for Randy to reach the opposite side of the bridge, but everyone was thankful he did it without drawing fire. Keeping his rifle pulled to his shoulder, Charlie kept his scope up, scanning for tangos on the rooftops and from elevated windows, but everything looked clear for the south and west side of Blue Island. The track, once again elevated above the roads crossing it, gave them a better field vantage point than the horror of Gary or East Chicago.

In Alsip, they crossed Cicero Avenue, and Robbie felt his heart skip a beat. "We don't have much further now," he whispered.

At 115th Street their luck ran out, and Randy threw up his fist before dropping to the rough gravel of the rail line. A crowd, gathered in the middle of the intersection, burned a pile of tires doused in gasoline and dragged people from their homes. The gang lacked any real central control, but they did have one thing in common. They all had a weapon of some type. Randy watched one man blow another man's head off with a point-blank discharge from a shotgun. The man pumped the action of the weapon and pointed it at a second man.

"Aw, fuck this," Randy grumbled and opened up on the gang from his position. Charlie, watching the action before him, didn't hesitate to join in. Not able to get clear shots, Robbie and Cody moved up and joined in on the action.

Each time his reticle centered on a target, Randy brushed the trigger twice before rolling to the next target. In ten seconds, he felt his bolt lock back and ejected the magazine and slapped in another while watching three trying to get away, and moved his reticle over to the furthest, brushing the trigger twice. Not watching the man collapse, Randy said hello to his friends and then moved to another firing position.

Watching the gangbangers dropping like flies, Charlie thought about the saying, 'Paint the town red' as he rolled to another position after dropping three. Aiming at another tango, Charlie thought the four former Rangers were doing an adequate job, and the town would have enough 'paint' for at least two coats.

Feeling his bolt lock and changing locations, Robbie dropped an empty magazine and reloaded with his prosthetic faster than most people with two functioning hands could. The team ceased fire with all their targets on the ground and changed their magazines without being ordered to do so.

"You see any more targets?" Robbie asked, sounding bummed.

Slowly, Charlie searched with his scope. "Nope. I see civilians trying to get the hell out of our firing solution, but I don't see any active targets."

"Clear the scene or haul ass?" Robbie asked and noticed Cody had never moved from his original firing location.

Picking empty magazines up, Randy stood and looked around. "We are close. Leave them here and let the civilians clean it up. They need the weapons anyway." When everyone nodded, Randy led them around the carnage. Passing the slaughter, Charlie did a quick count and came up with over thirty tangos down.

"I still didn't get to use my shotgun," Robbie whined.

Cody clapped him on the shoulder, "Cheer up, Blaster. We aren't there yet."

"Babyface," Robbie said in a low voice. "After you shoot, I want to see you move. You took down six targets and never moved from your spot."

"Their return fire wasn't even close," Cody shrugged.

"It's a bad habit that can get you, and us, killed. Shoot and scoot because you never know when the other side will pull an ace from their sleeve," Robbie told him, and Cody gave a nod.

The four men skirted the scene and avoided coming into contact with the few noncombatants left standing in the slaughter.

"Jesus, this crap is escalating too fast. Are all law enforcement pulling back and letting this happen?" Cody scowled and shook his head in disgust.

"They have families of their own to protect, Babyface. Just like we do. Come on," Robbie tugged at the younger man's sleeve and got him moving. They sprinted along the line and watched out for more pockets of gangs going after the local populace. They crossed the bridge taking them over 111th Street and saw cars on the road for the first time, but the low growl of diesel engines and machine guns mounted in cupolas had them ducking for cover and waiting for the convoy to clear the area.

"Somebody's moving in, and I don't like the looks of them," Charlie whispered.

"Who were they?" Cody asked.

"I shit you not, but those were United Nation Peacekeepers from the looks of them," Charlie replied.

Not buying that, Robbie snorted, "Bullshit! How the hell did they get here in only what, two days? We busted our asses to get here from Ohio."

Not getting into the discussion, Randy stood and led them on to Central Avenue. A used car dealership had a large party going on in the parking lot with music, drinking, dancing, and general mayhem. Nobody pointed guns at them or stopped gyrating long enough to notice the four leaving the tracks and running along the sidewalk to the high school. They turned right and raced across the open field until they hopped a fence behind the baseball field and disappeared into the line of trees.

Moving through the trees, none of them paused when they waded through a shallow stream and pushed through the low brush before climbing a low stone fence to enter yet another residential neighborhood. Holding up his fist for everyone to stop, Randy pulled out the map and checked the route planned by Robbie. "Eight more blocks. That's two miles. You think we can make it in thirty minutes?" Randy asked Robbie.

"Hell, man, that's slow. If we pick it up, we can make it in half that time. Fifteen minutes for two miles is a leisurely stroll for recruits in boot camp," Robbie replied and checked their rear with his night vision goggles. Folding the map, Randy pushed ahead for two blocks, then they turned north and followed Laramie Avenue for two blocks until they hit 103rd Street. The roadblock at Cicero and 103rd Street had a massive spotlight shining up Cicero to the north, but they crossed in the dark without incident. They heard gunshots ahead, and they all increased their pace.

From half a mile away, they heard the boom of a shotgun blasting away while the lower pops of handguns and the sharp bark of rifles they knew were ARs sang a deadly serenade. Randy tried to surge ahead, but Cody and Charlie stayed on his heels. Trying to keep up, Robbie lost ground with the rest of the team, but he still had them in sight when they turned right and then left toward Kristi's street.

The gunshots became louder with each step. Robbie felt his heart racing as suppressed shots rang out when Randy had turned onto Kristi's street. When he hit the intersection a block south of Kristi's house, he heard the familiar suppressed snaps as Charlie and Cody engaged targets in front of Kristi's home. Rounding the corner, Robbie raised his rifle and saw a knot of men trying to load up in an SUV. Pulling his AR to his shoulder, Robbie raced in and cut them apart before they could speed away. When the AR ran dry, Robbie let it hang while he transitioned to the shotgun. He hammered away at the remaining crew trying to escape until he'd emptied his magazine. He pulled his Glock and ran around the house to find three men trying to steal his motorcycle. Never pausing, Robbie shot all three and ran down the alley, looking for anyone else who wanted to fight. Reloading his pistol and shoving it back in the holster, Robbie transitioned back to his AR and changed magazines.

Grabbing his PTT, Randy called over the radio, "Blaster, clear out back?"

"I think so. The garage door is screwed up, and I don't think I can secure it. My bike is out in the alley, but I don't have time to mess with it."

"Come back around front, the back door is barricaded." Randy cut the transmission.

Trembling in rage, Robbie took the narrow yard between Kristi's house and the Ramirez property. Around front, Robbie got his first good look at the pile of bodies on the porch and strewn across the front yard. Based on the fact that several of the men showed signs of close range shotgun blasts, Robbie figured Jerome had put Wheat's shotgun to good use. What he didn't expect to see, lay at the base of the porch stairs.

Jerome had taken multiple gunshot wounds. The most severe, a chest wound, leaked a thick line of blood down his bare side. Kristi and Charlie were trying to keep the man alive, with Kristi doing chest compressions and Charlie tying a combat bandage around another bullet wound to Jerome's right thigh.

Robbie stepped into a spreading pool of blood and his feet kicked aside spent shotgun rounds.

"Kristi, are you hit?" Robbie asked.

"No. Jerome stopped them down here and held the door. We were upstairs trying to cover him. When Tabitha and Ryan showed up, we let them in, but this gang tried to rush the door," Kristi told Robbie and Charlie while she administered compressions.

"Your sister brought them here? The attack was caused by her coming to your home?" Robbie growled with a snarl.

"I didn't get into it with her, but she thinks they saw them driving around the neighborhood and just followed them to our doorstep. I'm sorry, but I couldn't just leave them out there. I'm such an idiot." Kristi stopped and checked Jerome's pulse. "Charlie, you can save the bandages. Jerome is gone." Kristi wiped her hands on her pants and left dark smears of Jerome's clotted blood on her thighs. "Everyone else is safe upstairs. Clark and Emily were shooting from their bedroom windows, but the men pushing in the door were covered by the porch." Kristi stood, and Charlie saw her hands shaking from the shock of seeing combat play out in her once-safe suburban domicile.

"Kristi, let us deal with Jerome. I don't want the kids to see him like this." Charlie stepped to the door and tried to lock it, but the damaged metal door would not close. The shotgun blasts to the hinges from the outside had warped the frame.

Kristi looked at Jerome for a second. "It's too late for that. Clark and Emily saw it all happen," she announced to the dark room lit by candles and smelling of spent gunpowder and blood. "They were in the fight, too. A lot of those bodies in the yard were cut down by them." Her words caught in her throat and she shuddered, "My babies saw Jerome fight for his life, and I couldn't do anything to help him. He told me to stay upstairs and wouldn't take my AR." Kristi stopped and let out a low moan, and Robbie caught her in a hug. He moved her into the kitchen and sat her down at the table.

"Jerome may not have been a Ranger, but he fought like one of my brothers. He fought for this family because he loved you as much as we all do. You have a job, Kristi; keep Clark and Emily safe. Let that be your focus. I'm going to give Jerome a proper burial, and then we need to get the hell out of here. Ranger on, sister." Letting her go, Robbie's voice broke as he stood and gave Kristi another one-armed hug. He wiped at his eyes and walked back to the living room. Relaxing when he saw Charlie had the front yard under observation, Robbie moved over beside him.

"Shadow and Babyface have it covered from the upstairs windows," Charlie said without looking away from the yard.

"Shouldn't you be on overwatch, Book?" Robbie asked as he dropped his pack and unbuckled the shotgun from his vest.

Stepping back from the door, Charlie shrugged, "I told them I'd help you bury Jerome. You think by the pool? He *did* work his butt off on that deck."

"I think he would like that," Robbie nodded, then paused before continuing, "I don't even know how to repay him. His boys are out there, and I have no idea how to find Charlene's crazy ass. He was here to get his sons clear of the violence. He wasn't ready for this."

"We do what we can, Blaster. Here," Charlie said and handed over a pile of blankets from the couch. "I raided the linen closet. You want to take him out the back door?"

"Yeah, I don't want to try to carry him out there and stumble on his handiwork. Good God, he piled those bastards up like wood," Blaster complimented Jerome's last stand at the door. "Shotguns are good until it comes time to reload."

Looking at the pile on the porch, Charlie nodded, "If I'm going out, whoever gets me is going to stumble on a mound of spent brass and bodies. Your friend did good."

Robbie and Charlie half-slid and half-carried Jerome's dead weight to the back door and disassembled the barricade made of a shelving unit and a table shoved into the rear entrance. A white security bar was jammed under the doorknob and secured to the floor with a rubber anti-skid pad. Someone had nailed a thick spike into the hardwood floor to further reinforce the simple bar. Inspecting the work, Charlie kicked the bar aside and unlocked the deadbolt before removing the chain. "I don't think they even tried to force their way in back here."

"They got distracted with my bike in the garage. They weren't bright, but their numbers made up for their lack of skill," Robbie grunted as he navigated the door. The two paused and pulled their goggles down.

Grabbing his PTT, Charlie called upstairs to Cody and Randy, "Are we clear out back?"

A few seconds later, Cody replied from above, "Yeah, Shadow has the front covered, and there's nothing moving in the alley. Shadow reports twenty-six tangos down out front."

Charlie nodded to Robbie, "I don't want to sound ungrateful, but we have to be expeditious about this. We can't delay here very long, Blaster."

"Just help me get him under the ground, Book. He deserves something for his devotion to the family," his voice cracked, and Charlie thought Robbie shook slightly as they shuffled Jerome's body down the steps and over to the aboveground pool. "I'll get some shovels," Robbie mumbled before he jogged to the garage and rummaged around the yard tools, returning with two long-handled shovels. "We can both dig and cut down on time. Let Babyface worry about watching our six."

With no more words, Robbie and Charlie dug at the soft sod until they had a grave deep enough to protect the body from roaming dogs. The two lowered Jerome's form into the shallow grave and covered him with the fragrant soil. Robbie gathered paving stones from around the pool and covered the disturbed soil.

"You want to say some words?" Charlie asked.

Looking at the stones they'd placed, Robbie asked, "What do you say to a man who lays down his life for someone else?"

Feeling Robbie's pain, Charlie's eyes welled up. "You call him 'brother'," Charlie said with his voice breaking.

With a long sigh, Robbie nodded. Together, the two stood in silence and said their own personal prayers for their departed friend. A pain neither wanted to feel again filled them: losing a friend in combat.

Lifting his head, Robbie looked around at the yard and remembered the good times they'd all shared in that place with the kids, Kristi, and each other. "This place will always be special to me."

"Maybe one day we can come back and give him a better funeral. His kids should know his bravery," Charlie suggested. "This place will have a very special meaning now."

"Yeah. One day," Robbie sighed, then walked off to return the shovels to the garage and they withdrew back to the house.

Chapter Twenty-Six

Chicago, IL

Once inside, Charlie and Robbie took the time to barricade the back door before heading back to the front of the house. They found Kristi at the table, redistributing camping gear into two new packs.

"I thought you already had that sorted out?" Charlie asked as he took a seat and worked at reloading magazines from his own pack. Unlike the others who'd refilled their packs from Kristi's safe, Charlie couldn't. Kristi didn't have 7.62 and he'd never kept any here. There had never been a reason for him to have rifle ammo stashed at the house.

Dropping into a chair, Robbie checked the action of the shotgun, swabbed the chamber and action with a rag from his kit before pushing rounds into the tubular magazine. The room smelled of death, blood, sweat, and gun oil as they worked to get their weapons ready.

Kristi sighed and stopped packing the bags. "These are for my sister and her husband. They ran from their building on the Gold Coast and drew that gang to us. Tabitha didn't know better, so don't take it out on her. They have Chase with them, and he's freaking out."

Not looking at her, Charlie inserted a fresh magazine into his rifle and hit the bolt catch. A fresh round stripped from the magazine and loaded the chamber. He safed the rifle and leaned it against the side of the table.

"That gang would have never shown up on your doorstep, except for your useless sister. Jerome died because they had nowhere else to go. Am I right?" Charlie snapped in a low voice, feeling his blood pressure rising.

With the shotgun in hand, Robbie stood up from his chair and headed for the stairs.

"Robbie, don't!" Kristi called out. She tried to cut him off, but her feet slipped on the coagulating blood. Robbie skipped over the streaked pool of Jerome's life-giving fluid and pounded up the stairs. Waiting, Randy met him at the top landing with his hand outstretched like a crossing guard.

"When we get out of this shit, I promise, you will get first shot at kicking their asses," Randy said, then pulled Robbie to Clark's bedroom. The boy was kneeling on his bed, scanning the street below with his AR. Never letting Robbie's vest go, Randy pulled Robbie back into the hall. "We protect the kids and Kristi first. I dislike, no, I despise Tabitha and Ryan, but their kid is blameless in this. It's a shit sandwich, but Kristi demands that we help get them out with us."

Taking a deep breath, Robbie started to protest, but Kristi grabbed his ear and pulled his head around. "Robbie, we are not abandoning my sister if we can help them."

"Why the hell did they just show up out of the blue? Don't they have their own fancy building with security?" Robbie asked with a scowl.

"As an alderman, Ryan got advance notice that the city was becoming unsafe. When he called the doorman of the building, he found out the security team the city paid for had walked off the job. They panicked and headed here, since Tabitha knew we had food and guns," Kristi explained.

Trembling in rage, Robbie shook his head, "So, like the Pied Piper, they drew an armed mob to your doorstep? How many anti-gun rallies have they attended? But when their sheeple world became scary, where did they run?"

"They blew through a roadblock the gang had set up. The gang saw a flashy SUV and gave chase," Kristi shrugged. "Tabitha and Ryan have no practical experience with what's going on, but she *is* family."

With a menacing gaze, Robbie looked around, "So, where are they? Are they ready to go?"

"They are in the spare bedroom. I didn't want Chase to see Jerome like that, so I told them to stay there until I came to get them." Kristi pushed past Robbie and Randy in the narrow hallway to reach the door. She pulled out a key and unlocked the knob to the room. "Hey, guys? It's time for us to go."

A man's voice whined, "But, why? Aren't we safe here?"

Robbie rolled his eyes at Randy, "Will you back me capping that whiny bitch now and save us time?"

Randy chuckled, "You'll have to deal with Kristi's wrath if you kill her brother-in-law right now. Later? Outside the city? Hell, I'll flip ya for it."

"What if we just left them behind?" Robbie asked.

Kristi coaxed the disheveled adults from the room. Tabitha had Chase by the hand. The pale nine-year-old boy shivered in fear, and he tried to bolt back into the room when he spotted Blaster and Shadow standing in the hall. Only seeing camouflage, low-cut ballistic helmets with night vision monoculars flipped up, knee and elbow pads with full tactical vests and an assortment of weapons, they didn't look like anyone Chase knew and Kristi stopped Chase from running back into the room.

Dropping to his right knee, Randy spoke to the boy, "Hey. We are here to help. Don't act like you don't know us. Your Aunt Kristi is a friend of ours, Chase, and we came to get her out of here. Do you want to come with us or stay here, Chase?"

"Mom?" Chase implored Tabitha Dillon.

"Do you have a vehicle big enough for all of us?" Ryan asked, putting a hand on his son's shoulder.

"Nope. We are walking out of here. The four of us got in here on our feet, and that's the best way to get out," Randy said as he stood and eyed their footwear. Tabitha wore flats, and Ryan sported leather loafers. Chase had kid's sneakers. "Before we go, we have to make sure you can keep up. Kristi, do you have any shoes that will fit Ryan or Tabitha?"

"I don't know about Ryan, but I may have a set of hiking boots that will fit her." Kristi led her sister downstairs to rummage through her closet while Robbie and Randy looked at Ryan's feet.

"You know what they say about men with big feet, right?" Robbie chuckled at Randy.

"Yeah, you get a size eleven and suck it up, buttercup." Randy grumbled. Ryan looked at his expensive Italian shoes.

"I paid over a grand for these!" he complained.

With a somewhat sinister grin, Robbie shook his head, "I'm gonna be honest with you, bud. No matter what you think now, your feet are going to feel like hamburger, even if we find you boots that fit. We aren't going to stick to paved roads or graded walking paths. You either keep up or get left behind."

Ryan shook his head, "Why is this happening? The news said the gun nuts were rioting over water rights. How did it get to this?"

With disdain on his face, Randy looked at the pathetic excuse of a man with his son by his side. "You really have no clue, do you? I haven't checked on the news broadcasts in a few days, but it's got nothing to do with water rights or farmers protesting in the streets. Did the guys chasing you look like farmers to you?" Randy sighed. "Come on, Wheat had huge feet, and there might be something in the basement close to your size." Randy led Ryan and Chase down to the main floor and further down into the finished basement. Not wanting to be near them, Robbie stayed upstairs and checked on Cody watching the back of the house, and Clark keeping an eye on the front. He tapped on Emily's door and waited for her to answer.

He heard her unlock the door with a soft "click". Robbie pushed the door open slowly, and Emily almost knocked him down with a fierce hug. Turning to the windows that faced the front yard, Robbie saw empty brass casings were spread over the carpeted floor with two empty magazines.

"Uncle Robbie! Is Jerome okay? Mom sent me to my room and told me to stay here until it was safe." Robbie saw streaks down her cheeks from her dried tears.

"We got it under control. We are leaving soon. Do you have everything ready?" Robbie saw the pack leaned against the dresser with her pink AR birthday present leaning next to it. Emily had her "camping clothes" on. Looking down at her, Robbie smiled at the girl, "Okay, then. We'll come get you soon. Your Aunt Tabitha and Uncle Ryan need some better shoes for the trip. Did you pack extra socks?"

"I always do. Just like I was taught," Emily answered with a forced smile and Robbie gave her a hug, glancing back at the pink rifle. He saw a smudge of carbon from the rifle being used, and Robbie looked at Emily again.

"Did you have to shoot at anyone when Jerome was in the fight?" he asked softly, but the empty brass gave him the answer.

Like a switch had been flipped, Emily's eyes welled up slightly, and her lower lip quivered. Very slowly, she gave a small nod.

Robbie knelt down and gave her a long hug and whispered in her ear, "It's okay," as she sobbed into his shoulder.

Holding her tight, Robbie cried with Emily for her pain and the loss of Jerome.

"I know you are upset about having to hurt people, but you did the right thing," Robbie told her in a soft voice.

"I'm not crying over shooting those guys. I'm sad that I couldn't help Jerome more. The angle was off, and the bad guys had cover and I couldn't get to them from the landing. Clark tried to go down to help, but Mom told him to stay up here," Emily said with her voice turning cold.

Not liking the tone but very impressed with the tactical assessment, Robbie pulled back and looked at Emily. "She did the right thing. If they got past Jerome, you three would've had to hold out on your own. Don't be angry with your mother. She did the right thing."

"Jerome died, didn't he?" Emily asked bluntly.

Keeping his eyes locked with Emily's, Robbie nodded, "He's buried out back by the pool."

Robbie's radio crackled. "Get everyone down here. It's time to move," Randy's voice sounded strained, so Robbie didn't reply back over the radio.

"Come on. Uncle Randy sounds a little testy. We have to get out of here. First, you put this on," Robbie said and pulled out a bulletproof vest from the cops they'd killed. Helping Emily put it on, Robbie grinned to see it almost wrapped around her, then helped with her pack and headed out to check on Clark. "Hey, get your pack on. We are moving out." Clark set his AR down. Robbie moved over, giving Clark the other vest. Clark's fit better but was still big. Grabbing Clark's pack and helping him put it on, Robbie pulled the straps over his shoulders before bouncing him up and down, pulling on the adjusters. Robbie checked the AR Clark had used to stand watch and shook his head. Blaster unslung his shotgun and handed it to Clark.

"Your new weapon. It's got eight in the tube and one in the chamber. Only use it for stuff up close, but it works fine." Blaster showed him the safety catch and let Clark practice with it for a few seconds.

"This is a lot like Dad's shotgun, but I don't have to pump it. Where did you get it?" Clark asked.

"That shotgun there has a story. I'll tell it to you when we get to safety. Keep it for me until then." He fished around in his drop bag for a box of shells. "We don't have a lot of ammunition for that gun, but it's something we need to have in our arsenal on this hike. I know you like that AR, but I need you carrying something more lethal up close. We didn't bring your suppressors and we used more ammo than we thought we would coming in and took all there was here, so stay on that. Emily told me you guys had to shoot at the gang trying to get in."

"We didn't just shoot 'at them', Uncle Robbie. We hit several of them at the doorway and drove them off. Then we went to our rooms and shot at ones in the yard till we saw Uncle Randy run into the yard."

Reaching over, Robbie helped Clark adjust the sling on the shotgun and saw a younger version of Wheat standing before him for the first time. The boy had the same eyes as his father.

His radio earpiece crackled again. "You coming, or should I come up and get you?" Randy asked.

"Coming," Robbie replied.

Downstairs, Cody had taken up a position on the front porch and he scanned the street with his night vision. The Dillons milled around the living room and got in Robbie's way when he tried to don his pack. Kristi pulled extra bottles of water from the pantry and stuffed them into the side pockets of her own pack.

Patting his gear down, Randy glanced around the room. "I'm going out first. Cody will follow with Book. Kristi, get Clark and Emily with you. Ryan, take charge of your family and follow Kristi out. Blaster, you have the rear, as usual."

"Is that a crack about me personally?" Robbie joked.

"Hey, you said crack, not me," Randy smiled and stepped out the front door. He tapped Cody on the shoulder and said quietly, "Fifty yards for now."

Never taking his eyes off the street, Cody nodded and waited for Randy to take off down the way they'd come in before he followed at a slow jog. Charlie replaced Cody on the porch and used his optics to look down the street for Randy's heat signature. He located Cody and took off after them.

When Charlie took off, Robbie took his place on the porch and snapped his night vision goggles into place. "Kristi, get a move on. Go." He waited for the Wheaton family to clear the front yard before he called for the Dillons to follow.

"Come on! I can't leave until you get your asses in gear. Go!" Ryan tried to protest, but Robbie grabbed him by his pack strap and physically dragged him down the steps of the porch and out to the street. Tabitha and Chase followed. After pushing them in the right direction, Robbie turned around to check the street. "Stupid m-," Robbie started as he ran back to the house and shut the front door and paused before running to catch up with the Dillon family. They had already stopped running and were strolling along at a snail's pace.

"You have to keep going, people!" he hissed at Ryan.

Ryan pointed at Chase, "He can't keep up!"

"Then carry your son! What the hell is wrong with you?" He scanned the street and picked up the boy himself. "If you want to see your kid again, you had better keep up with me," Robbie snapped, and he took off running with Chase in his arms.

Tabitha screamed and followed him. Ryan, not wanting to lose his entire family, ran after his wife. Ryan caught up with Tabitha when they hit 98th Street and headed due west. Far ahead, Randy ran down the right side of the street and stayed as much in the deep gloom under the tree-lined avenue as he could.

"How are things back there, Blaster?" Charlie asked over the radio.

"Peachy, son. Just peachy. Are we running balls to the wall all the way back?" he asked.

"Stay off the net, guys," Randy warned. "The hills have ears."

The distance between Kristi and Robbie narrowed as he found his rhythm while carrying Chase. Ryan and Tabitha gasped and wheezed as they tried to catch up. Over a mile later, Randy turned left and caught another rail line going south and west out of the city. Randy moved along under the cover of the thick vegetation and slowed his pace to let the civilians in the group catch their breath.

When the group caught up, Randy signaled for Cody and Charlie to pull back into the trees, and he eased off to circle the area, looking for threats. Putting Chase down, Robbie snapped his fingers to get the Dillons attention.

Fighting the urge to punch them in the face, "We are taking a breather for now. Drink some water and check your feet. Those boots were broken in by different feet, so they will take time to adjust to you," Robbie instructed.

"Why didn't we take our car? We could have driven that in a minute, instead of running like idiots," Tabitha asked as she flopped herself down on the ground.

Gunfire erupted when a small sedan passed the tracks. The car accelerated away, but they heard a crash followed by another flurry of shots going off.

"That's why we didn't use a car," Randy explained, emerging from the shadows. "Did you see anyone driving while we ran down 98th Street? It's not safe, so for now, we step light and slow. With our night vision, we do better at night in the city. Stay close, and don't say anything."

"So, now what? We just walk out of Chicago?" Ryan sneered. "That sounds like a great plan!"

"No, you idiot. We are walking to Ohio. Pull on your big girl panties and embrace the suck," Robbie slapped Ryan on the back and chuckled. "I told you this was going to be painful. Shadow only has one foot, so don't complain about your feet being sore."

"Yeah, Babyface is the only one who came back with all of his parts," Charlie smirked as he stood from a crouch and scoped the train line. "We have a clear trail as far as I can see. How long are we going for this stretch?"

"We are going until the sun comes up. We will jump off this line before Palos Park and head due south to find a place to lay up during the day," Robbie explained. He had mapped the returning route multiple times and knew the lay of the land.

"Why there?" Kristi asked as a torrent of gunfire sounded to the west.

Turning to the west, Robbie figured the battle was about a mile away. Hearing that the battle wasn't moving to them, Robbie finally answered Kristi, "A major power line crosses the tracks, and the green space under it goes for miles. There are all sorts of places to go to ground along that stretch."

"So, is the plan to run like we just did all night? Because I don't think I can keep up," Ryan complained.

Charlie flipped his night vision up and got in Ryan's face. "Kristi and the kids are probably carrying packs heavier than yours, but you don't hear them griping. Blaster wanted to cap you back at the house for getting Jerome killed, but out of the kindness of our hearts, we talked him out of it. Continue in this same vein, and I will turn a blind eye when, not if, he bleeds you slow and puts you down. Your son needs someone to look up to, so earn his admiration or stay here and die. I don't care either way, dumbass."

"I'll keep them going, Charlie," Kristi stepped between Charlie and Ryan. "You worry about getting us to the retreat."

"Okay," Charlie snapped and stepped away, flipping his NVG down. Randy checked the map one more time before he headed down the line. The heavens opened, and a scattered rain increased into a full downpour. The early spring night, cool to start with, turned colder from the rain. The moisture soaked through their jackets first and spread down their legs. They stayed warm by picking up the pace, but poor Chase suffered the worst. Ryan opened his jacket and tucked the child next to his body, trying to stop the boy from shivering.

As the eastern sky began to lighten, they reached Palos Park, and Randy led them off the tracks and under the silent power lines.

"It's getting light, but I have a good idea where we are staying," Robbie told Kristi.

"Can I count on at least four stars and turn down service?" she asked.

Turning to Kristi, Robbie stifled a chuckle, "Nah, but you'll appreciate a warm fart sack and time off your feet. You look exhausted, sis."

"Yeah, I didn't get any sleep at the hospital and didn't get much sleep at the house. It was a nightmare." She wiped drops of rain from her face that had leaked down from her sodden hat. "Catching some sleep will do me wonders. With all of you here, I know the kids are as safe as they can be."

"Well, we should be there soon." Robbie noticed Cody's head bouncing along in the distance. "Shadow is picking it up for the last push. Babyface is jogging to keep up."

"I'll try to keep up, Robbie," Kristi sighed.

Robbie shrugged in the dark, "I'll carry you and the kids myself if I have to, sis." He picked up his pace while keeping a constant watch on their backtrail. His wide-angle night vision goggles gave him the advantage in the dark, but with the sky getting lighter, the team would lose their edge in another hour.

Moving surprisingly fast and quiet, they followed a bike path under the power lines and dodged multi-use fields and unused baseball diamonds until they reached Burr Oak Woods. The thick growth of trees gave them shelter from the blowing rain, and they set up two small tents and covered them both with a camouflaged tarp, held in place with a piece of 550 cord strung between two trees. The tarp gave them extra space out of the rain and kept the tents from taking on any extra moisture. They pulled out their sleeping bags from dry bags, got the kids to strip out of their soaked clothes and had them crawl into the sleeping bags.

Kristi slept with Clark and Emily in one tent. Ryan and Tabitha slept with Chase in the second. The boys took turns under the tarp, with Randy and Cody taking first watch while Robbie and Charlie slept. It was only a few hours later when Randy and Cody traded spots with Robbie and Charlie. The rain fell throughout the day with no sign of letting up.

Since none of them usually slept more than a few hours a day, five hours later, the four gathered up just outside of camp. "How are we on ammo?" Randy asked, looking around.

"We took everything at Kristi's and that barely topped us off," Cody answered.

"I have Clark on the scatter gun," Robbie sighed. "I only gave him and Emily two mags each for their ARs. From the brass on their bedroom floors, it looks like each one blew through a hundred plus rounds at the house. Kristi blew through a little more."

Nodding as he wiped water off his face, "That's good, Blaster," Charlie said. "We want them to think run and not gun. How much is Kristi carrying?"

"Two hundred rounds," Cody answered. "Wish we would've brought their suppressors from the camp."

"Babyface," Robbie smirked. "Wish in one hand and shit in the other, tell us which one fills up first."

Rolling his eyes, "Blaster, I just don't want them capping off rounds that could give us away," Cody grumbled.

"Babyface, we want them to be able to protect themselves but not get in the shit," Charlie explained, glancing around. "They know their guns are loud and won't shoot unless they have to."

"What about food?" Randy asked, and everyone groaned. "Yeah, that's what I thought."

"We eat from my stores first," Cody told them, and everyone turned to look at him. "I'm not stupid, the body requires ammo also."

Everyone just grinned at Cody as Robbie leaned into the circle. "What are we going to do about the dead weight?" Robbie snarled.

Turning from Robbie, everyone turned to Charlie. "Hey, I didn't invite them," Charlie snapped in a low voice. "We can't just cap them. Kristi feels bonded to her sister and none of us can judge Chase by his parents' actions."

"Okay, I'll give you the kid, Book," Robbie said, sitting back up on his heels. "But they cost us, I don't know how many miles last night."

"At least six miles," Randy sighed. "Kristi and the kids could've made it a lot further. I don't need to remind anyone how far they've hiked in a day."

"No shit," Cody scoffed. "Hiking the Grand Canyon, they humped our asses in the dirt."

"Can I make an offer?" Robbie interrupted, looking from one to the other. "They either keep up or get left behind. We set a pace Chase can keep up with."

"I can live with that," Charlie nodded, looking from Cody to Randy.

"Book, we can live with it, the question is, can Kristi?" Randy asked.

Softly clearing his throat, "For her kids, she will," Cody told them.

All of them nodded at that and Randy asked, "Who tells her?"

Suddenly, Cody saw three sets of eyes looking at him. "Why me?" Cody whined.

"You are the next up for a lecture," Randy grinned.

Reaching over and patting Cody's shoulder, "Babyface, I'm sorry to say, nobody can stay mad at you," Robbie smirked. "That's why we send you to Mom so much."

Leaning his head back and looking up through the limbs at the overcast sky as the light rain continued to fall, Cody gave a long sigh. "Mom raises an eyebrow, I run to Pop," Cody admitted.

"What, you think we don't?" Charlie chuckled. "So how about it, troop? You talk to Kristi?"

Tilting his head back to look at them, Cody nodded reluctantly. "Yeah, I'll tell her," he mumbled in a low voice.

Still exhausted, Kristi got up and worked on heating up food with the camp stove. The lightweight single burner and the small lightweight propane tank got the water boiling in only three minutes. She poured the water into the silver foil packets and let the dehydrated food soften. Looking up, she saw the boys walking back into camp and could tell they had been talking about stuff that bothered them.

Acting like the big sister she saw herself as, Kristi fed Randy and Cody first. After fixing a pouch for Charlie and Robbie, she woke up Clark and Emily for their meal to split. The breakfast food would give them each five hundred calories. She checked her pack and did some quick calculations before going to Randy.

"We don't have enough food at this rate, do we?" she asked.

Looking around them, Randy spooned out his own breakfast and passed the bag over to Cody. "No, the freeze-dried food will run out in a few days. Once we get out into the country, we are going to supplement our food with whatever we can scavenge. We are all going to lose weight doing this, but the adults have more reserve."

"So, keep the kids fed and let the fighters starve? How long can you keep that up? Until you start breaking down?" Kristi objected tactfully.

With a look of indifference, Randy shrugged, "We've done it before in Ranger school. Granted, we are older now, but it's going to get tight."

"I'm going to work on getting the kids' clothes hung up, but in this rain, I doubt they will get much better."

"You can wring them out and run another line under the tarp. It's better than nothing. Their boots are going to need to get dried too, if you can," Randy suggested.

"I'll do the best I can. Tabitha and Ryan are still asleep. I'll get them up and see if they want to help."

"Don't count on it," Randy took another bite from the shared packet.

As Kristi moved to leave, Cody reached out and grabbed her arm stopping her. "Kristi, hold on a second," Cody said, pulling her back down. "From now on, we are setting a pace Chase can keep up with. If Tabitha and Ryan can't match it, they get left behind."

Jerking her eyes over to Randy, Kristi saw him nodding. "Guys, they aren't used to this," Kristi almost cried out.

Raising his hand for her to lower her voice, "Kristi," Cody said softly. "The longer it takes us to get out of the city, the more danger you and the kids are in. There are only four of us to fight our way out. That's why we aren't taking the way we came in, you can hear the gunfire. It wasn't that bad when we came through. It won't be long and all of Chicago will be just as bad. Your job is to protect the kids from anything that gets past us. How much are you willing to risk for the kids?"

Hearing the words, they watched Kristi's breathing increase. Closing her eyes, Kristi slowly nodded, "I understand, but she's family," Kristi sighed. Slowly, Kristi stood up. "I'll tell them," she said and walked off.

"We are family too, Kristi," Cody told her as she walked away.

Chapter Twenty-Seven

Outside Chicago, IL

They took turns resting and standing watch for the remainder of the day. Kristi busied herself with getting the kids' clothes dried out and the gear sorted. The most important, or most frequently used items would end up either in exterior pockets of the bags or near the top once the backpacks were loaded up again. Now that he had time, Robbie took the kids aside and tried to fit the body armor panels they'd taken from the deputies at the roadblock. With Ranger ingenuity, Robbie used duct tape, a knife, a needle with fishing line, and paracord to make the gear work for the much smaller kids. He cut extra Kevlar panels and doubled the front and back armor thickness to cover their vital organs.

"It's the worst sewing job I've ever done, but it will stop a pistol round," Robbie grumbled to himself.

Ryan walked over and saw the makeshift body armor. "Is that going to do any good?"

"I don't know, Ryan, but I have the Kevlar, so I might as well try," Robbie shrugged, feeling tension building in his shoulders when Ryan stopped beside him.

Ryan looked at the stitching. "Not bad for a guy with only one hand. Where did you learn to sew?"

"Physical therapy. It's not part of the treatment program, but I needed something I could do that required a delicate touch. Sewing helped with my fine motor control. I can even thread my own needle." Blaster opened and closed the three-fingered claw for Ryan by flexing his left forearm.

"Why do you worry about threading a needle?" Ryan asked, involuntarily stepping back from the claw.

"Because I want a fine touch when I'm reloading ammo or pulling wire on a rehabbed house. I'm not much for sitting on my ass and letting someone else do something for me that I can do for myself," Robbie spat, slowly looking up at Ryan.

"You don't like me much, do you?" Ryan asked, squatting down. Robbie looked at the arrogance on Ryan's face and had to fight the urge to knock it off.

"After the screwing you gave me on that house in Lincoln Park, I lost respect for you. When you led a gang of murderers to Kristi's house, I decided I'll bleed you slow with much pain and watch the light fade from your eyes. It's just a matter of time, Ryan Dillon. All I need is a reason from you," Robbie spoke without inflection and cold eyes, locking his gaze on Ryan's eyes as he spoke. Suddenly very afraid of the man behind the claw, Ryan stood up and went back into his tent.

As the sun crept toward the western horizon, they broke down the tents and stowed the sleeping bags before taking down the tarp. Packed up, Randy led them out when twilight settled over the land. The miserable rain drenched them all within the first hour of the slow slog through the forest preserve.

They avoided the open fields and easy routes of travel like the plague and kept to the edge of the woods. The sounds of gunfire picked up from all around them as the daylight faded. At one point, Randy had them all dive into the bushes along the trail when a line of bicyclists flew by on the paved trail with their headlights shining their way, going away from the heavily populated cities. A single pop from a gun to the east started a crescendo of pops and cracks as a gun battle started and ended within an hour.

Lifting his hand, Randy slowed the pace and scouted ahead, leaving Charlie on point. Not even gone for half an hour, Randy met up with them and had them all stop.

Dropping to one knee as the team closed in, Randy glanced at each one, "We have to keep to the woods for now, and the shooting we heard earlier was a group attacking a house. The neighbors picked the attackers off from their own homes. People are pulling together and protecting each other. That's a problem for us. We can't risk going into any built-up areas and risk getting our tails shot up by itchy homeowners."

"What's your plan, Shadow?" Cody asked as gunfire sounded in the distance. "I'm amazed there is this much ammunition in the area for all the gunshots. This is Chicago, after all," Cody noted, and the others nodded in agreement.

"We hole up for another day in the Southern Green Belt Forest Preserve. It will be like yesterday. We stay quiet and sleep through the day, and pull out at dusk again," Randy laid out the plan.

"Why lay up so close, Shadow? We can make more distance than that tonight," Charlie asked, wanting away from this cursed city.

"We run out of forest. Our next night will take us through the suburbs, and we are going to need all of our energy and focus ready for that. For now, let's move out and find a place to rest up. We have to cross two different interstates in a short period of time, and those make me nervous."

Not getting any objections, Randy stood and flipped his monocular down. Adjusting the gain when the rain picked up, Randy let the light-gathering tube do its magic, then slowly eased off. The falling rain covered the sound of their passage through the stands of trees. When they reached an open field, Randy had them stay behind while he ran ahead to check for attackers.

Charlie provided overwatch for the group as they made mad dashes across the open spaces. At Interstate 80, they didn't pause when Randy jumped the barrier and sped across the divided lanes, but waited for a reaction before waving to Charlie and Cody. Charlie and Robbie watched as Cody sprinted across and joined Randy on the far side. With the four in position from each side, they sent Kristi across with the kids before sending the Dillons over.

Charlie ran over next, with Robbie finishing the crossing.

"Jesus! That made my butthole pucker," Robbie shivered.

"See? Every time you say something like that, I think of that time in Italy," Charlie poked fun at Robbie.

"Hey, not in front of the kids. A man has to have his secrets, after all," Robbie grumbled.

Knowing this banter could last awhile, Randy shook his head and rolled his eyes behind his monocular. "Can we move on? I don't like being this close to the highways."

"Why? It's empty," Tabitha pointed to the empty interstate.

Robbie scoffed, "It's empty, until you see a convoy of troops rolling along with thermal scopes and automatic grenade launchers. You don't want to be anywhere near that kind of trouble." Robbie

252

helped Chase stand up. "We gotta go." He herded the Dillon family in the right direction and listened to the rain pattering to the ground. "This shit never happens when the skies are clear, does it?" he grumbled to himself.

They pushed through the tangled scrub brush and thorns for hours until they hit the second interstate they had to navigate, in the middle of the Tinley Park Forest Reserve.

Randy halted them back in the woods. "Book, we have a team set up on a bridge down the interstate that I need you to take a look at."

"You think it's another blocking force?" Charlie asked.

"I can't tell. Your scope has better magnification than my gear, but if they are a threat, I want to avoid or eliminate it. We will be sleeping just on the other side of this interstate tomorrow, so I'd rather avoid any contact." Randy scratched at the beard coming in.

"Can we track back to the north and cross?" Cody asked.

Scanning behind them, Robbie sighed, "No can do, Babyface. The trees run out up there. We have to cross here or go south, which puts us closer to that overpass."

Charlie crept to the edge of the highway and settled behind a tree to scope out the men on the bridge. He switched on his goggles and scanned the light signature coming from the bridge, picking up a stray laser dancing along the highway. The laser passed through the rain and threw off sparks of energized light. Behind the goggles, Charlie sighed, "Well, shit."

He turned off the goggles and swung them up before settling behind the thermal scope. Randy came up behind him and asked, "Run or fight, Book?"

"Can't run, Shadow. I have to drop them here if we are going to cross."

"You want me to ease up closer, Book?"

"I can get them from here. It's only a little over two hundred meters. That's like shooting fish in a barrel," Charlie said, picking one heat signature and waited for his crosshairs to settle. He practiced moving to the four different targets and anticipating how they would move when they started taking fire. When he had planned out three different scenarios on the groups movement, he whispered to Randy, "Sending."

Within ten seconds, he had hit the four men on the bridge. The first two received headshots, but the next target took a round in the throat. The last member of the crew stood up and got drilled in the chest for his troubles. When he sat up, Charlie pithed him like a frog.

"Four hits, Shadow. Bring them over, and I'll watch for movement from up there," Charlie called out softly, pulling out a fresh magazine and replacing the partially expended one from the rifle.

Lowering his body, Randy prepared himself and then hurdled the guardrail, landing in a dead run. Leaping up, he jumped over the fence of cable running along the centerline and sprinted across the northbound lanes before hurdling the rail on the opposite side.

Diving into the trees, Randy gulped down air and moved over to a tree, looking across the road. Nobody had shot at him, so he chalked it up as a win. He waved for Cody to follow his lead, and the younger man easily crossed the interstate.

"Showoff," Randy ribbed Cody as he landed.

"Old fart," Cody chuckled. "You want Blaster to go up there and grab their gear?"

"That's not a bad idea. He likes going through dead men's pockets," Randy joked. He pointed to the overpass and back at Blaster. Pulling into a crouch, Blaster waved in understanding and took off down the side of the highway.

"I haven't seen him run like that since Kristi made biscuits and gravy," Cody chuckled.

Charlie stayed back and watched the Wheatons and Dillons scramble across the interstate and struggle to get the kids over the center fence.

Checking the surroundings, Robbie ran up the embankment and fell to his task of stripping the useful gear off the four dead men. He took the weapons, ammo, and night vision equipment still serviceable. Charlie had taken out one of the units with a shot to the head that had exploded the goggles before blasting out a chunk of his brain. Robbie grabbed extra batteries and rations from their bags. With the load of gear, Robbie crossed the bridge and looked around for a vehicle the dead team could've used.

Not spotting one, he ran back to the group gathered under a stand of trees. "I scored some night vision, batteries, ammo, and extra gear. They didn't have a vehicle, so someone will come check on them and change guard. We need to hustle."

Needing no encouragement, Randy took off and Cody followed. The rest of the group shrugged and started jogging on their heels. Robbie took up the rear and scanned behind for anyone following them. They went deeper into the forest preserve and put miles between them and the interstate. Randy led them to a spot by a small pond and found a potential campsite tucked back in the trees.

"Same drill as the last camp. Tarp it and set up the tents. We can try to fish in the pond, but only if we can stay out of sight. Sleep, eat, and try to get dry," Randy told them, then left the camp and searched the immediate area for threats while they set up camp. They threw the tarp and tents up first and under the cover, Kristi heated up water for another round of rehydrated food. Randy came back and sat under the tarp with Book.

"I hate being so close to where we hit that team, but I was right. This forest runs out at Vollmer Road. We are between the interstate and Cicero Avenue here," Randy grumbled and pulled out his map.

"We haven't made any progress yet to the east, have we?" Charlie asked.

"Nope. We had to come this way to avoid the worst areas. Like I said, tomorrow night is going to be tough, and we need everyone rested up for it. This is our little bit of luxury before it gets bad." Randy slid out from under the tarp and circled the area wider, looking for threats.

Going through the gear, Robbie gave the working night vision to Kristi and the kids to use. "We don't have unlimited batteries, so only use them when I say so. The harnesses are for adult-sized heads, but we'll have to make them work for now." Clark and Emily thanked him before they crawled into their tent.

Kristi waited until they were inside to ask Robbie a question, "You took these off some dead men, didn't you?"

"Where else would I get them? They didn't need them anymore," Robbie shrugged and slid over to check on the magazines he had taken from the dead men and divided the spoils among the four packs lined up along the inside of the tarp. He pulled out his poncho liner and wrapped himself up before falling asleep, laying in a bed of wet leaves.

Chapter Twenty-Eight

Country Club Hills, IL

Feeling a soft tap, Charlie opened his eyes and saw Cody over his face. "Shadow's back," Cody said softly.

Lifting his arm, Charlie glanced at his watch. "Damn, four hours. Almost a record," he mumbled, pushing his poncho off himself. Seeing the other three kneeling off to the side of the camp, Charlie moved over to them.

"Why did you let me sleep so long?" Charlie asked, buckling his helmet on and hearing diesel engines groaning in the distance.

"Book, if any of us sleep longer than three hours, it's a miracle," Robbie answered. "The only reason you're up now is Shadow came back with shit for news."

Turning to Randy, "When did you get back?" Charlie asked.

"Fifteen minutes ago," Randy shrugged.

With his face going slack, "You've been gone for over six hours?" Charlie grumbled, and Randy nodded. "I take it those engines we hear aren't good?"

Wiping the leaves away between them, Randy started drawing in the dirt with his gloved finger. "That huge field to our west, they are putting up chain-link fence like you see on construction sites. It's five hundred yards by five hundred yards. And they are putting another smaller one just north of it. It may be smaller, but it's two hundred yards squared," Randy told them and moved his finger over. "They moved the trains off from here two hours ago and four locomotives with a very long line of cattle cars pulled in."

Drawing in the dirt, Randy put I-80 to their north and I-57 to their east, which was only six hundred yards from them. "They have roadblocks where I-80 and I-57 meet to our northeast. Then here where Vollmer Road crosses I-57, they have another hasty roadblock, but it looks more like a command and control group," Randy explained, pointing at each area in the dirt. "They are detaining people at each site in large groups, in the clover loops the ramps make. There are vehicles on the ramps with manned machine gun mounts."

"Fuck," Robbie moaned as Kristi came out of the tent.

"Don't stop, keep going," Kristi said, walking over to join them.

"Who's manning the roadblocks?" Charlie asked, looking at the lines in the dirt.

Wiping the dirt off his glove, "I saw cops, feds, National Guard, regular Army and Marines," Randy answered, then looked over at Charlie. "And fifty German troops wearing blue helmets."

"How did they get here so fast?" Robbie gasped, but Randy never turned, keeping his eyes on Charlie.

"The German troops have their own equipment," Randy informed them with no emotion. "I saw six of their armored personnel carriers, TPz Fuchs."

Closing his eyes, Robbie knew better than to question what Randy had seen. "Maybe they flew them in at O'Hare," Robbie tried to reason.

"I know that's not all your news, Shadow," Charlie said, looking down at the dirt drawing.

"This subdivision here," Randy said, drawing small boxes just below Vollmer Road. "I watched troops driving along and emptying houses. The thing is, they weren't searching all the houses. A captain was directing the search from the cupola of an MRAP and holding a laptop. The convoy would stop, and the captain would point at a house. I watched them close on the house, then search it and the weird thing is, nine times out of ten, the house they were clearing was occupied. If those inside didn't come out, they were brought out or shot inside."

As one, everyone gave a shiver as Randy lifted his finger from the dirt. "How did they know someone was home?" Kristi asked.

"Wondered that myself," Randy nodded, looking at the drawing. "We've cleared enough houses, and nobody is that good. So, I went and talked to a sergeant, and asked him while he was taking a leak."

Kristi gasped as the boys waited for Randy to continue. "They were going into houses with active cell phone signals. That's what the laptop the captain has was for," Randy told them slowly. "After talking to the sergeant, I followed them a little longer and watched them pull a man out of a parked boat that was tarped up. One of the troops pulled a cell phone from the man's pocket."

"Where's the sergeant?" Clark asked, and everyone turned to see him standing outside the tent.

A twitch on Randy's face flared his nose as he stared at the dirt. "Last I saw him, he was laying down on the grass and looking up at the sky," Randy answered, leaning over and drawing more detail to the southeast.

Clark ran over. "He could tell!" Clark gasped in shock.

Shaking his head, "No. Poor soul cut his throat shaving," Randy grinned, continuing his drawing in the dirt.

"These young people today just aren't careful," Robbie sighed with fake remorse. "Shaving is an art that takes time to learn."

"That's why I use an electric razor," Cody nodded. Reaching back, Kristi pulled Clark beside her as Clark looked around the group.

Moving from squatting down to rest on his knees, Charlie watched Randy draw. "Okay, ten pounds of shit in a five-pound bag. What else?" Charlie asked.

"The troops have overwatches on the overpasses and are patrolling the roads five miles out," Randy added, and Charlie reached over, grabbing his wrist.

"You moved out five miles?" Charlie almost growled.

"No," Randy scoffed, looking up. "The sergeant told me."

Letting Randy's wrist go, Charlie leaned back on his knees. "Sorry, Shadow. I should've known you know better than that," Charlie said as Randy continued drawing. "I take it you're about to tell us how we get out of the FUBAR we're in?"

"*Try*, to get out, Book," Randy corrected in a dead voice. "Just be glad we didn't try to go the way we came in. That's where most troops are being set up. That's what was in all those UN vehicles we spotted."

"What else did this sergeant tell you, Shadow, before we go on?" Charlie asked.

Leaning back, Randy wiped the dirt off his glove and reached into his dump bag, pulling out five magazines. "This was all the sergeant had on him, and privates have less," Randy said, holding them up. "The sergeant was a buck sergeant, an E5. Only staff sergeants, E6 and above are issued radios. The sergeant was issued a standard M16A3," Randy stopped and looked around. "The lower troops have to use cell phones."

"Holy shit," Cody mumbled. "They don't trust their own troops."

"No, US troops," Randy corrected, putting the magazines back in his dump bag. "UN forces only have to keep cell phones but get full combat loads."

"Any idea on numbers of UN troops?" Robbie asked.

Shrugging, "The sergeant didn't know, Blaster, even for around here," Randy answered. "He just gave me some info on local areas, but did say more troops were arriving tomorrow to start sealing the city off, so people can't leave. They are only blocking large routes right now."

"Anything else?" Charlie asked, and Randy shook his head. "Lay it out then," Charlie sighed.

"I found a culvert that runs under I-57," Randy pointed at the dirt. "That only gets us to the other side, but we move down through these patches of trees and cross over Vollmer Road here, a mile and a half from the checkpoint."

Holding his hand over the map and pausing Randy, "Shadow, why not move further east? There's only suburbs," Charlie asked.

"Yeah, where the gunfire is coming from," Randy said, looking up. "Every suburb is under siege, either by roving bands of gangs or feds. The ones I want us to cut through, the houses are more spaced out. Granted, that means more affluent and bigger targets, but less people defending their homes."

Pointing off the dirt map, "Shadow, you aren't wanting to take us through Park Forest, are you?" Robbie asked.

"Can't, not even the military can get in there," Randy answered, then moved his finger along the map. "After we cross Vollmer, we have to haul ass for three miles to get to any area with a semblance of security."

"That sounds about right," Robbie nodded.

"Where is the stop point?" Charlie asked.

Looking over at Charlie, "I-65," Randy told him. "That is where we have to be before more troops show up. Twenty-nine miles, just past Orchard Grove."

Kristi's eyes got wide hearing that while the others looked at the map. "We have to move soon," Randy told them. "It won't be long until they devote manpower to clear these trees."

Holding his hand out, "Give me the map, Shadow, so I can go over rally points with Kristi," Charlie said.

Pulling the map out, Randy handed it over. "It's going to get bloody, but there's no way around it. Sorry, Book."

"Shadow, we eat the shit sandwich we are handed," Charlie grinned. "You can turn your nose up and nibble, or just Ranger up and gulp it down."

Standing up and stretching, "Well, I like my shit sandwich with a side of fries," Robbie said.

Looking over as Charlie pulled Kristi close, Randy turned to Robbie. "Blaster," he said softly, stepping closer and pulled the five magazines out of his dump bag. "Tell Clark to dump the shotgun and give them these."

Reaching out, dread filled Robbie's face as he took the magazines. "I'll talk to them and give them their rules of engagement," Robbie sighed. "How certain are you of this sandwich, Shadow?"

"I had to kill nine to move around," Randy answered, and Robbie's shoulders slumped. "I don't think even us four could sneak through without trigger time, there's just too many bodies in the way. My hope is we only run into marauders and not feds. There just aren't any clear paths out of here left for us to use."

"Shadow," Robbie said, looking off. "We are in one of the biggest cities in America. I'm surprised we haven't had more trigger time."

Putting on his clear glasses, "Have Babyface set to our south, I'll be on the north," Randy said, turning away. "We need to be in the wind in a few hours, sooner would be better. We can hold up near the culvert until dark."

Watching Randy walk off, Robbie moved over and whispered in Cody's ear and Cody suited up, handing him a food pouch and moved to the south. "Clark, go get Emily up," Robbie said, holding the food pouch.

Kristi looked up from the map at Robbie. "I'm giving them their rules of engagement," Robbie told her. "Book will give you yours."

Closing her eyes while trying to keep calm, Kristi nodded and turned back to the map as Clark led Emily out of the tent. Both were wearing ponchos over their pajamas and Robbie couldn't help but grin. Opening the pouch, he grabbed the pot of hot water on the burner and knelt in front of them.

"Clark, you are leaving the shotgun here," Robbie said, pouring water in the pouch. "Both of you will be on your rifles."

"Uncle Robbie, I only have two magazines," Clark said. "I used more than that at the house."

"I used three," Emily mumbled.

Rolling the pouch closed, Robbie shook it slowly with the claw as he looked at the two. "Clark, I'm giving you three more magazines and Emily, you're getting two, but you're not to use them unless your life or your mother's is in danger. Do each of you understand?" Robbie asked, looking at the two.

"So, if I see someone aiming at Momma-," Emily stopped.

"If she's not shooting at them, you aim and pull the trigger until they go down," Robbie instructed, trying to keep his voice from breaking.

Clark nodded, "I understand, Uncle Robbie."

"Guys, this is all the ammo we can spare for you, so use it wisely," Robbie said, handing over the magazines.

"I can carry the shotgun, so I can have more," Clark offered.

Shaking his head, "No, Clark," Robbie told him firmly. "You don't need the weight because we will be moving fast."

Both kids looked at the serious expression on Robbie's face and started to get worried. "Just do what you know and don't worry about the rest," Robbie stressed, unfolding the bag and pulled out two spoons. "Both of you will stay within five feet of your mom, no matter what. If you pee, you'd better be able to reach out and touch her."

Even now they could hear gunshots around them, but neither had been overly worried after the uncles had showed up. Charlie, Cody, Robbie, and Randy to them, were larger than life and scared of nothing. Now Clark and Emily could see, they were worried about them.

They both took the spoons and ate from the bag while Robbie held it. "Okay, Uncle Robbie, we'll do good," Emily said with a small smile.

Grinning at the two as they ate, "Of course you will, tadpole. Both of you always do great," Robbie said.

Glancing back, Kristi saw the kids eating and turned back to the map. "Honestly, Charlie, how bad?" Kristi asked softly.

Holding his finger over the first rally point, Charlie turned to her. "Shadow's worried and that's never a good thing," Charlie told her. "Your priority is the kids and that's our priority. I'm sorry, but your sister better keep up because we aren't stopping. We can carry you and the kids. One of us will even get Chase, but other than that, you can't ask for more."

"I'll keep Chase near me," Kristi told him, then looked down at the map. "They will keep up or get left behind."

Hearing her voice, Charlie didn't believe her, but continued going over the route and rally points to meet up at if they got separated for twenty minutes.

They both turned to see Emily and Clark taking down the tent and already dressed. "I know the area," Kristi said, getting up. "Let me get Tabitha up, so we can move."

Kristi opened the tent whispering, and Chase climbed out shivering. Watching Kristi continue to whisper into the tent, Robbie walked over and grabbed a leg and pulled. Ryan cried out when Robbie pulled him out of the tent.

Dropping down, Robbie moved his left arm opening the claw and putting the open claw over Ryan's throat. "I move my arm and the claw will crush your throat," Robbie growled as Ryan looked up at him with abstract fear. "Make another sound louder than a mouse fart and you'll never make another."

When Tabitha climbed out to stop Robbie, Kristi grabbed her. "Don't, and keep your mouth shut. Dangerous people are close," Kristi warned in a low voice and Tabitha's eyes got wide.

"I'll take my claw off if we understand each other," Robbie glared into Ryan's eyes.

Nodding rapidly, "Y-yes, sir," Ryan whimpered.

Standing up, Robbie moved his arm causing the claw to snap shut as he stood over Ryan. "You have ten minutes to get ready because we are leaving," Robbie told him and walked off.

Before Tabitha could say anything, Kristi grabbed her shoulders. "They are killing people around us, you have got to hurry. You have to keep up with us or we will leave you," Kristi said in a low voice and Tabitha's eyes filled with tears.

"You would leave me?" Tabitha whimpered.

Taking a deep breath, "You can't watch out for or protect my kids, so I can't die for you," Kristi told her. "I'll fight for you, but you have to dig deep to keep up, so I *can* fight for you."

With her arms wrapped around her chest, Tabitha barely nodded as Kristi walked away with her own eyes getting teared up. "We're ready, Mom," Clark said, and Kristi saw each had more magazines on their small vests.

"Where's the shotgun?" she asked, grabbing her gear.

"Uncle Robbie said we are leaving it because we have to move fast," Clark told her.

Seeing the tent was already tied to her pack, Kristi pulled her pack on. "Here's some food, Momma," Emily said, holding the remains of the package out Robbie gave them.

"I want you and Clark to eat it all. We have a long way to go," Kristi commanded. Both kids started to protest, then saw the stern look on Kristi's face. Watching the kids finish off the pouch, Kristi turned when Charlie walked over to Chase.

"You will eat half of this now," Charlie said, and Chase looked at Charlie in terror before taking the pouch. Grabbing the spoon, Chase started eating. "Slow down and take your time," Charlie told him, looking up at Tabitha and Ryan.

"You two will eat the other half when he's done," Charlie said, walking off as the rain picked up again to a downpour. "Try getting the food before Chase has eaten, and I'm sending the claw back over."

Reaching his rucksack, Charlie turned to see Randy moving toward them. "Blaster, get Babyface," Charlie said, putting his rucksack on. "Shadow's seen something he doesn't like."

"Whatever it is better stay the hell out there," Robbie mumbled. "The last time Shadow saw something he didn't like, our world got fucked up."

Randy moved over to Charlie as he tightened his pack up. "We need to sky out now," Randy told him. Buckling his helmet on, Charlie raised his right eyebrow. "They are starting to check the woods, but-," Randy paused and Charlie turned to Randy, swearing he looked nauseous.

"Book, they're killing civilians," Randy said with a distasteful expression. "That salvo we hear a few times an hour to the north? That's what it is."

Coming back with Cody, Robbie and Cody froze and everyone turned to Randy in shock. "Who's killing civilians?" Charlie asked, feeling his arms go numb.

"Feds," Randy answered, closing his eyes. "They are wearing blue windbreakers with FEMA on the back.

Moving over beside Charlie, Robbie grabbed Randy by the shoulder. "So, they are killing the marauders and looters?" Robbie asked.

"Blaster, I saw them shoot a little girl tied to her mother that couldn't have been over six years old," Randy leaned over and spit, tasting the bile at the back of his throat. "They lead a group over, tied together and hobbled, and shoot them in front of the fenced-off areas where others are being held. There's a speaker going off and telling everyone who isn't compliant will be led over next."

Charlie looked at Robbie, "That isn't our fight. We have our fight ahead," Charlie snapped.

"Book, this is America!" Robbie gasped.

Nodding, "And we're getting our little slice of America the fuck out of here," Charlie barked softly.

"We need to move," Randy repeated.

"Are they close to getting here?" Cody asked, getting closer.

Shaking his head, "No, we leave now before I go back," Randy told him.

"You go without me and I'll kick your ass, Shadow," Robbie growled.

"Shadow, we have our mission and we will not deviate from it," Charlie said, turning to Kristi. "You ready?"

"Let's get the hell out of here," Kristi said, gripping her AR.

Everyone pulled on packs, checking the area and making sure they hadn't left anything, then moved over to Charlie. "Shadow, lead us to where you want to hole up till dark," Charlie said, press checking his SASS (Semi-Automatic Sniper System) which looked like a beefier AR-15. Seeing brass, he let the bolt go and tapped the forward assist. "Blaster, you have the back. Babyface, you keep the packages close. I'll take slack with Shadow."

Without saying anything, Randy turned and headed east. The others fell in behind him and Randy moved through the woods, with the waters getting deeper the further they went. Everyone was shocked when Randy continued until he was wading up to his thighs.

"Keep your weapons out of the water," Cody whispered behind them. Clark and Emily held their ARs up, with the water up to Emily's chest.

Hearing the roar of diesel engines ahead of them through the trees everyone paused, but Randy never stopped wading through the water. They watched Randy continue toward the diesel noise as the engines moved north. Holding up his hand, Randy moved back and whispered to Charlie, then moved off.

Turning around, Charlie waved everyone up. "We are going under the interstate. Shadow's going to make sure we have enough room to breathe," Charlie told them, and panic filled many faces.

"Why aren't you going, Book? You're part fish," Cody asked, looking around.

"Shadow said hold," Charlie replied as the water tugged at his legs. Hearing Kristi let out a gasp, Charlie turned while pulling his rifle up, seeing Kristi turn away.

Ten yards away, the body of a little boy floated past as Kristi tried to block the view from Clark and Emily. "We can't leave him here," Tabitha wept softly.

"He's dead. There's nothing we can do," Charlie told her in a breaking voice. A few seconds later, two more bodies floated past them, but these were adults.

"Here comes Uncle Randy," Emily said. Her normal cheerful voice was replaced with a sorrowful moan.

"Dammit, why isn't Shadow this easy to read when we play poker?" Robbie mumbled, not liking the expression on Randy's face.

"Blaster's got to lead," Randy said, reaching them. "The current isn't fast, but it's enough to take you off your feet. We form up behind him in a chain and we will have to carry the kids."

"How much breathing room at the top we working with?" Robbie asked, moving to the front.

"Six, seven inches of air for a hundred and ten yards. But we wait much longer, and we won't have that with as hard as it's raining," Randy answered. "Book, you need to be right behind Blaster. We will be coming out in a drainage pond with trees all around, but the command area for the checkpoint is only a hundred yards away. Stay low in the water and move northeast. You'll see where the water is flowing out of the trees. Head there and lead us out to the right, and you'll see a clump of bushes on high ground."

Moving up behind Robbie, "How deep is this drainage pond?" Charlie asked.

"Five to six feet but keep low, like your head is a turtle moving across the water," Randy told him. "Try to push anything floating to the side."

"Not that many turtles up here," Charlie replied, watching another body float past. "Many of those?"

"I pushed what I could to float through the other culvert but yes, we will see more. A lot more," Randy sighed and moved over to Clark. "Clark, you're going to ride my chest and hang on my left side."

Too scared to argue, Clark moved up beside Randy. "Kristi, hold my pack because the water will be over your head. You'll have to bounce up with each step but don't splash. Babyface, you have Emily and the rear guard."

"Aren't you scared they will see us?" Kristi asked.

Shaking his head, "Not with all the bodies floating in the water," Randy told her, nodding at Robbie. "Ryan, carry your son and if I have to do it, you'll be floating downriver."

Following Robbie, Clark turned to Randy. "Uncle Randy, my rifle will get wet."

"We will dry it off. Just leave it across your back," Randy said, picking Clark up.

Ahead, everyone saw two dark openings going under the interstate. Taking a deep breath, Robbie chose the one on the right, since four bodies were floating out the left. With minimal light from the dark rainy sky, Robbie guided his feet to the center of the opening.

Not able to see the other side, Robbie fought the current by leaning into it as he plunged into darkness. "Screw this," he mumbled, reaching up and turning on his NVGs. When they warmed up, Robbie flipped them down and gave a startle.

"What?" Charlie asked behind him, feeling the startle while he held Robbie's rucksack.

Pushing the body to the side, "Floater," Robbie replied over the rushing water.

They had to turn their heads almost sideways to keep their mouths out of the water. Hearing a splash, Robbie stopped but didn't turn around. The current was nearly strong enough to take him off his feet. Even with his body acting like a barrier, Robbie knew the others were hard-pressed to keep their footing.

"It was Tabitha. She's fine now," Charlie whispered as Robbie pushed another body to the side. Feeling the current push against Robbie, Charlie was glad Robbie was the size of pro linebacker.

Each step Robbie took was slow and steady. When he planted his foot, he tested his grip before moving his back leg. "Oh, I'm gonna be killing something very violently for having to do this shit," Robbie mumbled, pushing more floaters away.

Moving for what seemed like hours and feeling like a Hobbit, Robbie gave a sigh to see light ahead finally. Flipping the NVGs up, "Book, twenty yards to the opening," Robbie whispered back.

"Okay, keep this pace," Charlie said, letting go and Robbie turned to see Charlie's head floating upstream with his helmet rubbing against the roof of the tunnel.

"I bet you wished you were that good of a swimmer at Benning," Robbie mumbled and felt a hand grab his pack. He turned and saw it was Tabitha, who like Kristi, had to bounce off her toes to get her mouth above water. Impressed that she wasn't ramming her head into the concrete roof, Robbie turned around and continued on.

Reaching the opening, Charlie moved to the side, putting his back against the wall and his feet down. Looking over at the drainage pond, he sucked in a breath at the mass of bodies dotting the surface. Hearing faint voices, Charlie lifted his hand out of the water in a fist and Robbie stopped back in the culvert.

Bringing his rifle up and keeping only his eyes out of the water, Charlie eased up while tracing the voices. On the north end of the drainage pond sixty yards away, he saw two men laughing and pointing out at the water at the hundreds of floating corpses. Scanning around the pond, he didn't see any more.

Catching the body of a woman as she floated past, Charlie moved out of the tunnel to look along this bank. Keeping his head beside the woman, Charlie walked out, slowly turning his head. Not seeing anymore, Charlie brought his rifle up and let the woman's body float away.

Pulling the stock into his shoulder, Charlie saw the men were drinking beer as they laughed at the body filled lake. Seeing one turn up his bottle, Charlie put his reticle on the other's face. Flicking the safety off, Charlie slowly squeezed the trigger.

The muffled shot gave a weird 'twang' as the water cooled the hot gasses and Charlie centered on the other just as the back of the first man's head exploded. The second man coughed up his beer bending over, and Charlie's shot entered the top of his head and blew out his spine.

Dropping his rifle under the water, Charlie moved over to another body and held it in place while he looked around, making sure the shots weren't investigated. With the rain, the roar of water, gunshots in the distance and engines at the checkpoint, Charlie didn't think there was a risk but still waited. After ten minutes, Charlie guided the floating body he was hiding beside to the front of the tunnel. Charlie lifted his hand out of the water, motioning Robbie to move.

Stepping out of the tunnel, Robbie felt sick to see the bodies dotting the water forming a solid sheet in places. He had one that wasn't floating almost take his legs out from under him when it rolled along the bottom. As he neared Charlie, he pointed for Robbie to lead.

Waiting while the others passed, Charlie stepped up to walk with Randy. "Give me Clark," Charlie said, grabbing Clark and pulling him to his side. "Go find out who the fuck those guys were," Charlie snapped, moving over so Kristi could grab his pack.

Ahead, Tabitha retched at the sight of hundreds of corpses and there wasn't anything anyone could say, except Tabitha did it quietly. Moving through a pond of floating corpses pushed them all to nausea. Feeling Clark shivering, Charlie glanced over and saw tears running down his rain-soaked face. "Don't look, Clark," Charlie said, following along.

Lifting his mouth out of the water, "They were shot," Clark whimpered softly.

"I know, Clark, I know," Charlie said, having to bend over now to keep just his head out of the water. "Can you walk and keep your head out of the water till Blaster gets out?"

Nodding, Clark let go and turned around to see Kristi wiping her mouth. "Puked under water. Don't try it," she gasped. When she caught her breath, she lowered back down so only her nose was out.

When Charlie saw Robbie stand up and wade out, he fought the urge to take off running to get out of this watery hell. Walking into the trees, he saw the clump of bushes Randy had spoken of. Charlie turned around and saw Randy out of the water at the two agent's bodies.

"Go," he whispered, waving the others past and kneeling beside a tree. It may have been wrong, but Charlie chuckled when he watched Randy strip the bodies and pull the naked corpses out into the water with the other corpses they'd just been laughing at. Keeping Randy covered, Charlie risked a glance back and saw everyone was in the bushes.

When Randy stopped beside him, Charlie looked in Randy's face. "Who were they?" Charlie asked.

"Homeland," Randy answered, holding up two badges.

Chapter Twenty-Nine

Outside Country Club Hills, IL

Moving to the bushes with the others, Charlie and Randy found Kristi stripping Clark and Emily in the small clearing. Cody was at the other end leaning back on his rucksack. "Who were they?" Robbie asked, taking his claw off. Sitting beside his mom and dad still shivering, Chase looked with wide eyes at Robbie's left forearm where the bullet had amputated his hand at the wrist.

"Homeland," Charlie answered, tossing the credentials over.

Looking at the badges on the outside of the wallets, Robbie dried his stump off and then shoved a towel down in the tube that fit over his forearm to hold the three-fingered claw. "For some reason, that doesn't surprise me," Robbie grumbled.

"Blaster, them taking people's property on fake charges is one thing, but to execute citizens is Hitler-era actions," Randy said, dropping down and taking his rucksack off.

"Shadow, some could say shooting them is more forgiving than throwing them in prison to rot away like animals," Robbie told him. "Any equipment?"

"Nah, only Glock .40s, and I tossed them in the drainage pond after I pulled the bodies in," Randy replied, opening his rucksack. Untying the waterproof bag, Randy pulled out his woobie and two cellophane packages. Ripping one of the packages open, Randy unfolded a silver heat blanket.

Walking over to Clark and Emily, who were standing barefoot in their underwear, "Here," Randy said, wrapping the heat blanket around both of them. They looked up with quivering lips.

"Thank you," Clark said, trying to keep his teeth from chattering.

Wrapping the camouflaged poncho liner around them to cover the shiny silver blanket, "Not everybody gets to use my woobie," Randy smiled at them.

"No shit! I tried to use it once and we got ambushed. Shadow starts fighting me, even with hadjis shooting at us," Robbie laughed.

Pulling his boots off, "I told you to leave Shadow's woobie alone," Charlie laughed.

Turning to Kristi, "Get under there with them," Randy said, then walked over to Chase. "Stand," Randy told him.

Huddled into his mom and dad, Chase stood up with his teeth chattering. Reaching down, Randy pulled the boy's shirt off and dropped it. As Randy undid Chase's pants, Ryan leaned forward but Cody grabbed his shoulder.

"Open your mouth, and I kill you right here, right now," Cody snapped, letting Ryan go and moved beside Randy, kneeling down and untying Chase's boots. "I'll deal with Kristi. She only stays mad for so long."

"Y-y-oo- you can k-k-kk-kill him if he says anything about helping Ch-chchch-ch-chase," Kristi shivered, with chattering teeth while crawling under with her kids.

Hearing Ryan was cleared for a lead injection, Robbie seemed to levitate off the ground. Robbie moved over and shoved Randy and Cody to the side. "I got this," he said, buckling his claw on his forearm. Chase looked up at Robbie, standing over him without a shirt. "You'll be warm in no time," Robbie grinned, looking at Chase's blue lips.

"Here, Blaster," Randy chuckled, holding out the other heat blanket package.

Taking the package, Robbie knelt to take Chase's boots off and then his pants. Opening the package, Robbie wrapped the shiny blanket around him, then picked Chase up and carried him over to his rucksack.

Pulling his own woobie out, Robbie sat down, taking the heat blanket from Chase and pulled Chase between his legs. Wrapping the heat blanket and woobie around both of them, Robbie grinned over at Ryan. "We're warm," Robbie grinned, praying Ryan would say anything.

Picking up Chase's clothes, Cody wrung them out. "Tabitha, I would advise you to get warm," Cody told her while tossing down a package and Tabitha saw it was a heat blanket. Before she could say anything, Cody walked away to hand Robbie Chase's clothes and boots.

"Tabitha," Kristi said, feeling warmth seep back into her body. "Get out of your wet clothes and put them under the blanket with you, so they will warm up some before we leave."

While Tabitha did what Kristi told her, Ryan glanced around in shock, since nobody seemed to care about him. Then he looked over at Robbie smiling at him, and Ryan noticed Chase wasn't shivering and was leaning back against Robbie.

"We need better rain gear, Momma," Clark said, feeling much better.

"Doesn't exist," Randy admitted, taking his prosthetic off. "Want to stay warm and dry? Stay out of the rain."

Drying his stump off, Randy dried the inside of the prosthetic boot off. "We have two hours till dark. I suggest everyone gets ready for a hell of a night," Randy advised, pulling his poncho out and putting it over himself.

"We have to..." Clark paused as he swallowed hard. "Move with dead bodies again?"

"Don't know, but we might. We will be moving along a creek on the other side of Vollmer Road," Randy told him. "Just keep your mind on the here and now. When your hands and feet get cold, move your fingers and toes like you do when we are hunting."

"Can we use our heat packs, please?" Emily begged from under the blanket.

Looking over, Randy chuckled to see Emily had the blanket pulled over her head in a warm cocoon with her mom and brother. "If you need to, but you'd better already have them out because when we start, the only time we stop is to make sure the area ahead is clear," Randy told her, then everyone heard a group of rifles off in the distance fire at the same time.

The smile fell from Randy's face. Gunfire sounded around them but now, everyone knew what the group firing was doing. "Shadow," Kristi snapped. "You aren't getting side-tracked, understand?"

All the boys turned to see the stern look on Kristi's face. "Kristi, I would never dream of such a thing," Randy grinned.

Cocking her head to the side, "You do realize my husband did talk, right?" Kristi asked.

Leaning back against his rucksack and getting comfortable, "Man, I *wish* we had Wheat for this," Randy mumbled, trying to scratch his back on the rucksack.

Watching the boys relax while preparing themselves mentally, Kristi sighed with a smile. "He's with us," she said under her breath.

Robbie looked over and saw Randy using his prosthetic foot to scratch the center of his back. "I ever see a woman that can scratch her back with her toes, I'll marry her on the spot," Robbie vowed, making everyone chuckle quietly.

They could hear diesel engines around them, moving on the interstate and Vollmer Road. The darker it got, everyone noticed the tempo of gunfire around them increased, but none of them mentioned it.

When Randy stood up and started dressing, Charlie sighed. "Get ready," Charlie said, grabbing his boots. Putting on dry socks, Charlie cringed to put his wet boots on.

Checking the straps on his prosthetic, "I'm checking the road," Randy said, grabbing his vest and pulling it on. Patting his gear down and strapping the drop platforms on, Randy press checked his AR. "Book, if I'm spotted, I'll meet up at the first rally point."

"They see you, we are fucking hosed," Cody moaned, getting ready. Not acknowledging he'd heard, Randy slipped through the bushes. "Man, if he's that quiet and fast on one leg, I bet he was a terror on two. I only got to see it once and to be honest, I only remember being terrified."

"Babyface, I watched him slip into an enemy camp and steal their teapot," Robbie chuckled, and Charlie snorted hard, trying not to laugh. "Two hadjis were on guard and five others were sleeping and Shadow just slips in, steals their teapot, brings it back, and we had tea."

"I thought Wheat was going to kill his ass," Charlie chuckled, wiping his eyes.

"Did Dad tell Uncle Randy he couldn't?" Clark asked, pausing as he tied his boots.

"No," Robbie chuckled as he dressed Chase. "Wheat told Shadow he couldn't make coffee. We were following that group to a meeting."

"Did the bad guys find out?" Emily asked. She was shocked when her mom answered.

"No. The seven hadjis got into a fistfight because Randy brought the teapot back ... empty," Kristi smirked, tying Emily's boots.

Grabbing his rifle and making sure his optics were good, "In all fairness, Wheat told Shadow to get rid of the pot," Charlie chuckled. "That was some good tea."

As Kristi moved over to check Clark, he leaned to her ear. "I like it when they talk about stories with Dad," Clark whispered.

Seeing his boots were tight, Kristi looked up with a smile. "You're getting old enough to hear them now," she told him, and Clark grinned in excitement. "Make sure you tighten everything down hard, so it doesn't rub you."

"Okay, Mom," Clark said, pulling his backpack on. Putting the waist strap under the magazine carrier strapped to the vest, Clark pulled it tight and then grabbed his AR. Looking over at Cody, Clark saw Cody patting his gear and then pull the six magazines on his vest out, tapping the side to seat the rounds before shoving the magazine back in. Looking down at his gear, Clark copied what Cody had just done.

Cody moved over, taking the head harness of the NVG Clark had and adjusted it. "Just keep it on tonight. I have extra batteries," Cody told him, putting the harness over Clark's head and buckling the chin strap.

"Can't I put it over my right eye?" Clark asked.

"No, you can't aim with it over your right eye," Cody explained. Reaching to his thigh pocket, Cody pulled out a boonie hat in A-Tac camo. "This will help keep water out of your eyes," Cody grinned at him, tightening the cinch up.

"Thanks," Clark grinned.

"Here, tadpole," Charlie said, walking over and putting his boonie hat on Emily after Kristi had put Emily's NV monocular on. Spinning Emily around, Charlie pinched the back of the cap to take the slack out and pinned it with a safety pin.

"Rangers keep the weirdest shit in their rucksacks," Kristi chuckled.

Putting his helmet on, "It only takes one lesson to learn what to carry," Charlie said as Randy eased back through the bushes. "Verdict?"

"We are going to have to cross in ones and twos," Randy mumbled, moving over and lifting his rucksack. "Don't know what's happening to the east, but MRAPs are rolling hard."

"As long as it stays east, we don't care," Charlie said, tightening his gear down. "I'll cross with Chase. Babyface, you have tadpole. Blaster, you come last with Clark. Kristi, you take Tabitha and Ryan can drag his ass across alone and if he hesitates for a second, the next MRAP down the road will run over his dead body."

Before Ryan could say anything, Tabitha popped his arm. "Shut up," she whispered, then turned to Randy. "It's still light out," she noted in the twilight filtering through the rain clouds.

"It won't be when we get to where we cross," Randy said, walking off.

Before Charlie moved to follow, Cody moved in front of him. "I don't like Kristi crossing with Tabitha," Cody barked in a harsh whisper.

"Babyface, they're Kristi's baggage and she will help tote it," Charlie replied, walking around Cody. Walking past, Charlie saw the shocked face on Tabitha but just looked away.

"Cody, he's right," Kristi said, pushing everyone to follow Charlie. "I'm the one responsible for them."

Watching them file out, Cody looked over at Robbie. "Don't look at me, Babyface. I'm waiting for my opportunity to bleed Ryan dry, very slowly," Robbie said, pushing him to follow.

Following Cody out, Robbie jumped when Randy's voice came over his earbud. "Radio check, over," Randy called out.

"Book up," Charlie called out.

"Babyface up," Cody answered.

"Blaster in the rear with the gear," Robbie smirked.

Weaving through the trees with standing water above his boots, Randy headed east while gripping his AR tight. "Rain is good, just not so much," he mumbled, careful not to splash as he moved. Off to his right, he saw a car burning in a parking area.

Impressed the car was burning with the steady rain, he scanned around. Moving further left, Randy veered away from the light.

When Randy turned south, he lowered his NVG over his left eye and turned the thermal on mounted in front of his scope. "Down and dirty," he mumbled, moving ahead and the trees became separated, but they left the standing water.

Crossing a pedestrian path, Randy sped up to a cluster of trees ahead. Pushing through the thick vegetation at the edge, he eased in and could see the four lanes of Vollmer Road through breaks in the foliage. Stepping up, Randy made room for the others as a large vehicle rolled past and he eased closer to see it was an MRAP heading east.

"Don't like the idea of fighting the side with armor," Randy mumbled, dropping to his knee. When he felt Charlie grip his shoulder, Randy moved up to the tree line slowly. Looking west, he could see the lights of the checkpoint over a mile away. Turning east, he saw the MRAP a half a mile away still moving quickly east.

Springing up, Randy sprinted over the four lanes feeling like eyes were everywhere, watching him. Running into the trees, he planted his right foot and skidded to a stop. That was one thing he had lost, there was no pivot on his prosthetic foot.

Moving through the bushes and around trees, Randy came to a fence wrapped around a backyard of a nice house. Not seeing movement, he grabbed his PTT box. "Clear," he said, then let the box go.

When he reached the tree line, he saw Kristi and Tabitha running over. When they broke through the bushes, Randy caught Tabitha before she ran face first into a tree trunk, because she wasn't wearing NVGs.

Startled with feeling an arm grab her, Tabitha pushed away while opening her mouth and Randy slapped a hand over it. "You scream, and it will be the last sound you make before reaching the Pearly Gates," he growled in her face.

Relaxing, Tabitha nodded and Randy let her go. He turned to see Ryan sprinting across. "He can hit the tree," Randy mumbled, but Kristi stopped Ryan before he plowed into the tree.

When Robbie and Clark ran over, Randy moved back to the fence and jumped over it. Looking to the next backyard, he moved his gaze around and then lifted his AR up to look around with the thermal. All the houses he could see were dark and looked intact.

After climbing two more fences, Randy held up his hand for everyone to stop and stepped back. "Book, we are moving through the front yards. I don't want someone turning an ankle jumping fences," he said in a low voice.

"Yeah, I was worried about that over the last one," Charlie admitted. "I haven't seen or heard anything from this neighborhood since we've been here."

Giving a nod, Randy moved up beside the house they were behind and looked around. Solar landscaping lights across the road looked like flares in his NVG. Taking a breath, he eased out and moved across the yards.

Keeping a steady pace, Randy moved across the yards and crossed a street. Staying as close to the houses as he could, he kept lifting his rifle up to scan with the thermal. Before reaching the next street, gunfire sounded to his front. Knowing it was only a few hundred yards away, he slowed the pace.

When the gunfire stayed to the south not moving, Randy picked up the pace, moving quickly across a road into some trees and slowed while looking at the swollen creek below. Seeing a worn muddy path running beside the small creek, he moved on it and followed the creek as it twisted through the neighborhood.

Seeing the creek running under the next road, he studied the square culvert the creek flowed through. Moving to the creek, he waded under the road and heard the others moving in, following.

Ahead of them the gunfire stopped, and Randy was very happy he'd taken the low road.

Moving to the bank when he came out from under the road, Randy turned to Charlie and gave a hand signal for him to hang back, giving himself a ten-yard lead. Seeing Charlie nod, Randy turned and moved ahead, still watching for the shooters.

From the sound, he knew three were semi AKs and a bunch of pistols, but there were a few in the barrage that sounded like big bore hunting rifles. Seeing the creek go under another road ahead, Randy stayed on the bank.

Over the rain, Randy heard laughter ahead and slowed before moving up the bank and easing through the trees. Across the road in the yard of a large house, he saw five men kicking someone on the ground. Lifting his AR, he sighted in on the one not really participating in the beatdown.

When the reticle held true, he squeezed the trigger and watched the figure fold over when the round slammed into his chest. Moving his aim as the other four turned to watch their buddy drop, he squeezed the trigger rapidly, dropping another as the rest realized what was happening.

They ran across the yard with one turning around to aim an AK in his direction and Randy squeezed the trigger, dropping him after the guy had squeezed off two shots. Swinging his aim, he shot the last two in their backs before they rounded the house.

Watching the figure the group had been beating struggle up, Randy kept his AR pointed that way while he grabbed his PTT. "Contact to the right of creek, five down. One they were beating is heading back toward house," he called in a low voice.

"Copy, staying low," Charlie said, and Randy moved back to the creek, going under the road.

As the others came out from under the road, a few could hear the moans of those in the yard above the rain. None really cared which group was in the wrong, only that Randy had taken out the bigger threat.

The further south they went, more gunshots sounded nearby around them. By the time Randy led them under Governors Highway, it sounded like a full-scale war was taking place around them. Occasionally, they would hear the whine of bullets over their heads or hitting a tree that lined the lip of the creek.

Reaching where the creek ran under Lincoln Highway, Randy groaned, looking at the culvert running under the highway as a body floated past. "We aren't crossing that road," Charlie told him, leaning to Randy's ear. "I don't know what's going on around here, but we aren't getting in it."

Nodding, Randy eased into the creek and was thankful the culvert was only half full, but the water was moving. Stepping in, he reached up and turned on the IR light on his monocular to give him extra light. Seeing a body floating rapidly toward him, he pushed it out of the way and moved through the culvert.

Before coming out, he reached up to turn off the IR light. Continuing on, Randy soon reached where the creek followed out from a neighborhood ahead. There were no trees and the creek flowed in a concrete ditch only a foot deep.

Moving to his right, Randy saw a trucking depot with an empty parking lot. Across the street, he saw a shopping center with hundreds of people running out of the stores with armloads of merchandise.

Feeling Charlie move up beside him, "Book, we have to risk that neighborhood, then try to cross the road," Randy said.

"I've only seen it on TV, but it's more sickening in real life," Charlie spat, watching people ransack the stores. "Agreed. We don't have the ammo to plow a road."

Moving back into the trees, "Tell the others to watch their spacing," Randy said, moving toward the neighborhood. Stopping before the trees fell away, "Book, some of these houses are occupied," Randy called over the radio.

"Which has fewer, the spring sale across the street or the houses?" Charlie called back.

"I'm going to have to keep us in the road here. I see people in the windows with guns."

"Shadow, I hear them hitting that truck depot, go!" Charlie snapped, and Randy took off in a jog.

Coming out of the trees, Randy saw a man hiding in the bushes aim toward him, and Randy lifted his hand for the man to hold. The man saw the others and lowered his rifle, seeing the smaller form of kids in the group. "Watch out for cars, they are riding through the area and shooting people," the man called out.

"They just hit that trucking depot back there, so watch out," Randy told the man as he ran past, and the man gave him a wave. Staying in between two roads that ran into the neighborhood, Randy kept scanning and seeing several people armed and outside. Many trained their weapons toward the group but accepted the adage; you don't shoot at me, I won't shoot at you.

When the roads turned east, Randy left them to take a small side street heading west. Half a block away, he saw a blacked-out car with the stereo blaring. Seeing weapons poking out when the car turned toward him, "Contact front," Randy barked, lifting his AR up.

Randy raked the front windshield with bullets as the car turned and Charlie moved beside him, shooting. A flash went off under the hood as Charlie concentrated on the engine, then moved his aim up to see the destroyed windshield.

Around them a torrent of gunshots sounded, making both drop down to the road and roll away. They looked up to see people in the houses pouring lead into the car and one person fell out of the car window. Charlie's mouth fell open, watching the body get hit over fifty times.

Seconds after it had started, the torrent of gunfire stopped. "Glad we weren't in a car," Charlie said, getting up on his knees.

"You from over on Tower Ave?!" a voice called out when Randy got up, staring at the flaming car.

"No, trying to get the hell out of this city!" Randy shouted back and saw people running up to the smoking car.

"You better hurry then, because I know of two more cars in the area shooting anyone outside," a man said, walking past them to the smoking car.

Without looking back, Randy broke into a jog running past the man. When Kristi passed the middle-aged man, he tilted his head to her, "Ma'am."

Feeling her heart beating hard, Kristi smiled as people started pulling the bodies out of the car and grabbing the weapons. Despite the rain pouring down, the fire under the hood of the car started getting bigger as she passed.

"Let it burn right here!" a woman shouted and before Kristi reached the end of the block, she looked back and saw everyone gone.

Keeping them in the middle of the street, so homeowners wouldn't shoot at them, Randy turned onto another street and further into the neighborhood, another torrent of gunfire sounded. "Talk about a neighborhood watch," he mumbled.

Reaching the exit to the neighborhood, Randy slowed and looked north to the shopping center and could see a ton of people in the road beside the center. Turning left, Randy crossed Governors Highway and moved to the grassy shoulder.

Everyone kept the jog Randy had set and ran through the dark rainy night. In a subdivision on their right, they could see two houses burning, but on the left, they heard gunfire from another subdivision.

When she looked ahead and saw Randy move into trees, Kristi sighed. "Contact rear," Robbie snapped, and she heard the thump of Robbie's suppressed shots. With Tabitha holding her shoulder, Kristi made sure the kids kept running as Cody's rifle joined.

She saw Charlie kneeling and aiming past her. When she entered the woods, she heard Charlie open up and turned to look up the street. A group of people were charging out of the subdivision they'd passed. Several were shooting, but Robbie, Cody, and Charlie were mowing them down.

She watched Robbie peel off, running past Cody and tapping his shoulder. "Get your ass in here," Randy barked, yanking Kristi into the woods. "Check the kids, we are moving."

Randy watched Cody running and tapping Charlie who was just aiming down the road covered in bodies. Many were rolling around and even through rain and distance, Randy could hear them crying out in pain. Pushing the cries out of his mind, Randy moved back into the woods when Robbie reached him.

"Shadow, hold up, I need to reload," Robbie said as Cody and Charlie came into the woods.

"What the hell did you say to them, Blaster?" Charlie asked, dropping to one knee and pulling a box of ammo off the side of his rucksack.

"I didn't say shit. I saw one just watching us and when we were a hundred yards away, he yelled out and they just poured out of that subdivision like water," Robbie replied, thumbing ammo into his empty magazines. "When I saw several raising weapons up, sorry, I had to turn on the heat."

"Nothing to be sorry for," Randy said, reloading his magazines. "They made the choice to take a dirt nap."

Shoving his reloaded magazines back in his magazine pouches across his chest, Charlie glanced over at Robbie. "Blaster, you up?"

Tapping the back of the two magazines he'd used, Robbie nodded. "Ready to get back on the clock, Book," Robbie said, putting the magazines back in his vest pouches.

"The Babyface is ready," Cody looked over, grinning.

"Shadow, lead on," Charlie said, standing up.

Moving past Kristi, Randy saw Clark trying to put on a brave face. "It's all good, lil' man," Randy grinned, walking by. With the adrenaline coursing through them, nobody felt the chill from the rain when they fell in behind Randy.

With a steady pace, Randy led them through the stand of trees and Kristi was shocked when they crossed a railroad track. "Is this a subway line?" Emily asked with a worried tone.

"No, baby. It's just regular train tracks," Kristi answered, feeling Tabitha still holding her shoulder and crying softly. Glancing back, she saw Ryan was holding Tabitha's hand and Chase had a hold of Ryan's belt. "Asshole," Kristi mumbled under her breath.

"Clark, let Chase hold onto your backpack," Kristi told him, and Clark moved back and pried Chase's hand off Ryan's belt.

"Hold on here," Clark told him, putting Chase's right hand on a loop from his backpack.

"Thank you," Chase said. Even with the rain and NVG monocular, Clark could see Chase's tears running down his face.

Turning away, Clark moved back in line. "Don't worry, we'll get out of here," Clark said, trying to convince himself as much as Chase.

Coming down from the tracks, Kristi saw a wooded field. "I hate drainage ponds," she sighed, seeing the reflection of the standing water in the field. Watching Randy wade in, she was glad it wasn't over his knees; and it wasn't covered with floating bodies.

Moving through the water, gunfire sounded all around them, but Randy was concentrating on the gunfire directly ahead. Seeing trees ahead, Randy veered course, moving to them.

Pausing at a road, Randy held up his hand in a fist for everyone to stop. Easing away from the group and up to the road, Randy froze when a group of people ran up the road. Seeing a mother carrying a toddler and glancing back, Randy dropped to his stomach and crawled up. As the group ran east toward Governors Highway, Randy scanned west, seeing a group of thugs chasing the people.

When one raised a rifle, Randy's NVG flared when the thug fired a shot. "Dying time," Randy said, pushing up to one knee and pulling his AR to his shoulder. Centering on the shooter, Randy squeezed the trigger and watched the thug fold over, letting out a cry he heard eighty yards away.

While Randy moved to the next target, he heard a suppressed shot beside him and watched a thug's head mist out. The other six stopped, looking at their two partners and Randy dropped two in quick succession. "Five oh!" one yelled, raising his weapon down the road, only to have his head disappear.

The last three took off away from them, but didn't make it ten yards before getting hit in the back. Keeping his rifle to his shoulder, Randy glanced back and saw the group reach the highway and head south. "Good luck," Randy mumbled, getting up.

Putting a full magazine in, Randy put the partial on his chest rig. When Charlie squeezed his shoulder, Randy moved across the road. Seeing a subdivision to the west that the group of people had run out of, Randy saw several houses burning with a lot of gunfire sounding from it.

Waiting for the others, Randy eased up and knelt down. Hearing the sound of full auto fire to his front, Randy dove to the ground. Not hearing rounds streaking overhead, Randy lifted his head up as the fire continued. "That's a Ma Deuce," Cody said behind him.

"With several M4s and at least one SAW," Robbie whispered.

Feeling Charlie crawl up beside him, Randy kept his face turned to the gunfire as it started to slacken off. "Hold here and let me see what's going on," Randy told him, and Charlie grabbed his arm.

"Don't get in shit unless called for," Charlie reminded him.

"I don't argue with the Ma Deuce," Randy scoffed, walking away while hunched over.

Charlie rolled on his side, giving hand signals to Cody and Robbie. Cody and Robbie moved to form a triangle around the others as the gunfire to the south slackened off, but the gunfire to the west picked up. Hearing bullets whizzing overhead, everyone laid in the mud under the trees.

Crawling up beside Charlie, "The gunfire to our west in that subdivision is changing," Kristi said in a low voice.

"Yeah, before it was just civilian weapons. Now military grade weapons have entered the picture," Charlie told her, but never looked over while his eyes scanned left and right.

283

Before Kristi could ask another question, they heard big diesel engines rolling down Governors Highway heading north, and a man's voice came over a loudspeaker. "Move to the parking area ahead at the corner of Governor and Sauk now. Any person not heading there will be viewed as hostile and will be engaged. Drop all weapons and proceed there now."

Charlie knew that vehicle was barely a hundred yards away and was about to move toward the group that had just passed them when automatic fire filled the air. He heard screams from Governors Highway and everyone laid their heads down, but the bullets weren't flying over them.

"Drop all weapons now and move!" the voice bellowed over the loudspeaker. "We will not tell you again!"

"Shit, we couldn't get away with that in Afghanistan and they are doing it here in our own country?" Robbie gasped.

One engine stayed while others rolled up Governors Highway and they heard a loudspeaker in the subdivision to the west make the same demands, but with more gunfire. Praying nobody would run into the woods to escape, Charlie started getting worried, hearing more gunfire to the north.

It was almost a half an hour later when Randy came back panting and dropped down beside Charlie. "We are so fucked," Randy mumbled, and Charlie motioned Robbie and Cody back up to them. Keeping their weapons aimed out, they listened to Randy's report.

"We have stumbled into a company-sized element rounding up people to the north. They are using a large parking lot to our southeast near the subway to hold them. At least a platoon-sized element is moving through the subdivision to our west, but they are just hosing people down. I saw another platoon-sized element heading up Governors to that shopping center and they just started shooting into the crowd before they'd even rolled up on the scene," Randy told them.

"How about we pull back and move west through that wooded area?" Charlie asked.

"And go where? There is nothing but big ass stores with big ass parking lots. I chose this route because there was some cover," Randy snapped. "Book, they shot that mom that passed us carrying the toddler. She was running to them for protection and they cut her down."

"Take your heart out of this and get your mind in the game, Shadow," Charlie snapped back. "Now, options?"

Shaking his head and taking a deep breath, "There's a large store to our north. We move behind it and cross Sauk in a strung-out group and hope they don't see us. Moving across in small groups, we stand a good chance of getting cut in half," Randy said, calming down.

"Who are the troops?" Robbie asked.

"I saw National Guard, regular Army, and Marine troops, with German troops wearing blue helmets," Randy said. "Those US troops are just scared shitless kids."

Turning and glancing at Randy's face, Charlie saw he was holding back. "What else?"

"Book, I didn't see that many senior NCOs amongst our troops. I saw one platoon sergeant that might have been twenty years old. Hell, I saw a marine gunnery sergeant that was younger than that. The youngest I've ever seen a gunny was late twenties. If that one I saw wasn't a teenager, I'll lick your boots clean," Randy said, shaking his head. "None of this is making sense."

"What about officers?" Charlie asked.

"Book, I've never seen so damn many officers in my life. I counted fourteen butter bars," Randy answered. "A lieutenant colonel is running the show from an MRAP set up in front of the large department store in front of us."

"Butter bars?" Clark whispered to Kristi.

"Second lieutenant," Kristi told him.

"A light colonel is running a company?" Cody asked.

Shaking his head, "No, Babyface, a company is right in front of us. We have platoons spread out around us," Randy answered, then looked down at Charlie. "Book, if we don't move soon, they will bottle us up. Granted, the troops aren't carrying much ammo on their person, but they can run back to the command area for more."

"Odds of making it across?" Charlie asked as the gunfire picked up in the subdivision.

"We hoof it hard? Pretty damn good," Randy told him as an explosion sounded to the north and Charlie looked at him. "Our troops don't have grenades, but the Germans do and to remind you, the sergeant I talked to was right. The UN troops are carrying full combat loads."

"Any other UN troops?" Robbie asked.

"I saw a British officer, but couldn't see his rank, Blaster," Randy answered.

"What's your play, Shadow?" Charlie asked.

"We move up and when we see a chance, haul ass across that road and don't stop running for several miles," Randy told him. "If we can get by this, we can move into cover. This is the last concreted area for us."

Giving a nod, "I agree, let's go," Charlie said, getting up. Grabbing Kristi's arm, "Tell the kids to stay with you and if one of us tells you to go, move to the rally point at Deer Creek. Do you remember?"

"Yes, bend in the creek, north of Crete-Monee Road," Kristi recited in a trembling voice. "Hold one hour, then move to next rally point at Plum Creek where it Y's. Wait one hour, then move to the next rally."

Holding up his hand, "No, after Plum Creek, you move to the campsite. If we aren't there by 1100, you head on," Charlie said and pushed his map into her hands.

Looking down at the sealed plastic bag holding the map, "You better make sure your asses get there," Kristi told him, then shoved the map in her thigh pocket.

"If we aren't there, we're dead," Charlie told her, walking off.

Hearing Emily take a breath to ask, Kristi held up her hand. "Don't ask, baby," Kristi said, grabbing Tabitha's hand and putting it on her shoulder. "Clark, Emily, in front of me."

With Chase still holding his backpack, Clark followed Charlie with Emily behind them. Shaking her hands Kristi opened and closed them, looking at her soaked gloves. "Please watch over us, baby," she mumbled, moving off.

Chapter Thirty

Richton Park, Illinois

Creeping through the thinning trees and making out a large building ahead, Charlie saw Randy dive to the ground. Dropping down, Charlie glanced back to see Tabitha dropping with Kristi and Ryan slowly kneeling. Cursing under his breath, Charlie looked forward and saw four MRAPs and several HUMVEEs in the parking lot of a giant box store.

Two large portable lights shined over the area and then Charlie turned, looking out further and saw a huge cluster of people in another parking area across Governors Highway. That parking lot was surrounded by portable lights while the people stood out in the rain. Looking at the massive crowd, Charlie knew it was thousands. Hearing voices to his front getting closer, Charlie slowly turned his head to see a group wearing Army fatigues walking along the building.

Counting seventeen, Charlie studied their faces in his NVGs and had to agree with Randy; they were young. When he saw a sergeant first class pin on the lead soldier, Charlie scoffed, knowing that kid wasn't even old enough to buy alcohol.

The group carried M4s at the ready and walked alongside the building to the rear and continued heading to the subdivision. The one in the lead lifted his rifle up and fired off three short bursts, and Charlie saw two people that had been hiding behind a house drop. "Any we see in this subdivision are hostile!" the young sergeant shouted out.

Forming up into two groups, the young sergeant guided them into the subdivision. Hearing gunfire to his left, Charlie turned and saw three people, who had run out from the holding area parking lot, laying in the street. Watching a soldier wearing a blue helmet walk over to one person rolling around and holding her leg, Charlie sucked in a breath when the soldier raised his weapon and shot the woman point blank in the face.

"This is medieval," Charlie mumbled and heard gunfire to his left. Glancing left, he could see the flashes playing off the houses from the gunfire in the subdivision. 'If we don't get out soon, we won't', Charlie thought.

Seeing Randy slowly get to his knees, Charlie did the same. He glanced back and saw everyone ready to move and reached up, squeezing Randy's shoulder.

Pushing up, Randy trotted from the trees and across the parking area on the side of the building, then stayed close to the back wall. With gunfire increasing on their right from the subdivision, Charlie and Cody held their weapons across their bodies, keeping the muzzles aimed at the houses.

Feeling very exposed, Randy fought the urge to just haul ass but slowed down when he reached the end of the building. Keeping next to the wall, he heard the unmistakable sound of a HUMVEE from the west. A few seconds later, the HUMVEE drove past and then slowed, pulling into the front parking lot.

Reaching back, Randy pulled Charlie close but kept his eyes forward. "I'm moving up. You see me cross, bring the others. I get spotted, pull back and wait. I'll meet up at one of the rally points," Randy breathed out. Acknowledging he'd heard, Charlie squeezed Randy's arm.

Taking a deep breath with a last look around, Randy ran from the corner and across the side parking lot until he reached a tree beside the sidewalk. Pausing for a second, he looked both ways and didn't see any vehicles or sentries and took off.

Seeing Randy take off, Charlie followed with the rest.

Clearing the road and running through the parking lot of the building across the street, Randy turned around and saw the group just reaching the road. Willing them to move faster, Randy pulled his AR into his shoulder, watching Charlie lead the group across the road.

Behind Charlie, Randy groaned to see a person fall and take out another. Seeing they didn't have weapons, Randy knew it was Tabitha and Ryan.

Kristi stopped and turned to grab Tabitha but Cody reached down, grabbing Tabitha by the hair on her head and lifted her up to her feet. As Cody let her hair go, Tabitha reached up to hold her head where Cody had pulled her hair, crying. Seeing Tabitha wasn't moving, Kristi reached back and grabbed Tabitha's arm, yanking her into a run.

As he ran by Ryan, Robbie grabbed his arm and yanked him up, then saw Tabitha fall down again.

"Halt!" a voice shouted from the subdivision.

Lifting his AR, Randy sighted in on the figure standing at the first house in the subdivision. Flipping his safety off, Randy squeezed the trigger and watched the figure jerk before dropping to the ground.

"On the main road!" another voice shouted deeper in the subdivision. Feeling the pucker factor increase tenfold, Randy turned to see Kristi dragging Tabitha across the road and Ryan was passed by both.

"Get the kids back," Charlie said, lifting his rifle up.

Hearing Charlie's rifle cough as it touched his shoulder, Randy moved off with Clark and the kids following.

Seeing a group of troops running out of the subdivision, Charlie opened up by snapping off quick shots into each target, just trying to slow them down. Snapping a quick shot, Charlie would move and then re-engage.

"Sniper!" one bellowed and the rest just aimed forward, holding down triggers.

Ten M4s opened up while Kristi pulled Tabitha past Charlie with bullets whizzing around them. Seeing her kids ahead of her and red tracers arcing around them, Kristi let Tabitha go and leaned forward, pushing her legs hard.

Cody dropped down prone and rolled while bringing his rifle up to center on the first flashing muzzle and squeezed the trigger rapidly until the figure dropped. Moving his aim, Cody kept squeezing the trigger, moving from target to target.

Robbie moved past Charlie while Charlie moved to a new firing position. Lifting his rifle, Robbie started engaging and saw only two still shooting at them. Hearing engines cranking up, "We have got to go!" Robbie shouted, shooting one of those left and Cody dropped the other.

"MRAP coming!" Cody called out, getting up and changing magazines.

When Cody passed him, Robbie turned and followed, running behind a shopping center. Then Robbie heard the heavy thump of a Ma Deuce over the growl of a diesel engine. He could hear the heavy bullets punching into the building beside him and glanced back to see the MRAP pulling down a small side street.

Skidding to a halt, Robbie dropped to one knee and lifted his rifle up until he saw the hot silhouette of the gunner. Squeezing the trigger rapidly, Robbie cursed when he saw his rounds hit the cupola. The gunner dropped down inside, and the Ma Deuce stopped firing. Jumping up, Robbie took off to see Charlie ahead and aiming back.

The MRAP slowed as the gunner climbed back behind the fifty. Lifting his head over the steel plate, the gunner's head snapped back, and the lifeless body dropped back down into the MRAP.

"Show off," Robbie said, running past Charlie.

Hearing more engines on the other side of the shopping center, Charlie turned and ran past Robbie. "We have to buy time," Charlie said when a fifty opened up on the other side of the building. They could hear the bullets punching through the building and blowing out the cinderblock wall behind them.

Hearing the cinderblocks exploding closer, they knew the gunner was just hosing the storefronts. With trees ahead, they pushed their legs harder, expecting any minute for a chunk of lead to knock them down. Just before reaching the trees, the Ma Deuce fell silent from the front of the store.

Running into the trees at full speed, they dodged the trucks and saw Cody and Randy ahead. They skidded to a stop, panting. "Have two more MRAPs and three HUMVEEs coming," Randy said with no emotion. "Kristi moved with the others across the train tracks."

"I'll deal with the armor," Charlie said, ejecting his magazine. Pulling a magazine from his left thigh platform, he seated it and ejected a live round when chambering the first round of the new magazine. "How much time do we need to buy?"

"Three minutes. Then pull back and buy another three, then disengage and try to break contact," Randy answered, moving north through the trees that bordered the parking lot of the shopping center.

"That better be AP you put in, Book," Robbie said, following Randy.

"API, Blaster," Charlie grinned. "I only care enough to send the very best."

They followed Randy up and saw the MRAP in the parking lot while the gunner reloaded the Ma Deuce. Lifting his gun up, Randy slowed his breathing down, keeping the reticle on the gunner's head. Squeezing the trigger, he watched the gunner jerk back and drop down inside the MRAP.

Charlie moved further down next to a tree, seeing the vehicles rolling down the road in front of the shopping center. Holding his reticle over the front windshield and aiming where the driver would be, because no thermal worked through glass, Charlie slowly squeezed the trigger.

The armor piercing incendiary round streaked across the distance, punching a hole through the thick glass and hitting the driver in the shoulder. The driver yanked the steering wheel to the left and the MRAP rolled over two small trees and then across a parking area before slowly rolling to a stop.

Moving to the next MRAP that was speeding toward them, Charlie held on the windshield when the gunner opened up, spraying the trees over Charlie's head. Squeezing the trigger twice, Charlie watched two holes appear in his thermal on the window.

The first bullet hit the driver in the throat and the second hit in the center of his chest. Fighting to breathe, the driver's foot pushed down while he grabbed at his throat and the steering wheel spun to the right sharply.

With the squeal of tires, the massive weight of the truck wanted to continue forward but the wheels cut sharply. The MRAP's left side slowly lifted up and gravity did the rest. With a loud crash, the MRAP flipped on its side, throwing the gunner out of the cupola.

Turning to the next vehicle while he moved to a new spot, Charlie gave a sigh to see it was a HUMVEE, then he noticed dozens of troops moving across the parking lot and heading for them. Squeezing the trigger, Charlie watched the rounds punch through the window, but the HUMVEE kept coming and the gunner opened up with a machine gun. Flipping his safety on, Charlie relocated to another spot.

Watching a cluster of troops enter the parking lot, Cody dropped and opened up, working from the right. Dropping five, he changed magazines and started back up.

Seeing the forms charging into the parking lot, Randy started working from the far left on those closest to the building. Dropping two, he moved to another spot and centered on another while Charlie set back up and shot the gunner of the HUMVEE heading for them.

The driver had been ducking down in the seat and when his gunner dropped down missing most of his head, the driver slammed on the brakes and tried to turn around. With the side of the HUMVEE toward him, Charlie bracketed the passenger door with six shots, hitting the passenger and killing the ducking driver.

Lying prone now in the same spot with his bolt locked back again, Cody changed magazines and then started back up when the line of troops reached halfway into the parking lot and dove down, realizing over half of them were gone. They aimed at the trees and just cut loose. "Babyface, you have got to move!" Randy shouted, diving to another spot.

Seeing someone climb up on the MRAP in the parking lot to reach the Ma Deuce, Cody swung his rifle over to squeeze off three rounds, catching the figure in the side. Watching the figure roll off, Cody turned back to the line and saw the last HUMVEE weave off the road after Charlie had shot the driver. Seeing the gunner still in the cupola, Cody squeezed off three rounds.

Watching the gunner grab his arm and drop down inside, Cody moved his aim back to the line of troops laying prone. Shooting two more, Cody rolled to the side, pulling a magazine off his chest and slapping it home as the empty dropped out.

"Babyface, I know you heard Shadow. Move after you shoot!" Robbie shouted, running past him before dropping down and firing.

Grabbing his empty magazines, Cody dropped them in his dump bag and then ran a few feet, dropping back down. Lifting his rifle, Cody heard the bullets impacting around him. Hearing the fast fire of a SAW, Cody moved his aim and found the SAW gunner laying prone, popping his feed tray open.

"Time's up," Cody said, squeezing the trigger and watching the figure jerk from the two impacts.

Emptying his magazine into the stalled vehicles, Charlie paused while looking north, hearing a buzz. "Oh, you have got to be fucking shitting me," Charlie growled, dropping his magazine in his dump bag and pulling another magazine from his thigh. "Chopper coming in!"

Randy lifted his aim and saw the chopper in his thermal as a spotlight turned on, lighting them up. "Oh, you have FLIR," Randy groaned, and he steadied his aim when the chopper slowed.

With bullets whizzing around him, Charlie knelt down while taking slow breaths and holding on the bubble of the chopper. Slowly squeezing the trigger, the rifle bucked and then Charlie held on the chopper, squeezing the trigger rapidly to bracket the body of the small chopper.

Randy saw the chopper dip and a small explosion go off under the blades before the chopper started spinning wildly. With the co-pilot trying to get the stricken bird out of there, smoke poured from the engine and the wild spin started getting faster when the body started counter-rotating with the blades.

Watching the small chopper spin to the earth, Randy lost sight of it when it crashed behind the shopping center. "Damn it, Babyface, will you fucking move after you shoot?!" Robbie bellowed.

Dropping two he'd seen get up, Randy turned and saw bullets impacting all around Babyface as he lay prone, still firing. Turning to the troops, Randy started firing while Robbie ran over and grabbed Cody by his arm and jerked him up. Robbie pushed Cody into the trees as Charlie yelled, "Time!"

Moving his aim and seeing a troop stand up, Randy saw the group of detained people in the parking lot holding area swarm out. The troops running to back up those they were engaging, turned and opened fire, but were swarmed over by sheer numbers.

Still seeing the troops in the parking lot of the shopping center advancing, Randy spun around and took off. Changing magazines, Randy patted his vest and felt six empty slots. "Okay, now I'm pissed," Randy said, dropping his hand to his left thigh and pulling one of the four magazines there. Slapping it in, Randy passed by Robbie as he continued to bitch at Cody, "You shoot and move, not take up residence!" Robbie shouted.

"Blaster, we are in a firefight and trying to get away, so lower your voice," Randy snapped as he passed by.

"You only have one foot! How can you run that fast?" Cody snapped, and they heard the troops entering the woods behind them.

Running past Charlie, "Yeah, you shot down a chopper, but it was a little one, so don't get a big head," Randy said, moving into the lead.

"Eat me, country boy," Charlie chuckled, hearing a diesel engine growling.

Skidding to a halt, Randy moved up to the road and saw the first MRAP that Charlie had shot at, backing up from the railroad embankment. "You better have more bullets because it's coming," Randy said, running out on the road.

He ran across, dropping in the ditch to see troops running down the road, firing. Lifting his AR up, Randy started sending hate downrange. "Contact rear," Robbie called over the radio as Cody dove out past Charlie and landed in the ditch. He looked over when Randy moved up the ditch, then started shooting again.

Lifting his rifle, Cody saw the MRAP turning toward them and centered his reticle on the figures running down the road. Calming his breathing as much as he could, Cody squeezed the trigger, dropping one charging. Seeing another shooting from the hip, Cody moved his aim and sent three rounds into the figure and watched him face plant on the road.

Changing positions, Charlie saw someone climbing up in the cupola and aimed at the driver's spot, sending two rounds through the window, but the MRAP never changed course. The Ma Deuce started her thumping and Charlie dove to the side as bullets chewed up the tree he was near.

Hearing the thump of the fifty, Cody changed magazines, watching the last man he'd shot get run over by the MRAP. Seeing the line of tracers hitting around Charlie, Cody aimed at the cupola and seeing the gunner was ducking behind the armor shield, pulling the trigger rapidly, Cody watched his bullets ricochet off.

The gunner heard the pings off the armor shield and rotated the gun, never letting off the trigger.

Cody saw the stream of lead moving toward him and pulled up on his knee to run across the road.

"Uhff," Cody gasped when a truck hit him in the center of the chest. He looked down at a hole blown through his chest plate and could feel the blood pouring out his back.

Getting up, Charlie held his reticle on the turret and emptied his magazine, punching holes in the steel until one hit the gunner. When the body fell inside the MRAP, the driver stomped the brake and put the MRAP in reverse. Backing away, a line of troops using the MRAP for rolling cover had to jump out of the way before they were run over.

Randy started shooting into the group, moving rapidly from target to target. Feeling his bolt lock back, Randy rolled down the bank while yanking a magazine out and slapping it home.

Cody looked up twenty yards away and saw two troops running at him, firing from the hip. Lifting his AR up with one hand, Cody squeezed the trigger as fast as he could and watched the first one jerk before all strength left his arm.

Falling back, Cody felt a sharp pain in the side of his head before he landed on the grass, struggling to breathe. "Sorry, guys," Cody gurgled, with blood coming out of his mouth. Feeling his mind go cloudy, Cody relaxed.

As his eyes closed, calmness filled Cody's being and a small smile creased his bloody lips as he used his last breath, "Hey, Wheat."

Chapter Thirty-One

Randy turned and saw a man charging Cody and swung his rifle over, shooting the soldier in the side of the head. He watched the soldier fall and changed magazines, then his heart stopped. "Man down!" he bellowed, running across the road.

He dove into the ditch and saw a hole punched in the center of Cody's chest. Feeling for a pulse, Randy saw where a bullet had hit Cody behind the right ear and removed the base of his skull. "Can you patch him up?!" Charlie shouted, shooting into the woods while Robbie pulled back.

Swallowing a lump in his throat, "Man down," Randy said softly and looked up the road as the MRAP that was backing away was swarmed by the prisoners.

Taking Cody's pack off, Randy rolled his body onto his shoulder. "Road is clear, we are leaving!" he shouted. "Grab Cody's ruck!"

Robbie ran out into the ditch and saw Randy running up the embankment of the railroad tracks with Cody over his shoulder. Grabbing Cody's ruck with his claw, Robbie pumped his legs as hard as he could. Reaching the tracks, he stopped before dropping the rucksack and lifted his AR up, grabbing his PTT. "Book, peel," he called out.

As Charlie ran from the trees, Robbie saw two hot spots in his thermal and pumped rounds center mass until both dropped. "Last mag," Robbie called over the radio and Charlie picked up Cody's rucksack as he passed Robbie.

Seeing troops further back but creeping ahead slowly, Robbie turned and followed Charlie. Grabbing his sling, Robbie undid the clip from single point to double and let the AR hang across his chest. Reaching back with his right hand, Robbie pulled out a bandolier.

Running down the opposite embankment, Robbie snapped the speed loader and fed the first stripper clip in. Using his claw, Robbie shoved the ten rounds in, knocking the stripper clip off as he grabbed another.

Seeing Randy ten yards ahead and running through water, Charlie reached down and felt one magazine on his chest and none on his left thigh. Unable to reload carrying Cody's rucksack, Charlie splashed through the water.

With a dark subdivision on their left and the tracks on their right, Charlie and Robbie struggled to keep up with Randy. Looking ahead, Charlie saw they were headed into a field with a small stand of trees. Letting his rifle hang, Charlie grabbed his PTT box. "Shadow, stop in the trees, so we can work on Cody," Charlie called out.

"KIA," Randy called back, and Charlie's legs faltered, sending him crashing to the ground and sliding in the mud.

Running up, Robbie grabbed Charlie and yanked him up, "Come on," Robbie growled in a broken voice.

Forcing his legs to move, Charlie ran on.

Clearing the field, Randy shifted Cody on his shoulder as he ran onto a golf course. Behind him, the gunfire was increasing to battle field tempo but wasn't moving and he pushed on.

***

"We need to move," Tabitha said, gripping Kristi's arm.

Yanking her arm away, "Tabitha, we wait for thirty more minutes," Kristi snapped.

"Kristi, you heard all that gunfire! We need to leave," Ryan snapped, getting up and storming over to Kristi. "There is no way they could make it through that."

Kristi froze, hearing the unmistakable 'click' of an AR being taken off safe. "Get away from my mom," Clark snarled, and everyone turned to see Clark aiming at Ryan's head.

"Clark, you put that gun down now!" Tabitha snapped.

"Sit back down, Ryan, before I shoot," Clark said calmly.

Tabitha took a step toward Clark and he swung his gun over, aiming at her. "I feel threatened, so I can shoot," Clark said coldly. "And I will because you aren't my family."

"Tabitha, sit down and shut your mouth," Kristi said, grabbing her arm and forcing her to sit down.

"My knees are skinned up and bleeding," Tabitha whined.

Ryan went to move and saw Clark swing his aim back to him. "Five, four, three, two," Clark started, and Ryan dropped to the ground before Clark reached one.

"Kristi, you will tell Clark to stop pointing that gun at me!" Ryan barked.

Giving a sigh, Kristi turned back to look out over the field they had crossed. "Clark, if he gets up again, just shoot him in the face," Kristi said, and Ryan went pale.

Glancing at her watch, Kristi saw they had twenty minutes before they had to move. Seeing movement at the edge of the field in her NVG, Kristi caught her breath. "Momma, I see someone," Emily said beside her. "It's three people."

"Everyone, get behind a tree," Kristi commanded.

"I told you we should've left, dammit," Ryan hissed, moving behind a tree.

"Emily, Clark, don't shoot unless I do," Kristi said, kneeling down.

As the figures neared the trees, the second one reached up and Kristi saw an IR light flash three times. "Kids, it's them, don't shoot," Kristi said, jumping up and running out of the woods. As Randy got closer, Kristi reached up and covered her mouth, seeing a body over his shoulder.

She looked back and saw the second form and knew it was Charlie, and then the big form of Robbie. "Oh god, Babyface," Kristi gasped.

Never pausing his stride, Randy jogged right past Kristi. She turned and jogged after him. "How bad?" Kristi asked, trying to lift Cody's head up and seeing a chunk of his helmet ripped away. Then her eyes moved to Cody's back and her pace faltered, seeing a hole blown out through the back trauma plate.

Stopping in a small clearing, Randy kneeled and then gently took Cody off his shoulder. Kristi caught Cody's head as it flopped back and guided it to the ground. Hearing a sharp intake of breath, Kristi turned and saw Emily looking down at Cody's lifeless body.

Gulping in air, Randy undid his rucksack and let it fall off his back as Charlie and Robbie jogged up. Dropping Cody's rucksack, Charlie undid his, letting it hit the ground followed by Robbie's. The three formed up around Cody.

Kneeling beside Cody, Randy placed his hand on Cody's shoulder. "Why did you stay with us, Babyface? You should've found greener pastures," Randy mumbled with tears rolling down his face.

"He was with family, Shadow," Charlie sighed, wiping his eyes. "He died on his feet for his family. What any man would want."

Kristi knelt at Cody's head and saw the gentle smile still on his bloody lips. "You were a great man, Cody," she said softly and caressed his cold cheek.

"We're cursed," Randy declared, leaning over and started taking gear off Cody's vest. Emily moved over, hugging Kristi while Clark just dropped down beside his mom. A thousand questions filled Clark's mind, but the loss made his body numb.

Grabbing Cody's AR, Randy held it up and saw the ACOG scope and thermal attachment had been shattered by bullets. Then he saw a half inch hole through the housing made by a fifty-caliber bullet. Unclipping the AR, Randy grabbed the suppressor and twisted it off.

"Put this on your rifle," Randy said, tossing it over next to Kristi.

"We need to leave!" Ryan snapped, stomping over with Tabitha. Randy lunged up with bloodlust and felt a bull hit him from the side, taking him down.

Trying to spin away from his attacker, Randy felt a tree trunk wrap around his throat. Spreading his legs to spin around and face his attacker, Randy felt someone jump on his legs, holding them together. "Shadow!" Charlie snapped as Randy struggled to get out of the chokehold Robbie had him in.

Feeling Randy trying to rotate his body, Robbie wrapped his legs around Randy's abdomen. "Easy, Shadow," Robbie said softly, relaxing the chokehold.

When he felt Randy's body relaxing, Robbie let up more on his grip, but didn't release it when Charlie leaned into Randy's face. "Shadow, now isn't the time. We have pissed off the world," Charlie said, patting Randy's chest. "We need you to get your head to the here and now, troop. When our number comes up, no matter where you are, it's time to pay for the party. Cody went out fighting. He stood tall with his team."

Taking his eyes off Ryan and Tabitha, Randy turned to Charlie. "We've done this once already and got the t-shirt," Randy snapped with tears coursing down his face.

"We embrace the suck, troop. Life decides what the suck will be, but you can lay down and take it or embrace it and fight against it," Charlie said, slowly unwrapping his legs from Randy. Seeing Randy continuing to relax, Charlie nodded at Robbie.

Unwrapping his arm from Randy's neck and his legs from Randy's body, "Shadow, it could've been any of us and Babyface knew that. He charged into the dragon's den willingly and stood tall," Robbie said, letting Randy sit up.

Getting up, Randy turned to Ryan and Tabitha as Robbie prepared to get between them. Not because he wanted to protect them, Robbie knew Randy needed to unleash, but would feel guilty later. Otherwise, Robbie would've handed Randy his knife to bleed the garbage dry.

"Open your mouths again and you will eat your tongues before you die." Randy glared with fire at the two.

Moving over to Cody's rucksack, Randy took a deep breath when he knelt. He looked at the front and back and saw the round had passed completely through the rucksack. Opening the top, Randy started laying out gear as Charlie and Robbie moved over beside him.

"I'll carry him next," Charlie said, kneeling down and helping Randy sort the gear.

Reaching into the rucksack, Robbie pulled out clothes and looked in the bottom. "Good lord!" he gasped. Charlie and Randy leaned over, looking at the bottom to see it was packed with freeze-dried packages.

"That's why he had us eating from his supply," Charlie smiled remorsefully.

"He didn't want Momma on our asses about not eating," Randy said in a breaking voice.

Putting a hand on Randy's shoulder, "I'll tell 'em," Charlie sighed, and Randy nodded, pulling out the food.

With the stuff laid out, Randy stood up. "He only has one top for a stretcher, get one out of my ruck," Randy said, turning around. "I'm going to find some saplings."

"Clark, Emily," Charlie said, turning around and holding up Cody's two woobies. "He would want you to have these."

They moved over, taking the poncho liners and Kristi moved over to help them pack what they were taking. Randy came back with two six-foot-long saplings he'd cut and using two button-up jackets, they made a stretcher. "We carry him to the state line where we were going to hole up and bury him," Randy said, and Robbie turned around. "I'll come back on the horses and bring him home. We don't have the manpower to do that again, and we aren't young roosters anymore."

"I'm coming with you," Robbie said, daring Randy to say otherwise.

"Me, too," Charlie added. All three bumped fists and then moved over, taking Cody's tactical vest off. When Charlie moved to take off the helmet, Kristi stopped him.

"Don't," she said, grabbing his hand. "Let Cody keep it on."

Seeing the back of the helmet, Charlie just nodded and helped Robbie put Cody's body on the stretcher. "Tabitha, you help me carry the front. Ryan, you carry the back and if you complain, you leave right then," Kristi warned.

Kristi turned to see Randy tucking Cody's poncho around him like a blanket. "You were a good friend, kid," Randy said, getting up.

"One of the best," Charlie nodded.

"A brother and a Ranger," Robbie finished.

Chapter Thirty-Two

Indiana

With her left hand gripping the handle of the makeshift stretcher, Kristi looked over at Tabitha. "Don't drop it," Kristi said in a low voice.

"It's heavy," Tabitha whined.

"Tabitha, I'm carrying one end by myself," Ryan huffed, trying to let Kristi know he was tired.

"You two set him down, then you can leave," Kristi told them while the eastern sky started to lighten. Flipping her NVG up, Kristi turned to see Emily walking beside the stretcher and holding Cody's pale hand. "Emily, I need you in front of me."

Covering Cody's hand up, Emily wiped her face with the back of her glove and moved in front of Kristi with her head hanging low. "Emily, you need to help keep an eye out," Charlie said, slowing his pace.

Lifting her head up, Emily wiped her nose with her sleeve. "It's not fair," she mumbled, and Charlie reached over to flip her NVG up and turned it off.

"I know, tadpole, but life is rarely fair," Charlie said, letting his hand rest on her shoulder. "All you can do is your best and hope that's enough."

Looking ahead, Kristi still didn't see Randy. "When is Randy coming back?" Kristi asked.

"He's waiting for us at the campsite," Charlie said over his shoulder. "He wanted to make sure there were no surprises close."

"Uncle Charlie, is it going to rain forever?" Emily asked, looking around as the rain fell. They were walking along a fence row that bordered a field.

"Tadpole, I'm beginning to wonder that myself," Charlie told her, then cupped his hand over his earbud.

When Charlie dropped his hand, Kristi asked. "Was that Randy?"

"Yeah, he said there is military traffic on I-65, but it's light and we should be able to sneak under at the overpass," Charlie told her. "He's also got food going."

"I'm starved," Tabitha moaned.

"And lucky to be alive," Robbie mumbled behind them.

Moving up beside Charlie, Clark looked around. "Uncle Charlie, since we are in Indiana, will we still have to worry about the military and police?" Clark asked, sniffling.

"Clark, if they see us, I'm sure they will shoot first and ask questions later, so let's just avoid them," Charlie answered.

They stopped when they reached a fence and passed the stretcher across, then continued on. Charlie looked at his watch and saw it was already 1000 when he looked up and saw a stand of trees ahead. He tapped Emily's shoulder. "There's where Shadow is waiting on us."

Looking at the trees in the distance, Emily tried to smile but couldn't.

Reaching the stand of trees an hour later, they found Randy waiting for them and led them under several massive oak trees. Charlie saw an animal on a spit over a bed of charcoal briquettes. "Where did you get the charcoal?" Charlie asked while Kristi directed Tabitha and Ryan on where to put the stretcher down.

"Stole it," Randy shrugged.

Smelling the roasting meat, Tabitha moved over to the warmth of the charcoal. "Is that a baby deer?" she asked, holding her hands over the glowing coals.

"Dog," Randy said, moving to his rucksack.

"Mom said Dad ate dog," Clark said, taking off his backpack.

"More than once," Randy chuckled. "That man could cook some dog."

"And you expect us to eat that?" Ryan asked, walking over.

With dead drooping eyes, Randy locked onto Ryan's face. "I don't expect shit from you, except being the burden you are. I can honestly say; you and your wife are the two most worthless people I've ever met. If both of you dropped dead right this second, the world would be a better place," Randy told him.

Ryan took a breath to retort as Kristi moved over, seeing the corners of Randy's mouth twitch in a grin. "Ryan, you eat it or starve," Kristi snapped, knowing Randy was baiting to kill.

"I hope it's the latter," Randy said, staring at Ryan. "Yeah, you're worthless. You whine and bitch like you've done all your life. Expecting everyone to do *for* you. You don't like guns, but where did you run when your world fell apart? You ran to someone who had some because in the real world, a person is responsible for their own safety. The cops come after the crime. But know this, you do for yourself now or you walk. We've lost enough because of you."

"Ryan, go get warm," Kristi said, seeing Ryan's face turn pale. When Ryan walked away, Kristi turned to Randy. "They are doing their best," Kristi told Randy.

Shaking his head, "No, they aren't," Randy replied, bending over and picking up a folding shovel. "Kristi, I love you like a sister, but if your decision of letting those two continue on ends up hurting Emily and Clark, I'll never forgive you."

Kristi gasped as Randy walked around the large oak tree and got on his knees. Folding the shovel out, Randy started digging plugs of grass up.

Walking up behind Kristi, Charlie grabbed her arms gently, startling her. "Go get warm and put the tents up, so the kids can start getting dry," Charlie told her and then let her go, dropping his rucksack beside Randy's.

"Charlie, I would never endanger my kids purposely," Kristi mumbled while Charlie pulled out a folding shovel.

"Forest for the trees, Kristi. Forest for the trees," Charlie said, moving over beside Randy and started digging out plugs. "You already have."

As she stood there, Robbie came over while unfolding a shovel and dropped a poncho down. Moving back over, she helped the kids set up the tent and then was about to set up the other for Tabitha but stopped. "Tabitha, set your tent up," Kristi snapped.

"I don't know how," Tabitha whined.

"Learn. We've set it up twice for you and that's it," Kristi said, shoving her backpack into the tent. When she turned to usher the kids inside, Kristi saw both helping the boys. The plugs of grass were set in lines, just as they'd been taken out of the ground and now, they were throwing dirt on the unfolded poncho.

Kristi moved over, getting on her knees and helping the boys dig. When they laid Cody in the grave, Randy covered Cody's body with his poncho. "We'll be back, brother," Randy vowed. "You will be at the retreat with us forever, Babyface."

"Uncle Cody doesn't like being alone," Emily said, crying.

Pointing at the bracelet on her wrist, "Why don't you leave that with Cody until they get him to the retreat?" Kristi told Emily.

Taking the bracelet off, Emily moved up beside the grave and Randy pulled the poncho back, placing the bracelet under Cody's hands. Stepping up beside Emily, Clark took off his dad's dog tags. Looking at the tags, "Let Uncle Cody hold these till he gets home," Clark said, holding them out.

Randy took the same dog tags he had pulled off Wheat a lifetime ago. "Babyface will like that," Randy said with tears on his cheeks. Stepping up, Kristi took off a necklace that held Wheat's wedding band.

"Cody can watch this for me until we get him back," Kristi said, and Randy laid it under Cody's hands.

"You watch that stuff for them," Randy said, covering the body and stepping away from the grave. He came back with a yellow box and sprinkled powder over the poncho and Charlie looked at the box, seeing it was baking soda.

"Shadow, I hope you didn't hurt anyone in taking that," Charlie said in a low voice.

"Never knew I was in the house," Randy answered, getting on his knees. The others helped cover the body and then put the plugs of grass back where they'd come from. When they were done, Kristi looked at the spot and couldn't tell Cody was buried right in front of her eyes.

With the excess dirt in the poncho, Robbie carried it off and sprinkled it around.

Moving to a small stream, they cleaned up and ate. When they left at dark, there wasn't any dog left.

The End

Thank You for Reading, Please Remember to Leave a Review

Check out the Webpages Below to see more work by

Thomas A Watson, William Allen & M. C. Allen

Join Watson on Facebook A-Poc Press Page

www.facebook.com/groups/apocpress

Check out Watson's Website

www.apocpress.com

Check out the Allens at Malleus Publishing

www.malleuspublishing.com

The Sacrifice Tree" is a series set in Louisiana (and beyond).   Juliet didn't expect for her family to have secrets from her. Her life takes a dramatic turn when she discovers she has the ability to jump across dimensions.

Find Books 1-3 on Amazon

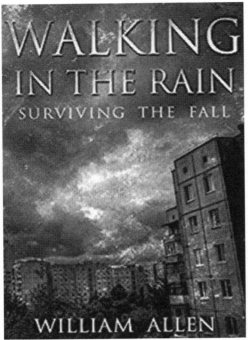

This is not a romance tale, or a zombie story, or a book about the end of the world. The world will still be here after civilization falls. This is a story about a boy who becomes a man in the most trying of times, and this story is filled with the violence of those lawless times.

Book Seven Will Be Available in 2018

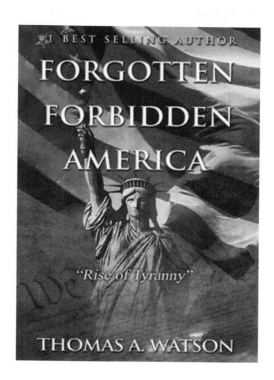

When the stock markets in Asia crash, this family knows that it is time to pull together with their circle of friends and get to their safe zone. But nothing worth doing is ever easy.

Look for Books 1-4 on Amazon